D0469419

JULIA LONDON

SEDUCED
by a SCOT

ISBN-13: 978-1-335-62942-5

Seduced by a Scot

Recycling programs
for this product may
not exist in your area.

This edition published by arrangement with Harlequin Books S.A.

For questions and comments about the quality of this book, please contact us at CustomerService@Harlequin.com.

® and TM are trademarks of Harlequin Enterprises Limited or its corporate affiliates. Trademarks indicated with ® are registered in the United States Patent and Trademark Office, the Canadian Intellectual Property Office and in other countries.

www.HQNBooks.com

Printed in U.S.A.

CONTENTS

Mackenzies of Balhaire

John Armstrong,
Lord Norwood

Anne Armstrong

Knox Armstrong *(bastard son)*

Bryce Armstrong

Margot Armstrong, b. 1688 ——— Cailean Mackenzie, b. 1711

m. 1706

m. 1742

Daisy Bristol, b. 1713
Lady Chatwick

(previous marriage)

——— Georgina Mackenzie, b. 1747
——— Ellis, *Lord Chatwick*

m. 1751

Arran Mackenzie, b. 1680

Avaline Kent, b. 1732

Conall Mackenzie

——— Vivienne Mackenzie, b. 1713

Jane Mackenzie

m. 1733

Marcas Mackenzie, b. 1710
(distant relation)

——— Maira Mackenzie, b. 1735
——— Bruce Mackenzie, b. 1736
——— Gavin Mackenzie, b. 1738
——— Nira Mackenzie, b. 1741

——— Aulay Mackenzie, b. 1714
Captain Mackenzie

m. 1752

——— Beathan Mackenzie, b. 1753

——— Carbrey Mackenzie, b. 1755

Ivor Mackenzie

Lottie Livingstone, b. 1729

Lilleas Mackenzie

——— Rabbie Mackenzie, b. 1715

m. 1750

Bernadette Holly, b. 1721

——— Ualan MacLeod *(Mackenzie)*,
b. 1743, *adopted 1750*
——— Fiona MacLeod *(Mackenzie)*,
b. 1744, *adopted 1750*

——— Isobel Mackenzie,
b. 1748, *adopted 1750*

Griselda Mackenzie, b. 1685
Jock Mackenzie, b. 1679

m. 1713

Nell Grady, b. 1690

——— Catriona Mackenzie, b. 1722

m. 1755

——— George, b. 1756

——— Louis, b. 1756

Nichol Bain, b. 1726
Counselor to Duke of Montrose ——— Hamlin Graham, b. 1716
m. 1759   *Duke of Montrose*
Maura Darby, b. 1734

One of the truly wonderful things about the writing profession is meeting so many readers from across the globe. We start off with a shared love of books, and some of these acquaintances become deep friendships. A special thanks to Bridget Costedot from France, and Sandra Schwab from Germany, friends and fellow readers who helped me with the bits of French and German in this book.

CHAPTER ONE

Stirling, Scotland
1758

CALUM GARBETT WAS not allowed to know happiness. No matter how close he came to it, his wife and daughter would swoop in at the last moment to destroy any chance of it.

The scene playing out in the drawing room was the crowning blow. He could feel all his hard work slipping through his fingers. To think of all the money and time he'd spent bringing Carron Ironworks to life. It had been a Herculean feat to forge a relationship with Thomas Cadell, an Englishman with a successful ironworks of his own, who could teach the Scots the latest techniques. Techniques that would save time and money, that would enable Calum to employ more Scottish men.

He'd positioned himself to become one of the premier industries in Scotland. If that were not true, would the Duke of Montrose be sitting beside him now, willing to invest his own money and influence into the endeavor?

Yes, Calum had bargained his daughter's hand

in marriage as part of the deal, but then again, he'd done her a great service, as her prospects for marriage had not been dazzling. Frankly, his daughter leaned a little to the homely side of things, and when young, randy men of marrying age were presented with the prospect of a potential mate who made them wince when imagining the marriage bed, they tended to shy away altogether.

Well, he'd found someone for his daughter, Sorcha, and now, she would ruin everything with her mother standing firmly beside her, all because the young rooster she was set to marry was enamored with the far fairer, and much more elusive, Maura Darby. Calum's ward.

Calum had taken Maura under his wing twelve years ago when her father, his oldest friend, had died. The lass was quite alone in this world, and Darby had appealed to Calum's generosity and sense of decency. Calum had been happy to do it, particularly as the lass had come with a nice bit of money, and her presence would not affect him in any way.

But he'd severely underestimated how slighted his daughter, Sorcha, would feel about it. Or, perhaps more importantly, his wife. She was quite set against the lass from the moment she arrived.

The resentment only grew over the years. As the girls became women, no matter what Calum's wife did to improve his daughter's looks, poor Sorcha was destined to live her life with a bulbous nose and slightly crooked eyes, while Maura blossomed into a woman with appealing ink black hair and eyes the same blue as a winter sky. The more alluring Maura became, the more his wife tried to push her aside. As it happened, Sorcha had been the first to receive an offer of marriage—with the help of Mrs. Garbett, who had resorted to all but locking poor Maura away.

The lass had borne it well enough, with little complaint. She'd become accustomed, he supposed, to wearing hand-me-downs, having her things taken and given to Sorcha—a kitten when she was thirteen, a muff a few years later, a fichu that was given to her by a friend on her twentieth birthday. And those were the things Calum knew about.

But what had happened in the last fortnight under this roof had turned Sorcha into an entirely unreasonable wee shrew. This, Calum decided, was a bloody disaster.

As he understood it, a chambermaid witnessed a kiss between Maura and his daughter's fiancé, Mr. Adam Cadell, and knowing this to be an unpardonable affront to her mistress, had run to the housekeeper, who in turn had run to Calum's wife, who had then screeched down the stairs and into the study where Calum and Adam's father, Thomas Cadell, were finalizing their agreement in the presence of the Duke of Montrose.

Mrs. Garbett was followed closely by a wailing Sorcha, whose sobbing had the unfortunate affect of making her nose look even larger. She was followed by the young man's mother, Mrs. Cadell, who vehemently denied her son had done anything wrong. Last, and certainly least, a sheepish Mr. Adam

Cadell, who insisted that the older woman, Maura, who had just turned four and twenty to his twenty years, had thrown herself at him and he had not known what to do.

Bloody randy rooster would have them all believe he was a poor wee lad who had been accosted.

A tribunal of three confused men—Calum, Thomas Cadell and the duke—was quickly assembled in the drawing room. Calum insisted the maid be brought forth to give her account. Maura, the accused, was also ushered in, and stood defiantly against the wall, her arms crossed over her body, her fair blue eyes flashing with defiance at the lot of them.

"I seen Miss Darby with her back to the wall, and Mr. Cadell kissing her," the maid said with her eyes firmly affixed to the floor.

"I am certain it was the other way around," Adam said hopefully.

Calum looked at Maura. "Miss Darby?"

"It was precisely as Hannah saw it, sir, aye."

It didn't sound to Calum as if she'd thrown herself at Adam, not with her back to the wall, but she'd confessed to the kiss, and he didn't know precisely what to do. "Well, now," he said uncertainly. "You must promise you'll no' do that again."

"Mr. Garbett!" his wife shrieked with great hysteria. "Will you no' defend your daughter's honor, then?"

Dear God, did she propose that Calum call out the young man? Duel to death in their drive? To think of the scandal, not to mention the mess that would need to be tidied up.

"Pappa!" Sorcha's shriek was identical to her mother's. "I will no' marry him! I *hate* him! I *hate* Maura! Why ever did you bring her here?"

Calum felt the weight of this unmitigated disaster bearing down on his chest. Plus, his head itched beneath his peruke, and he longed for a stick or something to shove up in there and scratch so he could bloody well *think*. If there was no marriage, there would be no deal. His ironworks, destined to be the economic jewel of all of Scotland, would circle the drain. He slowly gained his feet. "Let us not act in haste, darling."

"Haste?" Sorcha cried. "It is the second time she has kissed my fiancé!"

Oh right. The first time, Maura had said the lad had caught her outside, in the garden where no one could see them, and had kissed her. The lad, unsurprisingly, had flatly denied it. The two families had sided with him.

"I didna kiss him," Maura said, her voice surprisingly calm given all the female hysteria floating about them like an ether. "He caught me in the hall unawares and kissed me, sir." She looked at the young fool. "Please tell the truth, Mr. Cadell."

"How dare you!" Mrs. Cadell cried. "Know your place!" But then she swung around and hit the back of her son's head with the flat of her hand so hard that he was knocked forward a pair of steps.

"She is a temptress, on my word!" Adam said

frantically, looking around him, no doubt hoping to find a sympathetic face. He would find none.

"I donna want her here, aye, Pappa? I donna want her anywhere *near* me!" Sorcha insisted.

Calum exchanged a look with Thomas, who looked just as befuddled as Calum felt. Calum truly didn't know what he was supposed to do with Maura. It wasn't as if he could tuck her away in a trunk and put her in the attic.

"Mr. Garbett!" his wife said. "You must send her away!"

"Aye, all right, all right, I understand that feelings have been hurt," he snapped, and tried to think. His cousin? He'd not seen David Rumpkin in many years. He lived in what had been his father's manor near Aberuthen. He was an old charlatan, had never made an honest living, but Calum suspected he would take Maura in for a fee until this debacle blew over.

He glanced at Maura, who steadily returned his gaze, almost as if she was silently daring him to believe that wretched lad and send her away. Her icy stare sent a small shiver down his spine. "I'll send her to my cousin for the time being, aye?" he said, his gaze on Maura. "In Aberuthen. A tidy manor house near a loch. Do you no' like the sound of it, then, Maura?"

She did not flinch. She did not say a word. But the injustice radiated off her, heating them all.

"Send her away with all the privileges we have extended to her these many years, then?" his wife said angrily. "She has destroyed my daughter's happiness, and for that, she should be made to repay the kindness we've shown her."

"Indeed," Mrs. Cadell sniffed. "She should be made to pay the consequence of using her wiles on an innocent young man."

Innocent, his arse. "What would you like, madam?" Calum asked his wife. "A pound of her flesh? For she doesna have a farthing to her name." Technically, she did, but he was not prepared to part with the stipend.

"She has a necklace," his wife said.

Maura gasped. *"No,"* she said.

"No?" Calum's wife repeated, her eyes darkening with rage. "When I think of the gowns and the shoes and meals that have been bestowed on you!"

"The gowns and shoes belonged to Sorcha first, did they no'?" Calum tried, but no one was listening to him.

"That necklace has been in my family for years, aye?" Maura pleaded. "It's all that I have of them."

"Thank goodness for it, then, for you may repay your considerable debt."

"Mrs. Garbett," Calum said firmly.

"What, Mr. Garbett?" she snapped.

It was no use. His wife was livid, Sorcha was still tearful and Mrs. Cadell was trying to persuade her husband they should return to England. All of this in full view of the Duke of Montrose, who remained completely stoic and silent.

What he must think of them. A lot of bumpkins, that was what. Calum was so mortified by this display that he would do anything to have this over and done rather than prolong it another moment, and looking at his wife, he knew that if she didn't have her revenge, there would be no end to it. He said to the maid, "Fetch the necklace, aye?"

"*No,*" Maura cried frantically. "You canna have it!"

But Hannah had already scurried from the room to fetch it.

Calum flinched when he looked again at Maura Darby. The pain this caused her was obvious; for the first time since the trouble with Adam Cadell had begun, unshed tears of helplessness filled her blue eyes.

"It pains me to say it, lass, but you must gather your things. 'Tis best you go away until the wedding is done, aye?"

"There willna *be* a wedding," Sorcha tearfully announced, and pushed past Adam as she flounced from the room, her red nose leading the way.

Maura slowly straightened from the wall. She gave Calum a look he was certain would terrify any man as she took her leave.

"Thank the saints," Mrs. Cadell said when she'd gone. "You shouldn't have that sort of woman in your house, Mr. Garbett, if you'll not mind me saying. She's a temptress."

The coward Adam nodded.

Calum desperately wanted to defend Maura, but the stakes were too high. When the wedding was done, he'd send for her. He'd put it all to rights with her then, and she would understand.

Maura was dispatched that very afternoon.

Unfortunately, the rift between the Cadells and the Garbetts was not so easily dispatched, because Sorcha and her mother refused to listen to reason or apology.

Two days later, Thomas Cadell and Calum Garbett met with the Duke of Montrose again to advise him as to the status of their joint venture. They were both flummoxed as to what to do. "My wife will have my head if I agree to it," Thomas said.

"My wife will have my balls if I do," Calum added glumly.

The Duke of Montrose, who had remained uncomfortably silent through the detailed explanation of their ordeal finally spoke. "There might be a way to salvage it yet, aye?" he said. "I know a man who is very adept at solving problems."

Calum and Thomas eagerly looked up. "A man? What man?" Calum asked.

"Nichol Bain," the duke said. "He is a man of incomparable skill in matters such as this." He picked up a quill, dipped it in ink and jotted down his name and location. He slid that across to Calum. "You may no' care for his methods, but you will be pleased with the results. Send for him straightaway if you want your ironworks, sir."

Calum sent a messenger to Nichol Bain at Norwood Park in England that very night.

CHAPTER TWO

MR. NICHOL BAIN was hoping for a bit more of a
challenge in his latest engagement. A problem that
would require ingenuity and considerable discre-
tion to resolve. A situation with far-ranging consequences, such as the problem he'd solved for the
Duke of Montrose a few years ago, when the duke
had been rumored to have murdered his wife at a
time he was to be named to the House of Lords. Now
that was a problem with twists and turns and a bit
of meat on the bone.

He'd even settle for the sort of problem he'd solved
for the mild-mannered Dunnan Cockburn, the sole
heir of a Scottish linen dynasty who had somehow
fallen into a gambling ring and had gotten himself on
the wrong side of London moneylenders. Dunnan's
estate was entailed, which meant it was not his to sell
as he would like, but held for future generations. It
had taken a monumental feat of cunning to find a so-
licitor who could navigate the complicated history of
the entail and carve out a wee bit of Dunnan's land
to sell to pay his last debt, which had been an astro-
nomical sum of three thousand pounds.

And then he'd needed a great deal of finesse to

strike a deal with the naïve Dunnan and some rather unsavory characters in London.

But the problem Mr. Garbett and Mr. Cadell presented him was none of those things. He'd been summoned from England to the Garbett mansion near Stirling to resolve a young lover's quarrel. The problem should have been sorted out by the adults in the room, in Nichol's opinion. Unfortunately, rational people sometimes acted from passionate feelings rather than reasoned thought. Mr. Garbett and Mr. Cadell didn't need his help—they needed to step away from the turmoil and their wives, and *think*.

So, Nichol had taken advantage of their weakness and negotiated a very hefty fee to solve this child's play for the two iron barons. He considered the work a diversion, a bit of a lark. An exercise that would keep the machinery of his mind well oiled before he moved on to his next engagement that involved a wealthy Welsh merchant and a missing ship.

Nichol first met with Miss Sorcha Garbett, who, in his estimation, was as immature as she was plain. He asked her if she would be so kind to explain how her engagement had ended. Hopefully without tears.

Miss Garbett was quite eager to tell him and railed for a half hour about the unfair treatment of her person by one Miss Maura Darby, who had, for all intents and purposes, been banned from the Garbett house, and who, if Miss Garbett was to be believed, had been persecuting her for *years*. In the entire half hour, Miss Garbett mentioned her fiancé only in passing. She presented him as a rather un-

sophisticated gentleman who did not understand the
wily ways of a woman. But Miss Darby was another
matter entirely.

"Your father's ward sounds like a dangerous en-
chantress," he remarked, more for his own amusement.

"She's no' *so* enchanting," Miss Garbett sniffed.
"She's no' as clever as she thinks, and neither is she
a true beauty."

Miss Darby's looks had not been mentioned at
all. "I see," Nichol said, and oh, did he see. "Might
I inquire, Miss Garbett—do you love Mr. Cadell?"

She put a handkerchief to her considerable nose
and shrugged delicately.

Bain clasped his hands behind his back and pretended to examine a porcelain figurine. "Does the
notion of being mistress of a grand house appeal to
you, then?"

She slanted her eyes in his direction.

"I have seen the Cadell house in England, and I
can say without reservation that it is grander than
Kensington Palace."

She dropped the handkerchief, and her eyes went
wide. "Grander than a *palace*?"

"Aye."

She bit her lip and glanced at her lap. "But he
loves Maura."

"No," Nichol said. This was where he did his best
work. He squatted down next to the lass, took her
hand in his and said carefully, earnestly, "He does
no' love Miss Darby."

"How can you be certain?" she asked tearfully.

"Because I'm a man, aye? I know how a man thinks in moments of raw desire." He watched the twin puffs of red bloom in her cheeks. "He was no' thinking of the rest of his life, you may trust me. When he thinks of *you*, he thinks of compatibility and the many happy years before him spent in complete conjugal felicity."

That might have been too much, he thought lazily.

Miss Garbett sniffed again. "I suppose I could give him one more chance, aye? But I'll no' give Maura another chance! Never! Donna even ask it of me."

"I would never," he assured her.

"But you will," she said tearfully. "Because my father esteems her verra much. More than *me*."

"He could no' possibly," Nichol said soothingly. "You must believe me, Miss Garbett—your father likes the ironworks deal far better than Miss Darby. And he loves *you* much more than that."

She straightened in her seat and with a weary sigh, she looked to the window. "Is the Cadell house in England really as big as a palace?"

Problem solved. Nichol rose to his feet. "Bigger. Eighteen chimneys in all."

"Eighteen," she murmured.

From there, Nichol walked into the small study to speak to Mr. Adam Cadell. Although he was twenty years, he had not quite yet grown into his gangly arms and legs. He eyed Nichol warily.

"Well, then," Nichol said, and went to the side-

board to help himself to port. He poured one for the
lad, too. "You've gotten yourself into a bloody fine
predicament, aye?"

The young man looked uncertainly at the port,
but took it, and downed it with unnecessary determination. "Yes," he said hoarsely.

"Do you love Miss Darby, then?"

The lad colored. The knot at his throat dipped
with his hard swallow. "Of course not."

Of course you do. Nichol sipped casually at his
port, then asked, "What is the size of Miss Garbett's
dowry, by the bye?"

"Why?" the young man asked, and when Nichol
didn't answer, he fidgeted nervously with the hem
of his waistcoat. "Quite large," he said in a manner
that seemed to suggest he thought he'd be asked to
forfeit it.

"Large enough to build a house in town?"

"London?"

"Aye, London, if you like. Edinburra. Dublin."
He shrugged.

Mr. Cadell's brows dipped with confusion. "What
has that to do with this wedding?"

"I should think it obvious."

The lad looked at him blankly. Nothing was obvious to him but his raging lust.

"If you were to build or purchase a house in any
of those towns...you would undoubtedly meet many
pretty debutantes who would be eager to befriend
your wife, aye?"

Adam Cadell kept his gaze fixed on Nichol.

"*Scads* of them," Nichol added for emphasis.

The young man sank down onto the settee and clasped his hands together before him. Nichol had his full attention. "I donna understand."

Nichol put aside the port. "What I am suggesting, Mr. Cadell, is that you get your heir, then live your life. She will have the bairn she wants, the house she wants, all the gowns she wants, and you will have…" He made a flourish with his hand. "Society, aye? You will save your father's important business arrangement and everyone will be made happy once again."

"Ah," Adam Cadell said, and slowly nodded. His eyes brightened. And then dulled. "But Sorcha will not have me, not with the ward about."

So now Miss Darby was merely the ward, was she? "She is no' here at present," Nichol pointed out.

"No, but she'll come back. Mr. Garbett is right fond of her, he is. He'll not leave her put away. She'll be part of this family yet."

Nichol pondered that. "If the ward was put in a circumstance—one that Mr. Garbett would approve, naturally, but one that would keep her from this house for the foreseeable futur—could you see your way to making a proper apology to your fiancée?"

"Yes," the young man said, nodding enthusiastically. "Of course. Miss Darby will be utterly forgotten."

"Then leave it to me," Nichol said, and extended his hand.

Mr. Cadell took it with the grip of a small child and shook it weakly. "Thank you, Mr. Bain."

The solution, Nichol realized, was one that would solve two problems at once. This was perhaps the easiest thing he'd tackled in fifteen years.

He left the Garbett house with a bounce in his step, and returned to the inn in Stirling where he was residing. There, he penned a letter to Dunnan Cockburn, the former client and someone Nichol might consider a "friend." Nichol didn't have friends, really. For one, he never stayed anyplace for long. Two, he had learned at an early age to keep his thoughts to himself so they'd not be used against him. And three, he'd discovered that friendships relied on the ability of one to share feelings. He did not share his, and as a result, he had few friends.

He supposed he might count Lord Norwood as a friend. He'd met the earl in the course of his work for the Duke of Montrose. Norwood was the uncle of the new Lady Montrose, and had been either amused or impressed with Nichol's handling of her and Montrose's business. Whatever the reason, he had kept Nichol close and seemed to enjoy his company, although he did frequently dispatch Nichol to help his influential friends.

Nichol counted Dunnan simply because they'd spent so much time in each other's company. Dunnan was eager to please and possessed a good humor, in spite of his considerable troubles. He resided in a sprawling estate with his widowed mother, and while he'd conquered his gambling problem, he and

Nichol had both agreed that he might be less tempted to engage in such behavior if had he a proper wife to comfort and advise him and frankly, to keep an eye on him.

"You'll find a wife, then, will you?" Nichol had asked the last time he'd seen Dunnan.

"Oh, I will, I *will*," Dunnan had assured him. "It is on the very top of my list of things that simply must be done."

Unfortunately, the last he'd heard, Dunnan hadn't been successful in his quest. So this seemed the perfect arrangement for all involved—Dunnan needed a wife. The temptress needed a place in this world that was out of sight of the young lovers but one that would meet with Mr. Garbett's approval. Miss Darby would be well cared for and, Nichol suspected, honored by her husband. Doted upon. Smothered with affection. Dunnan seemed quite eager to have a wife.

Nichol sent off his letter, then spent the next two days awaiting a reply in the company of a bonny little wench who left scratches on his back.

Dunnan's reply was an exuberant *Yes. If you recommend her, Mr. Bain, I will consider myself the recipient of very good fortune and shall open my arms, my heart and my home to her.*

Precisely the reception Nichol had expected from a man who was overly enthusiastic about things as mundane as perfectly toasted toast points. In this case, he thought Dunnan might have been a little more circumspect, as he'd not even laid eyes on the lass, and matrimony tended to be for life. But that was not the problem he'd been hired to solve. He'd been hired to solve the problem of the ward, and he was very pleased with himself for having done a fine job of it.

It had gone so well, in fact, that Nichol was considering carving out a bit of time to call on the brother he'd not seen in many years. The distance between them, both literally and figuratively, had been weighing on Nichol of late. He had a soft spot in his heart for Ivan. His brother resided at their family home, not far from Stirling—or he had the last time they'd corresponded. Unfortunately, Nichol's letters in the last few years had gone unanswered, the messengers sent away.

Nichol wasn't entirely certain why, but he was entirely certain he would never know if he did not go to his brother himself. It would be a shock to Ivan, as it had been more than a dozen years that Nichol had been gone from home. That was another matter entirely, one that had no easy resolution. But where Ivan was concerned, Nichol would have liked to understand what had happened.

Perhaps now was the time to see him. Perhaps things had fallen into place for that very reason.

But first things first. Nichol said goodbye to the wench, hired a lad to act as his groom, then rode out to explain to Mr. Garbett and Mr. Cadell his plan to mend this rift between families once and for all.

As he suspected, his plan was welcomed by everyone, with the singular exception of Mrs. Garbett, whose thirst for vengeance apparently knew no bounds. She believed that Miss Darby should not be allowed to enjoy the privilege of marrying well, but faced with the prospect of her husband's ward being returned to them, reluctantly agreed to the scheme.

By week's end, Nichol and Gavin, his groom, were provisioned for several days of travel and on their way to a manor near Aberuthen to retrieve Miss Darby.

By noon the following day, they'd reached their destination. Fragile flakes of snow were whispering down from the sky, scarcely visible in the light of a weak sun that peaked in from between the clouds. The lad was shivering in his saddle, even though Nichol had tossed him his plaid to drape over his coat. "Still with me, Gavin, are you?" he called over his shoulder.

"Aye, sir."

"We'll be there soon enough," he assured him as they rode out of the small village of Aberuthen, armed with Garbett's directions to the Rumpkin abode. A half hour later, they arrived.

Nichol had expected the house to be something on par with the Garbett house, but was unpleasantly surprised to find a much smaller house, one that could scarcely be called a manor, and one that looked in serious need of repair. It had a single vine-covered tower at one end, and a house appended to it shaped like a box, as if the builder had struck out to build a castle, and had changed his mind in favor of a smaller house midway through.

A weak trail of smoke rose from only one of four

chimneys, and Nichol could see at least four panes of glass had been broken and replaced with wood. He and Gavin came off their mounts and stared up at the house. No one came to greet them. Not even a dog.

Gavin looked at Nichol expectantly.

"Aye," Nichol said to the lad's unspoken question. "I'll see if I can rouse someone, then." He handed the reins of his mount to Gavin and nodded in the direction of a stable or barn—another dilapidated building. "Feed and water the mounts. There is food in the bag for you, aye? Eat. Warm yourself. We'll ride out as soon as all is settled here."

With the leads of the two horses in hand, Gavin trudged off in the direction of the building.

Nichol pulled his greatcoat around him and looked again at the house, taking in the yellowed weeds that grew under the darkened windows. Had it been abandoned? That would be an unwelcome twist to his plan. With a grimace, he started for the door.

On the doorstep, he used the brass knocker three times with no response. He had about decided that the house was indeed empty when he heard the sound of someone fumbling on the other side of the door, which was followed by the door suddenly swinging open. A man, holding a lamp aloft, peered at Nichol. He was wearing a dressing gown over a sleep shirt that was stained with spilled food. The man was obese and stood with his legs braced wide apart, apparently to hold his girth aloft. He had not been shaved, and long scraggly hair floated about his head and shoulders. Even more hair sprouted from his ears.

Nichol had to swallow down his surprise—it was nearly two in the afternoon and the man looked as if he'd been roused in the middle of the night.

"Come for the lass, have you?" he asked gruffly.

Nichol couldn't say how he'd guessed it. "Aye, I have."

The man stuck out his hand, palm up. "I'll have the money first, then."

Diah, but it would appear that Garbett's cousin was a boor. "May I come in? It's rather cold."

The man grunted. He stepped back and bowed with mock deference as Nichol swept past him into a hall crowded with cloaks and boots and stacks of peat, of all things.

The man closed the door, then shuffled into a room just off the hall.

Nichol followed, but he felt a wee bit as if he was entering at his own peril. The room, a dining room, was disgusting. It reeked of spoiled food and dog feces, which, when Nichol glanced down, were scattered about the floor. Uneaten food had been left to rot in bowls around the table, attracting flies even in the cold. Two dogs lay at the hearth. One of them, a long-legged lanky thing, lazily pushed himself up and wandered over to have a sniff of Nichol before returning to his place at the hearth.

Nichol glanced around him and asked, "Has your housekeeper died, then, Mr. Rumpkin?"

"Amusing," the man said. "Has my cousin sent

you to entertain me, or to compensate me for keeping the *bampot*?" He held out his hand again.

Nichol withdrew the pouch of coins from his coat and put them in Mr. Rumpkin's outstretched palm. Mr. Rumpkin, in turn, set aside the lamp, opened the purse and dumped the coins onto the table, quickly counting them, and biting into one to assure himself it was gold. When he was satisfied, he pointed to the stairs across the hall. "She's up there, she is. Barricaded herself in."

Nichol could scarcely blame her. "How long?"

"Two days," he said gruffly. When Nichol didn't respond due to his surprise, Rumpkin glanced up at him. "*Och,* donna look at me in that manner! I sent food up to her but she'll no' touch it."

No doubt she'd feared contagion of the plague. Nichol couldn't believe Mr. Calum Garbett had sent his ward to this hell, of all places. His conscience demanded that he remove the lass from here as quickly as possible. "Which room?"

"The tower," Rumpkin said grumpily, and heaved himself into a chair at the table, picked up a spoon, and resumed eating whatever was in a bowl there.

Nichol turned away before he gagged. He stepped out into the hall, over a block of peat, then jogged up the stairs and paused on the landing. There was only one door to his left. Sitting outside the door was a tray of food that had been covered with a cloth.

He strode down the hall and knocked firmly on that door. "Miss Darby, please do open the door. I

am Mr. Nichol Bain and I've been sent by your benefactor, Mr. Garbett."

Several moments passed before he heard movement. He waited for the door to open, glancing
around that dark hall to perhaps identify the source
of the odor he smelled up here, and was abruptly startled by the crash of what sounded like glass against
the other side of the door. Had the lass just hurled
something at the door?

Nichol put his hands to his hips and studied the
door, thinking. He stepped forward, knocked a little more softly. "Miss Darby…lass. Mr. Garbett has
sent a proposition for you that I am confident you
will want to hear. He should like to see you removed
from this…place as soon as possible, aye? Open the
door. Please."

Silence.

He braced his hands on either side of the door.
He had not anticipated having to convince her to
leave. He would think she'd come bounding out of
the room, her bags packed, grateful for the opportunity to flee. "On my word, what I have to tell you
is better than anything you will find here."

He heard the scrape of something heavy against
the floor and realized she was pushing something
that sounded like a heavy piece of furniture against
the door.

"I warned you, I did," came the man's voice from
behind him. Nichol glanced over his shoulder. Mr.
Rumpkin had come up the stairs with a bottle in one

hand. He put that bottle to his lips and took a long swig before saying, "Bloody heathen, that one."

Nichol turned back to the door and decided to try authority. "Enough of this, Miss Darby, aye? Your benefactor is quite eager to arrive at a solution for you, and what he proposes will surely satisfy you. But you must open the door to hear it."

Silence.

Nichol was feeling his patience leak from him, and he never lost his patience. He tried the door, but as he suspected, it was bolted shut. He slammed his hand against it in an uncharacteristic display of frustration. "Miss Darby, I must insist you come out at once!" he said sternly.

He heard something and pressed his ear to the door. Was he imagining it, or did he hear a low laugh from the other side of that door?

He definitely heard another chuckle behind him.

Patience deserted Nichol altogether. He prided himself on his ability to stay completely calm when others were at sixes and sevens—it was necessary to the sort of work that he did. But this annoyed him. He could feel the uptick of his heartbeat, the surge of heat to his neck. He would not be treated in this way by a young woman with nothing to recommend her, with no one to help her but him. He would not accept her bad manners in light of what he meant to do for her. He whirled away from the door.

Mr. Rumpkin was still standing there, still drinking. He dragged his sleeve across his mouth and said, "Told you."

Nichol squeezed around him, then strode down the stairs.

He had also learned in his many years of solving problems that if one avenue for resolution closed, there was always another. The trick was to find it.

And oh, he *would* find it.

CHAPTER THREE

MAURA BRACED HER hands against the door and leaned in, pressing her ear against the rough wood, listening to footsteps receding.

When she couldn't hear them any longer, she pushed away from the door and smiled wryly to herself. How *dare* Mr. Garbett send someone for her? How dare he not come himself to deliver his apology? Did he truly believe she would simply walk out of this spot of hell with a stranger? Go meekly along after all that had happened? Not without an apology, she would not, and she felt quite determined to never leave this room until she had it.

Except that she was even more determined to leave this wretched place, just as soon as she figured out how. She would not remain one night longer under Mr. David Rumpkin's roof than was absolutely necessary.

Oh, how she despised that man! At first, she'd tried to make the best of it, and though she could hardly stomach her surroundings, she'd tried to be pleasing and accommodating. Just as she'd tried when she'd been taken in by the Garbetts.

On his deathbed, her father had told her to always be kind, to be grateful to the family that would take her in, to be as accommodating as he knew she could be. He'd reminded her that she had no standing in this world, and her existence depended on the benevolence of a man who was not her father. Maura had tried to be all of the things her father had recommended, but she was not their kin, and Mrs. Garbett had hated her from the moment she'd laid eyes on her. Mr. Garbett had been indifferent to her for the most part, even though from time to time he would defend her. Still, Maura had always believed Mr. Garbett liked her. Now she believed he had been precisely what he'd shown her: indifferent.

Given her experience in Stirling, perhaps she should have known that being grateful and accommodating would not serve her here, either. Rumpkin had shown himself almost at once to be an impossible, slovenly beast with no regard for her or that hapless lass who came from Aberuthen to cook his stews.

Still, she might have born it. She'd even had thoughts of tidying up the house a bit for him, as she was reluctant to sit on any seat. But it was Rumpkin's drunken pawing of her that had prompted her to barricade herself in the room. She'd been caught completely off guard by it—he'd come up behind her, had put one hand on her arse, another on her breast and his greasy mouth on her neck.

A shudder ran through her as she recalled it.

Maura had found a strength she had not known she possessed in that moment. She had shoved the mountain of a man with all her might, and he'd stumbled backward, falling into his chair. "Donna be a *shrew*," he'd slurred, and as he'd tried to lever himself to his feet she had fled to her room at the top of the stairs, had bolted the door shut, then had pushed a bureau in front of it for good measure.

The next day she'd had to remove the bureau to accept the bit of food the lass had brought her and left outside her door. She'd taken the bread, had left the bowl of stringy stew untouched.

Oh right, she'd almost forgotten—she was starving just now.

Maura turned away from the door and looked at her prison. She had a small stack of books that were keeping her occupied, but which she'd soon finish. She was running out of wood for the hearth, her clothes needed washing and she'd lost all manner of decency. The clothes she'd been wearing the night he'd put his hands on her were discarded onto the floor, where they would remain, unless she resorted to burning them for warmth. She hadn't bothered to dress her hair or don a gown over her stomacher and petticoat in days.

She fell onto the chaise longue at the end of the bed, and stared morosely at the ceiling with its peeling paint. She couldn't survive in here much longer. Last night, she'd concocted an elaborate plan in her head, whereby she would will herself to make it to spring when the days would be warmer. She could simply walk out of this house once Mr. Rumpkin had fallen into unconsciousness with his fingers wrapped tightly around a bottle. But then she'd grown sullen, for spring was too far away, and there was an entire winter to endure.

She needed to devise another, better plan.

She had only a few coins, some shoes that were worthless for anything other than dancing or strolling around manicured gardens, one decent gown and one serviceable gown. The third gown she'd been allowed to leave Stirling with was the one lying in a heap on the floor.

As she lay there contemplating, she heard a sound that she would have thought was a rat scurrying by had it not come from outside the window. She slowly sat up, staring at the window. It couldn't be. He *wouldn't*, this Mr. Nichol Bain. Maura shot up from the chaise and hurried to the window. She opened it slightly, just enough to see out.

All she could see was an auburn head of hair as the man picked his way up the thick vines that covered the tower.

Bloody bounder. Mr. Garbett must have paid him handsomely to ferry her off to yet some other hell. She closed the window and latched it shut. If he thought she would open it to him, he was a fool. She went back to the chaise and plopped down onto her back, one bare foot on the moldy carpet, one arm slung across her body, waiting for the inevitable moment that he pounded on the window demanding entrance. She hoped he fell and landed on his arse. She hoped his fingers ached so much that it brought a tear to his eye.

She did not expect him to punch his fist through the glass, but that's what he did, shattering the pane into a rain of chunks. That same fist reached through the opening for the latch and swung the window open. Maura was so stunned by this that she couldn't move, and watched, dumbfounded, Mr. Nichol Bain's acrobatic entry into her room. He paused just inside, brushed off his clothes, ran his hand over his bobbed hair, and then leveled a gaze on her that suggested he was quite perturbed at having to make an entry in this manner.

Neither of them said a word. Maura didn't know what stunned her more—his bold entrance or his fine looks. His eyes were the palest green, his hair the shade of autumn. He stood well over six feet, and broad shoulders that looked even broader in a greatcoat tapered into a trim waist. He was perhaps one of the most handsome men she had ever seen.

But his expression was thunderous as he surveyed her lying there—she was still incapable of movement—and said, in a deeply timbred voice, *"Feasgar math."*

He had just wished her a good afternoon in Gaelic. Maura stared at him. Had he come from the Highlands, then?

"Now I see what caused Adam Cadell to lose his mind," he said, and bowed gallantly.

For the love of Scotland! Men were degenerates, the whole bloody lot of them. Whoever this man was, or whatever he wanted, Maura didn't care. She had gone well past the point of caring in Stirling

and straight into unyielding fury with the world
and everyone around her. She did not want to be reminded of Adam Cadell, that bloody coward. She
sighed with impatience, cast her arm over her eyes,
and silently willed this handsome stranger from her
room.

He did not leave her room. No, he was moving
about, pausing here and there. When he next spoke,
she realized he'd walked the entire breadth of the
room to the other window. "Allow me to introduce
myself again, aye?" he said coolly. "My name is Mr.
Nichol Bain."

She didn't care what his name was. Did Mr. Garbett think she would trust *anyone* at this juncture?

"I understand you must be mistrustful."

Mistrustful? Aye, sir, mistrustful and furious. She
was teeming with raw, unabated fury. She had no
wish to discuss what she was or thought and muttered under her breath, *"Sortez maintenant, imbécile,"* telling the fool to get out of her room.

There was a long pause before he said, *"Pas avant
que vous n'écoutiez ce que j'ai à dire."*

Not until you've heard what I have to say. Surprised, Maura removed her arm and turned her head
to look at him.

He had squatted down onto his haunches a couple
of feet away from her and was watching her closely
like a hawk, his eyes sharp and focused, his movement very still.

Maura pushed herself up on her elbows and glared
at him. All right, so he'd been schooled in French,

too. He thought himself clever, she could clearly see it in his eyes. *"Mir ist es gleich was Sie zu sagen haben."*

She gave him a very pert smile. She's just told him that she didn't care what he had to say, and silently thanked her late father for insisting her education include languages.

Mr. Bain's smile was slow and almost wolfish. "Aye, you have me there, lass. My German is no' as good as that. Nevertheless... *Wollen Sie von hier fortgehen?*"

She gasped softly. This man, whoever he was, was a formidable opponent. She sat up, putting both feet on the floor, her hands clutching the edge of the chaise on either side of her knees. She gave him a good look, appraising him, before she answered his question. "Aye, I want to leave here," she said. "But no' with you."

Mr. Bain stood up, clasped his hands behind his back and said calmly, "At present, that would seem your only choice."

"It is no' my only choice. I could leap from the window you've so graciously opened for me, aye?"

He shrugged. "If you meant to leap from the window, I suspect you would have done so on the day you felt it necessary to barricade yourself in this room."

Well, then, he was a perceptive man. He should be heralded for it among women—*Look here, lassies, all of you, a perceptive gentleman! Come quick, for you'll no' see this again!*

Maura stood up. She was at least a full head shorter than him; he had to look down. And when he did, he unabashedly looked directly at her bosom before lifting his gaze to her eyes.

She glared at him. "What do you want, then?"

"To take you from these…accommodations, first and foremost."

She folded her arms across her body. "And then? Where do you mean to take me? To Mr. Garbett? Or am I to have the pleasure of visiting yet another cousin?"

He glanced at her mouth. Maura considered kicking his shin. "To Luncarty," he said.

"Luncarty. What the devil is a Luncarty?"

"It is a small village and an estate. It is also an opportunity."

She laughed at him. An opportunity! How naïve did he think she was? "*Is* it? What sort of *opportunity* would it be, then, Mr. Bain? Am I to defend myself against the advances of another man I've never met?"

"Pardon?" he said, and had the decency to at least look slightly horrified. "Did Rumpkin—"

She clucked her tongue at this fool. *All* men were fools.

But this fool's expression turned slightly murderous. "I would no' put you in a situation that might cause you harm, Miss Darby. There is a house in Luncarty that I think you would verra much like. A big wealthy house."

"Ah. Someone's mistress, then."

He seemed taken aback by her direct manner. "No

one's mistress. You are Mr. Garbett's ward, aye? He has vowed to do right by you."

She cast her arms wide. "Does this look right to you, sir? Aye, go on—if I'm no' to be a mistress, what am I to do at Luncarty?"

"Marry the laird."

She gasped with shock. And then laughed with sheer delight as she gathered her tangled hair and pulled it over her shoulder. "You must be mad! Or you must believe *I* am mad."

"What I am is determined to find a suitable situation for you."

"Well, that is no' one!" she said, and laughed again, this time with a twinge of hysteria. "I will no' *marry* someone I've no' met!"

"Of course you will meet him before you decide," Mr. Bain said with the patience of a parent. "The gentleman is an acquaintance of mine. He's kind, he's in need of a wife and he will treat you like a princess."

"I suppose you think that's all that is required!"

Mr. Bain shrugged. "What more would you like, then?"

"What *more*? Love? Compatibility?" All the things she was desperate to know, given that she'd spent the last twelve years of her life searching for even the slightest bit of love or compatibility. For the slightest hint of affection. Since her father died, Mr. Garbett was the closest she'd had to knowing any sort of affection, and even that was sporadically applied in the way of a pat to the head or a squeeze of the shoulder.

"Love and compatibility," he scoffed. "All verra lofty goals for a lass who is locked in a tower with no prospect of anything more than servitude."

Maura's breath caught in her throat. Her fury and disbelief dulled and she felt the truth in his words settle like a weighted mantel about her shoulders. She sagged, dropping her arms.

"Will you at least allow me the opportunity to explain?" he asked.

"By all means," she said dryly. "You've gone to the trouble of climbing the wall and smashing the window after all." She walked away from him, to her wardrobe. She pulled out a shawl and wrapped it around her shoulders. The broken window was letting in a north wind and flakes of snow. "You were saying, Mr. Bain?"

"Dunnan Cockburn is heir to Scotland's largest linen manufacturer. He lives in a grand house with only his widowed mother. He is a good man."

Maura eyed him with skepticism. "Why has he never married, then?"

"He is no' particularly adept with the fairer sex."

What did that mean? Was he hideously ugly? A happy drunkard? "I would guess that you manage the *fairer* sex with aplomb, aye?" she said. "Perhaps you ought to instruct him."

One corner of his mouth tipped up. "I am hoping that you will come along and make that task unnecessary, Miss Darby."

"What if I agree to meet him? When will I leave this wretched place?"

"Tonight."

That caught her attention—she could leave *tonight*? A flurry of thoughts began to race through her mind, not the least of which was that she had a way out of this house. That was the first step. She didn't know what she intended to do once she was freed from this prison, but she did not intend to marry some faceless man.

What she wanted was to get her mother's necklace back. That necklace was the proverbial straw that had broken the camel's back. Maura had done everything the Garbetts had ever asked of her, including moving to the small servant's room at the end of the hall to be "out of the way." She'd remained at home when she and Sorcha had been invited to parties so that Sorcha could shine. She'd tried to keep to the shadows when company came. She'd said *please* and *thank you*, had never asked for anything, had done everything she knew to do to be a grateful, accommodating girl. And for that, they'd accused her, called her a liar and, the ultimate insult, had taken her necklace.

They should not have taken it, and Maura should not have let them. She'd done nothing wrong. It was all she had to her name, and she intended to have it back.

She didn't have a plan for that, either, but the first step was getting out of the hell Mr. Garbett had sent her to, and Mr. Bain was offering her a way out.

Whatever would come next, Maura couldn't

guess. But it would not include marrying a man in Luncarty who was "not adept with the fairer sex," whatever that meant. But in order to escape, Mr. Bain had to believe that she would be foolish enough to agree. So she mustered up all the charm she could manage, looked into the pale green eyes of the man standing before her and said, "Aye, all right."

His brows dipped into a dubious frown. "All right?"

"I'll go."

"Just like that?"

"Is that no' what you wanted? I've changed my mind."

His frown grew even more dubious, but he said, "Have you a bag? Anything to carry your things?"

She nodded.

"Fill it with what you can carry. Clean yourself up and meet me in the drive when you're ready."

"Any other commands, your highness?"

"Aye. Dress warmly." With that, he turned away from her, easily pushed the bureau from the door, unbolted it, and strode out.

Maura's heart was suddenly beating with excitement. It occurred to her that this opportunity could disappear, and she could be prevented from escape. She had not a minute to spare and ran to her vanity.

CHAPTER FOUR

Nichol was no stranger to the dithering of young ladies at their wardrobe, and had expected to be kept waiting a good hour or more for Miss Darby. But here she came after only twenty minutes, bundled in a cloak lined with fur, with her hair bound haphazardly at her nape, and her leather bag—stuffed to the gills by the look of it—banging against her leg.

On her heels was Mr. Rumpkin, who had found a pair of trousers and a coat. He had not found the waistcoat or neckcloth, but at least he'd removed the offending soiled nightshirt.

"Is this how you'll take your leave, then? Without so much as a fare thee well?" he'd shouted at Miss Darby as she strode toward Nichol.

She ignored him. Did not pay him the slightest heed. *This woman.* Nichol didn't know if he ought to be appalled by her lack of civility or impressed with her courage to stand up to Rumpkin. And to him, for that matter.

She arrived before him and dropped her bag. He glanced at her shoes. Silk, by the look of it. "Those will no' do for a long journey, Miss Darby," he said, nodding in the direction of her feet.

"They will have to do, Mr. Bain. They are all I have. When I was banished from the home I've known for a dozen years, I was no' permitted the luxury of time to consider all that I might need, aye?"

Nichol's opinion of Garbett was rapidly deteriorating.

"Is this it, then? After feeding you and putting a roof over your fool head?" Mr. Rumpkin demanded.

Miss Darby looked up at the sky, at the dusting of snow that was beginning to fade away. She looked at Nichol, then at the groom. "Where is the carriage?"

"Carriage!" Mr. Rumpkin said with a sputter. "You think too highly of yourself!"

Miss Darby looked at Nichol.

"No carriage," he said simply.

She studied the horses, then young Gavin in his saddle.

"Where is the maid? Surely I'm no' to travel without a female companion."

"I'm afraid Mr. Garbett's resources did no' allow for a maid. We'll be but a day."

Her eyes widened with alarm. "Where is my mount, then?"

Nichol patted the rump of his horse.

Miss Darby stared at the horse, then at him. Her mouth dropped open. She looked at the groom again, but the lad studiously avoided her gaze. "Do you mean I am to ride with *you*?" she asked incredulously. "Without chaperone or a lass?"

"Aye."

"You never said I would ride *with* you, on the same horse!"

Nichol bowed his head. "Quite right you are. Allow me to correct the oversight—you are to ride with me, on the same horse. Without chaperone or a lass."

She gasped. "I will no'!"

"*Och,* I knew she'd no' go," Mr. Rumpkin said. "Too lazy, she is. She's had it easy."

With that remark, something flashed in Miss Darby's brilliant blue eyes. She slowly turned and glanced at the offending man over her shoulder, muttered something that sounded French, then picked up her bag. For a moment, Nichol thought she meant to return to her room at the top of the tower, but she suddenly threw the bag at him.

Nichol caught it with one hand. She stomped forward, presenting herself to be seated on the horse. How odd, Nichol thought, that at this moment, he was having to fight a small smile. Her defiant spunk amused him.

"What's this?" Rumpkin demanded as Nichol lashed her bag onto his horse. "You mean to go with him, then?" he demanded of Miss Darby. "Have you any idea the sort of talk you will cause if people see you riding off as if you were a dead fox draped across his lap?"

Miss Darby looking imploringly at Nichol. "Will you please be quick about it?"

He cupped his hands and bent at the waist to give her a lift. She slammed her foot into his hands, and he vaulted her skyward. She landed lopsidedly on the saddle and cried out with alarm, but managed to catch herself before she slid off the other side and landed on her bottom.

"Go on then, ride out of here like the slut you are, aye?" Mr. Rumpkin shouted.

Nichol turned, walked calmly to where Mr. Rumpkin stood swaying to keep his balance. He caught him by the open neck of his shirt. "You've caused enough harm, aye? No' another word, sir, or I shall put my fist in your mouth and shove it all the way down your gullet to make sure you never utter another word again." He shoved Rumpkin away, and the man stumbled backward. He was drunk enough that he went down onto his arse with a great *thud*.

"You'll no' treat me in this way!" he screeched, but made no move to pick himself up. "You will compensate me for the broken window, that you will, or I'll have the proper authorities searching for you ere you leave Aberuthen!"

Nichol walked back to the mounts, put his foot in the stirrup and launched himself onto the horse, directly behind Miss Darby. He hitched the horse about and nodded at Gavin. They trotted out of the drive while Mr. Rumpkin dumbly watched them go.

Miss Darby did not look back once.

"Donna sit so close," she said, and wiggled, trying to put some space between them. "I donna want to be so familiar with you, aye?"

"Do you want to be difficult?" Nichol asked casually.

She snorted. "You may depend on it, Mr. Bain."

"Good," Nichol said, and spurred his horse to canter. "I like a challenge."

She shot him a look over her shoulder. He arched a single brow and smiled. Her gaze moved quickly over his face, and then she abruptly turned, shifting her body forward so she would not touch him. But the horse was moving too fast, and she would bounce right off. Nichol put his arm around her waist to hold her in place.

"I beg your pardon!" she said angrily. "Is this part of Mr. Garbett's scheme, too? Did he think I deserved to be carried off like so much luggage?"

An actual response to her question did not seem necessary, particularly when she immediately asked another question.

"Where are we going? It will be dark soon. You canna mean to carry on in the dark."

His hope was that they would reach Crieff before it was too dark, but before he could answer, she said, "It is apparent that I've traded one wretched situation for another, is it no'?" Nichol sensed she had asked her question of the heavens, and not of him. He was right.

"I will be forced to ride like a hostage across all of Scotland and for what? Another man who might abuse my sensibilities?"

"You have my word I will leave your sensibilities verra much untouched," he said.

She clucked her tongue. "You will pardon me for no' believing you, Mr. Bain. In my experience, a man's word is hardly reliable. Mr. Garbett once vowed I would always have a home with him, and yet, here I am, cast out. In the dark," she added, looking about with a wee bit of nervousness.

Nichol didn't say anything to that, but it was true that he might know more about being cast out of a home than he was willing to share.

"I know what you think," she continued. "But on my honor, I didna kiss that man. You canna know how impossible it is to breathe when no one believes you. What motive would I have to lie? *Och,* but I hardly expect you to understand," she said with a shake of her head.

Nichol opened his mouth to argue that perhaps he could, but Miss Darby barreled on. "I canna be blamed that, on the *rare* occasion I was included in a gathering or a call with Sorcha, that gentlemen often looked to me. I never invited it and did my best to avoid it, on my word! But gentlemen believe themselves to be irresistible to the fairer sex and canna possibly believe that a lass would no' desire his attention, and seek to right that wrong. Even when a lass's lack of desire is clearly stated, aye? Mr. Cadell was the *worst* offender! I was quite clear that I didna want his attentions, that he was no' to touch me, that I would scream if he did, and do you know what he said? He said, 'You donna mean that,' and put his hands on my shoulders and pushed me against the wall and bloody well kissed me."

She paused, cast a quick glance at Nichol over her shoulder. "I beg your pardon for my choice of words," she added demurely. "I feel passionately that I've been wronged, I do."

"I would—"

"*Och,* donna give me platitudes, I beg of you. I've heard enough of them in the last fortnight, I have. And besides, I can guess easily enough what you think, Mr. Bain—that a man's desire canna be denied or some such foolishness."

"That is no'—"

"But what of a woman's desire, I ask you? Am I to have no say in it? Must I be subjected to him because he canna help himself? I tried to warn Mrs. Garbett and Sorcha about him, on my life I did. I meant it to warn her, to relate something of vital importance that she verra well ought to know, aye? But instead of thanking me for my honesty, Mrs. Garbett accused *me* of inviting his attentions. You'd no' believe what they said!"

"You donna—"

"They claimed that I've long had a habit of walking and speaking and smiling that serves only to invite male attention, and for that reason, I was often left at home, for I couldna be trusted. I swear to you, Mr. Bain, I swear on my father's grave, that I walk and I speak and I smile in the only manner I know how, and it is *no'* to invite attention, it is to get from one place to the next."

He silently arched a brow, uncertain if he was allowed yet to speak.

Apparently it was not yet his turn, for Miss Darby sighed, then drew a deep breath to launch once more.

Nichol guessed that she had not had the opportunity to say these things to anyone, and all her feelings about what had happened in Stirling were pouring forth.

"If that were all of it, I would find my peace with it, on my word, I would. But that was no' all of it, oh no. The Cadells were guests for more than a fortnight, and Mr. Cadell could no' be avoided. He sought me out at every opportunity, even though he was affianced to Sorcha. Mrs. Garbett said I purposely seduced him. No' only did she accuse me, they cast me out, and then took the only thing of my family that belonged to me. I would have gladly returned the gowns that were passed down to me and kept with the two muslins Mr. Garbett commissioned for me, but they took my *necklace. My* necklace, *my* heritage. Left to me! Can you believe the gall of it? After all these years, after trying so desperately to stay in the shadows for the sake of Sorcha, and they took my necklace!"

Nichol hadn't heard of any jewelry. "What necklace?"

"My necklace, my necklace!" she said impatiently, as if she'd explained this to him before. "It was a king's gift to my great-grandmother, handed down to my mother and then to me. It's quite valuable, but believe me when I say it's worth canna compare to the sentimental value it holds for me, aye? It is the only thing I've left of my family, the only thing that ties me to my name."

Something shuddered through Nichol. He understood better than this young woman could possibly imagine what it was to want to belong to a name. He understood how deeply unsettling it was to feel the snap of that thin thread. "This is the first I have heard of a necklace, Miss Darby. Had I known, I would have bargained to have it returned to you."

"*Och,* but you would have lost that bargain," she said sullenly. "The depravity there is surely beyond your ability to comprehend, Mr. Bain."

"On the contrary, I comprehend quite well," he said, and left it at that. It would be impossible to explain to her how or why he comprehended it as well as he did.

She twisted about so that she could view him fully and with unconcealed skepticism. "Donna tease me, Mr. Bain. You are no' acquainted with me, and it will no' be apparent to you that at present, I am in a very foul humor and likely will take offense. I canna even promise that I'll no' hit something *quite* hard."

She seemed very serious indeed, and Nichol made an effort to keep any sort of smile from his face. "I've had an inkling to your state of mind," he said, thinking that might be obvious, seeing as how she would not answer the door, then tried to keep him out by locking a window. "You've made it abundantly clear to all, then. I'd no' tease you, Miss Darby. Mr. Cadell is a coward and a scoundrel. Desire that is not mutually shared between a gentleman and a lady is pointless and vulgar."

She blinked, her gaze on his mouth, as if she didn't believe he'd actually spoken those words.

"Unfortunately, what I believe doesna change your situation. I have endeavored to find a solution that suits you. No' Mr. Garbett. *You*."

She snorted and shook her head, and turned her glittering blue eyes away from him, and Nichol felt a tiny little flicker of regret that she had. "There is *nothing* that will suit me, Mr. Bain. My patience and accommodating nature are at an end!"

He didn't think it his place to persuade her otherwise, and even if he'd been so inclined, he would not have the opportunity. Now that Miss Darby had been freed from the wretched conditions in Aberuthen and the Garbett house and, apparently, her silence, she had a long list of complaints.

"They forced me to leave all behind," she said again. "It was vindictive. It hardly mattered that all these years I endeavored to be pleasing, to stay well in the shadows, to keep to my room. But Sorcha and her mother were determined to lay blame and hardship at my feet, they were. What would be the harm, I ask you, in bringing along my needlework?" she demanded, her voice full of anger once again. "It was only half finished, useless to all of them, aye? *Och,* I donna care, Mr. Bain, I donna. I will start anew."

Nichol exchanged a look with Gavin, who seemed unduly wary, as he if he expected her to start anew here and now and somehow involve him in it. Nichol was glad he wasn't called upon to assure the lad otherwise—she did seem quite determined.

Her list of complaints against the Garbetts went on for a good quarter hour more, at which point, Miss

Darby seemed to have aired all her grievances and had lost her thirst for the airing. She seemed spent, taxed by the work of saying it all aloud, to have God and the world know how she'd been wronged.

She said no more until Nichol signaled Gavin that they would stop for the night, having decided they would not reach an inn before dark. He remembered a hollow they'd passed, where they could make camp, sheltered from wind. And it was on the banks of a creek so the horses could drink. He led them there.

It had stopped snowing, but the sky remained a dull slate gray turning to dark blue. Miss Darby did not hesitate to leap from her perch when Nichol reined to a halt, landing awkwardly on all fours, then disappearing into the woods. Gavin looked at Nichol with alarm, but Nichol shook his head. What would she do, run into dark woods with no place to go? She needed a moment of privacy, that was all.

Nichol was pulling the saddle from his horse when she returned to the small clearing. She looked with confusion at the saddle in his hands. "What are you doing, then?" she demanded.

"We'll bed here for the night."

"Here?"

"Aye, here," he said. "It's too dark to carry on, aye? I'll no' risk injury to one of the horses."

She looked around her. "But we're in the middle of nowhere!"

"That is no' entirely accurate. We are between Aberuthen," he said, pointing to the north, "and Crieff," he said, pointing to the south. "No' as much as a day's ride to Stirling, aye?" he added, pointing in the direction of Stirling. "We are indeed somewhere, Miss Darby, and this is a good place to water and graze the horses."

She gaped at him. Then at Gavin, who kept his head down and avoided her gaze. "Has my reputation been so irreparably damaged that you give no thought to it, sir? Am I to be humiliated further?"

"I mean to protect you, Miss Darby, no' harm you. Necessity demands adaptation, and I rather doubt you will be thought of any less for having slept under a night sky than an inn's roof." He unfurled a bedroll and laid his plaid on top of it. He bowed, and gestured grandly to the pallet he'd made. "You may avail yourself of this accommodation."

Miss Darby lifted her chin. She pulled her cloak tightly around her. "This is hardly *accommodation*," she muttered.

"I am confident you will weather it."

"Oh, I shall weather it, Mr. Bain. I have weathered *much* worse." With a dramatic swirl of her cloak, she fell onto the pallet and rolled to her side, facing away from him.

Nichol gazed down at her, sprawled on his plaid in a snit. She really was quite beautiful in his eyes. Her hair was inky black, and her eyes the color of a robin's egg. She had a lush figure that, in any other circumstance, would have caused his mouth to water. He thought she would be quite bonny if she ever felt like smiling again. He would like to see that, personally, but rather doubted he would be afforded the pleasure, given the nature of what would be a very short acquaintance. Her situation was not going to miraculously improve overnight and make her suddenly happy.

Nichol glanced at Gavin. The poor lad's eyes were nearly bulging out of his head. He looked at Nichol, as if expecting him to explain a woman's scorn. But that was beyond Nichol's considerable talents, and he shook his head, then instructed Gavin to gather wood for a fire.

CHAPTER FIVE

MAURA WOKE WITH a start, a swell of panic filling her throat as she frantically tried to sort out where she was or what was happening to her. A moment or two of blinking and sputtering against leaves stuck to her lips brought it all back to her—she was asleep on a forest floor. Her bones ached from cold and one arm tingled with a loss of feeling.

How long had she been asleep?

She recalled the surge of annoyance at this unexpected turn of events, then dropping onto the pallet Mr. Bain had made for her, and then…and then her eyes had felt scratchy, her lids heavy and her body so grateful to be off that horse.

She smelled smoke. Maura rolled onto her back, her gaze landing first on the small ring of fire, and then on Mr. Bain sitting beside her, his back against the trunk of a tree. He had one leg bent at the knee, the other stretched before him. He was holding a book.

Maura blinked. The man was reading by the light of the fire, as if this was a lazy summer evening.

Without looking at her, he held out a linen handkerchief.

She looked at the offering.

"You've half a forest pressed to your face," he said matter-of-factly.

Maura took it, then groped about for his arm to pull herself up. She gave him a good once-over, astonished that he could look so relaxed in the same forest with cold settling in. She wiped the dirt from her mouth. "How it pleases me to find the journey has posed no hardship for you, Mr. Bain, and that you are verra much at your leisure."

"I assure you, I am no' at my leisure, but merely attempting to pass the time." He deliberately turned a page.

Maura's stomach suddenly growled.

"Awake *and* hungry, then, are you?"

"Aye, famished," she said, and tossed the handkerchief onto his leg, annoyed that he should look so comfortable when she was freezing.

She looked around their little campsite. It must be quite late—the lad was asleep on the other side of the fire, his body turned toward the warmth of the flames. She could see the horses near the banks of the creek, blankets draped across their backs. "How will you keep the horses from wandering away, then?" she asked curiously.

"They're hobbled."

Maura peered at the horses, and could just make out the belt around their front legs.

Mr. Bain put aside his book and dragged a saddlebag onto his lap and began to rummage inside it. Maura glanced at the book, now lying between them.

"*'An Enquiry Concerning the Principle of Morals,'*" she read aloud. "How interesting. Perhaps your book will hold the answer as to the principle of morals in *this* particular situation, eh, Mr. Bain?"

He smiled wryly, and handed her a bundle wrapped in cheesecloth. "I've some dried beef and hard biscuits," he said.

Maura gasped with delight—she'd not expected food. She eagerly took the bundle from him and put it in her lap, brushed the tresses of hair from her eyes that had come undone with all her rolling about on the ground and which were apparently hosting a fair amount of leaves. But she paid no heed to her hair—she untied the cheesecloth and surveyed the food. As she had not eaten properly in days, this was a feast. Her stomach growled again.

She picked up a hunk of bread and bit into it, eating heartily, without regard to manners or attempting to conceal the sounds of pleasure she was making.

As she gnawed at a strip of beef, Mr. Bain nudged her and held up a skin. Whatever was in it, she hardly cared—she took it from him with a small grunt of thanks and drank.

Mr. Bain gave a small chuckle.

Ale. Strong ale at that, but she managed to keep from coughing it up and sighed when the warmth of it slid through her veins. When she had drunk what she could, she gave him the skin and resumed her meal.

Mr. Bain watched her with equal parts awe and amusement. "Am I so amusing?" she asked as she licked her fingers. "You'd be famished, too, that you would, had you been in the company of Mr. David Rumpkin. I've been desperately hungry—I dared eat scarcely a thing in that house."

"I donna blame you," he agreed. "I've no' seen a more despicable home."

She swallowed a mouthful of bread, thinking about the nightmare of the last fortnight. It would ruin her meal to describe the filth of that house, but she said, "I donna exaggerate when I say it was wretched, Mr. Bain." She glanced up, her gaze following a spark that flew up into the night sky. "It's much better here, really," she said brightly, having just decided it. She felt more optimistic with a bit of food in her belly. "Aye, quite cold, that it is. But better." She stuffed the rest of the beef in her mouth, gestured to the empty cheesecloth, and said, "Thank you for the food."

"You are verra welcome, Miss Darby. I have no' seen anyone enjoy hardtack and dried beef quite so much."

All right, then, she'd eaten like a sow, but she didn't care. She pondered her savior. Or was he her captor? A wee bit of both, she supposed. Either way, he was quite handsome. His hair was the color of autumn leaves, a mix of brown, dark red and gold. His eyes were pale green and when he looked at her, there was a certain sparkle in them.

Aye, he was a handsome man.

Yet she had the sense that there was something curiously distant about this handsome man. Perhaps it was because he knew everything about her, and she knew nothing but his name and that he liked to read books about philosophy, apparently. "Who are you?" she asked curiously.

He arched a brow. "I've told you."

"Aye, you've said your name, but who are you really, Mr. Bain?"

He gave her a slight, enigmatic smile. "Does it matter?"

Ooh, a *secret* then. Maura twisted about so that she was facing him. "Aye, it matters who, exactly, is spiriting me away to marry a man I've never laid eyes on. You could be a thief or a marauder for all I know."

"A *marauder*?"

"A highwayman?"

"That is no' an improvement."

"Well? What is your secret?"

"I've no secret."

"But you are a friend of Mr. Calum Garbett, and yet, I've never heard your name."

"Because I've only recently made Mr. Garbett's acquaintance."

"Really?" she asked skeptically.

He leaned forward, looked her directly in the eye and said, *"Really."*

"Then how...?"

"I'm what one might call an agent, aye? Let's agree that gentlemen often find themselves in uncomfortable situations, and I put them to rights."

Maura had never heard of such a thing. What gentlemen? What uncomfortable situations? Were there so many of them that a man might make it his occupation? "I beg your pardon?"

Mr. Bain leaned back against the tree and stretched his legs before him, crossing them at the ankle. "It's no' as strange as it sounds."

"Aye, it *is*," she insisted.

He smiled, lazily, indulgently, and it made her feel…warm.

"You are a young woman, Miss Darby. You would have no call to know that there are times in a man's life that he might need help disposing of a complication. I happen to be adept at that."

He spoke with such confidence! She was rather envious of that sort of confidence, really, particularly as she never felt entirely confident of anything. Well, except that she was not marrying a stranger in Lumparty, Lunmarty, wherever it was he was taking her. She was entirely confident in that. "What do you mean?" She suddenly had the idea that he meant something quite nefarious. She leaned forward and whispered, "*Are* you an outlaw, Mr. Bain?"

He blinked. He glanced at the lad as if to assure himself he could not hear, then leaned forward, so that he was only a few inches from her, and whispered, *"No."*

She swayed backward. "Then how is it you are adept at disposing of another man's complications?"

He leaned against the tree again. "I just am. In this particular instance, I was once employed by the Duke of Montrose. He is an acquaintance of Mr. Garbett and put forth my name."

Maura had seen the duke when she'd been called into Mr. Garbett's drawing room to account for her alleged crime. She knew of Montrose—everyone knew of him. But there was something more that tickled at her memory. What was it that was said of him? She suddenly recalled and blurted, "That's the man who murdered his wife!"

"He didna murder his wife, Miss Darby. It is true that the lady is no longer his wife, but she is verra much alive. When I said *complications*, I didna mean unlawful ones. I meant, simply…uncomfortable situations."

"Is that what I am, then? An uncomfortable situation?"

"Aye." He shrugged, as if that were plainly obvious. "If it eases you, you are the sort of uncomfortable situation that is easily put to rights."

"If it eases me!" she exclaimed. "It *offends* me that my uncomfortable situation is so easily put to rights! And never you mind, Mr. Bain—you may be adept with someone else, for I'll put my own uncomfortable situation to rights, thank you."

"*Will* you," he said skeptically, and gave her a hint of a smile that made his eyes shine even more. "And how exactly will you do that, Miss Darby?"

"Never you mind," she muttered. She had only a vague idea of how she'd go about it. It wasn't as if she'd ever been allowed to chart her own path. Until a month or so ago, she had been quietly biding her time until Sorcha married. Once, she'd inquired of Mr. Garbett if he might find her a position in a good house as a governess, or even a tutor. But Mrs. Garbett had seen her request as yet another example of how Maura meant to take attention from Sorcha. On the contrary, Maura had meant it to be helpful. She'd assumed Mrs. Garbett would want her gone.

Everything in the Garbett house depended on Sorcha making a proper match. Nothing else mattered. Maura had assumed that when Sorcha married, then she might be allowed to pursue a marriage of her own, or a position in a house that at least gave her something to do. Some place she might go where she felt wanted. And safe. She hadn't broached it again with Mr. Garbett, not with Sorcha's trials in attracting a suitor. She'd told herself to be patient, to stay in the shadows, to give Sorcha all the room she needed to accomplish this family goal. And then Adam Cadell had come along, the bloody bounder.

Maura had never imagined anything as ignominious as this. It mad her feel stupid to have waited so patiently for her turn, to have trusted the people who had sworn to look after her, only to have her turn upended into something as wretched as the circumstance she found herself in today.

No. She would think of something.

She looked across the fire to the lad. "Is he your son, then?"

"No. He's a hired hand."

"Have you a son?" she asked.

"No."

"A daughter?" She glanced at him from the corner of her eye.

He shook his head.

Her back was beginning to ache, sitting like she was, and Maura looked at the tree that held him up. The trunk was big enough for the two of them, so she scooted herself up and sat next to him. "A *wife*, then?"

He chuckled softly. "No."

"Have you anyone, Mr. Bain? Anyone at all to miss you?"

"I donna need anyone to miss me."

"Anyone who claims no' to need someone to miss them is a person that needs someone to miss them the most. I've no one to miss me, either, but I *need* someone to miss me." She punctuated that with a sniff of superior understanding of the ways of the world. Didn't need someone to miss him, indeed!

He gave her a discerning look, and Maura imagined how it must feel to be on the receiving end of his esteem. A tiny unwelcome shiver ran down her spine.

"You're verra unusual for a well-bred miss. You've more than a wee bit of pluck. You remind me of another woman I know, a woman from the Highlands."

"Then perhaps it is no' so unusual at all to have a wee bit of pluck, if you are acquainted with two," she pointed out, and turned her head.

She didn't like the insinuation that there was something wrong with *pluck*. He would have it, too, had he no authority over his own life. Maura was desperate, she was hurt and above all, she was furious that she had no say in what was to become of her. None at all! Her father had once told her she could be quite stubborn when she was of a mind. Well, she was of a mind. She had already decided that she would retrieve her necklace if it were the last thing on this earth she would do. They could pry it out of her cold, dead hand if they liked, but they would not take it from her while she had a breath in her lung.

Maura suddenly realized what she had to do. There was nothing to be done for it. Turning the idea over in her mind made her quake with fear, but it didn't matter—she would not have another opportunity and she would not let this one pass.

She suddenly stood, brushed out her gown and drew her cloak tightly about her. Mr. Bain did not object. "There is a place to wash where the river pools, just there," he said, nodding with his chin. He picked up his book.

He thought her helpless. The Garbetts thought her helpless. Adam Cadell thought her helpless. She was naïve, that she was. But she was *not* helpless. Mr. Bain had no fear of her wandering about in the forest because he believed she was too frightened to stray far. Well, she was, but that wouldn't stop her. Fury did funny things to a woman.

She walked on, past the horses, pausing to have a look at their hobbles. And then down to the pool to wash as best she could.

When she returned to the fireside, she noted that he had smoothed the pallet and had put more wood on the fire. He was reading again, engrossed in his principles of morals, she supposed. She took her place on the pallet. "I'm tired," she announced.

"Good night, Miss Darby," he said, as if he were sending a child off to bed. She lay down on the pallet, on her side, her back to him. She felt him get up and move away. A few minutes later he returned and stirred the fire, put more fuel to it. It wasn't enough heat, unfortunately. She could hardly feel her fingers or toes—the cold was beginning to sink into her bones. Maura pulled her cloak more tightly about her, but she was shivering.

A moment later, Mr. Bain lay down right beside her. So close that her heart began to race. She didn't trust him—she didn't trust any man—and a very primal fear began to ratchet in her.

That fear soared when he said, "You're shivering, lass. Come here, then."

"No," she said, but her tongue was thick, and her protest sounded garbled. She gasped with fright when he grabbed her hand and tugged her toward him. Maura cried out, expecting to be kissed, or a hand to grope her where it ought not to—but as she rolled, so did he, and she rolled into his back, her arm tight around his waist. "What are you *doing*, then?"

"Keeping you warm, aye? I'll no' have you freeze to death."

She tried to free her arm, but he held tight.

"I'll no' accost you, Miss Darby, you have my word. I mean only to keep you warm. Go to sleep."

"You're mad if you think I can sleep like this!" she exclaimed.

"Suit yourself," he said.

He could sleep like this, quite obviously, for his breathing began to slow until he seemed to be asleep.

It took some doing, but Maura began to relax. There was something to be said for the strength of a man's body, all hard planes and scents of leather and cardamom. And *warmth*. For the love of Scotland, his body gave off the heat of a brazier. And, admittedly, she felt a wee bit safer beside him in the middle of this forest. So she snuggled closer to him, seeking more of his warmth. He grunted, laced his fingers with her hand and held her close.

She imagined that this was what marriage must feel like when there was a healthy esteem between two people. Sleeping beside a warm man each night. Feeling safe and warm. And wanted? She would like that, to feel safe and warm and wanted. Perhaps one day she would.

Maura closed her eyes. She was tempted to sleep, but she dared not. She had too much to think about, too much to plan, too much to accomplish that could not be done while he was awake and unbalancing her with his very calm and matter-of-fact demeanor.

CHAPTER SIX

IT WAS TRULY maddening that a man could be in complete control of his deeds, of his desires, of his thoughts, with no more than a wee bit of effort. But lie next to a beautiful woman and it took every ounce of willpower Nichol could summon not to touch her.

He was a lad again, fighting against his urge to taste the cake the cook had made. He was a greenhorn, desperate to catch the scent of a woman. He was a man who had denied himself the pleasure of flesh for an eternity.

None of these things were true, but nevertheless, he felt as if they were, and he thought he'd never sleep. He couldn't quiet his mind, couldn't stop feeling her presence at his back, all soft and warm and pressed against him, her breath tickling the back of his neck. He couldn't stop imagining her without a stitch of clothing, of covering her beneath the blankets on this starry night, his body in hers, his eyes on her clear blue eyes.

But sleep he obviously did, for when the sun made its first appearance over the tops of the trees, he roused himself from the unsettled rest, and into his conscience crept the realization that his back was cold.

Nichol rolled over. She was not there, bundled in her cloak, her hair spilling about her. A jolt to his heart sat him up, and he looked about, trying to make sense of it.

She was gone. And she'd bloody well taken his plaid.

Nichol sprang to his feet with a roar, startling the lad, who sputtered awake. "Have you seen her?" Nichol demanded as Gavin tried to disentangle himself from his bedding.

"Who?" the lad asked stupidly.

Perhaps she'd gone to the creek. Nichol whirled about, but what he saw there made his heart sink even deeper. One of the horses was missing. Bloody hell, why had he not remained awake? Why had he been so damnably complacent? He let forth a string of swearing that made Gavin's face turn four shades of red, but Nichol was livid. He didn't like surprises—*he* was the one to control the circumstances. If there was one thing he detested, it was when a client did not behave properly. He was furious with himself for assuming that a young miss would not have the sense or the courage to make a muck of his carefully laid plans. And he was absolutely irate because it was entirely possible she'd gotten herself killed by now.

And maybe he was grudgingly impressed, too, because he'd never known a woman who would run off in the middle of the forest in the middle of the night. He doubted he would have had the guts to do it, without anything to protect himself, without provisions. Could she even ride? How did she put herself on a horse that was at least two hands taller than her? How far did the wench think she would get before she was lost, or fell or was set upon by thieves?

"Aaaiiieee," he roared, and kicked a log with all his might.

"What's happened to her, then?" Gavin asked timidly, his dark hair sticking up in several directions.

"She's gone off, that's what."

"By herself?"

"Aye, by herself," Nichol bit out.

Gavin's eyes rounded.

Nichol stomped down to the brook, thinking. He looked around, for any sign of where she might have gone. There was the horse's hobble lying on the ground. But the saddle was precisely where he'd left it. He shook his head at her audacity.

He knew where she was heading, if she could manage to determine the direction. He knew because she had done quite a lot of talking yesterday. She was so angry, and she wanted to give Miss Garbett a piece of her mind. Had she not said so more than once? Nichol didn't pretend to understand how a woman's mind worked, but he'd been with enough of them to know that a woman scorned was like a dog with a bone.

He was entirely confident that Miss Darby was on her way to Stirling just now.

There was no question that he had to go and fetch her. He couldn't have her appear in Stirling on the back of a horse with nothing but her fury—his reputation would be ruined! Not to mention he would lose his fee. *Bloody stupid lass. Stubborn wench.*

He squatted down and splashed water on his face. She would have kept to the roads. He could ride through the forest and catch her before she reached Stirling. But he couldn't catch her if he was riding with the lad.

He stood up, hands on hips, and stared at the rising sun.

What was he to do with the lad? He couldn't send him back to Aberuthen—the inn there was too bleak. There was no question that he could not return to Rumpkin's house of horrors. Nor could he send the lad on to Luncarty, as that was too far away—Nichol didn't trust him to make it there on his own without a horse.

There was one other option, unthinkable until this moment—Cheverock, the home where he was born. A half-day's ride from here at most.

Nichol had been toying with the idea of paying a call to his boyhood home, but to appear at Cheverock in this way after all these years was not what he wanted. Ivan would not understand a lad showing up and claiming to have been sent by Nichol. The last Nichol had seen Ivan, he'd not quite reached his majority. What would he think? And why had Ivan grown silent? Had he forgotten Nichol?

He hoped it was no more than that.

But he sensed it was much more than that. All the messengers had been turned away.

Never mind that now—this sudden development

would force the issue for Nichol. He had no other viable choice so it would seem at long last, he was going home.

Gavin could walk there and arrive by nightfall if he set out now.

Nichol glanced over his shoulder—Gavin was watching him anxiously, twisting the corner of his plaid that he'd draped around his shoulders. What was he, fourteen years? Fifteen? Too young for this, that much was apparent.

Nichol turned around, and the lad blinked. He clearly suspected the news for him would not be good.

Well, then, there was nothing to be done for it— Nichol was in a corner. He trudged back to the campsite, stood with his legs braced apart, his arms folded across his chest, and eyed the lad. After a moment, he said, "I must go after the lady, aye?"

"Where's she gone?" Gavin asked.

"I canna say for certain, but I've a good idea where," Nichol bit out. "She's got a good head start on me, aye? I need move with haste."

Gavin nodded. "I'll gather our things."

Nichol stopped him with a hand to his shoulder. "Gavin, lad, I canna catch her with two of us on the horse."

Gavin's brown-eyed gaze filled with uncertainty.

"I mean to send you off to a place where you may wait for me."

Gavin's lips parted. *"Where?"* he asked, his voice faintly tremulous.

"The seat of the Baron MacBain." Perhaps Nichol was imagining things, but Gavin looked suddenly very pale. "I grew up there," he explained. "You will speak to my brother, Ivan, and he will see that you are looked after until I come for you, aye?" At least he prayed that was the case.

"Should I no' go to Stirling?" Gavin pleaded.

"It's too far to reach on foot, aye? Do you know how to shoot, lad?"

Gavin shook his head. He was beginning to breathe heavily, almost in a pant. *Diah,* but Nichol wanted to shoot something just then. He would not like to be without his pistol, but he would not rest knowing the lad had nothing with which to defend himself. So he withdrew his pistol from his waist and held it out to him. "Watch me closely, then. We've no' much time."

He showed Gavin how to load it, to cock it, to fire it. He made him do it three times until he was satisfied that he'd at least not shoot his own foot. "You'll no' need it, but you ought to have it. Now off with you, straight up the road. By day's end you will come to an old castle ruin. The road forks there—turn east. You'll be two miles from Comrie. Cheverock is about two miles more."

"What if I get lost?" Gavin asked, his voice shaking now.

"You'll no' be lost. Look at me, Gavin," he said, and went down on one knee before him. "You canna get lost if you follow the road. Walk until you reach the old castle ruin, then take the eastern fork," he said, pointing east. "Tell Ivan I've sent you and I'll come for you by week's end, aye?"

Gavin was trying very hard not to cry. He nodded and looked at the gun in his hand.

"Look here," Nichol said softly. "You're a brave lad and a clever one, you are. You have everything you need inside of you, Gavin. Everything is there," he said, tapping his chest. "You donna need me, no' really."

"What if they donna believe me, then?" he asked through a sniffle.

It was a fair point. Nichol suddenly stood and went to his satchel. He looked inside, in a pocket there, and withdrew a ring. It was an insignia ring, one that had belonged to his grandfather, a man he remembered with fondness. He turned back to Gavin and pressed the ring into his palm. "Give my brother this. Tell him I'd no' ask for his help if it were no' imperative. He'll believe you."

Gavin looked at the ring, then slowly put it in his pocket.

"There's a good lad," Nichol said. He patted him awkwardly on the shoulder, then handed him the bags. "There is food and ale. Put your pistol here, aye? If you see anyone on the road, hide in the forest until they've passed. You've nothing to fear, Gavin."

He hoped to God above that was true. Nichol didn't know what the lad might expect when he reached Cheverock, as the estrangement between him and his father, and perhaps his brother, made it impossible to know. But he believed Ivan to be a decent man. He would not turn the lad out.

Gavin looked up, and Nichol would have kicked himself squarely in the arse if he were able. He had no desire to send Gavin off into the deep of Scotland all alone, any more than he desired to ride like a thief across Scotland to catch Miss Darby before she ruined everything for him. "I must go—I canna risk losing the wench, aye? Go as quickly as you can. You'll reach Cheverock by nightfall if you donna tarry."

He turned away from the lad whose eyes were as big as moons, grabbed up his things and stuffed them into his satchel and strode to where the lone horse stood. In minutes, he was saddled. He glanced back at Gavin, who had at least gathered his bedroll and the bag. Nichol threw himself on the back of the horse and reined him around. "God's speed," he said to Gavin, and set the horse to a trot, which he would turn to a run as soon as he reached the road.

Miss Darby, that wee half-wit, would sorely rue the moment she stole his horse and escaped. Aye, he would make damn certain of it.

CHAPTER SEVEN

EVERY MUSCLE, EVERY SINEW, ached in Maura. She'd had to cling to the horse so she'd not fall off. Her progress was achingly slow—she was afraid to give the horse any room to run, afraid she'd be bounced right off and onto her arse and lose him.

How far could it possibly be to Stirling? She'd been sent to Aberuthen by carriage, but they'd reached it within a matter of a few hours. And yet she felt as if she'd been riding all night and all day. She'd kept to the road, so she didn't think she was lost. Could she have possibly gone the wrong direction? Hadn't Mr. Bain very clearly pointed in this direction? Still, it had been awfully dark when she'd sneaked away in the predawn hours, and perhaps she'd gotten a wee bit turned around.

She hadn't wanted to leave the warm cocoon of Mr. Bain's body and blanket. She hadn't really wanted to leave the safety of him, either. But she'd made herself go, the desire to have her necklace compelling her. Frankly, she couldn't believe Mr. Bain and the lad had slept through her departure. It had taken quite an effort to unbuckle the heavy hobble as her fingers had turned to ice. The horse, the smaller of the two, had snorted over his shoulder at her, annoyed with her clumsy attempt. But at last she'd undone it, and had tied a rein around it's neck—she'd been too afraid to attempt the bridle—and had led the horse along the brook until they reached the road.

It had taken her several attempts to put herself on the horse's back. She'd tried jumping up, grabbing his mane, but he kept moving away, unwilling to participate in such mischief. And then she'd spotted a rock near the edge of the road, and at last, with the help of that rock, she was able to claw her way onto the horse's back. At which point she found herself lying flat against him, holding on to his mane, the rein having been dropped as she'd tried to mount. She would not risk losing the horse by getting off to retrieve it. She had kicked the horse in the flank, and off they'd trotted.

How she wished for a saddle! But to take one of them would have been useless—she didn't know how to saddle the horse, didn't know if she could lift the thing over her head.

Eventually, she'd felt secure enough to sit, but she'd left the gait up to the horse. They'd moved along, sometimes ambling, sometimes trotting. Once even stopping when the horse seemed rather determined to have a rest.

The sun was high in the sky now, and Maura passed the slow progress picturing the scene when Mr. Bain woke to find her missing. She imagined he'd been quite cross, as men thought themselves superior to women in every way, and he was undoubtedly the sort to despise being taken for an utter fool by a woman. The question was, would he be angry enough to follow her? He seemed a proud man, aye, but she didn't know if he was too proud to chase after a woman he scarcely knew. He'd done his duty after all. He'd removed her from Rumpkin and he'd surely collected his fee. And while she was certain beyond a doubt that he'd been cross when he discovered her missing, he also seemed unflappable. Detached.

No, he'd not come after her, she decided. He'd pack his books and tell the lad the day was fine and they might carry on without her.

The horse snorted and tossed its head; Maura glanced up and made a little cry of joyous relief. Below her, she could see the chimneys and rooftops around Stirling castle. There was a bridge across the river, and at the bridge, an inn with a public house. She would stop there and try and repair her appearance as best she could. And she'd have to think of a plausible explanation for her return to Garbett House. *Aye, I've come back, Mr. Garbett. How could you send me off to such a reprehensible man, I ask you? I've been a good and loyal ward to you, sir, and I've tried my verra best to stay out of Sorcha's light. How dare you impugn me, how dare you dishonor me as you have!*

No, that wouldn't do. Mr. Garbett generally did not care to be wrong.

Mr. Bain removed me and then left me! He said he'd invented the whole thing, and that he hadn't the time to take me anywhere. He said that I might do

*as I please but I could no' return home. What was
I to do, then?*

Better. But still highly implausible. Mr. Bain had
come at the recommendation of the Duke of Montrose. Wouldn't Mr. Garbett take his complaint directly to the duke?

*We were set upon by thieves and they took Mr.
Bain! I managed to escape and came straightaway
home, as I knew you would want me to do.*

That might work.

The horse suddenly began to canter. He probably
sensed the end to his ordeal was near or had caught
the scent of oats. But whatever the cause of his sudden burst of enthusiasm, Maura gave a little shriek
and grabbed onto his neck to keep from being tossed
off as they passed through a copse of trees.

She saw the horse's interest then—just ahead was
the public inn, and two horses at the trough that hers
was determined to join. If she ever saw Mr. Bain
again—which she would not, but if she did—she
would compliment his very fine horse and thank
him for the use of it.

At the trough, the horse muscled in between the
other two. As he dipped his head to drink, Maura slid
off his back, wincing when she landed. Her legs felt
as if a thousand knives had scraped up the insides of
them. Her hair was loose, and she wrapped it around
her fist, then tied it in a knot. She had to find some
place to tidy up—she could hardly walk into the public house looking as if she'd been dragged through

the forest. She tried to see over the horses. There was the inn, its door standing open, through which she could hear the voices of many. Beside the inn a smaller building. An office, she guessed, where mail and passengers paid for the coach. And behind that, a slightly larger building. The stables? That was it, then. She'd slip inside, attempt to tend her hair and shake out the wrinkles from her cloak and gown.

Maura stepped out from between the horses, glanced nervously toward the public house, drew the hood of her cloak over her head and hurried around the trough and down the path where horses were brought up from the stables. She quickened her step, and at the corner of the office, she paused to take one last look behind her before turning the corner, but was suddenly yanked backward by an unseen force, and a gloved hand clamped down over her mouth.

Maura desperately tried to find her footing, but was lifted off her feet, spun around and shoved up against the wall of the office.

It all happened so quickly that she hadn't had time to breathe, much less scream, and when she looked into the pale green eyes of Mr. Bain, her heart tried to leap through her throat and flee.

His eyes were shimmering with undiluted fury. He held her with his body against the wall, his hand firmly anchored her mouth closed, and with his free hand, he lifted a finger. "No' a word, aye? No' so much as a sound from you, or I will bring the men of the public inn down around your ears and tell them you're a whore who stole my purse."

She would have gasped with shock if she'd been able.

"Do you understand me, then?"

She didn't know how she was supposed to answer seeing as how he was holding her mouth shut, but managed to nod.

He slowly let go his hand at her mouth, but kept her pinned to the wall. It was rather awkward—he was mere inches from her, half his body pressed against half of hers. "I'll no' scream, I swear it," she said. "Will you step back, then?"

He laughed, and the sound of it was not pleasant. "No, you bloody wench—I donna trust you."

"At least I've no' accosted *you* against your free will."

"No, *you've* gone sneaking off in the dead of the night. What in bloody hell were you thinking, then?"

"I owe you no explanation, Mr. Bain, as you have no say over me, but *obviously* I was *thinking* I needed to escape!" she said incredulously. "Do you blame me? I donna care to go and marry your Mr. Whatsit."

"Have you a *better* idea what to do with you?" he scoffed.

"As it happens, yes!"

He snorted. "You may trust me that confronting Miss Garbett with hysteria is *no'* a better idea."

Fury replaced her fright, sweeping through her with such force that Maura was surprised it didn't lift her off her feet. *"Hysteria?"* she repeated loudly, and kneed him as hard as she could just below his knee.

"Ouch. Damn you, that hurt."

"I donna suffer from *hysteria*—"

"No, your malady is madness, quite obviously. I am trying to warn you that confronting her will no' improve your—"

She shoved him away from her. "I'm *cross*, Mr. Bain! Verra cross! You canna imagine how it feels to believe yourself part of a family, at the verra least a valued servant one moment, and then in the blink of an eye be cast out as if you are *nothing* to them! To be thought of so little that all your things are taken from you! To be made a vagabond! I am *cross*," she said again, and to her horror, tears sprang to her eyes. "It's humiliating," she said, her voice falling low. "I've felt only two things since the day they sent me away, and that is either quite lost or quite angry, and at present, I am choosing *angry*."

"Nevertheless, there is no need to resort to violence."

"Do no' condescend to me, sir!"

Mr. Bain reached into the interior of his coat and withdrew a handkerchief, which he held out to her. "It doesna follow that because I find your actions rash that I am condescending," he sniffed.

She took the handkerchief. "Why must men *always* believe they are superior to women in intellect and deed?"

"Oh, I donna know," he drawled, and folded his arms across his chest. "What in blazes would bring you back here, where you are clearly no' wanted, with no hope of having your side heard? Only a fool would take such a risk. A *risk*, I might add, that might have seen you killed, aye? And for *no* possible gain. It defies logic."

Maura rolled her eyes and blew her nose. "I would no' have been *killed*, Mr. Bain. But if there was the slightest possibility, do you really think I would risk my life to speak to Sorcha? I donna care what she thinks of me, on my word! And if you're so clever, why did you no' tie me up or keep watch over me? Why did you assume you knew how I'd respond to *your* decision for my fate?"

Mr. Bain glared at her. He pointed a finger at her. He looked as if there was much he wanted to say, but hesitated and said, grudgingly, "Fair point. I should have been more vigilant, aye. But the doesna change the fact that running off like you did could have seen you killed or worse."

"Worse!" She laughed and pushed hair, come undone again, from her face. What she wouldn't give for a few pins.

"Does that amuse you, Miss Darby? Has it occurred to you what sort of man might roam these hills, then? You canna talk or charm your way out of everything, and if a man is of a mind, he will do with you what he likes, aye?"

That sobered her. She'd thought of it, but only vaguely. It sounded much more real when he said it.

"You've made a bloody fix of things, aye, you

have," he added quite unnecessarily. But, she had to note, not unkindly.

"They are my things to fix," she said petulantly.

He sighed. "Tell me true, aye? Why did you do it? What do you hope to gain?"

"Freedom."

"Forgive me, Miss Darby, and at the risk of being accused of condescension, you are a *woman*. And one without means, aye? Freedom is no' yours for the taking."

She could not dispute that. "'Tis more than that."

"Go on," he said, gesturing for her to speak. "What more?"

"My necklace. I must have it back."

He frowned. "A necklace?"

"Aye, I *told* you. The necklace belonged to my mother and her grandmother before her. It's all I have of my name, and they should no' have taken it. I did nothing wrong, Mr. Bain. They should *no'* have taken it, and I will have it back." She held up her hand before he could speak. "Donna think you can stop me."

He studied her. No doubt he thought her foolish, or mad. She'd not be surprised if he marched her back to Garbett House and demanded Mr. Garbett pay him even more than he already had for all the trouble she'd caused him. "'Tis neither here nor there, but aye, I do understand," he said.

Maura pressed the used handkerchief into his palm. "How could you possibly?" she asked with weary skepticism.

"The depth of my understanding is too tedious to explain, Miss Darby," he said as he grimaced at the handkerchief before tucking it into his pocket. "Suffice it to say that I know what you are experiencing, far better than you could possibly imagine."

It was an odd thing for him to say. Did he truly think that a man as dapper and capable as himself could understand her woes? He was a man, after all, very much in command of his destiny, as all men were. *He'd* never been cast out. *He'd* never been humiliated as she had.

"You've every right to be cross," he added quietly. "But if you want your necklace, you must sing a sweet song."

"A song?" That made no sense to her. "What are you talking about?"

He held out his hand, palm up. "Come."

"Where?"

"You could do with some food, I suspect, as could I. We'll discuss your necklace."

Still, she did not take his hand. "I will brook no discussion, Mr. Bain. I mean to have it," she said firmly.

He leaned forward, touched a bit of hair that had attached itself to her eyelash and moved it aside. "Aye, Miss Darby, you've been exceedingly clear on that point. We'll discuss how to get it, then."

They *would*? What was this? What treachery did he present her now? Maura stepped back from him. "I donna want to discuss it with you—I donna trust you."

He suddenly chuckled, and the pleasant sound of it tingled through her. "I hardly trust *you*, either, but I should like to know on what grounds you will no' trust *me*, as I've given you no cause. What have I done or said that was no' true?"

He had her there. She sniffed. She looked toward the road. She felt his hand wrap around hers. Dwarf hers, really. "Come, then, lass. I'm hungry." He smiled, and tugged her along.

MR. BAIN ORDERED kidney pies and tankards of ale for them, and as they dined, Maura told him more about the necklace. "It's a ring of diamonds, goes round the throat," she said, gesturing to her neck. "An emerald the size of a bird's egg hangs just here," she said, touching the hollow of her throat.

Mr. Bain's gaze settled on her throat for a long moment.

"My great-grandmother was a rare beauty, that she was, and a favorite of King Charles. He gifted her the necklace."

"Did he," Mr. Bain said, rather stoically.

"Aye. She had her portrait made with it. It hung in the drawing room. My mother would allow me to put it on and pretend to be a great lady." She smiled ruefully at the memory of herself prancing about her mother's dressing room, the necklace heavy on her neck. She was a queen in that necklace, the furnishings her court. She even insisted the maid curtsy for her. What an insufferable little beast she must have been.

She glanced up; Mr. Bain was watching her, his expression inscrutable.

"It was meant to be mine all along, to be gifted to me on the occasion of my wedding. But my mother died, and then my father, and everything was taken away."

She thought of the day men had come to cart off all the furnishings of the house to satisfy her father's creditors. She hadn't thought of it in quite a long while, but she recalled now how she'd trembled with fear that they would cart her off, too, and toss her into a debtor's prison, or worse, a workhouse. Mr. Garbett had appeared just in time to save her. "Oh dear," he'd said as he'd watched brusque men carrying out the pianoforte. "Oh *dear*."

She had believed the kind-faced man to be her knight. But he wasn't a knight at all—he wouldn't or couldn't save her from his wife. She shook her head to dislodge the memory. "I've nothing of my family, Mr. Bain, nothing at all save that necklace, and I will crawl to Garbett House if I must and take it by force."

"Force? What do you mean, a bit of kicking and shoving again?"

Maura didn't know what she meant, but she showed him her fist.

Mr. Bain looked at her fist, then slowly leaned back in his seat, his expression quite serious. "So you mean to punch Miss Garbett in the nose?"

"No!"

"The belly, then?"

She clucked her tongue. "I donna mean to strike her at all."

"Then what *do* you mean, Miss Darby?"

She *harrumphed*, and sat back, her arms folded across her belly. A smile appeared on Mr. Bain's lips.

"My plight is no' amusing!"

"I beg to differ," he said cheerfully. "The picture of you engaging in a bare-knuckle brawl is *highly* amusing." She tossed her head. She didn't really want to fight for it. The prospect frightened her. It would hurt, for one, and Sorcha was taller than her.

He suddenly sat forward, pushed his plate away and folded his arms across the tabletop. "I've a proposition that may suit you, if you'll allow it."

She eyed him with skepticism. "Go on."

"If I help you retrieve your necklace, do I have your word you'll give me no more trouble and carry on to Luncarty?"

"To marry your *friend*?" she asked with not a little exasperation. The notion galled her yet.

"Have you someplace else to go, then? Another benefactor who will take you in?"

Maura shifted uncomfortably in her seat. She was, in fact, friendless. "I donna need to be taken in, Mr. Bain. I can do for myself, thank you."

"Mmm," he said. "And you will do for yourself… how? The roof that you will need over your head—do you have a way of providing it?"

"I'll sell my necklace."

"Ah," he said. "The sentimental value may not be as great as the monetary value, is that it, then?"

"No! It's more valuable to me for the sentiment. But I havena any money."

"So you'll sell it, aye?"

"Aye."

"In Edinburra, of course, for you'd no' get more than a fraction of it's worth in Stirling. Better yet, you ought to sell it in London, where it *might* fetch its worth. And then you will use that money to, what… purchase the roof?"

She shifted again. She didn't like the direction this was heading. "Why no'?"

"Oh, no reason, really. Other than the bothersome fact that you're a woman, Miss Darby, and you are no' allowed to own property outright. You need a man to purchase your roof, and in spite of your youth and inexperience, I think you know as well as I do that men donna buy houses for women without a few conditions of purchase." He arched a brow at her.

Heat crept into her cheeks. He was right, she knew he was right. She had no power. She was an orphan in this world and could not provide for herself. She had no living relatives, at least none that could be found when her father had died. She was as helpless today as she had been in Rumpkin's home. She hated the feeling of being trapped, of having no say over her own life. She hated being at the mercy of men, who cared nothing for her, except her body.

Mr. Bain was calmly awaiting her answer with his arched brow and his mouth pursed.

How could she possibly trust him? He thought she ought to by virtue of the fact she'd not caught him in a falsehood in the space of the twenty-four hours or so that she'd been acquainted with him. Well, she was far less trusting than that—sometimes it took a person weeks or even *years* to betray another. And then again, she desperately wanted her necklace. It was the principle of it, not to mention the sentimentality. She might possibly want it bad enough to go along with Mr. Bain at the moment. She crudely drew the back of her hand across her mouth. "Verra well."

"We have a bargain?"

"*If* the necklace is returned to me, aye, we have a bargain. But donna think for a moment this means I trust you, Mr. Bain."

"Perhaps no' yet," he said amicably, "but you will. I've your solemn word, do I?"

He had her word. She would determine what to do to save herself from marrying his "friend" when they reached Luncarty. "From my lips to God's ears, you have my word."

Mr. Bain's gaze fell to her lips, and the shine of his eyes changed, and turned a wee bit darker, and for a moment, Maura's heart skipped around a beat or two. She shifted in her seat like a child in church, and looked anywhere but at those green eyes shining with something she didn't quite comprehend, but that felt dangerous. Like the sudden flare of a newly made fire. The sudden swell of an ocean wave.

"How do we do it? How do we get it back?" she asked the table.

He pulled his plate closer, picked up his fork and

resumed his meal. "Eat," he said, gesturing to her unfinished plate. "Can you repair your appearance?"

She looked down at her gown. It looked as if it had been dragged through the forest. She put a hand to her hair. "I'll need help with my hair."

He took in the tresses that fell wild around her shoulders, then glanced at his plate. "And you do understand, do you no', that you must be contrite when we arrive?"

"Aye, aye, contrite, then," Maura said irritably.

"If you want your necklace, if you want to be freed from the Garbetts, you must do as I say and trust that I know what I'm doing."

She frowned.

"*Och,* I know you donna trust me, but for the sake of this exercise, we'll both pretend that you do, aye? This sort of thing is my occupation, Miss Darby. I understand the way a man's mind works. We'll say you've come back for a few of your things. Your gown will prove that to be an imperative need."

She couldn't help a small, wry smile at that. "It will indeed."

He returned her smile with one that was a wee bit conspiratorial, and picked up his tankard of ale.

"All right, shall we go?"

"Patience. We must arrive late enough that Garbett will be forced to invite us to stay for the night."

"*What!*" Maura exclaimed. "I'll no' stay there, Mr. Bain! I'll no' risk another moment in the company of Adam Cadell or Sorcha Garbett!"

"Aye, you must. I need time, Miss Darby. We

canna waltz in and take the necklace straightaway. If I canna convince Mr. Garbett to return it, I'll need another solution."

"What solution?"

He shrugged.

"*What* solution?" she asked again.

"I donna know as yet," he admitted. "Do you know where the necklace might be, then?"

She didn't know for certain, but she suspected Sorcha had it close by, so that she could look upon it every day and gloat. "I've an idea."

"We must know the exact location as soon as possible, before I speak to Mr. Garbett."

It took Maura several moments before she understood him. She gaped at him. "Do you mean to *steal* it?" she asked in a loud whisper.

"Certainly no'," he said, as if that were preposterous, and then gave her a ghost of a smile. "Except, of course, if the Garbetts are unreasonable. Then, I'll have no choice." He winked at her, drained his tankard and set it down. "All right, then, your first task is to make yourself…" He paused and took in her disheveled appearance. "Tidy," he said. "Your second task is to determine the exact location of the necklace once we arrive."

Maura was still reeling from the idea that they might very well steal the necklace, an idea that both thrilled and appalled her. "What will be *your* task?" she asked.

"To help you with your hair," he said. His eyes

moved to her throat, to her décolletage. "Because something must be done."

His voice was silky, a warm caress, and Maura wasn't certain he was speaking of her hair. She imagined him using that dulcet voice with a woman in his bed. She imagined herself lying naked with him, and him whispering *something must be done.*

The unsettling image prompted a wave of sparks to sizzle through her. She was suddenly and acutely aware of every part of him. Especially his gaze, which was so intent that she could swear it singed her skin everywhere he looked.

You're being ridiculous. This man, who had appeared like a faerie with a fist through a window, had come with an absurd plan to marry her off. And yet, instead of seeking every way possible to flee as she ought to be doing, her regard for him was suddenly shimmering, her breath glistening in her lungs. *Stop it at once,* she commanded herself.

Unfortunately, it was harder to stop than she would have thought. Maura picked up her tankard and took a long drink of bitter ale to steady herself as he watched her with that potent stare.

All right, then. Verra well. She would join him in this mission, and she would, as she said, trust him. But the moment it was over, she would flee. She would not allow a pair of very lovely eyes to weaken and divert her.

He was still watching her, quite casually, like a cat watches a bird or a mouse, and Maura had the strange feeling that he was actually reading her jumbled thoughts. It rattled her, and she realized she had to be more mysterious. She could not have him guessing her plans.

So Maura smiled. She smiled like she'd not smiled in weeks. As if she were entirely happy with what was happening to her.

Mr. Bain's expression changed. His fine eyes took on an entirely new sheen as they locked with hers.

The sizzle of sparks in her began to blaze.

CHAPTER EIGHT

NICHOL ESCORTED MISS DARBY into the stable where he'd sent the horses to be fed and watered. He searched through his satchel and produced a comb.

"Have you any pins?" she asked.

"Quite obviously, I do no'," he said wryly.

"We'll need something with which to bind it, aye?" she said, twirling a tress around her finger. "Had you bothered with my bag, we'd have it."

Frankly, he was still uncertain if Miss Darby was a woman who had suffered an injustice, or was merely mad. "Do you mean I was to gather your things in my haste to intercept you?"

"I should think it was clear that I could no' have brought it."

Nichol thought about pointing out that she should not have escaped him at all, or how illogical it was to assume that he should have made certain he had all her things after she did.

She suddenly caught her breath, then said, "I've got it!" She reached for the horse's bridle, hanging from a hook on the wall. "A wee bit of leather will do the trick, aye? If you have a knife, we can pare off a few strings of it."

The reins were long enough, and it was the only practical solution, short of finding a ladies' shop. Nichol removed a small knife from his boot and cut a piece from the end of the rein, then pared that into tiny strips as she combed her hair with her fingers. It was something that was entirely necessary, and should not have been the least bit erotic, but Nichol couldn't tear his eyes from the process. There was something about a woman's hair that moved him, that separated him from the fairer sex. A gentleman had once opined in his presence that a woman's hair was the crown of her beauty. Nichol had never thought of it in precisely that way, but then again, he'd never been drawn to a woman's hair quite like he was drawn to Miss Darby's luxuriant tresses, black as a satin night.

When she had combed through the tangles, she began to knot her hair, making loops, twisting the loops into knots, then tying them with the bits of leather he handed her. When she had several knots, she handed him two of the longest strips of the leather. "Gather them all together and tie them, then twist the ends under and tie them there, aye?"

"Pardon?"

She pressed the leather into his hand and presented her back.

Nichol examined the knotted loops. He began to gather them, taking care not to pull the knots from their ties. The feel of her hair was soft as a kitten in his hands. How was it possible that the feel of a woman's hair could stir emotions and desires in him that had no place in this stable? How was it possible that a man as careful as he, who measured each word and deed, could feel her hair on his fingers and feel himself on the verge of losing all reason?

He followed her instructions, tying the loops under to make a unique chignon. It was hard to corral all that hair, and Miss Darby complained that he was pulling too tightly.

"Beg your pardon."

"Ouch."

"I canna tie it without pulling a little," he complained. "You're tender headed," he said accusingly as he worked the last tie around the ends.

"Why must you say it as if I am purposely so?" she demanded, her fingers fluttering near his as if she meant to assume control.

He brushed her hands away. "If you want this done, Miss Darby, let me do it, aye?"

With a huff, she dropped her hands.

"There," he said, and dropped his hands, too. He studied his work. The chignon was a wee bit lopsided, but it would do well enough. She could enlist the services of a proper ladies' maid at Garbett House and tidy it up then.

Miss Darby put her hand to the lump of hair at her neck, feeling all around it. Nichol's eye was drawn to a tiny ringlet that had stubbornly escaped the binds. It lay against her neck, floating there, and he had the sudden urge to sweep that ringlet aside and kiss the pale skin just beneath.

"It feels *odd*," she said.

He felt odd.

"Does it look a fright?"

"I donna…" He paused. Did it look a fright? It looked incredibly enticing to him. He wanted to pull each tress free, watch it tumble down her back. "It will have to do. My skill in hairdressing will no' miraculously improve as we stand here."

"Aye." She turned around. "Are we ready, then? Might we go and have this done?"

"In a moment. Do you remember what you are to do?"

"About what?"

He narrowed his gaze. "Be *contrite*, Miss Darby." She rolled her eyes.

"Precisely what I fear," he said, and couldn't help himself—he brushed a bit of straw from her stomacher. "You must be polite *and* demure. *Can* you be demure?"

"Of course I can *do* it, Mr. Bain. I was no' raised in the wild."

"Hmm," he said dubiously. "Do you remember what else?"

She put her hands on her waist and nudged the bare floor with her slipper.

"Well, then? What else did we discuss?"

She groaned to the ceiling. "That I've considered my crime and I am verra sorry for it!"

"Could you possibly say so without sounding as though you've been tortured into confessing it?"

"Could *you* possibly worry about your part in this

and allow me to worry about mine?" she shot back, folding her arms defiantly across her.

"I'll worry all the same, for you have a disposition that doesna lend itself to sympathy."

She gasped. "You're as bold as brass!"

He shrugged.

She took another deep breath, and he expected to receive the full force of her anger. But she suddenly released it into one long sigh. "Aye, all right, all right," she said, capitulating. "I will do my best to appear as sweet as honey, and as shamed as a dog caught chewing a shoe, on my word."

"See that you do. If you give them *any* reason to—"

She tossed her head and looked away, clearly unwilling to listen. Nichol dipped to her eye level, and with two fingers to her chin, forced her to look at him. "If you give them any reason to suspect your motives for returning, you will lose. Moreover, my livelihood depends on my reputation for repairing bad situations with as little dust as possible. To return now, with you, to fetch a bloody necklace, is a risk to that most excellent reputation, and I donna intend to have anything go wrong. Is that understood, then?"

"Then why are you helping me?" she asked suspiciously. "If it's so dangerous for your blessed reputation?"

He had asked himself that very question. He could truss her up and carry on as planned, which undoubtedly would have been the better path. But there was something about her plight that resonated with him. And there was something about the Garbetts that sat sourly in his belly. They were disdainful of her, for no apparent reason other than her beauty. "I told you," he said, his gaze flicking over her. "I like a challenge. I will ask again, Miss Darby, do you understand me plainly?"

She sighed again. "Aye," she murmured. And contritely, he noted happily.

"Then we're ready."

She turned to the railing behind them and picked up his greatcoat, presenting it to him. "I cleaned it for you."

He held it up. She had indeed brushed the dirt of the ride from it. It looked refreshed and it surprised him. "Thank you. How did you manage?"

"I used the same brush the lads use to brush the horse's arse."

Nichol snapped his gaze back to Miss Darby. One fine brow rose above the other, and her summer-blue eyes shone with delight. "It was convenient," she added.

That smile, that hair. *This woman!* He would be very glad to be done with her, for she was making a wreck of his bloody head. And yet, Nichol found it quite difficult to look away from her smile to don his coat.

The first time he'd seen her smile in the public room had knocked him back on his heels. He hadn't expected it to be so...*shiny.* When she smiled, the whole of her lovely face smiled with her. Eyes, lips—

even a delightful little crinkle at the top of her nose. Aye, she was very bonny when she smiled.

"Thank you," he said again, and shoved his arms into the coat with a verve that was entirely unnecessary to the donning of the coat, but necessary for discharging a bit of strange tension in him.

Miss Darby picked up her cloak and put it on. She had not been so diligent with the brush on her garment, and he removed a bit of hay from the hem.

Miss Darby gave him a pert smile and curtsied. "You are too kind, Mr. Bain."

"Mind yourself," he muttered as he straightened her collar and hood. But he was smiling, too. "Shall we?" he asked, gesturing to the two horses.

"Please," she said pleasantly.

Nichol led the horses out of the stable. He spread the plaid she had taken across her horse's back. He put his hands to her waist and lifted her up, then put himself on the back of his own horse. He looked at her for a long moment, wondering about himself, about this flash of what he could only call lunacy, before leading them out of the paddock and onto the road for Garbett House.

All right, then, he'd tied himself by his word to this woman for the next day or so. That was not generally his way of doing things. He was generally very careful about putting himself into such predicaments. The years had seasoned him, had made him the voice of reason and calm in more than one volatile situation. And yet here he was, being entirely unreasonable, riding off to take back a necklace that he couldn't say with certainty actually belonged to the young woman beside him. For all he knew, she'd invented the whole thing for reasons he could never guess.

But there was something about Miss Darby that seemed too earnest for dissembling. He couldn't say what it was, but against his better judgment, he trusted her.

Whether or not such trust would be his downfall remained to be seen.

CHAPTER NINE

WHEN THEY TURNED onto the long drive at Garbett House, the sky was turning leaden, slowly eating the sun as it sank lower. Maura was feeling a little leaden herself—she had no desire to be back here, to see the family that had betrayed her.

She followed Mr. Bain onto the circular drive. As he reined to a halt before the grand house, the door opened and Mr. Bagley, the butler, jogged down the steps to meet them, gesturing to a groom who had come running from the stables to take the reins.

Mr. Bain came off his horse and lifted Maura down. When he set her on her feet, he gave her a look that was fraught with warning. She understood him quite clearly without the benefit of words—did he think she would not honor her vow to him? She frowned with exasperation.

He smiled lopsidedly, almost as if he expected her to frown. Maura put a finger to his very firm arm, made a show of pushing him aside with that finger, and then strode forward. "Good evening, Bagley."

"Miss Darby," he said politely, even a wee bit blandly, seeing as how the last time he'd seen her she'd been escorted from the premises with nothing but a bag containing a few belongings and her dignity strewn behind her. "Mr. Bain."

Behind Bagley, Sorcha's nose appeared, followed by the rest of her. Sorcha was clearly angry. Her face was mottled red as she looked first to Maura, then to Mr. Bain, with an expression of incredulous fury.

"Good afternoon, Sorcha," Maura said.

Sorcha said not a word but whirled around and disappeared inside.

Maura gritted her teeth. To think of all the hours she'd spent sitting silently on that woman's bed, listening to her go on ad nauseam about the gentlemen she would marry, then allowing Sorcha to sob on her shoulder when said gentlemen were scared off, one by one. How could Sorcha possibly believe that Maura would want to steal her fiancé? She'd gone out of her way to avoid Sorcha's many potential husbands altogether.

She looked to the butler. "Bagley, will you kindly inform Mr. Garbett that I should like a word?"

Bagley never had a chance to reply, for Mr. Garbett was informed of her arrival by the unsettling shriek of Mrs. Garbett. That was followed by a thundering of feet, as Mrs. Garbett, Sorcha and Mrs. Cadell herded into the entrance, their gazes full of surprise and displeasure.

"What is the meaning of this?" demanded Mrs. Garbett. She was wearing a lace cap and a mantua that looked too small, as if it might pop open if she moved too abruptly. She looked directly at Mr. Bain. Maura may as well have been a ghost.

"If I may, Mrs. Garbett," Mr. Bain said, and stepped before Maura, as if to shield her from the waves of disdain rolling off the woman. "Miss Darby is in need of her things."

"What things?"

"Clothing. Shoes. As you can see, this gown has been ruined," he said, and stepped aside, gesturing to Maura.

She dutifully opened her cloak to demonstrate the ruin.

"What has that to do with us?" Mrs. Garbett cried, refusing to look at Maura's gown. "She should no' have come here! She is no' *welcome here!*"

Maura had heard this before, of course, but Mrs. Garbett's vehemence still stunned her. Did none of them hold the slightest affection for her? She suddenly thought of a Christmas, many years past, when Sorcha had received new shoes. Maura had been given Sorcha's old shoes. She'd always admired the used shoes and had been so grateful for them that she hadn't seen that which was so clear to her now. She'd been telling herself a lie all these years. She'd allowed herself to believe that while they did not wish her to interfere in Sorcha's social life, they still cared for her somehow. What a little fool she'd been.

"Her things are here, madam," Mr. Bain said evenly. "Certainly you will agree she canna meet the man who will marry her looking like a wee waif, aye? Once we've gathered her things, we'll be on our way."

"What's happening? What's this?" thundered Mr.

Garbett. He appeared behind his wife in his waist-coat and shirtsleeves. His wig was a bit crooked, as if he'd been sleeping. "Mr. Bain!" he exclaimed, pushing his way through the throng of women. "Ah, Maura, lass," he said fondly, as if he'd never cast her out, and held out his arms wide. "What a delight! I rather thought I'd no' see you again."

"Mr. Garbett!" his wife screeched.

Maura dipped a curtsy. "I beg your pardon, sir, I would no' have come back, for I am certain it displeases you," she said demurely. "But I beg you, sir, I am in need my things."

"Oh! Yes," he said, and cast an accusing look at his wife from the corner of his eye. "Yes, of course, Maura. We should no' have sent you away in such haste, aye? Come in, come in," he said, and shooed his wife and daughter out of the way.

Mrs. Cadell stood firm, however, glaring at Maura.

"Bagley, bring us tea, will you, or better yet, whisky. Whisky, eh, Bain? There's a nip in the air. For heaven's sake, Mrs. Cadell, do let them pass."

"Pappa?" Sorcha said, sounding like a wounded child.

Mr. Garbett ignored her.

"Thank you," Mr. Bain said, and stood aside, so that Maura could pass. She stepped up reluctantly—she did not miss how Sorcha glared at her as she squeezed past Mrs. Cadell, whose displeasure came off her like an icy northern wind.

Mr. Bain followed her into the foyer, and as Maura

removed her cloak to hand to a footman, the bloody
fool Adam Cadell appeared. His eyes lit when he
saw her, and he suddenly came striding forward, all
slender arms and legs. He looked like a mere child
beside Mr. Bain. "Miss Darby. You've returned," he
said solemnly.

"Adam." This warning from Mr. Cadell, who had
followed his son into the foyer. He put his hand on
his son's shoulder, as if to pull him away.

"Mr. Cadell," Maura said, with a slight bow of
her head. "Please forgive my intrusion."

"No need for that, Maura. You are welcome," Mr.
Garbett said, lifting his chin and purposely not looking at his wife. "Come into the drawing room, will
you? I was certain I'd no' see you again, and it warms
my— Good Lord, what has happened to your gown?"
he said, stopping midstride.

"What?" She glanced down. *What had happened
indeed. I was cast out to the hell of Mr. Rumpkin's
house, and then retrieved by Mr. Bain, whom you
hired, sir.* "Oh that," she said lightly. "Mr. Rumpkin
did no' have the services of a laundress, I'm afraid."

From somewhere in the distance, she heard Mr.
Bain clear his throat. Mr. Garbett colored. He pressed
his lips together, then proceeded into the drawing
room, gesturing for her to follow. Maura fell in behind him, and the rest of the party followed them like
a litter of puppies, all eager to be first.

"Mr. Bain has explained all to you, has he no'?"
Mr. Garbett asked as he marched toward the sideboard.

"Yes, sir. Everything," she said. "I…" Dear God, but her pride had a very bitter taste as she swallowed it. "I must commend you for taking such care of my future in light of all that's happened."

Mr. Garbett turned from the sideboard and looked at her with astonishment. So did everyone else.

Maura glanced uncertainly at Mr. Bain, who gave her an almost imperceptible nod.

She swallowed another heaping serving of her pride and said, "I am quite…" It was so bloody *difficult* to say what she must.

"Quite what?" Sorcha asked.

"Quite pleased that Mr. Garbett has made me a match."

Sorcha made a sound of disbelief and sank onto the settee. But her fiancé kept his gaze firmly affixed on Maura. She could only surmise he must be as dim-witted as he was thin, for there was nothing that could raise the hackles of his fiancée more quickly than his interest in her.

"Well," Mr. Garbett said, looking around at them all. "It was the least I could do, really. I hated so to see you go, I truly did, aye?"

Mrs. Garbett cleared her throat.

"But of course, it was necessary," he quickly added. "After…well, we all know, do we no'?"

Maura forced herself to smile contritely—she gave Mr. Bain a quick look so that he could see she was—and said, "We do, indeed, sir."

Bagley entered the room with a silver tray and tots of whisky lined up like little soldiers.

"Aha, there we are!" Mr. Garbett said. "Pass them around, Bagley, we'll have a drink to welcome our guests and then go about the business of gathering Miss Darby's things. Where are they, dearest?" he asked his wife.

"I hardly know," Mrs. Garbett said with a sniff. "I had nothing to do with it. I told Hannah to dispose of them."

Hannah! The same maid who'd gone running to Sorcha to accuse her of kissing Mr. Cadell? Maura would not be the least surprised to find her remaining clothing ripped through with knives, given the animosity that radiated from Mrs. Garbett.

"Well, then, someone summon Hannah to us, aye?" Mr. Garbett said, fluttering his fingers at one of the footmen. "We'll have accounting of what she's done with Miss Darby's things."

"Can you no' have the accounting in your study, Pappa? I donna see why we all must hear it," Sorcha said. She had one eye on her fiancé, another on Maura.

"I most certainly could, *mo chridhe*, but I prefer to do it here." He turned from her to Maura. "How did you find my cousin, then?" he asked amicably. "I've no' seen David in many years."

Maura blinked. How had she found that old lecherous drunk? Was she to be contrite in her response to that, too? She glanced again at Mr. Bain for reassurance, but he gave her no indication of what she was to say. "I found him...unwell," she said carefully.

"What?" Mr. Garbett said, his hand fluttering to his neck. "Has he taken ill, then?"

Maura shook her head. She would say no more than she had, for she didn't trust the words that might flow if she began. When she didn't offer more, Mr. Garbett swiped a tot from the tray Bagley was passing around. "As I said, I've no' seen him in some time."

"It was quite obvious to me that you had no'," Mr. Bain said coolly.

Well, *that* was surprising. She glanced at Mr. Bain, but he was looking pointedly at Mr. Garbett, who colored under Mr. Bain's stark regard before tossing back his whisky in one deep swallow.

Bagley had just finished handing out the whisky to the rest of them who would partake when Hannah was ushered in by one of the footmen. The poor lass stood scarcely more than five feet tall, and looked about the room with great trepidation.

"Hannah!" Mr. Garbett said gaily, as if they were having a party, "Hannah, lass, what have you done with Miss Darby's things, then?"

Hannah's eyes rounded. She immediately looked to Sorcha, who, Maura noticed, made a point of avoiding the maid's gaze. Whatever hand she'd had in it, she would leave Hannah to suffer this interrogation alone.

"Well, ah…there was some of them things that got put away into the attic, sir, that's what," she said quietly.

Some? What did that mean, *some*?

"Bring them down," Mr. Garbett said.

Hannah clasped her hands together at her waist and looked frantically to Sorcha once more, but Sorcha turned her head.

"What is it then, Hannah?" Mr. Garbett asked impatiently.

"It's just that I'll need someone to help me, aye, sir? It's a trunk, and quite heavy—"

"Take a footman, then," Mr. Garbett said with a flick of his wrist. "You should no' have put it in the attic to begin with, if it's so difficult to retrieve. Use your head, Hannah," he said, pointing to his own skull.

Hannah looked at Sorcha. "But Miss—"

"Please do as my father asks," Sorcha said crisply, before Hannah could say more.

"Go on, lad," Mr. Garbett said to the footman. "Help her fetch Miss Darby's trunk. In the meantime, Sorcha, *leannan*, I'm sure you've something in that vast wardrobe of yours that Miss Darby might borrow for supper, aye?"

"Supper!" Mrs. Garbett exclaimed.

"Aye, supper," Mr. Garbett said. "By my watch it is nearly half past five. We dine at half past six."

"Surely Miss Darby will have her things and be on her way," Mrs. Garbett suggested.

"Madam!" Mr. Garbett said sharply, and looked around at all of them as if they'd lost their minds. "It has grown dark. We canna in good conscience turn them out. Of *course* Miss Darby and Mr. Bain will dine with us, and first thing on the morrow, we shall see them off, aye? I'll no' hear another word! Include them in our number, Bagley," he said, and started for the door. "Mr. Bain, you may join me in my study, then. Sorcha, *you* will find something suitable for Miss Darby to wear, for I'll no' have her put me off my supper looking as if she was found beneath a pile of rubbish!"

Mr. Bain followed Mr. Garbett. He gave Maura the slightest wink as he went past, as if to convey that he thought things were going along swimmingly.

They were *not* going along swimmingly—Mrs. Garbett was clearly beside herself.

Mr. Garbett paused at the door. "Tom, Adam, you'll join us as well, aye? We'll have a smoke, we lads, and leave the ladies to their nattering and what no' as they put on gowns, then."

Nattering! Maura had to glance at her feet to keep her glare from being seen by all. Was that what he thought, that after all that had happened, she would return to Garbett House to *natter*? She wanted to kick something, hit something, at the very least scream her frustration. But when she glanced up she found three sets of eyes staring at her with unabashed disdain, and it did not seem the most expedient way to get her hands on her necklace.

Maura said nothing, but bowed her head demurely, waiting.

"I donna have anything for you to *wear*," Sorcha said disgustedly.

"Oh, I donna know about that," her mother said

coolly. "I'm certain we've *something* that will suit Miss Darby."

She smiled in a manner that left no question as to what sort of gown they would find for her. Maura sighed, already resigned. "Thank you."

"Oh, donna thank me yet," Mrs. Garbett said, and with an imperious tilt of her chin, led the ladies' procession from the drawing room.

CHAPTER TEN

NICHOL WAS RELUCTANT to leave Miss Darby behind with that pit of vipers. He'd always known that a woman's scorn could run deep, but was Mrs. Garbett so vengeful that she would deny them a meal?

Nevertheless, he had no doubt Miss Darby would manage—he'd been rather pleasantly surprised that she'd done as he'd advised thus far and had presented herself as truly contrite and apologetic. Had he not known her true feelings, he would have thought her remorseful for what had happened here.

In his study, Mr. Garbett went straight to the sideboard and poured more whisky for himself. "Well, then, *this* has been quite a surprise," he said, and cast a disapproving look at Nichol. "I had no' expected to see you again, Mr. Bain. I had expected to receive the news of your success via messenger."

"It is a surprise to me, as well," Nichol said. "I hadna realized the lass had been sent off with so few articles of clothing."

Mr. Garbett shrugged. "I thought she took quite a lot with her. 'Tis no' *my* fault my cousin has no laundress. I guess the things I've heard are indeed true, and he's gone to drink, aye?"

If you'd heard such things, why in God's name send a young woman to him? Nichol wanted to shout. "You've heard correctly."

One of Mr. Garbett's eyelids fluttered unnaturally. "Well, I hope it wasn't too terribly awful for her," he said with a cool indifference that made Nichol want to punch him in the jaw. But he bit back the cursing on the tip of his tongue, and said, quite casually, "Clothing was the worst of it. She is missing her jewelry, too."

"What jewelry?" Mr. Garbett asked.

What jewelry indeed. Nichol shrugged. "All I can tell you is that she said she'd left behind a few gowns, some shoes and a necklace."

Mr. Adam Cadell perked up at the mention of the necklace and looked expectantly at his future father-in-law. But Mr. Garbett was quick to reply. "No necklace, Mr. Bain," he said instantly.

"Did I misunderstand her, then?"

"No," Adam said quickly. "They've taken the necklace from her. Mrs. Garbett—"

His father shot the young man a dark look that effectively silenced him.

"Pardon?" Nichol asked, feigning ignorance.

"Mrs. Garbett," Adam said, his expression suddenly defiant, "has taken the necklace from Miss Darby."

"Quite enough, Adam," his father chastised him. "'Tis no' your affair."

"Is it no'?" Adam asked. "I'm to marry Sorcha after all and I want no part of this, I donna."

Nichol cast a questioning look at Mr. Garbett, wondering if he would admit his culpability in their thievery now.

"Verra well," Mr. Garbett said with exasperation. "Aye, we have a necklace that belonged to the lass. It has some value, and my wife and daughter thought it the least she could offer, given that she has received gowns and shoes and her keep from us all these years, only to betray us in the end."

"Aye, of course," Nichol said, nodding along as if he agreed with their thinking. Then he paused and looked curiously at Mr. Garbett. "But did you no' tell me that she came to you with a small annual stipend for her keep?"

Mr. Garbett glowered at him at the mention of the stipend. "It was *scarcely* enough for all that she's been given."

Nichol shifted his gaze to Adam Cadell. He was the reason that Miss Darby was in this fix, and if he had any conscience at all, he would insist the necklace be returned to her. Mr. Cadell seemed to understand his pointed look, for he said, "With all due respect, sir, I would request that you reconsider Miss Darby's jewelry. She did seem quite attached to it."

"Aye of course she was," Mr. Garbett said with a flash of annoyance. "It's rather valuable, is it no'? Need I remind you that my daughter has been gravely injured by the actions of Miss Darby?"

Adam Cadell swallowed and glanced at his feet.

"Nevertheless, I shall appeal to my wife on your behalf, Adam. I canna say how she might receive it, but I shall appeal all the same, then," Mr. Garbett said magnanimously.

Adam Cadell instantly deflated. It was astounding to Nichol that Adam was not meant to shoulder any responsibility for what happened here, and that it was, every bit of it, assigned to Miss Darby because of one mother's vindictive nature. Mr. Garbett was more spineless than Nichol had originally thought, with no control over the women in his house. Every man standing there knew that Mrs. Garbett's answer would be no. The woman would not give an inch to Miss Darby until her homely, unpleasant daughter was wed to this hapless, useless man. Good God, the woman's vision was alarmingly myopic.

Well, then, Nichol would find another way to retrieve the necklace. He would not be put off by the likes of Mrs. Garbett. He realized, as he stood there listening to the men now speak of iron or some such, that what he was thinking was unlawful.

That was not like him in the least.

Nichol prided himself on being meticulous in his business dealings, to never giving anyone reason to criticize him or distrust him. His reputation of living up to his word in all things, of doing what he said quickly and effectively, was what recommended him to men like Garbett, over and over again. The only reason he had indulged Miss Darby in the quest for her necklace was because he knew all to well what it was to cling to a remnant of a life, to be reviled by people who were supposed to love you. He knew because it had happened to him. It bothered him that

Miss Darby, through no fault other than her beauty compared to the homeliness of Miss Garbett, was made to suffer the same hurt he had.

And he did like a challenge. This situation was certainly that.

Miss Darby would have her necklace if he had to scale another tower to get it.

AN HOUR LATER the household gathered in the drawing room before supper. As the gentlemen entered, Miss Darby stood from her seat on the settee to curtsy to Mr. Garbett. She was dressed in a gown of bright yellow that made her skin appear sallow. It was two sizes too large and hung on her body, dragging on the floor behind her. Nichol also noticed that her hair, which he had labored over, thank you, had been bound rather badly behind her head. And yet, she still managed to outshine every woman in this room. They could take all that she owned and cast her aside, but they could not take away what they resented most about her with their ill-fitting clothing or poorly arranged hair. She was still beguiling.

"Oh dear," Mr. Garbett said, looking her up and down, his expression one of alarm. "Have her things been brought down? Is there no' a gown that will fit her better than this?"

"There is no'," his wife said flatly.

Mr. Garbett looked to the butler. "Well? Where are her things?"

"We have no' as yet retrieved it, sir," Bagley said.

"We've sent to the gardener for a ladder tall enough to reach that section of the attic."

"What do you mean?"

"There is a wee bit of attic within the main attic. To reach it requires a ladder higher than we have available in the house."

"An attic within an attic," Mr. Garbett repeated skeptically, and looked to his wife.

"Aye, sir. It is the part of the roof above the kitchen. The ceiling, as you may recall, is higher there."

"I recall," Mr. Garbett said darkly, his gaze still locked on his wife. "What an effort it must have taken for the footmen to put it there, aye?"

"Aye, sir," Bagley stoically agreed.

"It might have been easier to have burned the trunk," he mused. "Well, then, Bagley, make accommodations for our guests this evening. I assume Miss Darby's room is still available to us? Unless, of course, it has been moved to the attic within the attic."

"The room is as Miss Darby left it, aye, sir. And we've the blue chamber for Mr. Bain."

"Verra good, Bagley. Mrs. Garbett, a word?" Mr. Garbett asked, and turned on his heel, stalking from the room. His wife lifted her chin and followed at a brisk pace, as if she meant to overtake him, as if she meant to have her say first. Their daughter looked around at those who remained and darted after them, as if she were afraid to be left alone with the rest of them.

Mrs. Cadell had no wish to speak to Miss Darby, or allow her son anywhere near her. She drew her son and husband aside to gaze out a window into the dark that blanketed the garden.

Nichol strolled past Miss Darby and indicated with his chin that she should follow. He walked to a painting at the far end of the room and said loud, "What is that in the distance, do you suppose?" and leaned forward, as if he was peering intently at some object portrayed in the Highland scene with a few sparse trees, an elk and a glistening loch beyond.

Miss Darby followed him, the fabric of her voluminous gown rustling around her. "It looks a wee bit like a bird," she said, and folded her arms across her body, her expression thunderous.

"Is that the best they could do for you, then?" he whispered, taking in her gown.

"No, Mr. Bain, it is the *worst* they could do for me," she returned in a whisper, and glanced furtively over her shoulder. "Mrs. Garbett said I'd no' ruin anything else that belonged to Sorcha, as I have ruined her engagement and quite possibly her wedding, and without a doubt, her life."

Bloody hell, that woman grated on him. He whispered, "Mr. Garbett is now, as we speak, inquiring of his wife if she will allow the return of your necklace."

Miss Darby snorted indelicately. "She'll no' allow it."

"No," he agreed, and glanced over his shoulder

to ensure that they were not being heard. "Do you know where it's kept?"

"Oh aye," she said, dispensing with the whispering. "Sorcha is *wearing* it."

Nichol slowly turned his head and looked at Miss Darby.

She nodded, her lovely eyes flashing with raw fury. "She keeps it in the jewelry box on her vanity," Miss Darby whispered. "Her mother wanted me to see it. To know it belongs to her now, aye? So she retrieved it and put it around Sorcha's neck."

That was so brazen that Nichol was rendered momentarily speechless. "Well, that presents a wee bit of a problem, aye?" he drawled. He stared at the painting, thinking. He considered that if he could, somehow, devise a way to get the necklace off Sorcha's neck, seeing as how he couldn't wrench it from her neck as he very much desired to do—but if he managed to find a way, he could very well be caught. That would be disastrous to his occupation—years of carefully building his reputation would be undone in one evening.

But then he glanced at Miss Darby. For the first time since he'd met her, she seemed defeated. There was such despair around her eyes that he winced.

He hated that look. He had felt it in himself long ago. He knew how hopelessness and helplessness gnawed at one's marrow. "Miss Darby," he said softly.

She looked up.

"On my word, you shall have it back."

"Mr. Bain?" Mr. Cadell said. "We've a question for you. Will you come to the window?"

Nichol gritted his teeth. He had no desire to keep the company of the Cadells—he had no desire to keep the company of anyone here but Miss Darby, a thought that was a wee bit unsettling. She had caused him nothing but trouble thus far, but by the same token, she was the most captivating of anyone here, and she was looking at him so hopefully right now that he could hardly turn away. Ivan used to look at him like that. It stirred strange feelings in him now. Uncomfortable, helpless feelings. "One moment, if you please," he said, and pointed to something on the painting and said, "A ship, I think, Miss Darby. Look closely." He leaned toward her and whispered, "Leave your bag, or whatever you have to carry your things, just inside the door of your room, and the door unlocked. Be prepared to leave at first light, no matter what else is said tonight, aye?"

"What?" she whispered frantically. "What do you intend to do?"

"Which room belongs to Miss Garbett?"

"You canna—"

Nichol touched his fingers to the back of her hand before she attempted to debate him. "You must trust me, Miss Darby, aye? Trust me, do as I ask and you will have your necklace. Which room?"

She bit her bottom lip worriedly, then said, "In the upstairs hall, next to the last room on the right. Mine is next to it."

He smiled. "Donna look so forlorn, lass," he murmured, and smiled as he moved away from her, walking across the room to address the burning question the Cadells had for him.

He noted that Adam Cadell watched him closely as he approached, his gaze moving between him and Miss Darby. Nichol thought nothing of it—the lad was too thickheaded to guess that anything was afoot. His thoughts were on that bloody necklace. He was a man who always remained above the fray, but he was uncharacteristically determined to retrieve it. Interestingly, he was growing more determined with each step.

He realized what was driving him as he reached the Cadells. That strange feeling in him—it was resentment. Something of great sentimental value was taken from him when he was a lad, and his soaring resentment at that was as fresh now as it had been then. It was billowing in him like a full sail, only now on behalf of himself and Miss Darby.

CHAPTER ELEVEN

MAURA HAD NO appetite for her supper. She vacillated between rage at the injustice of it all and pure despair that Mrs. Garbett and Sorcha despised her so. She'd never given this family the least bit of trouble, had been nothing but loyal to them. Now that she was back among them, it troubled her that they would turn so quickly, and it made her fear others would, too. If the people closest to her could find her so repulsive, what would people whom she scarcely knew make of her?

For whatever reason, and in spite of *all* the evidence to the contrary, Mrs. Garbett and Sorcha had somehow convinced each other that not only had Maura tried to steal the weakling Adam Cadell—who, by the bye, would not stop looking at her as if she were an exotic bird—but that Maura had schemed to steal everything of Sorcha's from the beginning. They had convinced themselves that a twelve-year-old girl, who had lost her father, who was frightened and uncertain, had somehow been wise enough to scheme against Sorcha. That a twelve- year-old girl who had hoped with all her heart that she and Sorcha would be friends, would share secrets and laughter, had come to them with a devious plan to take Sorcha's place. Maura realized now she'd been too hopeful and naïve to understand it then, but oh, how she understood it now.

"*Always* envious, were you no'?" Mrs. Garbett had said as she'd yanked one fine gown from the wardrobe after another, tossing them on the bed while Sorcha paced. She pulled a sage green gown from the wardrobe.

"I believe that one was mine," Maura had said very carefully.

"It was *no'* yours!" Mrs. Garbett had snapped. "None of this is *yours.* Even as a lass, you could no' be trusted."

"That is no' true," Maura had tried.

"It is!" Sorcha had exclaimed.

"Name one time—"

"My fourteenth birthday," Sorcha said. "You disappeared with Delilah Frank before cake and missed the celebration altogether. You were envious, that's what, so you stole my friend."

Had Sorcha lost her bloody mind? She'd been terribly envious of pretty Delilah and the attention the Campbell twins had lavished on her. "Have you forgotten, Sorcha? You didna *want* Delilah there, aye? You may have forgotten, but you asked me to walk with her in the garden, you did."

"That is a lie!" Sorcha had declared. "She is a verra dear friend, that she is."

"Aye, so dear that you've no' spoken to her in a year," Maura said before she could stop herself.

Sorcha gasped.

"This is *precisely* the sort of behavior we mean, Maura," Mrs. Garbett had said, and thrust a gown the color of bright yellow daffodils at her. "Either your memory is exceedingly poor, or you are quite comfortable dissembling."

"I have never lied to you," Maura had said evenly. "I came to you straightaway when Mr. Cadell—"

"Take it!" Mrs. Garbett had shouted, tossing the gown at her. Maura had caught it before it fell to the floor. "I will remind you, Miss Darby," Mrs. Garbett continued, drawing so close that Maura took a step backward, "that you are here by my good graces alone. Do *no'* test me, for you will no' like the response."

Maura had bit her tongue. She could hear Mr. Bain's calm voice warning her to be contrite. She'd looked down so that Mrs. Garbett would not see her indignation and said meekly, "Aye, madam. Thank you for the use of the gown."

"I hate that gown," Sorcha had said.

"Never mind, *leannan*, your gown is bonny," her mother had said, gesturing to the pale cream silk Sorcha wore. "Do you know what would go best with it?"

Sorcha shook her head.

"The necklace."

Maura's heart had skipped several beats. She'd slowly lifted her head and had looked directly at Mrs. Garbett, who was looking at Maura with a smirk.

"Aye, it's just there, in the jewelry box," the witch

had said, gesturing to the polished wooden box on Sorcha's vanity.

At least Sorcha had a wee bit of conscience left in her, because she'd looked stricken. "Mamma, I donna think—"

"Put it on. Maura, you may change in the dressing room."

Maura had hesitated, locking gazes with Sorcha, silently pleading with her, hoping that she would remember that Maura had always endeavored to be her friend.

"Go on, then," Mrs. Garbett had said sweetly to Maura, and pointed to the dressing room.

Maura had gone. She hadn't known what else to do, short of wrestling Sorcha for her necklace.

And now, here she was, in an absurd yellow gown, with no help for her hair, and Sorcha seated across from her, wearing her necklace. *Her* necklace. The necklace her mother used to whisper would be hers one day. *You'll wear it to the grandest balls, you will,* mo chridhe.

Maura seethed.

They were seated on either side of Mrs. Garbett at one end of the table, with Adam Cadell next to Sorcha. He looked a wee bit lost and weepy, as if he'd walked into a garden maze and could not find his way out. On Maura's left was Mr. Cadell, and across from him, Mr. Bain. Maura wondered if Mr. Bain was sleeping with his eyes open. She hardly blamed him—the meal was tedious and Mr. Cadell was droning on about the monthly progression of the moon or some such, and how he and his wife disagreed about the true length of the lunar calendar, to which Mrs. Cadell, seated next to Mr. Garbett, laughed roundly, as if that was the most amusing thing that had ever been said.

Maura couldn't take her eyes from her necklace as her indignation slowly filled every inch of her. The necklace was quite fetching on Sorcha's slender neck. It made her look almost…regal. The diamonds were the size of small beans, and glittered in the low light of the candelabra. The emerald at the center was the size of a robin's egg. The necklace was remarkably simple, and yet, at the same time, remarkably elegant.

These people were thieves. There was no legitimate reason for them to have kept her property from her. No matter what they thought of her, no matter what crimes they'd assigned to her, the necklace rightfully belonged to her.

How could Mr. Bain possibly retrieve it from Sorcha's neck?

"Have you no appetite, Maura?" Mrs. Garbett asked sweetly.

Maura looked at her plate. She'd hardly touched the roast beef. "I, ah…"

She was saved when the door to the dining room swung open and a footman entered. He bowed before Mr. Garbett and said, "The trunk has come down, sir."

"It must have come down by way of Edinburra, then. Bagley, you may escort Miss Darby to Han-

nah so that she might assist her to pack her things."
He sipped his wine and said to Maura, "Take what
you want from the trunk, aye, lass?" he said, gesturing to her.

"But she's no' eaten her supper," Mrs. Garbett
said. "What will we do with all this food, then?
Throw it to the dogs?"

"I donna see why no'. They will appreciate a wee
bit of beef." He gestured impatiently for Maura to
follow the footman. She reluctantly rose, and all the
gentlemen rose with her. She gathered the volumes
of gown around her and followed Bagley out of the
dining room with the rest of it trailing behind her.

Hannah was waiting for her in her old room. She
could not look Maura in the eye when she opened
the trunk, then stood back and nervously fidgeted
with the hem of her apron as Maura looked inside.

There was scarcely anything in the trunk. Perhaps
three gowns instead of the ten she'd left behind, a
pair of shoes that no longer fit her and a chemise that
looked as if it had been stained. "What happened to
my things?" Maura asked, mystified. "I left much
more than this."

When Hannah didn't answer, Maura looked up.
The lass's face had gone red. "What has happened
to my things, then, Hannah?"

"I didna ask for it!" Hannah cried.

"Pardon?"

"Miss Sorcha... Miss Sorcha said I should have
them," she said, suddenly tearful. "She said you'd no'
return and I should have them. I thought—"

"They gave you my things?" Maura asked dumbly, and looked into the trunk. "As if I'd *died*?"

Hannah bowed her head, ashamed.

Maura sighed. "*Diah,* donna cry, Hannah," she said. The only thing she truly cared about now was the necklace. "I'm no' cross with you." She pulled out one of the gowns and held it up to have a look. "Help me determine which of these might still be wearable."

They had determined that only two gowns of the three could be salvaged for her use, and Hannah tearfully, guiltily, offered to press them. Maura agreed, past the point of caring about Hannah's guilt. She was attempting to do something with her hair when the sound of raised voices and a commotion in the hall reached them. It was Sorcha, and it sounded as if she was crying.

Maura went to the door and looked out just as Sorcha and her mother turned into Sorcha's suite of rooms. Maura went to the door of Sorcha's room. "What's happened?" she asked. "Is everything all right?"

"No!" Sorcha cried. She had picked up a cloth and angrily swiped at the bodice of her gown, stained a dark red. Even from across the room, Maura could smell the wine. "Mr. Bain spilled wine on my gown!" she said angrily. "So stupid, so *clumsy* of him!"

Mr. Bain was anything but clumsy, and Maura thought immediately that he'd done it on purpose. He'd done it so Sorcha would be forced to change. But why? And then she understood as she watched

Sorcha remove the necklace and toss it onto her vanity as if it were costume, then began to struggle out of her gown, snapping at her mother as she tried to help.

"Hannah! Where is Hannah?" Mrs. Garbett shouted.

"Here," Hannah said, brushing past Maura to enter Sorcha's room.

"We need a change and fresh water in the basin!"

With the gown off and tossed onto the floor, Sorcha stepped behind a screen to remove the rest of her stained clothing, whimpering as she went along. "I canna believe it!" she cried. "It is my best gown, Mamma!"

"The Cadells are rich enough that you'll have all the gowns you need, Sorcha," her mother said impatiently, and fell onto an upholstered armchair at the hearth. That's when she noticed Maura, still standing there. "What do you want? Go on, then, off with you!" she said with a flick of her wrist, as if Maura were a pesky dog.

Maura slipped away, closed the door behind her, her mind racing.

Her necklace was there, on the vanity, in plain view. She had to let Mr. Bain know. Better yet, she ought to think of how he might come up and fetch it. But that would mean she should keep Sorcha and her mother occupied? How in blazes was she to do that?

She returned to the drawing room, her mind racing. She was not surprised to find Mrs. Cadell at the pianoforte. She seemed to think herself quite the talent, and even before Maura was sent away, Mrs. Cadell took a turn at music every evening.

Her husband and Mr. Garbett were standing together near the hearth, crystal snifters of brandy in hand, laughing together. Mr. Adam Cadell was seated in a chair, a book in his lap, a scowl on his face. He didn't look up when she entered. In fact, the only one to notice her was Mr. Bain.

"Would you care for a brandy?" he asked.

"Please," she said. She followed him to the sideboard, nodding in greeting to the gentlemen who looked up as she passed. He poured a bit of brandy into a snifter and handed it to her. She took it, looked him in the eye and said, *"Vanity."*

Mr. Bain clasped his hands at his back and bowed. "Aye, you're most welcome, Miss Darby," he said, and walked away, strolling to the other side of the room to join the other gentlemen.

Maura's thoughts were swimming in confusion, her heart hammering in her chest. Had he heard her? Did he understand what she meant to convey? If he'd understood her, if he actually found a way to take the necklace, he risked all. What if he were caught? What would Mr. Garbett do? He said his occupation was dependent upon his reputation—if he were caught, she could well imagine that Mrs. Garbett would make it known far and wide. She ought to help in some way, and as she tried to think of how, she turned away from Mr. Bain.

Her gaze landed on Adam Cadell. He'd stood from his seat and was standing near the sideboard now, watching her carefully. "Oh," she said, feeling startled. "Mr. Cadell. I didna see you there."

"Miss Darby." He had a strange look on his face, almost as if he was disappointed or annoyed. Had he heard her utter the word *vanity*? What if he had? It would mean nothing to him. Not unless the necklace went missing, and then he would think back to this moment—

He glanced across the room to Mr. Bain, then back to Maura. Her heart seized painfully. Surely he did not suspect they were plotting together. *Diah,* no. She would not permit Adam Cadell to ruin this for her, too.

She panicked, set aside the brandy without tasting it, and moved closer to him. "How are you, then, Mr. Cadell?"

"What do you mean?" he asked, his eyes moving to her mouth.

"How have you fared since…all that has happened?"

He lifted his gaze. "How do you think, then?" he asked. "Every day, every *moment* has been a challenge, aye? I have missed you, Maura."

What a ridiculous young man he was. Did he think she'd come back for *him*? Did he think she would tolerate his desire *now*, after all that has happened? If Sorcha saw him speaking to her like this, his expression so intent, standing so close…

"Mr. Cadell." She glanced around, uncertain what to say or do, but when she looked at Mr. Bain, she had a sudden stroke of genius. She knew precisely how to create a diversion. "Would you care to dance?"

Mr. Cadell looked as startled as if she'd just slapped his face. "I beg your pardon?"

"Dance," she said again, and glanced at his mother, who was so intent on her playing that she had failed to keep an eagle eye on her son.

"I donna… We ought no'—"

"What harm is there? I'll be gone on the morrow." She suddenly grabbed his hand and pulled him into the middle of the room. She dropped her hand and picked up her skirts, and began to dance the steps to a minuet, rising up on her toes, then down again, holding her skirts out and taking her steps around him.

"What's this?" Mr. Garbett said, having noticed them, and then laughed. "What a lark! You've no' enough dancers, Miss Darby! Adam, lad, Maura is an excellent dancer. Here, I'll join you," Mr. Garbett said, and stepped up to Maura's side and began to match her steps.

Mrs. Cadell turned to see what the commotion was about and instantly stopped playing. "What is the meaning of this?"

"Go on, woman, play the song," her husband said gruffly. "There is no harm in a small diversion."

Mrs. Cadell didn't instantly do as he said, and he thundered, *"Play!"*

She turned. She brought her hands down woodenly onto the keys and played. Mr. Garbett hardly seemed to notice. He was enjoying himself, either uncaring or oblivious to the notion that his wife and daughter would not care for the dancing, and gestured for Adam to join them.

As Maura came around again, she caught Mr. Bain's dark disapproving look, but then his expression shuttered and he regarded them as any guest might, with a bit of amusement, a bit of tedium.

He was surely angry, and of course there was no way she could pause to explain that she was helping him. She wasn't certain he'd even understood what she'd said at the sideboard. But Maura kept to her steps, knowing that Sorcha would return at any moment and find them dancing and would lose her fool mind, and thereby, create the diversion that Mr. Bain would need to retrieve her necklace.

She dipped, she twisted, she laughed gaily as if they were all having a grand time of it. So did Mr. Garbett, who was well in his cups, and far too jolly for the bit of terrible dancing he was doing.

Adam moved stiffly, clearly uncomfortable with the dance and too weak to simply walk away. "Have a bit of heart, lad!" Mr. Garbett shouted at him. Adam tried—but he was a terrible dancer, and he bumped into Maura, nearly knocking her off balance. His bumbling made her laugh out loud—this was absurd, the whole thing *absurd*.

Fortunately, it was very quickly over, for Sorcha and Mrs. Garbett entered the room just as Maura had linked arms with Adam and twirled around. Mrs. Garbett cried out with alarm when she saw what was happening, and Sorcha shouted, *"Adam!"*

"Mr. Garbett, how could you!" his wife exclaimed.

"How could I what?" Mr. Garbett asked, apparently truly mystified as to what his crime was now. Sorcha began to breathe erratically, as if her heart was failing her. Mrs. Cadell leapt from the pianoforte and swore to Mrs. Garbett that she had not approved, but had been commanded by her husband to play for them. That prompted Mr. Cadell to argue that had not been the case at all, and in the melee, Maura held her breath because Mr. Bain had slipped out, unnoticed, unremarked.

Maura couldn't say how long the arguing went on, with Mr. Garbett and Mr. Cadell insisting it was nothing but an innocent bit of diversion as Adam's face turned red. When it seemed that Mrs. Garbett might accept that, Maura said, "Then shall we dance again, Mr. Cadell?" which sparked another round of argument. Mrs. Garbett announced her decided opinion that Maura had returned expressly to steal Adam's heart at the same moment Sorcha tearfully accused Adam of not loving her and believing Maura prettier than she—all accusations Adam foolishly did not refute.

The arguing went on long enough that Mr. Bain slipped back in, picked up a brandy snifter and stood at the back of the room as if he'd never left it. It was remarkable. Impossible! Still, Maura wasn't entirely certain until his gaze met hers, and she would swear, would *swear*, that his eyes were shining with a smile.

Maura suddenly threw her arms wide. "Enough, I beg of you!" *Enough, enough, please, enough.*

Everyone stopped talking at once and turned to

her with varying expressions of outrage. "I beg your pardon. May I offer my sincerest apologies, Sorcha? I never meant to cause you strife, on my word, I did no'! I meant only to pass the time, aye?"

"You are *diabolical*," Mrs. Garbett said heatedly. "I will have you gone from this house at morning light and *never* shall you return, Miss Darby." She put her arm around Sorcha, who was sniffing as if she'd been tearfully contemplating her future without Mr. Cadell. But Sorcha had not been crying, as her nose was not swollen or red. She'd been stewing.

"I think it best if you retire," Mr. Bain said coolly.

"Aye," Maura said, and tried not to read too much into his tone. "Again, I do beg your pardon," she said with all the contrition she could muster. She tried to steal a look at Mr. Bain as she went out, but he'd turned his back on her. She kept walking, one foot before the other, the anxiety in her heart ratcheting with each step she took. What if this had all been for nothing? What if she'd come back to suffer this interminable evening, and would be forced to leave here without her necklace, sent off to marry a faceless man whose name she could not recall? What if every tie to her true self was severed here, tonight, by these awful people?

When she reached her room, she shut the door behind her and leaned against it, her eyes closed, taking deep breaths to calm her heart. Her bag was still where she'd left it, just inside the door, as Mr. Bain had instructed. She knelt next to it and held her breath as she opened it up. Her heart began to beat like a thousand wings when she looked inside, because there it was, her necklace, lying serenely on top of her few things.

She felt a swell of gratitude and esteem so profound for Mr. Bain that she sagged against the wall. She had her necklace and her pride returned to her, and she would never forget his kindness in this, the risk he had taken on her behalf.

Maura quickly rearranged things and put some clothing on top of the necklace. When she was satisfied it could not be seen, she changed out of the awful gown Mrs. Garbett had lent her and left it lying in a heap on the floor. She pulled on a moth-eaten chemise and one of her older plain gray gowns with a fraying hem and fabric worn bare at the elbows. She washed her face and hands, brushed her hair and braided it, then moved to the bed. She did not pull back the coverlet, but lay down in her clothing on top of it.

She was ready. As soon as there was light, she was ready to leave the Garbetts behind her forever. Funny, wasn't it, that a few weeks ago, she was desperate to stay. Now, she was so desperate to leave that it left her breathless.

She wished for Mr. Bain. She wanted to press her cheek against his chest and cling to him for warmth, for safety. She had trusted him. How remarkable it was that she had, for she hardly knew him. But of all the people in her life, she trusted him more than anyone. He was the only one who had not betrayed her in one way or another.

Mr. Bain was the only soul in this world who stood firmly in her corner.

At least for now.

CHAPTER TWELVE

NICHOL OUGHT TO be bloody furious with Miss Darby and her machinations, the wee little fool. Had she once considered that the engagement might have been called off because of her dancing? Had she once considered that her dancing would have not only risked their plan and his reputation, but could have seen them tossed out on their arses before he had an opportunity to fetch her bloody necklace? On one hand, it could have doomed him irreparably—not only would he have failed to have done as he promised, he'd have been the catalyst for the failure by bringing her back here.

But on the other hand, he had to give her credit. Her brazen bid to dance with Adam Cadell had ended in a predictable contretemps, which had created the perfect diversion for Nichol. He'd found the necklace precisely where she'd said, left carelessly on Sorcha's vanity.

Miss Darby had what she'd come for, and as soon as the sun rose above the tree line, they would be on their way. It wasn't yet dawn, but he'd already been downstairs to inform Bagley they'd need horses readied and brought around. He'd returned to his room, was lying on his bed fully dressed, his feet crossed at the ankles, his arms pillowing his head, thinking.

In hindsight, he wished he'd never mentioned the necklace to Garbett. Not because he was afraid he would be suspected—that was a given, just as soon as it was noticed missing. But because he didn't want Mrs. Garbett to have the satisfaction of knowing Miss Darby desired to have it back. In some ways, the woman reminded him of his own father. Unyielding. Willful. An insufferable inability to ever be wrong. Last evening had felt all too familiar to him—he'd lived in a home much like this, had been made to feel a stranger in that home, had been made to feel a trespasser.

A sudden image from his childhood popped into his head—his father standing in his room, staring at him, his expression murderous. In the open door, his younger brother, Ivan, was trembling. "What have I done, Pappa?"

He'd been ten years old. What could he possibly have done?

His father, cold as ice, had said, "Give me the pocket watch."

Nichol's heart had skipped when his father held out his hand for it. The pocket watch had belonged to his maternal grandfather, a man Nichol remembered with great fondness and warmth. His grandfather had given him the watch one bright summer day. *This is for you, lad*, he'd said. *Keep it close and you'll have a wee bit of me with you forevermore, will you no'?*

Nichol had scampered out of his bed, and at first,

had refused to hand it over. "It's mine," he'd said, which had earned him a hard slap alongside his head.

"It doesna belong to *you*, it belongs to my son. *Give me the pocket watch*," his father had commanded again through gritted teeth.

Nichol had begun to cry helplessly as he retrieved the pocket watch from his dresser and handed it to his father, and then in turn had watched him hand it to Ivan. Nichol had been confused by his father's remarks, for he was as much his son as was Ivan.

Ivan had looked startled and helpless. He knew what the watch meant to Nichol. His hand was shaking when his father had shoved him, had exhorted the eight-year-old to "be a man," and had pushed the watch into his palm. But Ivan had looked up at his brother and said, "I'll keep it safe for you, on my word."

"Donna be a fool," his father had chastised him. Nichol remembered the cold draft he'd felt as his father had quit his room, as if a ghost had left it.

He never saw the pocket watch again.

The very next morning, he was roused by a footman, told to bathe and dress. And without any explanation, he'd been sent away, to apprentice with the Duke of Hamilton. He'd had no inkling that he was to be sent off, no time to prepare for it, no time to say goodbye to his brother. He didn't know the Duke of Hamilton, and he'd been frightened. He'd stood on the drive, fighting tears, as his father railed at him not to cry.

But as he'd been handed into the coach, before

the footman could close the door, Ivan broke free and ran to him, clambering inside as their father shouted at him to return. "Here," he'd said, and had pressed something into Nichol's hand. "I shall miss you, Nic," he'd said.

That was all he was allowed to say before their father had removed him from the coach and the door was shut.

When Nichol uncurled his fingers, he saw their grandfather's signet ring, his gift to Ivan.

Nichol had been touched, and had pocketed the ring, keeping it on his person since then. Of course he'd always understood that his father favored Ivan, but Ivan had borne his own cross when it had come to their father. Everyone who knew the man bore that cross.

Nichol wondered idly how many nights he'd lain awake, trying to fathom his father's disdain for him. How many times had he tried to appease the old man, but to no avail? His father had, from the time Nichol could remember, resented his presence. When he returned to his boyhood home after his schooling at St. Andrews, he'd been met with hostility and an invitation to leave Cheverock and Comrie, the small village where his father, the Baron MacBain, presided. Ivan was a young man then, too, and he had tried to bridge a gap between Nichol and his father, but without success.

Nichol had left for good then, determined to make his way in this world. He'd changed his name to Bain so as never to be associated with William MacBain again. He'd wandered across Europe, in search of something, anything, to hold on to, to call his own, to cherish. But he found it difficult to trust others, and questioned the sincerity of others toward him. It seemed the closer anyone got to him, the farther away he wanted to be.

He'd eventually settled for his nomadic life, took some comfort in his work, which, incidentally, he'd fallen into quite by accident, when a friend, in a moment of drunken idiocy, had challenged a Frenchman to a duel. Nichol's handling of that debacle had recommended him to another Frenchman, who had a disagreement with his neighbor, a powerful count.

Nichol had hardly thought of his father these last few years, other than to wonder yet, from time to time, what he'd ever done to deserve his father's revulsion. It was still unfathomable.

But he'd made his own way. He needed neither his father's approval nor his money. After thirty-two years, Nichol felt nothing but dread when he thought of him. The only time he could be aroused to any emotion at all was when he was witness to someone else being treated poorly.

Nichol would never understand what Maura Darby could possibly have done to deserve her poor treatment at the hand of the Garbetts. She'd been a lass when she'd come into their care, and they'd had a moral responsibility to treat the child well.

An hour or more passed. He heard people moving about in the house, heard the horses snorting and shaking their heads on the front lawn. He rose, went to the basin, washed and combed his hair. He gathered his things and made his way downstairs, and found the household at breakfast. He had no interest in the food or anything else they had to offer—his only interest was in leaving here with Miss Darby, in finishing the venture he'd been paid to undertake, in moving on from the unpleasantness that he'd found in Stirling.

He asked a footman to send word to the kitchen that they'd need food to take with them. Then he walked into the breakfast room to make the formal declaration of their departure.

The family was seated and the tension between them all palatable. The Cadells hardly spoke, and Sorcha picked at her food.

"Mr. Bain," Mr. Garbett said cheerily. "Will you no' join us?"

"No thank you," he said. "As soon as the lass comes down, we'll be on our way."

"At the very least, break your fast, lad," Mr. Garbett tried.

Nichol shook his head. To sit with them was to convey approval of them, and he did not approve.

He heard the sound of someone on the stairs, and a moment later, Miss Darby was striding like a soldier down the corridor to him. She was wearing a plain gray gown that, at the very least, fit her well, but looked worn. Her hair hung in a long black braid down her back.

She stepped into the dining room and curtsied to

Mr. Garbett. "I beg your pardon sir, I should no' like to interrupt, but I should like to thank you again."

Mrs. Garbett muttered something under her breath as she buttered a slice of bread.

"Will you no' eat, Maura?" Mr. Garbett offered. He was obtusely ignorant of the animosity around that table—even Mr. Adam Cadell dared not look up.

"No, thank you," she said primly.

"Well, then," Nichol said, and exchanged a look with Miss Darby. "Shall we, Miss Darby?"

"Aye," she said, her voice low, her eyes glittering. He understood her perfectly—she was as desperate to be away from here as he was.

"Now?" Mr. Garbett asked, and pushed his chair back to stand. His napkin was still tucked into his collar. "Bring her cloak, Bagley."

The butler nodded and went from the dining room. He returned a moment later, the cloak in hand, and as he fit it around Miss Darby's shoulders, the chambermaid hurried in, scurrying around the table to where Sorcha was sitting.

Miss Darby turned her back on the room, as if she meant to leave then and there.

"Maura! You canna go without wishing us well," Mr. Garbett said. He opened his arms wide as if to embrace her. "How I shall miss you! You must write us, aye? We'll want to know how you fare as mistress of Luncarty."

Were the events of the last month completely lost in Garbett's mind? Did he truly think she was willingly, happily, going off to marry a man of her choice?

"Thank you, sir, but I donna think anyone will want to hear from me."

"Oh, donna fret about our Sorcha," he said gregariously as the chambermaid whispered in Sorcha's ear. "She'll be quite all right once she is a missus, that she will. That's the only bee under her bonnet."

Adam Cadell looked as if he might break into tears.

Adam's father stood from the table and offered his hand to Nichol. "Thank you, Bain, for repairing this predicament for us."

As though the lass's life was a mere complication for his son.

"Pappa!" Sorcha suddenly cried, and stood so hastily that her chair fell over. A footman scrambled to right it.

"*Diah,* lass, must you shout?" Mr. Garbett said, and pressed a thick hand to his chest, startled by her outburst. "Aye, what now?"

"My necklace!" she said, her voice gone hoarse. "It is *missing.*"

Nichol suppressed a groan. It was the chambermaid who'd told her, no doubt to save her own skin. He'd hoped for a bit of time to get away from Garbett House before it was discovered. He glanced at Miss Darby; the blood had drained from her face. She gripped her ratty bag so tightly that he could see the whites of her knuckles.

"You've only misplaced it," Mr. Garbett said dismissively, and turned back to Nichol.

"What do you mean?" his wife snapped, standing, too. "Hannah? What do you mean it is *missing*?"

"M-miss Sorcha, she left it on her vanity, she did. It's no' there now."

"It's been *stolen*!" Sorcha cried, glaring at Maura.

"Aye, Sorcha, we heard her, all of us! Will you please stop *shouting*? Now, Hannah, lass, I'm certain it is there. Go and have another look, then."

"I beg your pardon, sir, but it's no' there."

"She took it!" Sorcha said, pointing at Miss Darby.

"What?" Miss Darby said, her hand pressed to her chest as if she'd been struck. "On my word, I would *never*, Sorcha!"

"She *took* it, Pappa! That's why she came back, aye? She didna want her things, she wanted to ruin me and steal my necklace!"

How quickly the necklace had become the property of Miss Sorcha Garbett in her mind.

Mr. Garbett looked curiously at Miss Darby, but Miss Darby looked like a trapped animal, her gaze raking over all the faces staring at her now. "I did *no'* take it!" she insisted.

"What good is your word?" Mrs. Garbett asked with a snort. "Surely, husband, you'll no' allow her to leave without looking through her things. Your daughter is quite right—Miss Darby came here to take something from us. When she could no' have Adam, she took the necklace!"

"Donna be absurd," Mr. Garbett said. "We'll clear

this up here and now, shall we? Maura may have made a mistake or two," he said blithely, as if any of this could possibly be her fault, "but she's no thief. Let us have a look, lass," he said, and held out his hand for her bag.

Miss Darby's grip tightened. She looked helplessly to Nichol.

"Come on, then, Maura, let us have it, aye?" Mr. Garbett said again, and extended his hand closer to her.

Miss Darby looked as if she might faint. She glanced uncertainly at Nichol again.

"Give it," he said softly.

Her expression changed instantly, her gaze hardening, her mouth set in a frown of disgust. Of course she believed he'd betrayed her.

She slowly handed the bag to Mr. Garbett, who thrust it at his daughter. "Here," he said sharply. "If you accuse the lass, then you do the searching, aye?"

Sorcha took the bag and went down on her knees with it, placing it on the floor before her, pulling out the few articles of clothing within. When she reached the bottom of the pile, she turned the bag over. It was empty.

"There, you see? You accuse her falsely, Sorcha! That was badly done! There is no necklace in there, of course no'! Were I you, I'd ask your maid what she's done with it."

"How dare you accuse Hannah!" Mrs. Garbett said angrily. "What of *him*?" she said, pointing at Nichol.

"*Him?* The man we've paid so handsomely to take her away, then? You're mad, wife."

Nichol shrugged out of his coat and held his arms wide. "You may search all you like, Mrs. Garbett," he said.

The woman colored. She kicked the bag away from her daughter's feet, then drew Sorcha back to the table.

Nichol calmly bent down and gathered Miss Darby's things and returned them to the bag. "We'll take our leave now," he said, and with his hand firmly on Miss Darby's elbow, he wheeled her about and strode down the hall with her.

Miss Darby kept her head down, her jaw firmly clenched as they sailed out of the Garbett residence.

"Maura, lass, please," Mr. Garbett pleaded, walking after them with his napkin still tucked into his collar. "Donna be cross with us, aye? Any reasonable person might have made that mistake, is that no' so?"

"Goodbye, Mr. Garbett," she said, and turned her head when Nichol lifted her into the saddle. He strapped her bag to the back of the saddle, then put himself on the back of his mount.

Mr. Garbett hovered around them. "But…you will write, will you no'?"

Miss Darby flatly ignored him. Nichol took her reins, set their horses to a trot, and left Mr. Garbett standing in the drive with that napkin lifting in the breeze.

They rode in silence for a quarter of an hour, down the long drive, onto the road again. Nichol had things to explain, that he knew, but he thought they would stop at the inn at Stirling once more, fill their bellies, and he'd explain all.

Miss Darby had other ideas. She abruptly yanked the reins from him and then pulled her horse to a stop.

"What are you doing?" he asked.

Her response was to swing off the mount, landing awkwardly and bumping into the horse. Then she began to walk up the road. Actually, she strode off, her arms swinging, as if to war. Nichol watched her, curious as to how far she would go if he didn't stop her. "Where are you going, then?" he called after her.

"Away from you! I owe you *nothing*, Mr. Bain! I lived up to my end of the bargain, but *you*! *You* betrayed me! You're no better than them!"

Nichol hopped off his horse and walked after her. "If you will halt in your march, I'll explain—"

She gave a bark of hysterical laughter and whirled about. "Do you think me so feeble that I need an explanation? It is all quite clear! Did you lose your nerve? Did you deem me suddenly unworthy of your assistance? Were you so concerned about your *precious* reputation that *my* life and *my* concerns no longer mattered?" she railed at him.

Nichol went down on one knee.

"Do you know what infuriates me most of all, Mr. Bain?" she demanded.

"I've an idea, aye."

"You've *no* idea. What infuriates me most is that I trusted you! I *believed* you!" she shouted angrily as Nichol rose to his full height. "What a bloody fool I was for trusting *you*, a mere stranger! Everyone I have *ever* trusted has abandoned me, and I canna imagine why I thought you'd be any different. I should never have let you take me. I should *never* have—" She suddenly stopped shouting.

Her mouth gaped.

She stared at the necklace he held in his hand a long moment, then looked at him again. "When?" she asked simply.

"In the night." He supposed he should be relieved to discover that he could not think like a thief, but it had been a bit of bother not to know how to steal properly. It had struck him near two in the morning that the Garbetts would immediately turn to Miss Darby if the necklace was discovered missing before they escaped, and would look through her things, and therefore, he had to alter his first plan. He'd felt ridiculous, catting about like he had in the night. He'd sneaked down the hall, pausing when a board creaked. He kept to the wall, where the floorboards were not as worn and were taut. His heart had been in his throat, but he could not allow them to take that necklace from Miss Darby.

Quiet as a mouse, he'd opened her door. The bag was just inside, where she'd left it earlier. He could see her in her bed, lying on her side. Her long dark hair spilled behind her and he could hear her steady breathing. She'd looked so young to him, so vulnerable. It had made his heart ache in a peculiar and uncharacteristic way. She'd been dealt a rotten hand in life, that she had. Just like him. But to *feel* something about that, to find that he could not ignore it or push it away, had been unsettling.

He'd found the necklace easily enough. He'd looked at her once more before he slipped out—she'd looked almost ghostly in the low light of the hearth's embers, and he had suddenly imagined her hair sliding between his fingers. His lips on her neck. His hand on her breast.

"I thought you had lost your nerve and put it some place they might find it," she said meekly.

Nichol tilted his head to one side and gave her a curious smile. "Do I seem to you a man who loses his nerve easily, then?" He glanced down at the necklace in his hand for a moment to gather himself. "I feared something might happen, and it did. I realized that if they discovered the necklace missing before we'd taken our leave, they'd suspect you, aye?"

Her brows dipped. "So you...you came into my room while I was *sleeping*?" she asked with a tone that made it impossible to discern if she was angry or impressed.

"Aye." He held out his hand, the ends of the necklace dangling through his fingers.

Miss Darby slowly stepped forward, her eyes locked on the necklace. And then she began to move with alarming speed. Nichol braced himself—he believed she meant to tackle and pummel him. Indeed she did tackle him, but not in the manner he was expecting, and he was caught completely off guard.

Miss Darby threw her arms around his neck and

yanked his head down as she rose up on her toes, and kissed him.

He gave a short laugh of surprise into her mouth, which she flatly ignored while she kept kissing him. *This woman!* Was there no end to the ways she surprised him? She was igniting him, setting the blood in his veins on fire. She was taking risks she ought not to take, persisting when she ought not to persist, and he was a sudden conflagration of want. He slid his arms around her body, holding her to him to prolong this attack, and tangled his tongue with hers.

She felt unimaginably soft in his arms, tasted sweet as spring. He felt himself foundering in the sensual caress of her mouth against his, sliding headlong into the grip of his determined arousal. But she suddenly lifted her head, breathless, her eyes glittering. She laughed so gaily—or was it hysterically—and he was startled. He'd not seen this side of her.

"*Mi Diah,* what have I done?" she laughingly cried. Her arms slid from around his neck, her body slid down his as she put herself back on her heels. "I donna know what came over me, Mr. Bain, aye? I didna mean to do it, I swear it, and I canna explain it other than I am so *happy*," she said, and took the necklace that he'd threaded through his fingers.

He'd forgotten he was holding it.

"I thought it was lost to me forever! *Mi Diah,*" she said, again, pressing her palm to one cheek, then the other as if to calm herself. "Please forgive me."

He felt inwardly shaky. He was rocked by that kiss and at present, wasn't sure which way was up.

He ran his thumb over his bottom lip. "No forgiveness is necessary, Miss Darby."

Her eyes were still shining, but there was a different sort of light in them now. It was slightly seductive. More knowing.

"You are kind to no' take offense, Mr. Bain, for you would be entirely in the right if you did. I *do* beg your pardon. Contrary to what you might have heard from the Garbetts, I am truly no' in the habit of forcing my affection on gentlemen, unsuspecting or otherwise."

Affection.

She laughed, as if surprised. "I scarcely know myself." She pressed the back of her hand against her forehead. "I need a wee bit of air, that's what." She moved as if to walk away, but paused and looked at him sidelong, a funny little smile playing on her lush lips. "I apologize for my harsh words earlier. I was so terribly *angry.* But I am in your debt, Mr. Bain," she said, and turned away, walking up the road, rubbing her hand on her nape as if to wake herself from a long nap.

How odd, how discomfiting that the gleam in her eye should make him feel so outside himself. So bloody restless.

This was not like him.

No one disconcerted him, particularly not the fairer sex.

But here he stood, quite thoroughly disconcerted.

He shook his head, tried to dislodge the thoughts rolling about. He took the horses by the reins and led them to walk up the road where Miss Darby had stopped, standing in the middle of the road, staring off into the distance. He noticed she'd put on the necklace—the emerald flashed at him from the hollow of her throat.

"What do you think?" she asked, and turned, holding her cloak open so that he might admire it.

What did he think? That it was bonny. Almost as bonny as the fair neck it graced. That he would very much like to remove it, to feel her smooth skin beneath his fingertips, to slide his hands over her creamy shoulders.

"Do you think your friend will like it, then?" she asked, and curtsied deeply. "He might think me a fine lady, aye?"

Bloody hell, but Nichol had forgotten about Dunnan Cockburn altogether. "Aye, I think he will," he answered in all sincerity, and felt a slight swell of illogical resentment against Cockburn.

Miss Darby rose up, and Nichol reached for the open panels of her cloak. "Unfortunately, we'll no' know how Mr. Cockburn finds your necklace straightaway, for we must take a detour."

He hardly knew what he was saying. His plan was to hasten her to Luncarty and leave her there, dispose of this particular problem, his job complete. He'd then go around to fetch the groom and see his brother after all this time. That's what sentiment did to a man—it made him think of ridiculous things, and worse, act on them. Nichol hadn't been to Cheverock in years. This wasn't the way a son should return home, but his feelings for the lass were driving him to ignore even the slightest bit of common sense.

"Pardon?" she asked as he fastened her cloak at her neck.

"Do you recall the lad you frightened half out of his wits with your complaints?"

Aye, he was mad, then. A simple kiss had propelled him to say and do things he ought not to, all to allow himself a wee bit more time in Miss Darby's company. To what end? All for the sake of another kiss?

She tilted her head to one side. "Aye yes, I remember a lad, I do," she said. "Only vaguely, really. He said no' a word and I was no' of a mood to pay him any heed."

"Aye," he said, smiling in spite of himself. "I recall too well." He fastened the second hook on her cloak. "The poor lad was left without a horse, he was. I was forced to send him off for safekeeping until I could come and fetch him."

"Why did you no' bring him with you?"

"If I'd brought him with me, I would have lost you." He looked her in the eye. "And I could no' allow that to happen, could I?"

She smirked. "Mr. Garbett must have paid you *handsomely*, Mr. Bain."

"On the contrary, Miss Darby—he did no' pay me nearly enough." He smiled.

So did she.

Aye, he was mad. He would change his route, add two days to his time with her, arrive on his family's doorstep with a woman he could not explain, all for the sake of a kiss.

He dropped his hands to her waist to lift her onto the horse. But he didn't lift her right away. He was caught by the look in her eyes. Her head was titled back, and her eyes were filled with amusement. Her gaze drifted to his mouth. "I didna ask you to come after me, Mr. Bain. Therefore, I refuse to feel the least bit bad for you."

"I would be sorely disappointed if you did, Miss Darby."

"Where did you send him?" she asked, and placed her hands delicately on his forearms as he prepared to lift her up.

The warmth he was feeling began to cool as he thought about Cheverock. *His father.* He lifted her up onto the back of the horse. "Home," he said. "I sent him to my home." Even the words tasted bitter to him.

"Oh!" She looked surprised and even a wee bit delighted. "That's quite a risk, is it no', Mr. Bain? They'll think you've brought your mistress." She laughed at that, as if it were wildly impossible.

Nichol didn't laugh. He couldn't laugh. The dread had already begun to fill him, pushing against his ribs and his throat.

Miss Darby's smile faded. "I beg your pardon, my jest was in poor taste. What excuse will you offer for me, then?" she asked, averting her gaze. Her cheeks were turning pink. "I donna care what you say, if it helps you. No one's opinion can harm me now."

She had not met his father, he thought bitterly. "I donna know," he said truthfully. "I've no' been home in many years and I canna be entirely certain how either of us will be received. But I will no' see you harmed, Miss Darby."

"Oh," she said, clearly surprised by that. "But—"

Nichol turned from her horse and leapt up onto the back of his. He did not want to hear her question, did not want to explain, did not want to think of it at all. He set them off on a trot, away from the moments of tenderness they'd just shared, the warmth he'd been feeling, the *affection* she'd shown him.

It had been a lark anyway. What he'd just done was foolish—nothing would change the fact that he was delivering her to Dunnan Cockburn. Today, or tomorrow or the next day, it didn't matter, he would deliver her, because this was the way of his life. He made the acquaintance of women. He was intrigued by some. On occasion, he bedded them. But he always left them.

He was a rolling stone, without a home, without a name.

But that didn't mean he couldn't alter course and enjoy a day or two in her company.

Affection.

CHAPTER THIRTEEN

MAURA WAS SUITABLY shocked by her own actions, but she was in no way sorry for them. She'd gone long past the point of worrying about propriety. Who could blame her, really? She'd been overcome by emotion—she'd felt such crushing disappointment when they'd left, and she'd thought her necklace lost to her forever. When she discovered Mr. Bain had it after all, her heart had filled to nearly bursting. It had felt as if she and Mr. Bain were two rebels, fighting against tyranny and injustice, and she'd been so filled with gratitude and victory and relief that she'd not been able to help herself.

No, she wasn't sorry for it even a wee bit—she was glad she'd kissed him.

She kept thinking of his lips, how soft and pliable they were, and yet at the same time, rather demanding. Not in the same way Adam Cadell's torturous kiss had been demanding—his lips had been hard and unyielding. Rather, Mr. Bain's lips were the sort to demand by coaxing and teasing and molding her mouth to his.

Maura shuddered with longing that sizzled like fat in her veins. She'd not wanted to stop kissing him, and she supposed she might have completely abandoned her morals had that pang of consciousness not stabbed at her when it did. She was suddenly aware of what she was doing, of who he was. She was suddenly aware of who *she* was, or had been, up until a month or so ago when Adam Cadell had ruined her life. She'd been a woman who valued her reputation and was careful not to give offense to anyone. She was a woman who waited patiently for Sorcha to marry so that she might possibly find her own match.

She was most decidedly *not* a woman who threw herself at a man and kissed him so enthusiastically.

And she had been *quite* enthusiastic.

Her conscience had at last grabbed her by the hair and pulled her back from the brink of total ruin, and frankly, Maura still wasn't certain how she felt about her meddling conscience.

She watched Mr. Bain ride just ahead of her, his seat just as sure on the bare back of the horse as if he'd been in the saddle she now rode. His back erect, one hand curled into a fist and pressed against his thigh.

She had to stop thinking about that kiss. Practically speaking, she had to stop thinking about *him*. She hardly knew a thing about him, really. He had burst into her tower prison and had whisked her off, intent on marrying her to a perfect stranger. She was, by his admission, a problem he'd been paid to solve. And he would have handed her off without the slightest hesitation had she not escaped. The only thing she really knew about him was that he was a decent soul, because he'd agreed to help her retrieve her family heirloom.

A month ago, she would have been aghast by her familiarity with a man about whom she knew so very little. But as she was destined to be presented as a potential wife to a man she had not even *met*, she supposed her acquaintance with Mr. Bain was a deep one by comparison.

Once again, her practical side chimed in, reminding her that instead of musing about how well she did or did not know the man she'd so brazenly kissed, she ought to be about plotting her next escape.

Funny how the heat in her blood could drown out all reason.

She'd think of her next escape when the time came. There was no use pondering it until she saw what obstacles faced her.

So she would allow herself this bit of fantasy while she might. Soon enough, she'd not have the luxury of time to think of anything other than how to survive. *Let me have this,* she begged the practical side of her. Her practical side began to snivel, but her lustful thoughts banded together and crowded around it and pushed it off a bloody cliff.

Mr. Bain glanced over his shoulder at her, as if to assure himself she was still there. She smiled. He faced forward again.

What an interesting enigma he was. He was educated, refined in his manner. Maura would have guessed him the son of a vicar or a laird, a man from a respectable family. Why, then, had he not been home in many years? Why had he said he didn't know how he'd be received? It was odd—he presented himself so fully in command that she would think he'd be fully in command of his family, too.

No matter what he'd meant by it, it had cast him in a different light to her. He'd seemed rather black-and-white to her at first, but now he was varying shades of shadows and glimpses of bright light.

She wanted to know how many other shadows there were in Mr. Bain. Perhaps there were dark shadows, peculiar peccadilloes that would astonish her. Perhaps he was the sort to lust after a woman's foot. That was something Maura would have thought outrageous and impossible, but Delilah Frank had whispered such madness about Mr. Grant, a widower who'd married a lass who was thirty years his junior. *She said he likes to rub himself on her feet*, Delilah had whispered in Maura's ear one afternoon as they'd followed Sorcha and Adam about the garden.

"What do you mean, rub himself?" Maura had asked.

Delilah had giggled, her cheeks flushing red. "I mean *it*," she'd said with a furtive glance about and a nudge to Maura's side.

Maura fixed her gaze on Mr. Bain's back and tried to imagine it. The image forced a giggle, and she tried to swallow it, but that only made her want to giggle wildly, like a girl who'd gone off her head. She choked back more than one burst of laughter.

Mr. Bain turned his head. "Aye, let's have it, then. What amuses you?"

How do you like a woman's foot, Mr. Bain? She shook her head and bit the inside of her mouth to keep from laughing. It was absurd to even think it. "Nothing."

His gaze narrowed. He slowed his horse so that hers could catch up to his. "If you'll no' tell me, I will assume you are diverted by the plotting of your next escape."

Well, that was a wee bit uncanny. She would have been doing precisely that had she not kissed him and begun to imagine even more impossible things. "My escape!" she said gaily. "Whatever makes you think I plan to escape?"

"Because you've demonstrated a penchant for it, aye? And, you have your necklace now. I would guess that you believe the world is now yours for the taking."

He was not wrong. "Well, you're wrong, sir," she said. "You lived up to your half of our bargain, and I intend to live up to mine."

"And by that, you mean you will allow me to deliver you to Luncarty," he said with a lopsided smile.

"I give you my word, Mr. Bain, I shall no' attempt any escape until you've been long gone and canna be faulted." She smiled prettily at him.

"Verra considerate of you," he said with a touch to the brim of his hat. "However, I should warn you that while Mr. Cockburn may be mildly mannered, he is no' a fool."

"I'm certain he would have said the same of you. And yet…" She shrugged cheekily.

He laughed. "And yet. Touché, Miss Darby. Are you hungry, then?"

"Hungry? What has that to do with mild-mannered fools?"

"It has to do with the fact that this fool is famished, aye? I took the liberty of asking the kitchen for a bundle of food. We'll stop and water the horses."

"You do think of everything, Mr. Bain."

"Aye, lass, it's my job to think of everything."

In a quarter of a mile, he turned off the road and onto a smaller path. It led them through a thick copse of Scotch pine, alder and ash trees, crowded around the banks of a small loch that lay placidly between rolling hills. There was not a soul about, not even a crofter or fishing house anywhere to be seen.

Mr. Bain laid his plaid on a bed of pine needles, and Maura settled onto her knees. He unbundled a cheesecloth and spread it between them. The Garbett kitchen had provided cheese, the heel of a loaf of bread, and some ham. Mr. Bain went to the edge of the loch and pushed between the horses, who had ambled into the loch ankle deep, their tails swishing about them as they dipped their heads to drink. Mr. Bain dipped a flagon beneath its surface, filling it with water.

He could not have found a bonnier place to suit Maura. This vista was the very image of the Scotland that lived in her heart. The sun broke through the clouds on occasion, casting bands of light to skate across the water's surface. Overhead, the crossbills chattered at each other, and the only other sound was water lapping onto the shore as the horses moved about.

It was so peaceful, so serene, and Maura realized she hadn't been this at ease in weeks. Perhaps even years.

They took their meal in mostly silence, each of them lost in their thoughts. When they'd had their fill, Mr. Bain got up to feed the horses. Some ducks appeared above the loch, gliding down onto the surface, then paddling toward them. He took the bread they hadn't eaten and threw bits of it to the ducks, and Maura laughed as they frantically chased each bit around, their heads disappearing beneath the surface then up again.

When Mr. Bain had tended the horses, he returned to the blanket and eased himself down beside her. "You have the look of a woman who's no' slept, Miss Darby."

"Mmm," she agreed. "I didna sleep well at all, with the exception of the moment when a mysterious visitor entered my room, aye? For that, it would seem I was quite sound asleep."

He smiled. "I can be quiet as a mouse when necessary. Lie down and rest, then."

"What of you?" she asked. "Are you no' tired, then?"

He shook his head.

Maura lay down on her side and gazed out over the loch. She tried to imagine what it would be like to arrive on the doorstep of his family's home, uninvited, unexpected. "What is your home like?" she asked curiously.

Mr. Bain shifted beside her. He drew his legs up and wrapped his arms loosely about his knees. "'Tis a grand home. Or rather, it was the last I laid eyes on it. That's been many years."

"How many?"

"Many," he said vaguely.

"*Och,* but what of your mother, Mr. Bain? Surely she'd no' let you go so long without calling."

"My mother is long since gone from this earth."

Perhaps that explained it. Perhaps, like her, his parents were dead, and there was no reason to return to his childhood home. No one was there waiting for him. "Your father is gone as well, then, aye?"

He didn't respond immediately, then said, "No' that I'm aware." He said it as if he were talking about a distant relative or a public figure. There was a disconcerting lack of esteem or regard for his family and home that she didn't understand. "You truly donna know how he fares?" she asked, glancing up at him.

Mr. Bain's gaze was fixed on the loch, but Maura had the sense he was seeing far beyond it. "I truly donna know."

"Have you any siblings, then?"

He turned his head and smiled with a bit of impatience. "You are a verra curious lass, are you no'? Do they teach young lassies in the course of their studies to interrogate gentlemen?"

"And *you* are verra peculiar man, Mr. Bain. Of

course I am curious. You mean to take me to your home without invitation, a home you have no' seen in many years, and donna know who lives, and I am well within my right to know who I will meet and what I might expect, then."

"Aye, all right," he said, conceding. "A reasonable request. I've a brother, two years younger than me, at Cheverock. Ivan is his name."

"*Thank* you," she said, smiling. "Do you know how *he* fares?"

"I've no' received a letter from him in a few years. I assume he is well."

"Aye, I hope he is, for our sake," she said, and rolled onto her back. She stared up at the tops of the pines, admiring the way the gray light filtered through the needles, and waited for Mr. Bain to expound. Naturally, he did not. "Must I ask, then?" she playfully chided him.

"Ask what?"

She clucked her tongue. "Mr. Bain, I am *desperate* to know why you've no' been home all this time. You must oblige me or I will perish, here and now."

"I donna think you will," he said lightly, and leaned back, stretching his legs long before him, and propping himself on an elbow. "Must you know everything?"

"Aye, I must!" she said with a flick of her wrist. "I think you donna appreciate that I've been bargained away with no thought to my feelings about it, though I spent my life behaving as I'd been taught to behave. It hardly mattered. So now I am determined to understand the world around me so that I may make my own decisions. I donna care what anyone thinks of it." She flicked a leaf from her belly. "So why, then, have you no' been home for so long?"

He smiled at her impertinent question, which in and of itself was a revelation to Maura—there was no Mrs. Garbett to chastise her for saying the wrong thing. No Sorcha to roll her eyes. There was only Mr. Bain to smile at her.

"I canna answer all your questions, you wee upstart. My life has been rather complicated, it has."

Maura couldn't help but laugh at that. "It canna possibly be more complicated than my situation, Mr. Bain! You need no' choose your words with me. I'm in no position to pass judgment on you, aye?"

"Well, *that's* true enough," he agreed. "All right then, where shall I begin? I've no' been home in many years because I've had a difficult relationship with my father. When I was in my tenth year he sent me from home to apprentice with the Duke of Hamilton."

"Really," she said with delight, fascinated with this bit of information, and rolled onto her side to face him. She knew that it had once been very vogue for the Quality to send their sons off to learn how to be dukes and kings and earls, but it was not the habit of so many now. Nevertheless, she was under the impression that it was a practice of wealthy, important people, and therefore, she supposed his family must be important, too. "What was it like?"

Mr. Bain thought a moment. "Lonely," he said. "I

learned quite a lot from the old duke, that I did. But I was lonely without my brother. There was no one about but a few servants."

Maura understood how it felt to be deposited in a strange house. When she'd first arrived at Mr. Garbett's home, Sorcha had been thrilled to have a playmate, and one that would do her bidding at that. But even then, Maura had felt like an outsider, a plaything for the favored child in the house. There were years that were easier than others—when she was younger, before they were women—but she'd never felt as if she belonged, precisely. *Diah,* how she would cry herself to sleep at night, missing her father so achingly, and missing her governess, the cook, the entire staff. It had been a lot for a child to endure, really.

"From there, I was sent to St. Andrews."

"Ah, *that's* where you learned French and German, then."

"No. I spent quite a lot of time on the Continent when I finished my education, and learned the languages then. And you? How did you learn to speak two languages?"

"Oh, my father insisted," she said. "It was only the two of us from the time I was a bairn. He said he'd never have a son, and therefore, I would have to be both son and daughter to him. He taught me science, too." She smiled sheepishly as she recalled the child she'd been. "I fancied myself an astronomer."

"An astronomer!"

"Aye, why no'? I *like* the stars. Donna you like the stars, Mr. Bain?"

"Well enough," he said with a shrug. "I've no' given them much thought."

"What did you want to be?"

"A barrister," he said. "I was quite taken with my father's barrister, I was. He was handsome and fit, an excellent rider..." He glanced away. "And he was verra kind to me at a time when few were. I admired him."

Why hadn't people been kind to him? "You might still be a barrister, Mr. Bain. Perhaps you might even apprentice with him, aye?" she asked. "Is he near to you now? Where do you live?"

"I donna live anywhere in particular," he said. "And I should no' like to be a barrister. I like my occupation, such that it is."

"What do you mean, you donna live anywhere? *Everyone* has a home."

"No' everyone," he said, and touched her hand. "*You* donna have one."

She rolled her eyes. "I had thankfully forgotten that for a wee time." Moreover, in that moment she hardly cared. She would be perfectly content for the rest of her life to lie on that blanket, on the bank of that loch, with the crossbills chattering above while Mr. Bain stared off into the distance. "You're a wanderer, then, are you?" she asked on a yawn.

"Aye, I suppose I am," he said, as if the thought had just occurred to him. "I take residence in the homes of the people who engage my service."

"Like Mr. Garbett?"

"No' him. More like the Duke of Montrose, who I have served. Most recently, the Earl of Norwood."

"And now? Where will you go once you've tossed me off at Luncarty?"

He chuckled. "I'll no' toss you off, lass. I will hand you carefully. As for me, I've been summoned by a wealthy sea trader in Wales. He's lost a ship at sea and owes quite a lot of money. He has engaged me to go to France on his behalf and work out the terms of the debt."

That sounded intriguing to Maura. Exciting, too. She would like to flit about, living in one grand house after another, consorting with the Quality and solving their problems. "You have an exciting life," she said with a twinge of envy.

"It has been at times."

But he spoke without conviction. As if he wasn't entirely convinced of it. There was something about his demeanor that brought to mind a lad, sent to apprentice with an old duke. Was it possible he was still a wee bit lonely? It must be impossible to form friendships when one was constantly moving from one house to the next. "You've never married?"

"*Och,* you ask too many questions," he said, and playfully squeezed her arm.

"Aha, you've *no'* married, then," she teased him.

"Aye, you've discovered my darkest secret, Miss Darby. I have no' married." He grinned at her and brushed another leaf from her shoulder.

"*Hmm,*" she said.

"What do you mean by *hmm*?"

"Nothing."

"Liar."

"I *mean*, Mr. Bain, that it seems impossible you've no' married. An educated man who has served dukes and earls would be considered quite a matrimonial catch, I should think. Oh all right, I will confess it— I'm surprised you've managed to escape the clutches of mammas in search of matches for their daughters, I am. Mrs. Garbett would have fainted dead away had you been unmarried and so gallant anywhere near her, aye? But she would have rallied herself just in time to sink her clutches into you for the sake of her daughter."

"Diah," he said, one brow arching over the other. "I hadna realize how narrowly I've avoided the worst possible fate a man might endure."

Maura laughed gaily. "I wish *I* could have wandered and avoided the worst possible fate," she said. "Why is it that bachelors may do as they please, but unmarried women must be kept under lock and key?"

"'Tis the way of the world, lass. What of your suitors? I should imagine a line of them at the door of the Garbett house."

"Oh no," she said, with an adamant shake of her head. "Mrs. Garbett wouldna *hear* of it. She was determined that Sorcha would have her pick of any eligible bachelors in and around Stirling. But I didna complain, for the gentlemen she invited to dine would no' have suited me, I think. They were all for Sorcha. Alas, inevitably, her caller would inquire after my suitability for marriage and Sorcha's feelings would be hurt."

"It's quite understandable."

"But it's no'!" Maura insisted with a nudge to his shoulder. "I never encouraged *any* gentleman who came to call on Sorcha. I did my best to be absent as much as I possibly could and if I could no', as quiet as a ghost."

"Nevertheless, from a man's perspective, you are far more desirable, Miss Darby. I should think that obvious even to you."

She laughed with disbelief. "I donna see how any gentleman could have thought so! I scarcely said a word at all."

"Perhaps that was how?" he suggested, and laughed when she gasped with pretend outrage.

"You're bonny, you are. A gentleman's attention is no' at first drawn to words as it is to beauty. The attraction was undoubtedly immediate to anyone who had the chance to meet you. Your compatibility became obvious in the dim light of Miss Sorcha's company."

Maura blushed self-consciously at his praise. She'd been told before she was bonny—certainly Adam Cadell had said it more than once with a desperation that made her want to run. But when Mr. Bain said it, it felt more impactful. She did not want to run, she wanted to believe him. She wanted to believe he found her bonny, not just in looks, but in character. That he found her compatible in every way.

Och, but such wishful thinking was not her right,

and she glanced away, wishing she could stop imagining the impossible when it came to him. "On my word, I tried to give Sorcha her due, I swear it. But she can be unpleasant when things donna go as she likes. She's her own worst enemy, really."

"I'd offer that her mother is the bigger enemy."

Maura giggled. "Oh aye, she is wretched, that one. But then a match was made with Mr. Cadell and I thought *that* would be the end of it, I certainly did."

"It was only the beginning for you, was it?"

She nodded, then sighed wearily.

"He was besotted with you, you know," Mr. Bain said with a gaze so soft that it sent a fluttery little burst of feathers down her spine.

"He's a fool."

Mr. Bain's smile deepened. "Another fool."

She smiled. She'd not forgotten she'd called him a fool today. "*All* of you, really, donna you know?" She rolled onto her back again and tossed her arm over her eyes with a sigh. "How long until we reach Cheverock?"

"About five hours. Rest, then. We've an hour or so before we must depart."

She was feeling the ribbons of sleep spinning a web over her eyes. "What will you do, then?"

"I'll keep watch over you."

Those words, softly spoken, spiraled through her, and Maura moved her arm to look at him, uncertain of his meaning. Uncertain of her feelings.

His gaze was on her mouth, and the fluttering feathers began again. "I canna have you escape again, can I?" he asked. "It would ruin my excellent reputation."

"No, we canna have that," she murmured. "I promise I'll no' escape until I've napped, then." She closed her eyes and pillowed her head on one arm. Mr. Bain touched her face lightly, then brushed a bit of her hair from her cheek, tucking it behind her ear. She felt warm. She felt safe.

Donna be tender with me, please donna be tender.

It would only make her want harder.

It would only make it impossible to say farewell when the time came.

She wished he would not cause her to imagine any more impossible things this day.

Nonetheless, she groped for his hand, and when she found it, she wrapped her fingers around his all the same.

CHAPTER FOURTEEN

IT FELT AS if the sky was below him, the earth above him. It was neither winter nor summer, but somewhere between stillness and movement.

Nichol had never been here before. He didn't know what to do in this odd space or how to understand what was happening to him. He was not excessively prone to feelings of any sort. He'd kissed a dozen women in his life, and he'd kissed them in every conceivable way. But he'd never experienced a kiss quite like the one she'd bestowed on him today.

He'd never experienced a day quite like today.

He was surprised to realize that he'd been so invigorated by their little caper. Made to feel again, as it were, with a vague anticipation of something new and different around every corner. Had his life grown stale? Had he become so accustomed to the mundane familial and business problems gentlemen trapped themselves in that he'd forgotten what a wee bit of excitement felt like? How many times had his heart pumped in the last twenty-four hours? How many times had he felt the exhilaration of a risk he knew he ought not to take? How many times had he bloody well *smiled*?

And now here he sat, far longer than he ought to have done, watching Miss Darby sleep.

It was cold; the clouds were beginning to thicken and he could sense snow was coming. The horses could sense it, too. They were restless, moving about, bumping into each other as they waited. And yet, Nichol didn't move from that odd space.

He was uncomfortably aware that there was something about Maura Darby that had coaxed restless feelings to bloom in him. Feelings he was certain he hadn't felt before. He'd had paramours, of course. What man denied his most primal instincts? And while he'd been fond of one or two, he'd never *felt* things.

Like comfort.

Or an appreciation of the wreckage of his family. He'd never expected anyone to understand how he'd come to be the man he was—there were times he scarcely understood it himself—and while he assumed he'd not told her enough to truly understand, he had the sense that if anyone *could* understand, it was Maura Darby.

It wasn't just her kiss that made him feel. The kiss had been surprising and quite pleasant, but it was still just a kiss. No, what was rumbling about in him, untethered, unmoored, was far more than that.

He had decided, sitting there, that it was her spirit. It was her defiance and determination in the face of adversity that was not of her making, that was beyond her ability to control. She was young, at the beginning of her third decade, perhaps. She had not lived enough to know that life was forever unfair in ways that tested a man's resolve. She'd lived a sheltered life in the way all young women of her particular circumstance and social standing lived— protected by wealth and the men who ruled their lives. And yet she had not crumbled when faced with a sudden change in her situation. Neither had she gone along meekly. Maura Darby had instinctively, and with not a little grit, sought to take control of events that were quickly spiraling out of her control.

He had to admire her for that. Who wouldn't? Better to meet one's fate with a sword in hand than in one's back, wasn't it?

But Nichol understood that the sort of admiration he felt for her could lead to terrible trouble. He knew it very well, and yet he couldn't seem to take a step back from her.

It was half past twelve when he finally glanced at his pocket watch. He wanted to be in Cheverock before nightfall and reluctantly awakened the sleeping beauty. She pushed away from the earth groggily, blinking at the dull gray day. "I didna dream it, then," she said, her voice light.

"Dream what?"

She hopped to her feet, then stretched her arms high overhead with a yawn. "Nothing," she said, then threw out her arms and did a perfect little pirouette, as if that were perfectly natural in this circumstance.

Nichol kept looking at her as they rode, trying to separate his feelings from the truth of the situation that actually existed for both of them. There was a husband waiting for her, a Welshman waiting for him with a lucrative problem to be solved. He couldn't miss that opportunity. Miss Darby couldn't miss hers, either. With no one to sponsor her, no one to vouch for her, Dunnan would be her only opportunity.

Nichol knew all these things, but he felt a palatable foreboding when he thought of having to step away from her.

But at the same time, he felt incomprehensibly peaceful in this space between stillness and movement.

Miss Darby had awakened with renewed vigor, and she nattered along as they rode. She had an idea, she said. She was very adept at sewing and had decided, apparently between Garbett House and now, that she could take in work, perhaps even learn to make fashionable gowns for ladies of the Quality. "I would like that," she mused. "I should like verra much to make lovely gowns with the best fabrics from the Continent." She paused, her brow furrowed as she contemplated it. "I particularly like blue," she said. "What do you like, Mr. Bain?"

"I like blue," he said, as he'd given it no thought and blue—especially the blue color of her eyes— seemed almost divine.

She laughed as if she believed he teased her.

She spoke philosophically about the process of courtship. "It's impossible to know if two are compatible for the rest of their lives, is it no', when they've had only a bit of walking and talking here and there, and always in the presence of others. Think of it, Mr. Bain, if we'd been anywhere but in those woods, I could no' have asked you about your life, could I?"

"Are we courting?" he asked.

"If we *were*," she said with a pert little smile, "I should no' have gleaned nearly as much about you as I have today until the moment we were wed. It's astonishingly senseless! I'm quite certain that once Sorcha has her husband and her house, she might possibly be unhappy in the end, for she knows verra little of Mr. Cadell."

"I would argue that what she knows is enough to recommend against a union."

"Quite right, Mr. Bain!" she agreed imperiously. "And now *you* would have *me* marry a man with whom I've no' had the pleasure of even a single conversation!"

"You may have as many conversations as you like," he assured her. "Mr. Cockburn enjoys a rousing tête-à-tête."

"That's all verra well and good, then, for I've quite a lot to say."

Nichol couldn't help but laugh at that.

Then Miss Darby wondered aloud if there were any astronomers where she might apprentice, having apparently cottoned on to the idea of apprenticeships in general.

"In Scotland?" Mr. Bain asked idly.

"Aye. Mr. Ferguson of Rothiemay is an astronomer of repute, and do you know the best of it, Mr. Bain? He taught himself!"

"Aye, then perhaps you might write to him and implore him to take you under his wing."

"I should like that verra much, if my new husband would allow it," she said, giving him a side-eyed look. "Alas, Mr. Ferguson has gone to England to educate all the young gentlemen who are afforded the luxury of learning about stars and planets. I'm certain I'll be deeply occupied in determining the menu for the Sunday meal and embroidering hearts on my husband's handkerchiefs."

Nichol chuckled.

He enjoyed the ride to Cheverock. He listened to every word she said, which surprised him, for he'd found that the fairer sex had a perplexing capacity for words, and seemed to use far more than was necessary. But with Miss Darby, he listened. He laughed, he pondered the questions she raised to him. Time passed quickly, and it was with dismay when he realized that they were upon Cheverock.

Uneasiness began to ratchet in Nichol the closer they drew to his boyhood home, so much so that his hand began to ache from gripping his reins with such force his fingers were unrelentingly curled. His uneasiness grew into complete apprehension when they entered the drive to Cheverock. The clouds were thick now, mashing down upon the house, the gray shade that portended snow. Everything looked and felt as oppressive and heavy as the air around them.

The house, as magnificent and as dark as it had

existed in his memory all these years, showed hardly any light at all. The lawn was well manicured, and a flock of sheep grazed languidly in the fields as it always had.

Miss Darby had fallen silent, and Nichol risked a look at her. Whatever she thought of the house, she kept it hidden, but she stared up at it as if she felt the heaviness, too.

They rode around the fountain at the center of the drive, Nichol's eyes on the house, half expecting his father to come storming out, demanding he be gone.

"There's the lad, then," Miss Darby said, and pointed to a figure who'd come from the outbuildings. Gavin jogged toward them, halting just ahead of the horses. He swept his hat off and gave Miss Darby a bob of his head, and to Nichol, he said, "Aye, you came, then, sir."

He sounded relieved.

"Aye, lad, of course I did, I gave you my word." Nichol dismounted. "You found my brother, then?" he asked, mentally bracing himself for whatever Gavin might have found here.

Gavin nodded.

"All is well? You gave him the ring?"

Gavin nodded. "Aye, sir. I've been given leave to sleep in the stables until you come."

Nichol glanced back at the gloomy house and then reached up for Miss Darby to set her down. "He's here, then, is he? My brother?" Nichol asked uncertainly.

"Aye, sir." He suddenly dipped down, lifted the

hem of his trouser, and withdrew a pistol from his boot. He held it out to Nichol.

"What are you doing?" Miss Darby exclaimed with alarm.

Nichol shook his head, and slipped the pistol into his pocket. "'Twas a precaution," he said absently. "Take the horses, then, lad. Eat well, rest well, aye?" He glanced at Miss Darby and offered his arm. "Welcome to Cheverock, Miss Darby."

She looked at his arm, then her gaze flicked to his feet. "I'm a wee ball of nerves," she admitted.

He smiled thinly. He wished he could assure her, but unfortunately, he felt a wee ball of nerves, too. "I'll keep you close," he assured her. He escorted her to the front steps, then let go of her hand and jogged up to the landing. He used the brass knocker to summon someone. He wondered if Mr. Ross, the family butler, would answer, or if he would be greeted as a stranger in his father's home.

It was not Mr. Ross, but Ivan who answered the summons to the door. He swung it open and stood for a moment, clearly stunned by Nichol's presence. But perhaps not as stunned as Nichol was by his brother's appearance. He was two years younger than Nichol, having not quite reached his thirtieth year, and yet, he looked ten years older. Haggard. Worn down.

He was a wee bit taller than Nichol, and wore shirtsleeves and a waistcoat, as if he'd been hard at work on something. His peruke looked like the sort made from horsehair, and did not look as if it had been washed. He was thin, his shoulders stooped.

Frankly, he looked as if he'd been through hell.

"Nichol," Ivan said, his voice full of disbelief. He frowned darkly. "I didna believe it, but here you are, at our door, just as the lad said you'd be."

Nichol didn't know what, exactly, he'd expected, but he was not prepared for his brother's coldness. "I had no' planned it," he said. "I would no' have come had it no' been necessary."

"Necessary," Ivan repeated as he looked him over. "You're a right proper gent, Nichol, are you?" he said, but his tone was not complimentary. He gave a self-conscious tug on his waistcoat. "I thought—"

"Ivan?"

The woman's voice drifted up over Ivan's head, and he whirled about. "Finella," he said, and then to Nichol, "You've been gone so long that you've no' had the pleasure of making the acquaintance of my wife, then. I'm a married man now, aye? Mrs. Ivan MacBain," he said with a flourish of his hand. "You may call her Finella."

Nichol tore his gaze from his brother to the woman who stood beside him. She was a slight thing, with an upturned nose, and was holding a bairn in her arms. She had kind eyes, he thought. "Oh, but you must call me Finella!" she agreed cheerfully. "How do you do, Mr. MacBain?" she asked, dipping a curtsy as best she could. "You're an uncle, too, you are," she said, holding up the bairn.

Nichol glanced at the bairn. He or she screwed up its face and cried. It looked no more than two or three months old. "A lad, then?" he asked.

Finella laughed. "A girl! Britta is her name. Would you like to hold her, then?"

"No' now," Ivan growled.

"You look verra well, Mr. MacBain," Finella said happily, beaming at him. "I've long wondered after you, that I have," she said.

"Stop talking, Nella," Ivan snapped.

Nichol felt uncomfortable. Embarrassed. His brother's demeanor was hostile toward him. There was no affection left in him. That was Nichol's fault—he'd been gone so long that his brother had lost faith in him.

Two small children appeared, peeking out from behind their mother's skirts. Nichol was surprised and unnerved by them. It was as if a whole other life had played out here, one he had been removed from as a child, and one he removed himself from as an adult. "You've more children," he said dumbly.

"Aye, Geordie and Alice," Finella said. "We've been blessed these last five years, indeed we have," Finella said. "Is that your wife, then?"

Nichol suddenly remembered Miss Darby and jerked around. "*Diah,* forgive me," he said. He'd been so taken aback by his brother's appearance and demeanor, and his brood, for Chrissakes, that he'd forgotten her. "Miss Maura Darby," he said, stepping aside and putting his hand on her elbow to guide her up to the top step.

"No' your wife?" Finella sounded disappointed as she smiled at Miss Darby.

"Ah no… I am escorting Miss Darby to Luncarty."

"Luncarty!" Ivan said. "Whatever is in Luncarty?"

"My future husband," Miss Darby said, and curtsied. "It is my great pleasure to make your acquaintance."

"Miss Darby, may I present my brother, Mr. Ivan MacBain," Nichol said. "And his wife, Mrs. Finella MacBain."

"MacBain," she murmured and looked questioningly at Nichol.

"How do you do, Miss Darby?" Finella said cheerfully. "Look at us, Ivan, we've left them standing at the entry. Come in from the cold, now," she said, stepping back to make way, and tripping over the small children behind her. She clucked her tongue at the two. "You're to be in your rooms, are you no'? Go on then, go back to bed!" she said, and gestured toward the stairs, shooing them away like little chicks.

The children scampered off, pausing on the bottom step to have one last look.

Their mother hardly noticed. She'd turned back to Nichol and Miss Darby. "You must call me by my given name, Miss Darby. It's Finella. Ivan calls me Nella. Come into the parlor—we've a good fire to warm you."

Ivan stepped back, and Miss Darby followed Finella into the parlor. Ivan went, too, and Nichol was the last to enter, bracing himself, expecting to see his father's imposing figure there.

But there was no one else in the room. It was the same grand receiving room he recalled—at the center, two upholstered chairs facing a settee, a scattering of other chairs were set against the walls. Paintings of notable ancestors, of hunting scenes and landscapes, filled the walls. His father's books—his love of reading was the only thing he'd ever given Nichol—were stacked on a table beside the settee. Nichol picked one up off the top. *Treatise of Human Nature* by David Hume had fascinated him in that space he'd been home after his apprenticeship.

Miss Darby glanced at it, then looked at him questioningly. "I read it as a young man," he said quietly. "It made quite an impression." Nichol put the book down. Miss Darby ran her fingers over the spine of the book, curious.

"Shall I ring for tea?" Finella asked.

"'Tis no' a social call, Finella," Ivan said irritably.

Nichol glanced at his sister-in-law. "Have you any whisky, madam? As I recall, Ivan likes a tot now and again."

"Oh, that he does," she said cheerfully, and juggling the bairn, went to the sideboard to pour.

Miss Darby slowly followed as she took in the room. Nichol supposed she found it quite opulent compared to the Garbett house. Chandeliers hung from gold leaf medallions, the carpets were Belgian, imported at a dear cost. Nichol's father placed much emphasis on appearances. He was a baron; he was determined to be viewed as the most prestigious baron in Scotland.

A feeling of agitation began to build in Nichol as he stood in that room. He felt like he had many times as a child—anticipating his father's wrath for one unexpected thing or another, a blast of ire to catch him off guard. He wouldn't have been surprised to see his father suddenly leap from behind a velvet drape, or burst through the hidden servant's entrance into the room.

He watched Ivan clear the settee of children's toys and his wife's needlework. "How do you fare, Ivan?"

Ivan gave him a dark look. "Well enough," he said curtly.

Nichol couldn't see the boy he'd known in this man. Ivan seemed hollowed out to him, his spirit missing. "Where is our father, then?"

Ivan's expression seemed to gray a bit. "In his bed," he said.

"Is he ill?" Nichol asked, confused. His father would be an old man now—perhaps he took to his bed early in the evening.

"Ill?" Ivan looked at him, confused. "Is it no' why you've come, then?"

"Pardon?"

"You said you came because it was necessary, aye? Because he is dying."

"Dying," Nichol repeated, slowly taking the news in. He shook his head. "I didna know."

"Did you no'," Ivan said skeptically. "Consumption. He's no' long for this world."

"Miss Darby, whisky for you, then?" Ivan's wife offered.

"No, thank you," Miss Darby said.

"How long has he been ill?" Nichol asked quietly.

"A year or more," Ivan muttered. "If you didna

come to have a last go at him, then what has brought you?"

A last go? "To fetch the lad," he said. "I had a bit of a problem and no place for him to go. And to see you. Why did you no' write to tell me, then?" he asked. Through the years, Nichol sent word to Ivan as to his whereabouts.

Ivan snorted. "And send it where, then, brother? To whose attention? The last I heard from you was before my second child was born," he said bitterly.

Nichol clenched his jaw. Had so much time passed? "Aye," he said. "I should have written."

"Why would you? You donna care for anything but…" Ivan bit off what he would say.

"But what?" Nichol tried.

"I assumed you'd heard from someone else he was dying," Ivan said.

Nichol glanced at the two women. Finella was talking rather rapidly, and in a low voice, as if imparting some secret. Miss Darby was leaning slightly back, as if the force of Finella's words were pushing her.

"Nella, the whisky, then," Ivan said sharply.

"Oh aye," she said, as if she'd forgotten her task. She suddenly pushed her bairn into Miss Darby's arms, who gave a tiny mewl of surprise and stared down at the bundle. The bairn began to wail as Finella hurried across the room with two tots of whisky.

"Thank you," Ivan said, taking the tots from his wife.

The bairn wailed louder. Nichol wondered how his

father endured the wailing of Ivan's children. He'd certainly not been able to abide the slightest sound of despair when he and Ivan had been children. *Another tear and I'll beat you till you bleed, aye?*

"Where is that butler?" Ivan asked, and tossed back the whisky before marching to the bellpull.

"What happened to Ross?" Nichol asked.

"A long time dead," Ivan said curtly.

The door opened, and a very thin young man slipped into the room.

"There you are, Erskine. Tell cook we'll have two more for supper, aye?"

The young man glanced impassively at the new guests.

"Go on, then," Ivan snapped.

Erskine, or whoever he was, bowed his head and went out.

"We canna find proper help here," Ivan said bitterly. "Everyone fears the consumption. Erskine is no' a butler, but he is the best we can manage at present."

There was suddenly some commotion at the door, a lot of banging and things being moved about. Through the open door, they could see a man with a worn, dirty coat depositing the small bag Miss Darby had carried from Garbett House, as well as the two bags Gavin had carried to Cheverock.

"Donna leave them there, man," Ivan said irritably. "Put them at the top of the stairs, aye?"

The man muttered beneath his breath, then gathered the bags and began to shuffle across the foyer under their weight. The bairn's cries turned torturous. It was always like this at Cheverock—such anxiety amid such trappings of wealth. Nichol had been absent from it for so long that he found it jarring.

"Finella!" Ivan shouted.

"Oh, but she's a wee bit colicky, that's all," she said, and took the bairn back into her arms.

"Take her out!" Ivan said. "Nella, *leannan*," he said pleadingly now. "Take her out, I beg of you. I would speak with my brother now, but I canna think with all the wailing. Show Miss Darby to a guest room, aye?"

"Oh aye, she'll want to refreshen before we dine, will you no', Miss Darby? 'Tis time to feed this one, too. She's quite an eater, she is. I donna have a wet nurse, of course, no' here. They dare no' risk the consumption."

"Oh," Maura said. She looked stricken.

"But you need no' fear it, lass," Finella said. "Lord MacBain rarely comes down now. He's bedridden, he is. Come with me."

Miss Darby glanced at Nichol, and he gave her a slight nod. He needed to speak to Ivan. He needed to see his father.

When they'd gone, Ivan helped himself to more whisky. An awkward silence enveloped the room. "'Tis good to see you, Ivan," Nichol said.

"Is it?" Ivan said, glancing at him from the corner of his eye.

"Aye, of course. I've missed—"

"I donna know if Father will see you," Ivan said suddenly.

Nichol shrugged. The man in him was long past the point of caring, really, but a small part of him, yet a lad, wondered why a father would not want to see his estranged son on his deathbed. What could that son, who had never said an ill word, had never done anything but try and be the son his father wanted, what could he have done to be shunned even now?

Ivan suddenly rubbed his face with his hands. "It has been a trial, Nichol, a right trial, aye?"

"Tell me," Nichol suggested. "Start from the beginning." He wanted to know all there was to know if this would be the last time he faced his father.

Ivan sighed to the ceiling and said, "You'll want to wash before supper, will you no'?" He walked to the door and shouted, *"Erskine!"*

Nichol didn't know what had happened, but it was clear that his brother had come to hate him.

CHAPTER FIFTEEN

FINELLA CONTINUED TO chatter as if they were old friends as she and Maura climbed the stairs to a musty guest room. The furniture was covered in drop cloths, the hearth was cold. Finella opened the window to air the room, but it had begun to snow, and a cold wind slipped in on small gusts.

Maura didn't know what to think of this place. It was quite grand, as Mr. Bain—Mr. *MacBain*?—had said, but it felt empty. Bereft of any warmth. Even though people were living here, obviously, it felt as if no one really lived here.

Finella—or Nella, as she insisted Maura call her: "And what shall I call you, then, Miss Darby?"—sat on the bed, then hoisted a heavy breast from her décolletage and began to nurse her baby. "You donna mind, aye?"

Maura didn't mind. But she didn't know where to look, either, and decided a dedicated study of the bare mantle was her best option.

"My husband will be *full* of good cheer now that his brother has come, he will. I'm certain he's missed him terribly, although he scarcely mentions him, but he is his brother after all," she said. "When the lad came to our door with the ring, my husband wanted to know everything, and was verra distrustful of him, he was, but the lad, he'd only say that Nichol MacBain would arrive as soon as he was able."

"The ring?" Maura asked.

"Aye, a ring, a signet ring, that belonged to their grandfather. I canna know the significance of it, of course, for there is much that exists between two brothers that is no' to be understood by others, would you no' agree?"

"I donna—"

"We've no' had guests in an *age*," she said, lifting her bairn to lay across her shoulder. "Mrs. Garbunkle is to blame for it, if you ask me. She's said to all the village, even the old man who keeps a chicken in his cottage that he thinks is a cat, that the baron's consumption is contagious from even a distance of across the room. It is clearly no', aye? For we are all quite well. I'd no' have my children here if I feared it."

"Pardon?" Maura asked the mantle. She was having trouble keeping up with the exuberant Finella.

"Aye, my husband's father. He's a baron, did you no' know it? Baron MacBain, he is."

MacBain! Why had Mr. Bain changed his name? "How awful that he suffers from consumption," Maura said as she went to the window and closed it before they all turned to ice. She gingerly removed a drop cloth from a chair and sat, wondering if Mr. Bain had been aware that his father was ill before today. "Where is he, then, the baron?"

"Upstairs, in the master suite," Finella said, and fit the bairn on her breast once more. "Aye, he's quite ill. 'Tis but God's grace he's been with us as long as he has."

He was *that* ill, then.

"I've no' seen him in weeks! My husband willna allow it, for fear of contagion." She glanced at the open door, then at Maura. "But I'm no' sorry for it," she whispered. "He's a sour man, he is."

Maura was surprised the woman would be so un-guarded in her remarks with someone she'd only just met. Finella didn't seem to notice her surprise at all—she was cooing to her bairn.

"I donna know what will happen once he's gone," she said. "His heir is Mr. Nichol MacBain, of course, as he is the oldest male child. But my husband says we are no' to think of it, that God will guide his father's hand. I said, 'Our Lord has guided his hand all along, has he no', and the man is as tight as a drum!' My husband didna like that I said it, but I donna care. It's quite true."

Maura squirmed. She had no desire to hear Finella speak of Mr. Bain's father in this way.

"He doesna care, you know," Finella said.

"Pardon?"

"Finella! Finella, where are you, then?" her husband bellowed from somewhere below them.

"Oh!" Finella hopped up, lay her baby on the bed and fit her breast into her bodice. "I'll have Erskine bring a brazier, aye?"

A brazier! She'd freeze—the chill would not be chased from this room without a fire in the hearth.

"We sup at eight," Finella added, picked up her infant, and hurried out as the bairn began to cry again.

He doesn't care about what?

What was the matter here? Why were their names different, why did this house feel so cold in every possible way?

Unfortunately, Maura was not enlightened in the course of supper. She arrived at the appointed time wrapped in Mr. Bain's plaid. She was terribly cold, could not understand why the house was not properly heated. Were they poor, then? Did the baron not care for heat, either?

Mr. and Mrs. Ivan MacBain had dressed in their finest for the occasion, whereas Maura and Mr. Bain were still wearing the clothes they'd traveled in.

Mrs. MacBain was quite garrulous, and her husband brooding, which, Maura suspected, had to do with the amount of wine they consumed. Both of them seemed anxious, as if expecting something to happen. What could possibly happen? Finella continued to talk over everyone in her haste to tell Mr. Bain all they knew about Cheverock and the people around it.

Mr. Ross, whom Maura understood to be the former butler, had suffered from a failed heart in the middle of the night, and he'd gone peacefully. Unlike the milk lass, who went missing one December morning and was found some weeks later, frozen and still clutching her pail at the bottom of a ravine.

Mrs. Schill had taken great exception to Mr. Schill's adulterous affair, and had followed him to Falkirk to catch him in flagrante delicto. Mr. Schill's response to that had been to banish Mrs. Schill to some remote estate in the Highlands, where he claimed she would live the rest of her days, for he would not be questioned by a woman.

For some reason, Mr. MacBain found this tale to be quite amusing, and laughed as if it were some sort of staged comedy. Maura was infuriated by it. What could anyone find amusing about a woman who could not demand justice of a philandering husband, and was somehow made to be the villain? She was rather offended by the news of another woman who bore the blame of a man's doing, just as she had.

She wondered what Mr. Bain thought of it. That was impossible to know—he remained subdued throughout the course of the meal, listening intently, speaking only when addressed. Last evening at the Garbett house, she could feel his ennui. His silence had felt like impatience, which had been made evident to her by the way he drummed his fingers on the table, then had looked about as if seeking anything to divert him from the inane chatter of the Garbetts' supper table.

But tonight he seemed doleful. He listened to Finella's chatter and his brother's occasional concurrence. More than once he caught Maura's eye across the table, his gaze lingering on her a little longer than was necessary.

What was he thinking? Was she wrong that she

could sense something like anguish? But it was in the set of his mouth, the look in his eyes. He despaired. She knew it because she'd felt the darkness of it so recently herself. Last night, at the Garbetts', she'd felt entirely disillusioned by the people who had promised her father to care for her, and strangely heartbroken.

Mr. Bain had not been betrayed, not like her—at least she didn't think he had—but something dark had happened here, something from which none of them could return. She didn't know how she knew it, but Mr. MacBain was far too quiet, and Mrs. MacBain was falling deeper into her cups, as if trying to drown out the tension. And Mr. Bain only grew more sullen as the meal went on.

Maura felt a great deal of sympathy for him. Every time he caught her eye, she smiled as reassuringly as she could. She wished she could convey that she stood with him, that she understood his disappointment, even if she didn't understand the reason.

But she was also fairly certain that Mr. Bain didn't see her there. He didn't see her at all, really. Each time he looked at her, she felt his gaze go clean through her, to some point that only he could see.

She would be very glad when he came back from wherever that was.

CHAPTER SIXTEEN

AFTER SUPPER, WHEN the ladies had retired to the sitting room so that Ivan could smoke a cheroot, Ivan told Nichol that his father knew he had come. "He predicted it, aye? Said you'd come back before his demise."

"I didna know he was ill, Ivan. How could I?" Nichol said.

Ivan gave him a look very close to a sneer.

"Did he say any more than that?" Nichol asked curiously. He thought perhaps old age and illness had mellowed his father.

Ivan snubbed out his cheroot. "I'll no' repeat it," he said. "But he'll see you."

For a single moment, Nichol thought to tell Ivan that he had no desire to see the old man. But that wasn't true—he did want to see him. It was the last time he would see him, and some morbid curiosity had arisen in him. Could a man so near death still harbor such intensely unpleasant feelings?

"Verra well," Nichol said, and stood from the table.

So did Ivan. He walked to the door and opened it, cocking his head toward the main hall. "You'll be shocked how he looks, aye?" he said as they trudged up the stairs.

"I donna care how he looks," Nichol said, and he didn't. It wasn't as if he had any lingering hope for the old man. That had died years ago, along with his ability to believe that anyone would want him. He wasn't certain what he wanted to accomplish with this final meeting. He could have come to Cheverock and left without every laying eyes on the baron, and perhaps he would regret this after all. But something compelled him. Words were on the tip of his tongue, just beyond his reach, but wanting to be said.

They reached the door of the master suite, and Ivan glanced at Nichol. "I warned you, aye?" He opened the door and stepped back, letting Nichol go in alone.

There was nothing Ivan might have said that could have prepared Nichol for the sight of the ancient old man lying in that massive bed. He was perhaps fifty-five years, perhaps as much as sixty. But he looked much older from a distance.

As he stepped into the room, Nichol first noticed the scent of decay, of unwashed flesh. His father looked like he was part of the pile of bed linens, a shadow of a man, a mere skeleton of the man he'd once been. The baron had always loomed so large in Nichol's thoughts that it made him founder for a moment, unable to reconcile how this body could be the same robust, virile father he remembered. His skin was sallow, his lips gray and cracked. What remained of his thinning gray hair had bristled and spikes of it stood up from the top of his head.

But it was the same spiteful man—his eyes gave him away, as sharp and filled with disgust as they'd ever been.

He watched Nichol walk across the room to his bedside without any hint of emotion or thought. Nichol paused a foot or so away from the bed, unwilling to come any closer. He didn't want to touch him, didn't want to breathe the same foul air. So he stood back, observing the shell of the man who had once oppressed him so miserably.

"Ah, so you came to pick over my bloody remains like a vulture, then, did you?" his father asked hoarsely.

"I hadna planned to come at all."

"Then why did you?" his father snapped, the force of which prompted a spasm of wet coughing so hard and deep that Nichol cringed.

"To see Ivan," Nichol said evenly. "I hold no ill will for my brother."

"Only for me, is it?" his father asked, and with fingers turned crooked with rheumatism, he groped for the coverlet to pull over his chest.

"I hold no ill will for you, either, sir, and I never have. It's always been your ill will for me, has it no'?"

"*Mi Diah,* I hope you've no' come to cry at my deathbed about your ill treatment at my hand. If you expect an apology, you'll get none."

Nichol snorted. "What good would an apology

do now? I didna come for that, sir—you taught me well and early that I could expect nothing from you."

"You've found a wee bit of your backbone, then," his father said, and followed that with a spasm of coughing into a handkerchief that had turned rust brown from the blood he'd coughed up. "Aye, well, now you've seen me, and you've said what you would. Go and leave me be. Donna waste my time, for I have precious little of it. Donna think you'll have anything of this house or this estate, aye? I've left it all to Ivan."

This time Nichol chuckled. He had not once thought about what he might stand to inherit. He couldn't care less. What he thought about, what he still burned to know was why? Why, after so many years of being reviled by him, of having learned to accept it without understanding, should the remarks from a miserable old man's deathbed wound him so? And the window to understanding was closing.

Nichol stepped forward to his father's bed. "I donna give a damn about your house or your holdings, old man. I've made my own way, aye? In spite of you, I've done quite well for myself, and I donna need anything of yours."

"Good," the baron said weakly.

"But what I will have from you is why," Nichol said flatly, and leaned over, looming over his father's bed. "What could a lad, scarcely in trousers, have done to earn such vitriol and hatred from you, then? What could a lad have done that would cause his own father to turn his back on his flesh and blood?"

"I'm no father of yours!" his father said before coughing up more blood. "I should think that would be understood by now, you bloody dolt."

Nichol didn't understand him. "You are no father of mine, aye, but you gave me life—"

"I gave you *nothing*!" his father said with surprising force, and began to cough again. "I had naught to do with you!"

Nichol blinked as a thought that made little sense to him flitted through his head. How many times had his father referred to Ivan as his son, but never him? "What are you saying, exactly?"

"*Och,* are you so bloody thick? 'Tis that common blood that runs through your veins, that's what."

"What are you saying!" Nichol demanded loudly, and grabbed the coverlet his father held. "I will have the truth, spoken plainly."

"Your mother was a *whore*," his father spat. "The only thing she ever did for me was give me Ivan, aye? But *you*? *You* are the spawn of some common blackguard. You are no more my son than a bairn birthed in England!"

Nichol gaped at him. This possibility had never occurred to him. Not once in all the hours he'd spent agonizing over his father's hatred had Nichol thought that perhaps his mother might have had an illicit affair. It astounded him that it hadn't, particularly in the years he'd spent in his occupation, dealing with issues such as this.

His father chuckled unpleasantly, then coughed again, his whole body racked with the painful force.

"What a bloody fool you are," he said, his voice rough from the coughing. "Did you never wonder why I hated your whore of a mother?"

His mother had died shortly after Ivan was born. He couldn't possibly recall his father's treatment of her. "I never wondered because it is your nature to hate," Nichol said quietly. "Why did you never tell me, then? I should think it would have given you immense pleasure to tell me I am a bastard born, aye?"

"And have the shadow of scandal taint my son?" the baron snapped. "Have the stain of *you* his burden to bear all his life? *Och,* you're a bigger fool than I believed."

"If you meant that no one would know for the sake of Ivan, then why did you no' accept me as your own? I was a *bairn*, for God's sake."

"You were a *bastard*," he said roughly, and closed his eyes. "Every day I had to look at you was a day I was reminded of what she'd done to dishonor me."

Nichol let go of the coverlet and straightened.

He felt both agitation and relief. Relief that somehow, his life suddenly made sense to him, even if the truth was bitter. Agitation that he'd never known, had never guessed it.

He turned away from the bed, his thoughts spinning, his desire to be anywhere but near this man.

"That's it?" his father—rather, the baron—said to his back. "You've nothing more to say, then?"

Nichol clenched his jaw. He turned back to the bed and considered the old man lying there. *I am not him. I am nothing of him.* He could rejoice in that, at least. And because he was not him, he would not put himself on the same despicable level, either.

"I was a lad," he said calmly. "I was no' to blame for how I came into this world, aye? But you will have to answer to your Maker for how you treated me. I wish you well in that."

A sneer curled the gray cracked lips. "Do you think you can frighten me? I've a lot to answer for, that I do, but I donna have to answer for you," he said. "Your whore mother was held to account for that." He turned his head.

Even in death, the man would treat him ill. Nichol turned and walked out of the room, relieved that he would never have to lay eyes on him or hear his name uttered again.

But as he walked down that hallway, expecting Ivan to be waiting, but finding himself utterly alone, an old but familiar ache began to spread in his chest. For what might have been. For his mother, a woman he remembered only in snatches of images. For all those nights as a lad he'd cried himself to sleep, not understanding and feeling as if something was terribly wrong with him. Something heinous that he could not see. For the doubts he'd suffered as a young man, certain that something must be terrible about him. Unlovable. It had kept him from true intimacy, certain that anyone who got close to him would see the heinous thing that was so apparent to his father, but that he himself could not see. Where might he have been today with a loving father? Married? Children of his own? True friends? A brother who revered him yet, instead of looking at him with such rancor as Ivan did now?

Nichol took the stairs to the first floor, his thoughts tossing and twisting inside his head like so many snakes. He remembered how frightened he'd been when he'd been sent off to the Duke of Hamilton. He remembered coming home from that apprenticeship, certain that whatever had been wrong with him had been corrected. But he'd been treated with cold indifference by everyone but Ivan, who, even at that young age, already lived on the edge of his frayed nerves. The baron may have considered Ivan his son and one true heir, but he treated him scarcely better than Nichol. He'd set impossible standards for Ivan to reach, and when he failed, his father berated him.

It had aged Ivan. He was a prisoner here, unable to leave his ailing father, unable to find his own place in this world. Tethered to a bitter old man's side. Bitter himself now, it seemed.

And yet, through all the heartache Nichol had suffered in silence, Nichol had never lost hope that his father might one day have a change of heart. To think he might have set Nichol free years ago, might have spared him the burden, infuriated him.

It broke him, too.

He turned into the hall on the first floor and strode along, bound for his room. At the end of the hall a door was opened, and inside, the glow of a brazier. He thought it was Ivan, waiting up to hear how the meeting with the baron had gone. But then

Miss Darby stepped into the open door, her hand on the jamb. She looked at him expectantly. Anxiously.

Nichol paused. Had there ever been a bonnier or more welcome sight in a drab day gown? His bitter disappointment, his feeling of emptiness, slowly began to dissipate, and the memory of this day, of a beautiful woman lying lazily on his plaid beneath a winter sky, filled his thoughts. This woman was an unexpected port in the private storm that raged in him. There was no one else who might possibly understand his grief, no one else who could fathom what it was to be cast out without regard. No man, no woman, who had ever looked at him the same way she looked at him.

Nichol was suddenly moving again, his stride long, his need to feel her arms around him so great that he shivered with the force of it.

Miss Darby kept her place in the door's frame. She nervously dragged her fingers through her unbound hair as he neared her. "Is everything all right, then?"

No, everything was not all right. Nichol walked to the open door and hesitated. He took her in, from her winter-blue eyes, to the necklace of diamonds and emerald that glittered at her neck, to the fit of the worn gown, and the tips of her shoes, stained with the dust of the road. He watched her nervously suck her lower lip in between her teeth. She was uneasy. She didn't know what he wanted of her.

He didn't know what he wanted of her, either. He only knew that he wanted to be with her. It was imperative, as if she was the only thing standing between him and breaking into bits and pieces of angry flesh. He took a single step forward and put a hand on her waist.

She did not resist him. She kept her gaze locked on his as he tentatively pulled her closer, his hand sliding around to the small of her back. He cupped her face with his other hand. "Miss Darby."

"Maura," she said. "What has happened to you, Mr. Bain?"

He couldn't help his lopsided smile at the absurdity of the question. "What has no' happened to me, then?" He lowered his head and kissed her, quite tentatively, because he didn't know what he was doing or what he intended. *Everything was wrong.* This house. The baron. Kissing her. The fact that she was off to marry Dunnan Cockburn. Everything was wrong but the desire he felt for her with a fierceness that was unconscionable.

The fierceness bled into his kiss. The touch of her tongue glittered in every one of his nerves. Miss Darby—*Maura*—stood uncertainly at first, her arms hanging by her side, as if she didn't know what to do with them. Maybe she didn't know how to resist him. Maybe she didn't want this at all. But when he slipped his tongue into her mouth, she made a soft sound that sounded like *aha*, as if she'd been waiting for exactly this. She slid her arms up his chest and around his neck and somehow leapt onto him, hooking one leg around his back as he caught her. She took his face in both her hands and kissed him back with gusto.

Nichol was both surprised and emboldened. He kicked the door shut, then twirled around, putting her back to the door. "What are we doing?" he growled as he nuzzled her neck.

"This," Maura whispered, her eyes closed as she bent her neck to give him better access.

"We are fools, then, both of us," he said, and slid his hand to her breast, squeezing it. "This canna happen—"

Maura stopped him from finishing his thought— she caught his head again and kissed him fully, until white-hot heat was blooming in every muscle. Nichol was breathless with longing, and he knew that if he allowed this to continue, if he didn't drop his hands from her now, he would be hard pressed to turn back. *"Maura,"* he whispered against her cheek. "I am mad with desire, that I am, but I canna do this to you. There are consequences—"

"Diah, say no' another word, Mr. Bain!" she said, and caressed his face. "If I were a debutante and you a suitor, aye, there would be consequences. But we are no' those people. We are different than everyone else." She lifted her face, her lips just a moment from his. "We have our own rules."

"No," he said, and felt a crack open somewhere inside him. The truth of him, the baseness of him. "I have nothing, Maura," he said, surprised that he'd uttered the words aloud, that the truth would come tumbling out. "I have no home, no family." He gave a sudden laugh of bitterness and dropped his hands. "I donna even have a name."

"Of course you have a name—"

"I changed my name long ago so as never to be associated with the man who has caused me nothing but misery all my life."

"Your father."

Nichol laughed bitterly. "So I believed all these years, but no, he is no' my father. On his bloody *deathbed*," he said, gesturing wildly to the floor above, "the old man has at long last told me why he sent me away, why he could never abide the sight of me, aye? Because I am *no'* his son. I am a bastard born. My father is unknown, my mother unfaithful— and it appears that he has hated me for her sin all my life, has taken out his anger on me."

"*Diah,* Mr. Bain," she whispered. She reached for him, but he shook his head.

"I esteem you, Maura, *Diah* help me, I do. But I can offer you *nothing*. Do you hear me? I am *nothing*."

He meant to turn away from her, but Maura caught his arm. "I didna ask you to offer me a bloody thing, did I? I just want… *You* want…" Her voice trailed away and she looked wildly about the room, as if trying to find the right words to describe their mutual yearning.

"Aye, we both want," he agreed. "More than words can adequately describe."

"Aye," she whispered.

He tenderly stroked her face. "I will take you to Luncarty on the morrow—you know that, do you? I've no choice."

Her breath lifted her chest with each inhale. "I know, Mr. Bain. But I also know that no' everything is lost, for you *or* me. We still have a choice. Here and now, we have a choice." She tentatively moved closer.

"What you suggest is unconscionable, Maura. I canna deliver you to Luncarty a ruined woman."

She gave a short bark of bitter laughter. "The ruin already has been done. But this night, this *one* night, we who have nothing have each other, aye?" she asked, wrapping his hand in both of hers. "Night will most assuredly turn to day, and our lives will move on as they are meant, and this will be naught but a memory, but tonight, we have each other, Mr. Bain."

For a man who had honed his skill at being unaffected, for keeping himself at a distance from others, he was strongly affected by her words. They reverberated in him, constricted around his heart, breathed life into that old thing. He realized, as she clearly had, that they were two lost souls in this world, clinging to each other for one night before their lives whisked them away to solitary paths unknown. "*Diah,* Maura," he said low, and laced his fingers with hers, pulling her closer. "My name is Nichol. Nichol Bain." He clasped her head in his hands and kissed her with sudden and dogged determination to have this one night.

The kiss felt different than any kiss he'd ever experienced. It was full of intense desire, of lust. But it was also full of extraordinary yearning for the affection he'd never had. The desire for that was so powerful that he had to check himself, slow down, gentle his touch. He was tumbling off a cliff, and flailing along into the rough business of wooing.

He was astounded by his intense emotions and didn't know how to interlace them with the pure lust surging through his blood. His heart beat like a drum; he grabbed Maura's hands, lifted them over her head, and pinned them against the wall. He greedily moved over her, his mouth against her skin, acquainting himself with her body.

Her breathing raced along as he moved over her. She remained pressed against the wall, her eyes closed, her mouth parted slightly with the force of her breath, her skin rosy from her desire. It astonished him how starkly this woman could arouse him. He felt impossibly virile, his heart pumping with lust enough to fill a loch, his blood burning with ultimate desire.

She pulled her hands free of his grip overhead and ran her hands down his arms, and then into his coat, pushing it from his shoulders. He helped her, shrugging out of it as he dipped to press his mouth to her throat. Then lower, lightly nibbling the swell of her breast above the bodice of her gown.

Maura gasped softly, her breath hot on his skin as she began to work on the buttons of his waistcoat. Nichol's body was hard with want, and he pressed against her pelvis.

She looked into his eyes when she reached the last button of his waistcoat and pushed it from his body. He saw no trepidation there, nothing but want, and he was happy to oblige. He grabbed a handful of her gown and began to pull it up, gathering more and more of it as he hiked it higher, until he could slip his hand between her legs.

Maura's lips parted with the sharp intake of her breath. She was slick, and he was lost. He buried his face in her neck as he slipped his fingers into her body. He was beyond himself, in a space that was an explosion of soft light and primal scents. He cupped her face and kissed her gently in what felt like a futile effort to pace himself, to go gently.

Maura mewled with pleasure so softly in the back of her throat that Nichol all but disintegrated. He had surrendered to his blood, had lost all perspective, and reached for her waist, unbuttoned the robe of her gown from the petticoat beneath. Maura shimmied out of it, letting it pool at her feet, then removed her stomacher as Nichol, his eyes locked on hers, removed his shirt. Her eyes widened at the sight of his bare chest, her lips parted, and she reverently ran her hands from his abdomen to his collarbone.

He pulled the tie of her chemise and it fell open, revealing her breasts. He took them both in hand, kneading them. His need was desperate, and he slipped his arm around her waist, lifting her off her feet, turning around to the bed behind them and setting her down again. His unspoken question rose up between them: *Are you certain? Is this what you want?*

Maura sat on the bed. She took his hand, kissed his palm, his knuckles. It was the answer Nichol needed. He moved over her, pressing her back onto the bed.

Whatever doubts played at the corner of his mind were being strangled by his own desire and her ardent response to him. He felt like an unearthly king, invincible, as if he alone could summon the tide or slide the moon across the sky.

Her hands were on his body now, inflaming his heart—it beat hard without restraint. He had never met a woman who aroused such improbable passion in him. He pulled her petticoat from her, then the chemise. She wore nothing but the necklace, a symbol of their extraordinary journey together.

His expedition of her body was slow. His hands searched, his mouth explored. He touched her everywhere, aroused by the little moans she made, the grip of her fingers in his skin. She explored him, too, her hands running over the planes of his back and hips, her mouth on his neck and his chest, until Nichol had disappeared entirely into sensation.

She was panting, groaning, her body pressing against his, silently demanding more. They were moving together, these two who had nothing, both of them lost in this night and in this moment. He pressed the tip of himself against her soft, wet entrance, and released a silent cry into her hair. They were desperate for each other, desperate for release. He lifted his head and looked down at her. "Now?" he asked, uncertain what he meant by it.

But Maura answered him with a single caress of his brow and a nip of his bottom lip. She opened her legs, wrapping one around his back, and then locked her gaze on his as he slowly slid into her, fraction by fraction, allowing her body to open to him. Only when he pressed against her maidenhead did she close her eyes and swallow.

Nichol stopped moving. He gritted his teeth to hold himself back, but it was no use. Her body was a siren call, and he pushed past her maidenhead with a groan of relief.

Maura's breath caught, but after a moment, she began to breathe again, and she began to move against him, wanting what her body knew it wanted. Something in Nichol's chest fluttered. His heart was a slow boil, and he moved slowly, carefully, his strokes matching his caress of her face, his desire pressing hard and long into her, the anticipation unfurling. He wanted to prolong it, to stay here, with her, in this moment. He tangled his fingers in her hair; she scraped her fingers down his back, as if trying to hold on. He slid deeper and deeper into a fog, and she slipped with him, moved with him.

Nichol reached his hand between them and began to stroke her in time to his body sliding inside her. Maura groaned and arched into him, dug her fingers into his shoulder as if she feared she might fly away. He kept up his ministrations until she gasped with the release of her body.

He thrust hard one last time, then quickly pulled away, spilling onto her thigh.

For several moments afterward, neither of them moved as they struggled to catch their breath.

Nichol finally shifted his weight from her, falling onto his chest beside her. He felt a profound sense of esteem for Maura Darby. A press of affection.

Affection.

There it was again, that thing that had eluded him all his life. But he felt it thrumming through him. Her affection for him. His for her.

Everything was not lost.

Maura sat up and leaned over him. She kissed the back of his neck. "What do we do now, then?"

"Now?" he asked, and rolled onto his back. He pushed her hair behind her ear, let his fingers trail down her body and breast. "What do you mean, *mon trésor?*"

She smiled brightly at his endearment. "Do we couple again, *mon Roméo?*"

He laughed. He gathered her in his arms against his chest. "Aye, again. But first, we rest," he said, and kissed the top of her head.

We have tonight. The night will turn to day and we'll have only the memory, but we have tonight.

CHAPTER SEVENTEEN

NOT A MONTH AGO, Maura would not have considered giving herself to a man who was not her husband. She had believed in chastity, had believed in the sanctity of marriage. But then her world had been made a shambles, and everything she believed felt no longer true. She was glad she'd done what she had. It was a night she would never forget, an experience that would be branded into her heart for the rest of her life.

She was remarkably sanguine about her sin, to her great surprise. She would rather give herself to a man she cared about and desired than a faceless man who needed to marry her because he couldn't make his own match. She had no idea what to expect at Luncarty, but she knew very well what she had in Nichol Bain.

She believed he cared about her—he'd certainly been very tender with her through the night, and the light that had shone in his eyes was real. She believed he was the first person to *truly* care about her since her father had died. She could see that now, could see that Mr. Garbett cared more for himself, and Mrs. Garbett and Sorcha never had, not really. But Mr. Bain…

Ah, Nichol.

She was swimming in a profoundly bottomless well of emotion. She felt things that were extraordinary, new and fresh and eye-opening. Never in her life had she felt such ease in the company of another person. Confident and desired, sheltered and warm. Perfectly compatible in every way. It was perfection.

Was she wrong about this? Had that exquisite feeling, that lightness of being and deep regard for him been anything less than perfect?

She had admired his physique as he lay next to her. He looked almost sculpted to her, like the drawings of the Greek statutes in her father's books she'd studied as a child. But then he would move, put his arm around her, pull her into his side and kiss her forehead or her mouth, and he was warm, and he was soft and hard at the same time, and she was deliciously sore and had a secret and she never, never wanted this to end.

During the night he'd told her about the baron, the man he'd believed was his father. He'd told her about the bitter cold of his boyhood, and that the baron had rejected him over and over again for so many years. He told her about his nomadic life after he'd come of age. Anywhere, he said, but Cheverock. How he'd changed his name, and kept his true identity to himself, had let his patrons believe of him what they would, had told only one other person who he was, and even then, he confessed, in a moment of weakness when too much wine had loosened his tongue. It was a secret he'd meant to carry to his grave, for he couldn't bear to admit to anyone that his father despised him.

And now, it hardly mattered at all. He belonged to no one. He had no one. He was a man completely unto himself.

Maura's heart broke for the lad he'd once been. She understood the despair he must have felt, perhaps better than she ought to have understood. Unfortunately, she knew what it was to be unloved, unwanted and to feel utter desolation. No wonder Mr. Bain had held himself apart. No wonder his facade was so hard to penetrate. *No wonder, no wonder, no wonder.*

He had confessed the truth about himself without the casual regard she'd come to expect from him, but with true anguish. None of it changed her opinion of him. None of it made her esteem him any less. If anything, his heartbreak endeared him to her more.

Neither did she care that he didn't have a family name. Or a place he would call home. He was like her, wasn't he? Had there ever been two people more perfectly suited to each other?

She woke up just as the sun was peeking above the horizon and admired him again, stretched on his side, his back to her. He was magnificent, God's perfect creation of the male form. She wished she had a pencil and paper to capture this moment, fearful that one day she might possibly forget just how magnificent he was.

Nichol made a sound of wakefulness. He stretched, then glanced over his shoulder at her, his expression sleepily confused for a moment. But then he grinned and reached for her, rolling her onto her back and coming over her. "What a scandal we've caused, Miss Darby," he said, and kissed her.

"'Tis no' a scandal if we're no' discovered," she reminded him, and put her hands on his waist, sliding down his hips.

"We'll be discovered, donna doubt it. I suspect Finella and her maid will visit your room as quickly as they discover my bed has no' been slept in, aye?"

Maura giggled. "This bed has no' been slept in, either, Mr. Bain."

He kissed her more earnestly, crushing her to him as if he were afraid she would flutter away.

It was astounding how quickly corporeal desire could envelope a person, how thoroughly it could push all rational thoughts from one's mind. Nichol's touch was bedeviling, and no matter how thorough his touch, she was left panting and wanting more. There was something about his reverence of her that scored her soul quite deeply. Her skin shimmered when he touched her, her body quivered where he kissed her. She clung to him, her desire as deep and fervent as breath.

His pleasure was as obvious as her own, she was happy to note. She'd been transformed, from an innocent to a wanton, and she wanted him to want her.

Nichol nipped hungrily at her lips and swirled his tongue around hers, and Maura eagerly met his kisses, her hands sliding over the stiff curves of his body, her fingers tangling in his hair. She stroked his bristled cheek and slid her hand over his hips. She pressed a hand against his chest to feel the heat in his skin, the steady and strong rhythm of his heart. She realized that the tingling she felt in all her limbs was her craving for his sex, and she pushed her body into his without thought, with only raw desire.

But Nichol faltered in the heat of it. Maura opened her eyes, uncertain what was happening. Nichol was gazing down at her, his green eyes seeming much darker than normal. His jaw was clenched, and his hair dipped over one eye. He brushed his knuckles across her cheek. "How bonny you are, Maura," he said. "How…how cruel life can be at times."

She thought she knew what he meant. Their coupling was intense and so full of need. It was cruel to need so much, to want so much.

He bent his head, nibbled at her earlobe, then carefully slid into her body with a soft groan of pleasure.

Maura sighed with contentment and slid her hands over the corded muscles of his back. She would never have imagined it was possible to feel as if she and another person were truly one. This was where the two of them belonged, she thought hazily. Together.

There was no question in her mind as her desire grew more imperative, no question as she wrapped her arms around him, pressed against him and let herself go. There was no question when he followed her release with his own, his breath hot in her hair, his hands possessive on her body. *No question, no question, no question.*

Nichol brought her back to the land of the living with a soft kiss, then touched his fingers to her lips. "We must leave, aye? As quickly as we can, then."

She opened her eyes, and the feeling of bliss began to fade away like a dream. She didn't move for a moment, unwilling to let the night turn to day just yet.

"Maura, *leannan,*" Nichol said, and stroked her face, kissed her breast. "We must leave before we are discovered."

She made herself get up to dress.

They cleaned up the room as best they could— the bed linens presented something of a problem, but Nichol bundled them together for washing. They crept down to the drive, where Gavin was already waiting with the horses saddled. He looked apprehensive, as if he were anxious to be gone from Cheverock.

They did not manage to make their escape before Ivan MacBain stumbled out the door in his dressing gown. "Nichol?" he said, his voice full of confusion, his expression one of disbelief. "Do you intend to depart like a thief in the night? I expected you to come to my father's study last night after you spoke to him."

"*Your* father," Nichol said and sighed. "Then you know."

"Know that you seek to use an old man ill?" Ivan said. "Aye, I know."

Maura gasped.

Nichol gave her a grim look. "Stay here," he said, and walked across the drive to his brother. Maura watched as he put his arm around his brother's shoulders, which he immediately shrugged off. Nichol gestured for him to walk, and the two of them turned away from the horses, walking together a few steps. But then Ivan halted his step and glared at his brother.

"Mi Diah," Maura muttered to Gavin.

There was an exchange between them—Ivan's voice louder, Nichol's voice unflappably calm, and then Nichol strode across the drive to the horses and without a word, lifted Maura up onto the saddle. He swung up behind her, told Gavin to ride ahead, then reined his horse to follow.

Maura glanced back at Ivan, still standing in front of the house in his dressing gown and bare feet. Still staring after them, his face contorted with anger. "What did you say, then?"

"The truth," Nichol said quietly. "That I want nothing from the baron."

"But he's so cross," she said. She would think Nichol's brother would feel his devastation.

"He believes what my father has said of me," he said, and gave a soft, bitter laugh. "I have missed him all these years and all the while, he was learning to hate me."

"Surely not," Maura tried, glancing back again. "You canna leave him like this." Ivan was striding up the steps to the house.

"Perhaps I'll return one day after the baron is gone, aye? Until then, there is no point in it."

"But—"

"*Och,* lass, let it be," Nichol begged her.

She turned her head from the sight of Ivan MacBain as they rode away.

It was apparent to Maura that the meeting with his brother on the drive troubled Nichol. But for her, the day was a confection of rainbows and blue skies. She talked, more to fill the silence than anything, for she couldn't bear how quiet he'd become. Nichol smiled at her. He responded when she questioned him, he hugged her close when the horse cantered to catch up to the lad. Oh, she was babbling like a mad hen, she knew she was. But it was the only way she knew to keep the dark edges of reality from ruining her day.

She was, in spite of everything, and in spite of Nichol's quite demeanor, strangely happy. Her head was full of delicious memories, filling over and over again with images of being cherished, and the feeling, still so fresh, of the physical sensations. She could not help herself from imagining what could be. How could she? She was so keenly aware of him at her back. So keenly aware of the strength in his body, and how secure and happy she felt in his arms.

Did he not feel it, too? Could he so easily push aside the night? But clearly, the news from Cheverock weighed on him. As the sun rose higher and higher above them, he sank more into quiet.

Maura inwardly tried to reason with herself as she nattered on about the sky, the trees, the birds overhead. The revelations of his father had been profound, and she couldn't forget that he'd come to her in a moment of raw need. He'd needed desperately to lean on someone. Perhaps she'd read too much into his desire. Was it possible a man could do all the things he'd done with her last night and not feel that ache in his chest as she felt in hers?

Whatever he felt was heavy enough to suppress the air around them.

Still, Maura was not heavy. She refused to allow it. She'd had her first taste of love, and she was not willing to let it escape. She thought of all those nights she'd spent lying in that awful hovel of David Rumpkin's house near Aberuthen, uncertain what to do, how to think, which way to turn.

Well, she knew what she wanted now. She knew what to do, how to think, which way to turn.

What she wanted was to be with Nichol. On a forest floor, in a ramshackle house, with no home, with no name, she didn't care, as long as he was with her. It seemed rather romantic to her, really.

She did not yet know what to do about that.

In the early afternoon they stopped at a public inn. Nichol sent the lad inside to eat while he tended the horses. "Luncarty is no' two hours ride from here," he'd told the boy. "Eat, rest a wee bit, then go and tell Mr. Cockburn we've come, aye? He will be expecting us any day now."

For the first time that day, the smile faded from Maura's face. Of course she'd known where they were bound, but to hear him say it aloud soured her soaring spirits.

When the lad had gone, he smiled at Maura and

gestured to the inn. "A bite to eat, aye?" he asked, and escorted her into the public room of the inn and to a table near the back wall. He helped her from her cloak, then asked the lass who brought them ale to bring them stew. As they waited, he looked around the room, and Maura wondered if he was avoiding her. "Will you no' look at me?" she asked him.

Nichol shifted his gaze to her. "Of course I will."

"You've scarcely looked at me all day, Nichol."

"Ah," he said, and sighed, pushing back into his seat, one fist against the table. "On the contrary, I have looked at you all day. I canna take my eyes from you, in truth. But I've been a wee bit preoccupied." He smiled reassuringly.

Maura surged forward, both arms on the table. "I donna want this to end."

Nichol reached across the table for her hand. "Neither do I, *leannan*." He took her hand in both of his, holding it tightly. "You have my word that I'll see to it you are properly settled before I go, aye?"

That was *not* what she wanted him to hear. "Donna say that," she warned him.

"I must say it," he said. "I told you what would happen, and you agreed, Maura. Nothing has changed."

"*Everything* has changed," she argued. "My entire life has changed, and so has yours, if you'll only admit it."

He smiled sadly. He brought her hand to his lips and lingered on her skin. He did not act like a man who would "see her settled."

"I am forever a changed man, aye, I am," he agreed. "As much as I wish it were no' true, our circumstances havena changed—I am still a man with no name. You are still a lass with no prospects."

"Stop—"

"You've no' seen Luncarty, Maura. You will like what you find."

That remark vexed her, and she yanked her hand free. "How can you say such a thing after what we've shared! Do you believe a fine house will appease me? I've been in big houses, Mr. Bain, and I have found them wanting. There is no love, there is no warmth in them. Garbett House was a fine house and it was full of hostility. Cheverock was frigid. I donna care for fine houses."

"You would care verra much after a few nights on a bedroll, I can assure you."

She gaped at him. "Do you feel *nothing* for me, then?"

"*Mi Diah, leannan*, I feel everything for you," he said pressing his palm against his chest. "*Everything*. And it pains me beyond measure that I canna give you what you deserve. I canna give you an honest name or even a home of your own."

"But you could," she pressed.

He shook his head. "You canna know how it destroys me to know that I am a man whose occupation it is to put to rights things that have gone horribly wrong, but in this one thing, the thing that matters most, I canna repair it. I canna fix this problem, because the problem is me."

"I donna care," she said stubbornly.

"Aye, you do," he said calmly. "You may no' realize it yet, but you do. You want to believe you can bear never knowing where the next bed is, or the next meal. You want to believe you can bear living under different roofs or no roof at all, aye? You want to believe you can forgo children for it, because there would be no roof for them, either. You want to believe you can bear all of that, but what if you find it impossible? What if I get you with child? There is no escape once you've stepped onto that path, Maura. There is naught I can do to help you if you find it unbearable. I canna find a better situation for you. I canna make it right. Do you see, Maura?" he asked plaintively. "Do you see my torment?"

Of course she saw it. She knew what he was saying was true. She'd known it even last night. But she hadn't expected to feel like this. She hadn't expected her heart to be so full. And she couldn't very well empty it out because he said so.

Maura tilted her head to one side and considered what he'd said. "What if your friend doesna care for me, then?"

Nichol smiled wryly. "If he doesna care for you, he's a bloody fool. He will. You will charm him as you've charmed me."

"What if he doesna offer for me? I can hardly hide my esteem for you. I certainly canna hide the fact that I've been tossed out on my arse."

His smile grew deeper. "What are you about, then,

lass? Are you plotting? Do you mean to cause me trouble again?"

She shrugged.

"He will offer. He already has, in fact."

"'No' to me," she said, and folded her arms. "He must extend an offer to me, then, and I must accept it for it all to be legal and proper, aye?"

"I will tell you once more, as I've told you numerous times in our short, but significant acquaintance—you must trust me. He will offer."

Maura looked away from him. She absently fingered her necklace.

"Maura?"

"Mmm?" She glanced at him from the corner of her eye.

"Donna even think of it. It will no' go well for you if you do."

"Think of what?" she asked innocently.

He smiled wryly—he knew her well. "If you do something that forces Mr. Cockburn to call off, I will deposit you on the side of the road without your necklace, aye?"

Maura smiled saucily. "You'll have to take it off me, Mr. Bain."

He leaned forward and whispered, "I command that you donna smile at me like that. It makes it bloody well difficult to think." He lifted his hand and stroked her cheek. "Why you, Maura Darby? Why now?" he murmured.

"Why *you*?" she whispered, just as mystified. Her vision blurred as unshed tears filled her eyes. "Why now?" This was a tragedy. A Shakespearean, gut-wrenching tragedy of epic proportions, and Maura knew her heart would never recover from this break.

If there was a break. She didn't know how, but she was determined to find a way to convince him.

CHAPTER EIGHTEEN

THERE WAS SO MUCH Nichol wanted to say to Maura that he had no right to say to her, especially since he'd already done the worst damage. *I esteem you, I admire you, I want you. I want to give up all and plant fences around us, Maura. I want you.*

He bit his tongue and said nothing. This was his fault—in a rare moment of despair, of feeling lost, he'd turned to her, had let his desires push aside all reason. He'd done something unthinkable, especially for a man like him, who valued his integrity and honesty above all else. He'd acted on emotion rather than rational thought, had been made weak by the very hint of affection toward him, and as a result, had created a quagmire for them both.

I want you. I want you. I want you.

The words chanted at him over and over in his head as they rode along.

He wondered what Maura was thinking. *I hate you*, perhaps. He deserved it.

He deserved her complete disdain.

Whatever she thought, she said very little in those two long and final hours to Luncarty. It was strangely disconcerting—she'd been exuberant all day, her skin flushed with happiness, her eyes sparkling...all the telltale signs of blossoming esteem. She'd had affection for him so true that he'd felt it in his bones, had experienced it in his arms and he craved it like a dying man craved salvation.

And what was he to do with himself now? Watch her walk into the embrace of Dunnan Cockburn? Ride for Wales as if nothing happened? He had no idea how he would manage the shambles he'd made of his thoughts and emotions.

The day grew colder, the skies leaden. He suspected more snow, and felt Maura shivering against him. The day was deteriorating, right along with his heart.

Nichol desperately needed more time to sort things through, but unfortunately, they arrived in Luncarty before he was able.

"That's it, then?" she asked, her voice small.

"Aye, it is." He had pulled the horse to a halt on a hill above the estate. Luncarty was as grand and imposing as he'd told Maura it would be.

"It must have twenty chimneys," she said, her voice betraying her awe.

"Twenty-four by my count."

"Why has he never married, then?" she asked curiously.

A fair question—one did not reside in an estate like this and lack the attention of eager parents and their unmarried daughters. "He is clumsy," Nichol said simply. "Awkward in the company of the fairer sex. He deserves compassion, for it is no' from a lack of trying that he has failed. He is a good man, aye? But he is quite shy."

"That is the *oddest* thing I've ever heard," she said curiously.

It was indeed odd, but then again, Maura had not yet met the unique Dunnan Cockburn. She would come to understand, just as he had. Hopefully, she would come to esteem Dunnan in some way.

In *some* way. It was madness to think of it, but Nichol's single hope was that she would never esteem Dunnan as she had esteemed him.

He spurred the horse to carry on, and they moved down the road to the drive. When they reached the house, Nichol came off the horse and helped Maura down. He took the reins of the horse, his intention to tie them to a hitching rail, but the pair of tall wooden entry doors suddenly swung open, and a host of people began to spill out of it and onto the drive and lawn, looking at Nichol and Maura as if they were two exotic creatures.

Maura took a step backward.

There were a dozen or so souls, all of them in towering powdered hair, in perfectly curled perukes, in brightly colored silks and satins. Nichol couldn't fathom what this was. They looked as if they were preparing for a ball. But their clothes were more... exaggerated than that. *Bloody hell*, what was Dunnan about?

"Who *are* they?" Maura asked nervously, stepping back again and bumping into the horse.

"I donna know," he said irritably.

A lad came rushing forth from the crowd, his wig set back on his head so far that Nichol worried it might fly off. He wore white gloves with his livery, bowed deep and said, "I'm to take the mount, milord."

Nichol reluctantly handed him the reins. The lad tugged on the horse, who stubbornly refused to budge, but then Gavin appeared from somewhere behind Nichol and took the reins from the lad. He nodded at Nichol, as if he knew precisely what he was to do—care for the horses and wait.

The horse followed Gavin willingly, and the lad with the white gloves made a sound of exasperation.

Just then, Dunnan appeared on the top step of the entry, his mother on his arm.

Those two were inseparable, a fact he had failed to mention to Maura. Nichol would have to speak to Dunnan about that. It was time for him to be inseparable with another woman.

"Is that him?" Maura whispered.

Nichol couldn't tell from her voice what she thought of him. "Aye," he muttered, and took in Dunnan's round figure, his freshly powdered peruke. He was reminded that the last time he was here, Dunnan had chastised him for wearing his auburn hair in a simple queue.

"I donna have a place to keep all the accoutrement that a peruke would require, aye?" Nichol had said with a laugh.

"But this," Dunnan had complained, gesturing at Nichol's hair, "'tis no' *fashionable*, Bain."

Dunnan was fashionable, all right, in his new suit of clothing: a gold brocade coat with very large sleeves, over a blue silk waistcoat that had been embroidered within an inch of its life. His cuffs and neckcloth were fine lace, his stockings pristine white, his shoes highly polished. At least he'd dressed for the occasion of meeting the woman who would be his wife.

But Nichol noticed something else—Dunnan's face was florid, as if he'd exerted himself to appear in this manner. Nichol knew Dunnan, and knew that to be a sign of nerves. Dunnan's nerves were easily frayed.

Dunnan stood on the top step, one leg stretched before him, his smile cast to those below him.

Nichol glanced at Maura from the corner of his eye, who was staring at Dunnan with a look of pure wonder. "Brace yourself, *leannan*," he muttered, and strode forward to greet Dunnan.

"Bain!" Dunnan cried gaily, as if he'd just this moment spotted him. He promenaded with his mother down the steps to the drive, then bowed over his extended leg, an affectation, Nichol noted, that was new since the last he'd seen him. "You've come as promised, that you have. Dearest, you recall Mr. Bain, do you no'?" he asked his mother.

"Of course I do!" she trilled happily. She was likewise dressed in new clothing. Her fichu was so delicate that it looked as if her large bosom might possibly devour it. "Mr. Bain, it is a great pleasure to welcome you to Luncarty once again," she said, and curtsied. "Look!" she added gaily, and cast her arm wide. "We've made a party for you!"

A *party*. Nichol wanted to strangle Dunnan.

"You were no' to tell him, dearest," Dunnan pouted. "I wanted it to be a surprise."

"How could it be a surprise when the troupe is all here, dearest?" his mother shot back.

Troupe?

Dunnan reached for Nichol's hand and shook it with great verve. He had yet to look at the woman he'd said he would marry and acted as if she wasn't even present. But Nichol knew by the determined way in which Dunnan was still shaking his hand that he was very much aware of Maura. How could he not be? She was bonny.

"Dunnan…let go of my hand, then," Nichol murmured.

Dunnan instantly let go and stepped back. He smiled uncertainly. He glanced at his mother, who was gazing at him with foolish pride. "'Tis been a long journey for you, has it, Bain? How did you find the roads, then? I've heard they are terrible, quite impassable. Did you no' say the roads were impassable, Mr. Givens?" he said, turning his back to Maura to face his little crowd.

A man wearing silk trousers of pale blue looked startled. "I said no such thing, I'm certain of it," he said, and looked at the others around him. "Did I say it?"

"Well, *someone* has said it," Dunnan insisted and looked at the others accusingly. "I am *certain* of it—"

"Mr. Cockburn, if I may," Nichol interrupted. A snowflake flitted its way to the ground between them. "May I introduce Miss Maura Darby?"

Dunnan jerked around as if Nichol's presence had startled him, in spite of having just greeted him. "Pardon?"

"Miss Maura Darby," Nichol said, glaring at his friend. He turned to Maura, who had not moved a muscle, her blue eyes wide as she took in this crowd. "Miss Darby, if I may, Mr. Dunnan Cockburn of Luncarty, and his mother, Mrs. Cockburn."

"How do you do," Maura said demurely, and dipped into a curtsy. Dunnan stood there stupidly.

Maura rose and glanced at Nichol.

"Well, are you no' a bonny lass, Miss Darby," Mrs. Cockburn said enthusiastically, having clearly taken no notice of her son's oafish behavior. "Is she no' a bonny lass, dearest?" she asked, presumably of Dunnan, but she was still studying Maura, her gaze taking her in from top to bottom, her gaze fixing on the necklace.

"Ah. She is indeed." Dunnan cleared his throat. "Good evening, Miss Darby," he said, and bowed over that leg again. "Welcome to Luncarty," he said solemnly, and with a flourish of his hand, indicated his house. He seemed oblivious to the snow that had begun to fall lightly. He cleared his throat again and looked anxiously to the group assembled behind him.

"Thank you," Maura said. She was studying Dunnan as intently as his mother was studying her.

Dunnan shifted his weight onto a hip. He forced

a smile. Was he put off by the sight of Maura? That
was impossible—there wasn't a man in Scotland who
could be put off by the sight of her. But Dunnan was
acting a fool.

As if he understood what Nichol was thinking,
Dunnan glanced uncertainly at him. It was as if he
didn't know what to do. "Perhaps you might invite
us in," Nichol suggested, arching his brow. "It has
begun to snow, aye?"

"What?" Dunnan looked up. "Well, then, it has indeed! Aye, of course, of course!" he said, and waved
his arms at the others. "It's begun to snow! Look will
you, it is snowing! We should all be inside, should
we no'? Where is Fillian, then? Mr. Fillian, where
are you?" he called, seeking his butler. "We'll need
the hearths refreshed!" He put his arm around his
mother's waist and hurried her along inside behind
his guests, who had noticed the snow well before he
had, and were eager to return to the warmth of his
grand salon.

Nichol watched them all fleeing inside in a rain-
bow of blues and golds and greens and pinks. He realized that Maura had not moved and risked a look
at her.

She slowly turned her head and glared up at him.
"You must be mad," she said.

"It is entirely possible," he agreed. "Give him a
wee chance."

She stared at him in disbelief.

"Donna judge him too harshly," Nichol begged.

"As I said, he's rather awkward. He'll come round, he will."

Her eyes narrowed with sharp skepticism. "*Will* he?"

Nichol knew better than to respond to a woman in a full fit of pique. Not that he had an answer for her. A fortnight ago, this scheme had all seemed perfectly reasonable and logical. He'd had no regrets, had even mentally congratulated himself for having killed *two* family crises with one stone, so to speak, and for a handsome sum at that.

But now? He was questioning everything he'd ever known.

Maura knew it, too, because she muttered impatiently beneath her breath and struck out, her cloak billowing around her as she strode to the door while snowflakes danced merrily about her.

Nichol didn't blame Maura for her fury—he was rather furious himself. Dunnan had made an unforgivably bad impression. How could a man grown be so bloody *inept*?

He reluctantly followed Maura inside.

Maura was still in the entry. She'd removed her cloak and had handed it to the footman. Her gray day gown seemed quite plain in comparison to what the other ladies were wearing, and yet Nichol thought she was the bonniest of them all. Her cheeks, rosy from the cold, made her appear more youthful and vibrant than anyone else. Her hair, poorly bound at her nape, was a dark crown to her pale skin. To the casual observer, she might have looked as if she'd

come from the village, but for the priceless necklace
she wore around her neck. She had not removed it
since he'd returned it to her.

She shot a dark look at Nichol over her shoulder
as he shed his greatcoat, then turned and walked into
the salon, halting just inside the door. Nichol walked
to stand behind her.

Dunnan's salon was a sight to behold, overdone
with its velvet draperies and gold braided ties, the
fresco paintings and banquet scenes that hung in
thick burnished frames around the room, and the
elaborate plaster ropes and medallions that covered
the ceiling. Maura seemed riveted by it as her gaze
traveled overhead, then to the thick carpets, and
around the paintings and consoles with the various
works in marble.

Dunnan's guests were milling about, and the at-
mosphere was quite gay. Oddly enough, it reminded
Nichol of a carnival he'd attended in London. Footmen moved between them with glasses of wine and
whisky, all of which were snatched up with eagerness.

What the devil was in Dunnan's head? He knew
very well that Nichol was expected with Maura. Had
he changed his mind about marriage? Did he think he
could hide behind all these people? As Maura took
in her surroundings and shyly accepted a glass of
wine from a footman, Nichol took the opportunity
to have a word with Dunnan Cockburn.

He was standing with two admirers, his laughter
at whatever they said so loud and long as not to be

believed. Nothing could be that amusing. As Nichol reached Dunnan's side, he noticed a trickle of perspiration had escaped his wig and was making its way down his temple and cheek.

"Mr. Bain! You've not yet had the pleasure of making the acquaintance of my friends—"

"Aye, and I look forward to it, I do, but might I have a word first?"

"Oh," Dunnan said. He smiled uneasily at the two standing beside him. The female half of the pair smiled saucily at Nichol and flicked her gaze over him in an overtly appreciative manner.

"A word, then?" Nichol pressed him.

"Aye, of course," Dunnan said, and moved awkwardly from the couple, as if he was still uncertain he ought to step aside. So Nichol did it for him. He took him by the elbow and wheeled him about, forcing him to walk several feet away and out of earshot of anyone else.

"What in bloody hell is the matter with you, then?" he demanded sternly.

Dunnan's brown eyes widened. "Pardon? Whatever do you mean?" he asked, and self-consciously put a hand to his wig, as if Nichol was complaining that it was crooked.

"You do realize, do you no', that Miss Darby is the woman for whom I received your favorable reply to consider offering for her hand in marriage?"

It seemed impossible, but somehow Dunnan's round face grew redder. "Aye, of *course* I do. I'm no' a bloody ninny."

That was observably debatable. "Then act like it, man!" Nichol barked at him.

Dunnan swiped at the trickle of perspiration, which had now reached his chin. "Aye, I will," he said firmly, then hesitated. "But what am I to do?" he added uncertainly.

"*Diah,* for the love of all that is holy, *talk* to her. Ask after her journey. Anything at all would be better than the way you've received her thus far."

"Aye," Dunnan said nodding. "I will. I *will*."

"What are all these people doing here, then?" Nichol demanded. "They are a distraction to the business at hand, are they no'?"

Dunnan looked at the group as if he'd not noticed them before. "Performers," he said. At Nichol's puzzled look, he clarified. "They are members of a theatrical troupe. I've seen them perform and they are quite exceptional, they are. I thought they might perform a musicale in Miss Darby's honor, aye?" He spoke hopefully, as if perhaps Nichol would understand his reasoning and suddenly think it a brilliant idea.

Nichol did not think it a brilliant idea. He thought there was something fundamentally wrong with Dunnan's block of a brain. "Dunnan, lad, think of it—you canna host a musicale in her name if you've no' met her. You donna yet know her *name*. It is premature to do something so grand for someone you've yet to greet properly, do you no' see? She is no' prepared for this, Dunnan, of course no'. She's only just arrived, has only laid eyes on you for the first time."

"But I... I thought she might rest, naturally. We'd have the performance after supper. After I have... learned her name," he muttered.

Nichol clamped his hand onto Dunnan's shoulder and squeezed hard. "Heed me now, lad. The woman doesna know you, and she doesna have a proper gown. She might forgive the impulsive gathering, but she will *no'* forgive being the least well dressed of the evening, do you understand? Do you know *anything* about the fairer sex?"

"Precious little," Dunnan admitted with a sigh. "They donna seem to care for me."

"You must postpone the musicale—"

"Postpone it! But they've come!" Dunnan exclaimed, and gestured to the assembled persons. "I sent all the way to Glasgow for them!"

Nichol had a renewed urge to strangle him. "Aye, all right. Then find her something suitable to wear, and do no' claim the performance is in her honor."

"I must *what*?" Dunnan whispered with a horrified expression.

With his chin, Nichol indicated Maura, who was still standing at the door of the salon, sipping at a glass of wine and speaking to a young woman whose hair was adorned with flowers.

Dunnan looked in the direction Nichol had indicated. "Ah. I see," he said. "I have just the thing, Bain. She might borrow—"

"By all that is holy, if you say your mother's gown, I shall put my fist through your fool mouth," Nichol muttered.

Dunnan swallowed down whatever he might have said. He cleared his throat. His cheeks were nearly purple. He looked as if he meant to argue, but Nichol held up a single finger in warning. And still, Dunnan leaned forward to whisper, "But *how*?" he whispered.

Nichol looked around the room. He pointed to the woman who was speaking to Maura. The one laughing so deeply that she had both hands on her belly. "That one, then. She looks to be the size of Miss Darby. Tell her that the luggage has no' yet come, and you would consider it a personal favor if she would assist Miss Darby."

"A personal favor," Dunnan repeated, and nodded.

"And then you will show Miss Darby to a room. Let her rest, let her bathe, let her prepare to meet these people properly, but for God's sake, you best act as if you are verra pleased to have her here, aye, Dunnan?"

"Aye," Dunnan said, nodding furiously now. "Aye, of course, of course. I understand."

Nichol placed both hands on Dunnan's shoulders. "Look at her," he commanded.

Dunnan did as Nichol bade him, and rose up on his toes to see over Nichol's shoulders, and looked at Maura. He nodded, as if the prey had been sighted.

"You canna possibly marry better than her, Dunnan. No' even if you were the bloody king of England."

"Aye," Dunnan agreed.

"So show a wee bit of interest in her."

"I am!" he said. "I will."

"And donna hide behind your mother's skirts." He removed his hands and turned to take his leave. He could do with a bath, a fresh change of clothes.

"But...but what shall I talk about?" Dunnan whispered with a hint of desperation in his voice.

He really was the most hapless person Nichol had ever known. "She is fond of astronomy."

"Astronomy," Dunnan repeated in a whisper, and then, "Oh dear." His face fell as he undoubtedly realized he knew nothing of astronomy.

"Think of something, man!" Nichol said sharply.

"You may depend on it, Bain!" he said, nodding hard again. "You'll no' be sorry."

Nichol hardly cared if he was sorry or not. What he couldn't abide in the years to come was the notion that Maura hated him.

No, he couldn't bear that.

But he rather thought he'd hate himself enough for the both of them.

CHAPTER NINETEEN

MAURA HAD DRUNK two glasses of wine on an empty stomach, and was feeling a little woozy and a little feisty when at last Mrs. Cockburn, her supposed intended's mother, asked if she might escort her to a room.

"Aye," Maura said. Anything to escape this salon. She felt sorely out of place, a weed among flowers. She had been ignored for the most part, the merry-makers unconcerned with her.

Neither was Mr. Cockburn terribly concerned with her. Actually, he had seemed to avoid her at all costs, although he had approached her like a man might approach a snake he wasn't certain was venomous, creeping up slowly and her eyeing her suspiciously. "How did you find the journey, Miss Darby?" he asked.

She stared at him. She didn't know where to begin. Perhaps she should start with having been cast out of the Garbett house the first time. Or perhaps she ought to skip ahead and commence with fleeing the Garbett house the second time. But instead of saying anything, Maura accepted her second glass of wine from the footman and said, "Quite well, thank you." She reminded herself she was a proper young miss, brought up to be unfailingly polite and demure. To not shine too brightly, lest she burn Sorcha to the ground.

"Verra well," Mr. Cockburn said, and seemed relieved that was all she had to say. He flitted off after that, disappearing into the whirl of people moving about the room.

She had drained the second glass and was searching the room for Nichol when Mrs. Cockburn had appeared before her. Gone was her friendly smile that she'd worn on the drive. She peered closely at Maura with a mix of fascination and what seemed like a wee bit of disgust. Did she look like a lightskirts? Perhaps she did.

"I'm to show you to a room so that you might rest, aye?" she said.

"*Thank* you," Maura said gratefully with more eagerness than was probably necessary.

"Follow me," Mrs. Cockburn said, and sailed out of the salon with Maura close on her heels. But she did not turn left to go up the grand staircase. She walked straight through the foyer and into another long corridor. "Our dining room is here," she said, and paused at an open door so that Maura could see into a cavernous room with a table as long as a small ship at the center of it. "As you can see, we may dine with forty if we like."

"Mmm," Maura said.

Mrs. Cockburn jerked her gaze to Maura. "I beg

your pardon, are you *accustomed* to such tables? Do you *dine* at tables of forty often?"

The tone of her voice startled Maura. "Pardon? No, madam, I donna at all."

"I thought no'," she said with a sniff, and carried on.

Maura trudged after her, exhausted and a wee bit in her cups, quite honestly.

"Here is our morning room. The ladies take their tea here. We dress for tea, Miss Darby."

"Aye," Maura said, afraid to say any more than that for fear of offending her further.

"And there is my son's study. He is no' to be disturbed when he is there, aye? He is a verra busy man. *Verra* busy."

That suited Maura just fine. Perhaps he wouldn't notice when she sneaked away.

"This room," she said, opening the door to a room that was so full of chintz that at first Maura thought it was a storage room, "is *my* study."

"Oh. Aye, it's…bright."

"I've done the decorating myself," she said smugly. "Dunnan insisted we bring up a young man of some repute from Salisbury. He has decorated all the finest English houses, he has."

"His work is bonny, aye," Maura absently agreed, and made a note to never allow this person to decorate one of her rooms. One could become positively lost in all that floral patterning.

But once again, Mrs. Cockburn turned a cold gaze

to her. "*He* didna do it, lass. *I* did. This is all my own doing."

"Oh. Aye, it's bonny," Maura said again, and noticed, for the first time, that Mrs. Cockburn's dress was also made of floral chintz. She hadn't realized until this moment that someone could be so enamored of floral chintz. Frankly, it was a travesty of chintz, and she almost smiled at the absurdity.

"Aye, it is," Mrs. Cockburn said pertly. "My study is right small, it is, but 'tis the envy of everyone in and around Luncarty, you may rest assured."

Maura would rest assured if that's what it took to lie down before she collapsed.

Mrs. Cockburn continued on, pointing to a painting she'd created, or the lace doilies on the consoles in the long hallway. She was responsible, she said, for all the draperies, as she had traveled to London to choose the fabric herself.

At her son's insistence, of course.

She led Maura up a narrow stairwell, and they emerged into another long hallway. "This is the north wing where we house our guests. We often have guests. My son prefers to surround himself with his friends rather than travel. He oversees a vast linen enterprise, I'm sure you've heard, then."

Maura tried to remember if she'd heard that. So much had happened in the last week.

This hallway was rather crowded. There were a few people going back and forth between the rooms. Chambermaids dressed in matching striped mantuas went back and forth with them, carrying linens and clothing. Maura followed Mrs. Cockburn down the hall until they came to a room at the end of the hallway.

"We've only the two rooms left, then. Mr. Bain prefers the one across the hall, as it has a view of the gardens and a private sitting room. You'll no' mind the smaller one, aye?" she asked, and opened the door.

It wasn't a room, it was a closet. It scarcely fit a bed and small bureau within its walls. Maura was so fatigued she hardly cared if it was a closet, and yet, she couldn't resist giving Mrs. Cockburn a look. This seemed a curious choice of rooms to assign to a woman who would be her future daughter-in-law. Perhaps Mrs. Cockburn hated the idea of her marrying Mr. Cockburn as much as Maura did.

Mrs. Cockburn smiled in a manner that suggested she dared Maura to say something.

"*Thank* you," Maura said, inclining her head. "This will suit me perfectly, aye?"

"I thought so," Mrs. Cockburn said with a gaiety that did not match her expression. "Miss Fabernet has generously loaned you one of her best gowns," she said, and gestured to one lying across the bed.

Maura had met Miss Fabernet downstairs. She'd brought her a glass of wine and had told Maura she looked very well for having come so far. The gown she'd left was pale blue silk, with a white petticoat embroidered with tiny red flowers, as well as a matching blue stomacher. It was quite bonny.

"Oh," Maura said appreciatively. "I must thank Miss Fabernet."

"A footman will bring a tub for you and a maid will bring water for bathing."

"Thank you again," Maura said, feeling a surge of delight at the possibility of a bath.

Mrs. Cockburn shrugged indifferently. "Mr. Bain said we must."

Why must the lady sound so resentful? Maura couldn't begin to guess why, and didn't really care to try. She was exhausted, she was a wee bit drunk and she wanted her bath. "When I see Mr. Bain, I will thank him for insisting on my behalf," she said, and gave Mrs. Cockburn a flash of a pert smile.

Mrs. Cockburn did not smile. "We dine at seven, Miss Darby. By the bye, where *are* your clothes?"

"In Stirling," Maura said. She did not offer that Sorcha was wearing them. Or that she'd been tossed out without a thing to her name.

Mrs. Cockburn's gestured to her neck. "You've come with no clothes, and yet you wear that," she said.

Maura put her hand to her necklace. "It belonged to my great-grandmother and has been handed down."

"Well, at least there is *some* dowry, then. I told Dunnan he must insist on a dowry," Mrs. Cockburn said.

Maura stifled a laugh. She rather thought Dunnan shouldn't insist on anything. "He's no' offered marriage," she pointed out with as much civility as she could muster. "And I've no' offered a dowry."

"Aye, he's no' offered, and you ought to keep that in mind. My advice to you, Miss Darby, is to be on your best behavior. My son is no' an impressionable man."

Maura didn't know what he was, other than he had a cloying air about him.

"You must always ask me if you are uncertain of anything," she added.

Maura tilted her head to one side as she tried to make sense of that. "Uncertain of what?"

"Anything to do with my son. What he would like. What he would *no'* like and such."

It took a moment for Maura to understand that this mother hen was not ready to let her chick go. This was precisely the sort of thing Mrs. Garbett might have said, and Maura was not going to be meek about it this time. She didn't intend to stay here, and she certainly didn't intend to stay if Mr. Cockburn's mother ruled the house. She smiled sweetly and asked with feigned innocence, "Should I no' inquire of Mr. Cockburn himself what he likes or doesna like?"

Mrs. Cockburn blinked. Her cheeks began to pinken. She stepped forward, so close to Maura that she could see the tiny crumb in the corner of her mouth. "I should no' like us to set off unpleasantly, Miss Darby, aye?"

"Neither would I, Mrs. Cockburn," Maura said. She would not apologize and she would not submit to the thumb of this woman. It was bad enough that she had to subject her life to the enormous thumbs of men, but to another woman? It was Mrs. Garbett all over again, only in another form, another gown, another estate, and it was *not* to be borne.

Mrs. Cockburn smiled coolly. She very carefully tucked part of Maura's hair over her shoulder. "Let us have an understanding, shall we, Miss Darby? You have come to us because we are indebted to Mr. Bain for his considerable help in another matter, aye? He said you were involved in an unpleasant quandary and were in need of saving."

"I donna need to be saved—"

"We are doing you a favor, aye?" she said, interrupting Maura before she could argue. "You should be thankful that you have a roof over your head, and a fire in your hearth and a wench to help you bathe."

Maura swallowed down the retort she wanted to give Mrs. Cockburn. She wanted to tell her that the most unpleasant quandary of all was being made to do as men bid her, with no say of her own, to being subjected to the sort of treatment she was receiving at that very moment by a woman who had concluded she was far superior to her in every way.

But she was thankful she was not sleeping on a forest floor while snow fell, and she reckoned it wasn't yet too late for that to happen. She swallowed again. This time, it was the bitter taste of her pride. "Aye, of course. My apologies, Mrs. Cockburn."

Mrs. Cockburn's smile was heartless. "There now, that was no' so hard, was it, lass?"

Harder than crossing a desert, which Maura had read about in one of her father's novels before Mrs. Garbett had them carted off with the excuse they put too many ideas in Maura's head. Harder than living in David Rumpkin's house for a fortnight. Harder than being powerless and alone in this world and beholden to someone like Mrs. Cockburn. Nevertheless, she smiled sweetly, as if she had seen the error of her ways and was prepared once again to portray a saintly young virgin in want of a husband.

Mrs. Cockburn had the gall to pat Maura's cheek as if she were a petulant child. "Penny will come round and help you dress, she will."

"Thank you."

Mrs. Cockburn turned away. She eyed the gown that Miss Fabernet had left her, ran her hand over the silk. "Oh, it's bonny, that it is," she said, and went out.

Maura waited until she was certain she was gone before she whirled around and kicked the bedpost as hard as she could, then winced with the pain that caused her toes.

"Are you injured, then?"

Maura whipped around—she'd not heard the petite young woman come to the door. She was just at the threshold holding two pails of water.

"Where am I to put it, then?" a male voice asked behind her.

"By the hearth, Mr. Gils, what do you think?" the maid said, and stepped aside so the footman could wrangle the wooden tub into the room. When he had it in front of the hearth, he bowed to Maura and went out.

The girl poured the water into the tub. "I'm Penny," she said cheerfully. "Madam said I was to tend you at your bath."

Maura didn't know if she trusted Penny, but the prospect of water and soap convinced her to take her chances. She began to unfasten her gown.

Penny shut the door to her room, then bent down to the small bureau and rummaged around. When she stood, she held a linen cloth.

"Thank you," Maura said. "I'm desperate to bathe. I've been riding for days, it would seem."

"Where'd you come from, then?" the girl asked.

After the discussion with Mrs. Cockburn, Maura thought the less she said the better. "No' far, really." She stripped down and eased into the water. She closed her eyes and sighed.

"Oh, but 'tis a lovely gown, is it no'?" Penny said from somewhere near the bed.

"Mmm," Maura agreed. "I must thank Miss Fabernet for her kindness."

"You may thank her soon, you will. She's coming round to dress your hair."

"Pardon?" Maura asked, and opened her eyes.

"She said your hair was a tragedy—I beg your pardon—and that you couldna dine with it so, and she means to help you dress it." She glanced over her shoulder at Maura. "She's an *actress*."

As if on cue, there was a knock at the door. Penny rushed to answer it before Maura could cover herself, and in swept a woman with a tower of powdered hair dotted with silk flowers. She had a fine figure and light brown eyes. The kohl that darkened her brows and lashes made her skin look almost white.

"There you are!" she trilled as she swept in. "I've caught you at your bath, have I?"

Miss Fabernet was English, judging by her accent, a fact that had escaped Maura earlier. "Ah…"

"You must not mind me, darling." Miss Fabernet held up a pillowcase whose contents made some interesting lumps. "I've come prepared to dress your hair. I would not wish to intervene, and I'm certain that any lady Dunnan means to marry would have her own dresser, but I presume yours has not yet come? I've taken pity on you."

Maura didn't know how to respond. Was it common knowledge that she'd come here to accept an offer of marriage?

"You mustn't feel as if you need answer," Miss Fabernet said, and walked to the bed to dump her things next to the gown. "The room is rather small, is it not?" she asked, looking around. "Ah well. You'll be warmer than the rest of us, I suspect. Now then, let's wash your hair. It looks quite…untidy," she said, and shivered.

Maura slid deeper into the water. What *was* this place where Nichol intended to leave her?

CHAPTER TWENTY

NICHOL DID NOT see Maura enter the salon at the dinner hour—he was preoccupied with Dunnan. He knew the Scot well—Dunnan was typically quite carefree and in a mood to be diverted. But tonight, he was subdued. And he'd been whispering with a gentleman whose hair was slicked back in a thick black queue for a quarter of an hour and he seemed uncharacteristically agitated.

Nichol moved about the room with the intention of cornering Dunnan and asking him what he was about. But when he stepped away from the wall he'd been leaning against, he saw Maura. She was in the middle of the room speaking to the woman whom he'd suggested to Dunnan should lend her a gown. He was momentarily dumbstruck—she was a vision in the pale blue gown. *Boideach. Bel. Schön.*

He looked around at the others in the room, certain they'd been struck by her comeliness. Was he the only one to notice? Why wasn't everyone assembled in that room gazing at her now? Her hair had been put up in a dark tower and bluebirds nested at the top. He couldn't help but smile at the whimsical dressing—she seemed far too practical to allow bluebirds to nest in

her hair—but the affect was charming. The gown fit
her like a second skin and made her seem even more
womanly. The blue of it was dazzling, the white petticoat with bits of red eye-catching.

Aye, she was the bonniest woman he'd ever
known.

Alas, the dolt that was Dunnan Cockburn hadn't
noticed her, Nichol realized, so he walked across the
room to greet her. He had also bathed and changed
and was wearing a plaid and formal coat for the evening. She turned her head slightly as he made his
way across the room, and her eyes lit with delight.
She turned to face him fully as he neared her and
the other woman. "Mr. Bain, a plaid? I didna know
your affinity for the Highlands."

"Aye, 'tis a true affinity," he said. "The plaid was
a gift from the Mackenzie clan. Perhaps one day you
will be fortunate to see Balhaire for yourself." His
days spent at the Mackenzie estate of Balhaire in
the Highlands were some of the very best of his life.

"I've not heard of it. Perhaps, I will," she said,
smiling wryly. "May I introduce Miss Fabernet? She
has lent me a gown and helped with my hair." To
Miss Fabernet, she said, "Mr. Bain."

"Enchantée," the woman said, and with a sultry
smile, she held out her hand and sank into a curtsy.

Nichol took her hand and bowed over it, "A pleasure, madam."

She rose up and let her gaze slide over him, lingering on his tartan. "*I* should like to see the Highlands, as well," she said silkily. "I've heard that the

gentlemen there are formidable." She lifted her gaze to him. "In every way."

Nichol smiled. A fortnight ago, he would have read the invitation in her eyes and would have acted on it. Tonight, he wished she would go away. He wanted only Maura.

"I must say, sir, that you wear a plaid *very* well," she added.

Ah, but he did admire a brazen woman. He turned his attention to the most brazen of them all and smiled. "How bonny you are this evening, Miss Darby. Miss Fabernet has been verra generous."

"I can be more generous than that," she purred, and sidled closer to him.

"Shall we say good evening to Mr. Cockburn, then?" Nichol suggested to Maura, and offered his arm.

Miss Fabernet sighed. "Go on then, the two of you," she said, flipped open a fan, smiled at Nichol over the top of it, then glided away.

Nichol offered his arm to Maura. "You look verra bonny, lass," he said to her as they walked along. "But until tonight, I had no' thought you a woman given to bluebirds."

She laughed. "Miss Fabernet thought my hair was distressing and could scarcely contain her glee at dressing it. She said it would make me more appealing to my future husband." She glanced at him from the corner of her eye. "Do you think that is true, Mr. Bain?"

"You could no' be more appealing. It would seem Mr. Cockburn has summoned the town crier."

"Aye, it would," she said. "I wonder if he will offer at all, in truth. His mother doesna esteem me."

"She does," he said.

"Oh, but she does no'," she said quite adamantly. "She made it clear that Mr. Cockburn is hers and I'm no' to have a say in him at all."

Bloody Dunnan and the apron strings he clung to. "I'll speak to him."

"Donna trouble yourself, Nichol," she said, and looked away. "I am acquainted with the likes of Mrs. Cockburn. She'll have her way, and there is naught you can do to change it."

Nichol swallowed down a lump of guilt. He had never questioned the plans he came up with to solve the problems of those who retained his services, but he was questioning them now. But still, his misgivings were tempered with Dunnan's wealth and his generally affable demeanor. He was a good solution for Maura.

Wasn't he?

They reached Dunnan, who was standing alone, the man with the dark queue no longer with him. When Dunnan looked up, he stuttered backward, startled by Maura's appearance. "Oh! Oh my! Miss Darby, how *well* you look!"

Maura laughed a little. "I must have looked a fright when I arrived," she said, and self-consciously touched her hair.

"No' at all, no' at all," Dunnan said, trying to recover from his surprise.

"Miss Fabernet has been verra helpful. Thank you for requesting her assistance."

"Aye, well, I thought I ought," he said, then caught himself. "No' that I thought *you* needed help, madam, no. But to make you welcome, do you see? My mother and I wanted to make you welcome." He glanced at Nichol. A dewy sheen of perspiration had erupted on his brow.

Diah, but Dunnan was as maladroit in the company of the fairer sex as he was round. Nichol found it annoying—how could he fumble every little thing?

"Thank you," Maura said. "Your mother has been…"

"Oh, she is a dear. Lives to serve, she does." Dunnan took a tiny step closer to Maura. "Might you, Miss Darby, if I may be so bold to impose, would it be at all possible if…"

For the love of Christ, man, say it.

"Would it be possible if you were to sit beside me at supper?"

"Oh, I—"

"'Tis a verra long table, you see, and if you're verra far away, I'll no' be able to speak to you. Or… or hear you."

"I'd be delighted, Mr. Cockburn. And Mr. Bain?"

"What? Bain? Oh! Aye, aye, he'll be there, too. Aye, that he will, I'll see to it." He hesitated and touched a finger to his lips. "I best see to it, aye? I'll have a word with Fillian then. He has set the

places but he will arrange it. Will you excuse me?"
He smiled grandly, as if he was very pleased with
himself for having worked it all out.

Maura dipped a curtsy as he hurried off. When
he had disappeared into the crowd, she asked, "Is he
in possession of *all* his faculties, do you suppose?"

Nichol was distracted by the way Dunnan hurried across the room as if a fire had engulfed it, but
had been stopped in his progression by the same
gentleman who had been whispering with him before. What in the devil was Dunnan about?

"Is there wine?"

Nichol glanced at Maura. She was looking down,
removing a piece of lint or something from the
gown. She was so beguiling to him that he felt an
unexpected swell of emotion in his chest. It was a
gush of warmth. He was afraid to name that swell
of emotion, afraid to give it legitimacy.

"I'll fetch it," he said low, and walked away from
her before she could pierce him with her blue eyes
and force him to give a name to that warmth—he
could not bear to name it, he could not afford to name
it. He would *not* name it.

By the time he returned to her, he'd slung down a
tot of whisky, and Miss Fabernet had found Maura
once again, this time in the company of Mr. Johnson,
who was, Nichol gathered, the leader of this group
of stage performers. He had a bombastic manner of
speaking, as if he believed every sentence an oratory.

When supper was announced, they all trooped to
the dining room in a garbled promenade. Mrs. Cock-

burn was shouting at who should escort whom, but
most of them ignored her instructions. In the dining
room, Dunnan had forgotten his intent to instruct
Fillian to rearrange the place settings, and once he
realized it, caused quite a hullabaloo over moving
everyone around so that Maura would be seated on
his right. In the ensuing melee, Nichol found himself
far down the table, next to an elderly woman who
claimed to be a dear, dear friend of Mrs. Cockburn.

It was the second meal he'd had to suffer the tedium of small talk, which Nichol had never been
adept at, and of late, rather impatient with. He
couldn't keep his attention from Maura. Dunnan
was doing a great deal of talking—he could be quite
verbose with a bit of wine in him. She seemed to be
conversing with him, too, and even managed a smile
now and then.

She was trying.

By the time the meal was over and the crowd had
moved back to the salon, several of them had fallen
deep into their cups. Those who hadn't yet were not
far behind. The boisterous performers gathered at the
pianoforte and broke into bawdy barroom songs that
reminded Nichol of a French salon. For some reason,
an image of the Garbetts came to mind, and Nichol
could not help but smile at how properly scandalized
they would be if they were here tonight.

If Maura was scandalized, she didn't outwardly
show it. She was with Dunnan and Miss Fabernet,
was laughing at something one of them said. From
time to time, she would look around the crowded

room, rising up on her toes, seeking him. And she would smile with something that looked a wee bit like relief. Comfort that he was still here, still watching over her.

"We must have a dance, aye?" Dunnan suddenly shouted. He stood up and looked eagerly about the room. "A dance! You there, in the plaid, my good sir! You must show us a Highland jig, aye?"

Nichol laughed. "Show us yourself then, Mr. Cockburn," he said back to him.

"But you must," Dunnan said. He was swaying a little on his feet.

"I'll stand up with you if you like, aye?" Maura offered pleasantly, and walked forward.

This offer was met with risqué remarks and laughter. Only Mrs. Cockburn seemed offended. Her son was amused.

"Aye, Bain, you must have the first dance with Miss Darby, then," Dunnan said, clearly delighted.

Maura curtsied and began to sway her hips, swinging the hem of her skirt one way and the next.

Nichol watched her a moment, marveling at her resilience given the events of the last several days. He felt the press of his worries, the turmoil of his emotions. He was exhausted, spent…perhaps what he needed was a diversion. Perhaps he needed to dance.

He pushed away from the wall he'd been holding up and walked to the middle of the room. "*Mi Diah,* how do any of you expect us to dance a jig or a reel with no music, then?" he demanded.

Dunnan eagerly clapped his hands. "Music!" he

shouted, and gestured for the gentleman at the pianoforte to play, who instantly struck up a jaunty tune.
Nichol looked at Maura. "I am no' a fine dancer,
Miss Darby. You might have done better with one
of the gentlemen here."

"You'll never be a fine dancer if you donna try,
Mr. Bain." She grabbed a handful of skirt in both
hands, lifted the hem, and began to dance.

Fortunately, Nichol had had a wee bit of practice
at Balhaire. Catriona, Lady Montrose, had insisted
upon it, in part as punishment for what he'd done to
her when she'd fallen in love with the Duke of Montrose, and in part because despite all that had happened, Catriona esteemed him in some small way.
He was grateful to her now, for he managed to keep
step with Maura who was, much to his chagrin, a
fine dancer.

Others joined them, dancing a jig and whirling
around the room, bumping into each other with gales
of laughter. Nichol eventually begged off, and he
and Maura collapsed against a wall, breathless. Her
cheeks were flushed, her eyes sparkling with glee.
She could be happy here, he thought. She could ad-
just to this life.

Nichol looked around the room, determined that
Dunnan would have the next opportunity to dance
with her. But Dunnan was nowhere to be seen.

"Come!" shouted a gentleman, and grabbed Maura's
hand, pulling her into the fray again. He whirled her
about in a reel, passed her to the next partner.

Maura was laughing. She was dancing with the

abandon of a woman who had nothing left to lose, kicking up her heels, twirling this way and that. Nichol watched her, fascinated. Captivated. He watched as a bluebird went sailing out of her hair, followed by another one that bounced off the shoulder of a woman who never noticed it. If Maura noticed her hair was toppling down, she didn't care. She kept dancing, kept kicking up her feet, flying around in the reel and relinquishing the tight grip she'd kept on herself in the days that had preceded this one. It was almost as if she were shedding all that had happened to her.

She laughed as her hair tumbled down and the net of filling that had held it up in the tower hung from a tress of her hair. She laughed wildly, when one man plucked it up and stuck it on his head. The sound of her gay laughter filled Nichol's heart to the point of bursting.

He didn't know what to do with his heart. It needed to burst, to let go the pressure, to sink back to the hard little fist it had been before he'd met her. If it burst, it would kill him. This could all kill him. He could die of longing.

Someone threw open the terrace doors to give the dancers some air. The snow was piling up ever higher outside, which relieved Nichol. It meant that he didn't have to decide tomorrow what he would do next. It meant that his swollen heart did not yet have to burst. He'd been given a reprieve, and it was enough to cause a grown man to dance. He entered the reel, grabbed her hand, and laughed with her.

CHAPTER TWENTY-ONE

LONG AFTER EVERYONE had gone to bed in the wee morning hours, Maura lay in her small bed, staring at the pile of snow on her windowsill. Her room was freezing, the fire in the tiny hearth having gone out before she'd ever come up from the salon.

She burrowed deeper under the covers, but she could still hear the whispers, the sound of feet running down the hallway. This theatrical troupe was ending their evening in each other's beds. She thought of Nichol, and the warmth of his body. She thought of him in his plaid, a compelling figure with strong legs and broad chest.

She'd enjoyed herself tonight. She enjoyed the company of the bawdy troupe. But mostly, she enjoyed dancing with Nichol.

She did not allow herself to think of Mr. Cockburn or his mother. Oh, he'd been pleasant enough at supper. He had not the faintest clue how to engage in conversation, and seemed to be most at ease when someone else did the talking. She had the sense that he was somehow intimidated by her. Afraid, perhaps.

But she didn't think about him. She thought of Nichol. He was constantly in her thoughts, filling her with a desire so powerful that it made her feel weak, as if she hadn't eaten enough to sustain her.

She didn't want to say farewell. She didn't want to go on with her life as if this thing between them, whatever it was—*was it love?*—had never happened. Maura didn't know what would come next—the snow made it impossible for anyone to leave on the morrow—but she would escape this place, one way or another. She could not bear it without him. And she didn't think she could possibly marry Mr. Cockburn, not after what she'd experienced in Nichol's arms.

She rolled over onto her back and fingered the necklace at her throat. She would not remove it, although it was heavy and rubbed against her skin when she slept. She trusted no one but Nichol Bain. Only him.

She glanced at the snow again and suddenly wanted him with a fierceness that robbed her of any rational thought. She threw off the coverlet and wrapped her arms tightly around her body and the thin chemise she wore. One thing was certain—when she got to wherever she was going, she would have proper clothing restored to her. She opened the door of her room a small crack—a rush of cold air hit her squarely. She slowly opened it wider and glanced down the hall. No one was about at the moment, although she could hear someone giggling down the hall.

She stepped out into the hallway, pulled the door shut behind her, then tiptoed across the hall. *Diah,* she hoped that Mrs. Cockburn was right, that he was in here and not some other guest who would think she'd come to pay a visit in the middle of the night. She rather imagined Mrs. Cockburn would appreciate any excuse to banish her.

She slowly turned the knob and pushed the door open. She saw instantly that the draft caused the fire in the hearth of this room to flare and dance. She slipped into the room and shut the door.

Nichol was in bed, but he'd come up on his elbow, watching her.

Maura stood frozen, looking at him, unsure what she ought to say. But then he held up the coverlet on his bed, revealing his naked body and silently inviting her in.

Maura ran across the room and climbed into his bed, and climbed on top of him.

"I feared it might be Miss Fabernet," he muttered as he kissed her.

She giggled. She felt no remorse, no guilt. She felt nothing but need for him to hold her, to kiss her, to fill her body. "*Mi Diah,* Mr. Bain, but you have captured me completely, you have," she said, and slid her mouth to his neck, then down his chest, to his nipple. "I donna know how to keep from being captured again, day after day."

"*Criosd,* Maura, donna stop now," he said roughly, and grabbed her head between his large hands and lifted it from his body so that he could kiss her.

She was disarmed, so completely powerless. He could do to her what he liked and she would welcome it. She didn't want to think, she wanted only to feel. She wanted him to love her as man and woman loved.

His breath was warm on her skin, his body a fire against her. He untied the lace of her chemise and dipped his head, filling his mouth with her breast. Maura pushed her chemise from her shoulders and slid it down to her waist so that he could ravage her body. He growled with approval, wrapped a thick arm around her waist, and abruptly flipped her onto her back. He straddled her, moving down her body.

She arched her back, moved her legs against his hips, pressed her knee against his hardness. He caressed the flare of her hip, then the soft flesh of her inner thigh, then put his body between her legs.

Maura's breath was quick with anticipation. Nichol began to trace a hot line down her belly with his lips and tongue, nipping at her belly button, then lower, until his head was between her legs. This was new, this was astounding. She thought she would lose her mind and lifted her hips, then cried out when his lips closed around her sex.

She was beyond rational thought, sunk into a cloud of oblivious pleasure, her body pulsing, her fingers searching, her mind completely gone. He'd aroused her to the point of complete madness, and she began to pant, desperate for the release. When it came to her, it was hard and long, sending her tumbling down a slide into pure, ethereal pleasure. And even in the heat of the moment, she understood it wasn't just the physical release—it was something much bigger. It was a sense of finding absolute sanctuary in another human being. It was allowing herself to be so vulnerable with another person that she was made that much stronger.

She had been guarded for so long, it was absolutely freeing to let go and trust him.

The release shuddered through her until she couldn't bear it any longer. She wiggled out from beneath him, pushed him onto his back, and climbed on top of him, straddling him, eager to feel him deep inside her. She slid down his shaft and watched his eyes flutter shut. He grabbed her hips, pressed his lips together, and opened his eyes, locking them with hers. And he kept them locked with hers as they began to rock in unison.

She believed he felt it, too. That he felt as vulnerable, felt as powerful, felt all the things she was feeling, and he was the same as her as they moved against each other. When his release neared, he sat up and folded her in one arm, braced himself with the other, and carried them home.

He held her tightly to him for a long moment, then slowly reclined with her onto his back. She pressed her hand against his bare chest, felt the wild beating of his heart. He felt it, too, she supposed—he covered her hand with his.

After several moments, she slowly lifted her head. A swath of her hair covered half his face and she pushed it away, stroked his jaw.

Nichol's eyes were closed. He lazily stroked her back, up and down, his fingers running the knobs of her spine. He said something so softly that she couldn't understand him. "Pardon?" she asked, and kissed his cheek.

"I said, you have undone me." He turned his head to her, kissed her tenderly on the mouth. "Utterly, irreparably undone me."

Those words filled her with indescribable joy. "Should I no' have done?"

He smiled, closed his eyes once more. "You should no' have done."

She laid her head against his chest again, drew a circle around his nipple with her finger and asked, "What do we do now, then?"

"Now?" He caressed her shoulder. "Sleep. The sun will be up before long, aye?"

That was not what she meant. He knew that was not what she meant. "Donna leave me here, Nichol," she said against his chest.

His embraced tightened. "Ah, *leannan*. Where would I take you, then? What would I do with you?"

"You might take me to Balhaire. Where is it, then?"

"Ah, Balhaire," he said. "Far in the Highlands." He told her about this fortress above the sea. He told her about a woman named Catriona, who had married the Duke of Montrose in spite of his considerable efforts to prevent it. He told her about the lady's home for wayward women.

"Her what?" Maura asked.

He chuckled, and it reverberated in his chest. He explained it all to her, and the time he'd spent there with this family, and as he talked, Maura had never desired to be anywhere quite like she desired to be there. "I want to go there," she said.

"Aye," he agreed wistfully.

But Maura was quite serious. She had never been to the Highlands and it seemed as good a place for them as any. Tucked away from the world. Where men wore plaids and women…well, she didn't know what women did there, but she'd find something.

"How was your supper this evening?" he asked.

Damn him, he'd not entertain her fantasy. "Tedious," she said with a sigh. "He's quite strange. He doesna know how to have a proper conversation."

"Aye, he's shy, he is. And his nerves get the best of him around you."

She lifted her head and looked at him. "Do you really think so?"

"Aye," he said, and stroked her face. "I donna know what else to think. He seems unusually distracted to me."

"I donna care if he is," Maura whispered. "Donna leave me with him, Nichol—"

"Lass. *Mo chridhe*," he said. "I'm to be on a ship at the end of a fortnight, aye? I canna take you with me. I have committed to it and I canna risk my livelihood."

That stung her. "All right, then, you canna take me with you. No' this time. But you can come back for me, Nichol."

He looked at her strangely. "I suspect you'd be married by the time I returned."

She hated that he said it and squeezed her eyes

shut for a moment. How could he be so distant with her now? Had their lovemaking not felt as profound to him? "You said I undo you!" she said, and pushed up, sitting up beside him. "I said you have captured me! What more can two people say to each other to indicate their true feelings?"

"There is more," he said, and played with the ends of her hair as he watched her.

There *was* more. Maura wanted to say it. She longed to say it. But she was afraid—if she trusted him with those words, words she'd never used before in her life, would he toss them aside and leave her anyway? She didn't think she could bear another betrayal. Not this one. Not something that had settled so deeply in her soul.

Nichol slowly sat up. "Maura, listen to me, please," he said quietly. "As much as I desire things to be different, they are no', are they? I canna give you this life, aye? I canna give you a fine house and a theatrical troupe to amuse you. Think of it—you will be mistress of this house—"

"This house has a mistress," she shot back.

"*You* will be mistress here. You will have the freedom to come and go as you please. It is the best possible solution. Had I no'…" He paused, seemed to consider what he would say next. "Had I no' come to esteem you so completely, I would tell you that you are a fool, that you could not have hoped for better than this house and this marriage. Dunnan will put you on a pedestal, he will."

"His mother will knock me off it."

"She willna do so once you are married. Donna fret about it—I will speak to him. But this is the best for you."

She pushed his hand away from her and crawled off the bed. "I've had quite enough of men explaining to me what is best for me," she said, and grabbed her chemise from the floor. "*I* know what is best for me, Nichol, and until this moment, *you* were best for me, aye?"

"I am trying to help you understand, Maura, that I am no' the best for you—"

"It is no' for you to decide!" she said loudly. "*I* will decide what is best for me."

"All right," he said with infuriating calm. "Is no' having a home best for you?"

"I donna care," she said petulantly.

"You donna even know what it means," he scoffed, and swung his legs over the side of the bed.

"Do I no', then?" she demanded, casting her arms wide. "Look around me, Mr. Bain—I have no place to call home, and I've no' had one in nearly a month."

"Is it best that sometimes you will have a fortune, and other times no' a farthing to your name?"

"That could happen to anyone, could it no'?"

"Maura—"

"Donna say it," she said, throwing up a hand. "Donna say a word, then, because I donna care what you think is best, do you hear me? I know what is best for me, and do you know what else I know, Nichol Bain? You could use someone to love you as much as I could."

"Do you love me, then, Maura?" he asked thoughtfully.

Tears suddenly filled her eyes. The euphoria she'd felt only moments ago had disappeared. She wanted to say that she did, but pride and fear of betrayal stopped her.

"Do you?" he asked again and stood.

"Would it matter to you if I did?" she whispered.

He did not reach for her. He looked pained, aggrieved, as if she'd insulted him or told him he was vile to her. "It would matter," he said softly. "More than I have words to convey, aye? But I've told you, I have no home. I move from one opportunity to the next. I canna provide for you, and I donna know what I would do to provide if I didna do this. But even if I could change who I am and make a home for you, it's more than that now. I have discovered I am a bastard born," he said low. "I canna claim a title, I canna claim an inheritance. I canna even put you at my brother's home, for he has come to revile me as much as my father."

"He does no'!"

"Aye, he does. Do you know what he said to me on the drive? He told me to never come there again. That his father had warned him about me, that I would endeavor to take what was rightfully his, and he'd no' allow me to ruin the peace that he would finally, at long last have."

She was stunned. "What did you say?"

"I told you. I told him the truth. That I had no' abandoned him, I'd been sent away. That I only loved him, that I've no desire to take from him. That I've wanted nothing from my father or Cheverock. But it's too late—the well has been poisoned by my father. I willna see you poisoned, lass. I willna see the resentment build in you. You deserve more. You deserve better than that which I can give you. And moreover, Maura, I must also decide what is best for me."

Maura gaped at him. He looked as bereft as he had the night he'd learned his father had lied to him all these years. As if he'd lost something quite dear. She pulled her chemise on over her head and turned away from him, walking across the room.

Nichol didn't try to stop her. He said nothing as she slipped out of the room.

She closed the door behind her and ran back to her room. Through the window, she could see the first pink light of day peeking out over the horizon on a glittering world of white.

She was freezing, but she suspected all the fire in the world could not warm her now.

CHAPTER TWENTY-TWO

NICHOL HATED HIMSELF.

He was pathetically weak, unable to deny himself, or Maura, for that matter. But he should have. If he were a good man, a decent man, he would have sent her back to her room. He ought to apologize for it, atone for it, but he didn't know if she could be appeased.

He tried to convince himself it was Dunnan's fault for being so bloody feckless. He would have a strong talk with him, then, convince Dunnan that the only way to salvage the damage he'd done was to persuade Maura of his true desire to marry her.

The last time Nichol was here, Dunnan had been quite adamant that he wanted a wife. He *needed* a wife. He'd begged Nichol to help him. Well, he'd helped him all right, had put his own damn heart on the line, and Dunnan had been nothing but a fool.

He would fix this. That's what he did, he fixed things, and he had yet to encounter a problem that could not be repaired. He had said last night that she'd undone him, and that she had. But he would put it all back together again, by hook or by crook. He would fix this for her, he would fix this for him.

He would not think of how badly he wanted to tell her he loved her, too. He couldn't tell her, for if he did, she would not accept what must be. He had meant it when he said she deserved better than to be married to a homeless bastard. She deserved all that Dunnan could give her.

Nichol had stared out the window of his room for what had felt like hours, watching the sun melt the snow. In the distance, he could hear the rattle of wagons as men pulled flats of stones over the roads to pack the snow so that coaches might pass. Come the morrow, he'd have no excuse to stay any longer.

He leaned his forehead against the cold pane of glass and closed his eyes. *How would he do it?* He couldn't bear the thought of leaving her. Was it possible he could convince Dunnan no' to marry her, but to keep her here until he came back for her? Was it possible he could find a livelihood that would grant him the opportunity to be a husband, a father? Was it possible that for once in his life he could allow intimacy to flourish in him rather than shut it away?

Ah, but Dunnan had told everyone that he intended to marry her. And what if Nichol didn't come back? He was bound for France with a Welshman—anything could happen. He could be delayed, or worse, he could be killed. Then what? Would she live out her days here at Luncarty, unmarried, with no prospects, a prisoner in another house? At least if she married Dunnan, she could come and go as she pleased. She would make new friends. She could take a lover if she so desired.

The thought of her with another man made him feel nauseated. There were no answers that suited him. Nothing that put him at ease.

He remained at the window until the steady staccato of *drip drip drip* drove him mad. The sun was nearly overhead when he went down to breakfast.

There was no one in the breakfast room except Maura. She was once again dressed in her plain frock, her hair bound at her neck. She had the hint of shadows under her eyes, for she'd not slept. Neither had he.

She scarcely looked at him as he entered the room and calmly continued to butter a point of toast. "Good day," he said.

"Bonjour," she said briskly.

Nichol went to the sideboard and filled a plate with bread and cheese. He'd just taken his seat when Dunnan came in the dining room, his natural hair sticking up in unnatural directions, and wearing a free-flowing dressing gown. "Oh aye, you're both up, are you? Good morning."

"Good afternoon," Maura said without looking up from her toast.

"Pardon? Oh, indeed it is," Dunnan said. He sat at the head of the table and gestured to his butler to pour tea. "Quite an evening we had, did we no'? Did you enjoy yourself, then?" Dunnan asked. He was looking at Nichol, but Maura said, "Aye."

That was the moment Nichol lost all patience. If Dunnan had shown her the slightest bit of deference, they wouldn't be having this terribly awkward breakfast. Everything would have been settled. He wanted to shout at him to be a man for once in his life. "Where were you last night, if I may?" Nichol asked, in a voice curt enough to bring Maura's head up.

"Me?" Dunnan said, avoiding Nichol's gaze. "Oh, well, I was afflicted with the most terrible of headaches, I was. I thought it best to take a tincture and go to sleep."

He hadn't looked as if he'd had a headache when the dancing had begun. And he didn't look as if he'd slept any more than Nichol or Maura had.

"Did you see how thick the snow is?" Dunnan asked with sudden cheeriness. "You'll no' make your escape today, Bain. They'll need more time to clear the roads, aye?"

"That will give us time to have a proper talk, aye?"

"You and me?" Dunnan asked as he accepted his tea from the butler.

"The three of us—you, me and Miss Darby," Nichol corrected.

Maura looked at him. "Me?"

"Aye."

Maura frowned down at her plate.

"Fillian, please do tell Mamma that Mr. Bain should like a word—"

"Do no such thing, Fillian," Nichol interrupted sharply, and leveled a look on Dunnan. "Your mother is no' needed, lad. This is your business, and yours alone."

"Yes, of course," he said firmly. Then, "But she prefers to keep informed with household matters."

"This is no' a household matter. Your mother is no' invited."

"Ah." Dunnan shifted in his seat. "She'll no' care for that, no."

Nichol leaned across the table and pinned him with a look. "I beg your pardon, Dunnan, are you no' the man of the house? Or would that be your mamma?"

Dunnan paled and glanced sheepishly at Maura. "Of course I am the head of this house," he snapped. "I donna care for the insinuation, Bain."

"I'll say no more," Nichol said. "Shall we meet at half past two in your study, then?"

"Aye," Dunnan said quickly.

Nichol speared a piece of cheese. "Miss Darby?" he asked, and looked up.

"Aye," she said firmly, and folded her arms across her middle as she sank back in her chair.

"There then, it's all settled," Dunnan said, his good nature restored to him. "Fillian, build a fire in my study. It's so blessed cold in this house I donna think we'll ever see it properly heated." He began to natter on about the expense of heating this house in the course of the winter, and had thought to go to peat, as he'd heard it was far superior burning quality, even if it did have a rather pungent smell.

As he nattered on, Nichol looked across the table to Maura. Her gaze narrowed slightly, and he believed that she was silently challenging him in some way. But then she stood, causing Dunnan to nearly knock over his chair in his haste to stand. "Until half past two then," she said, and strode out of the room with the same determination he'd seen when she desired to leave Garbett House.

Dunnan slowly eased himself into his seat once more. "Now what have I done?" he asked plaintively.

There was no way to explain to Dunnan that what he'd done was to be himself, and he shook his head. "Just be there," he said, and stood, too. "Donna be late and do *no'* bring your mother, man."

"No," Dunnan said, his color draining.

AT HALF PAST TWO, Nichol was the first to arrive in Dunnan's study. He was restless, wanted this meeting over and done. He walked to the window and stared out. He wanted this marriage business settled once and for all, and by extension, his own fate. Then he would take his leave. Get on with it, so to speak. Push down the feelings as he had trained himself to do. As a lad, he had learned to mask his disappointment and hurt behind his unsmiling face. Once, the housekeeper had advised him to look in the distance and imagine something that pleased him. A puppy. A girl. As a man, he preferred to push his feelings down into a bottle of gin.

As he contemplated his fate, he noticed the tracks of two horses in the snow below the window along the path that led to the stables. He wondered idly who had tried to leave when the snow was so deep?

The door opened behind him, and Nichol turned

from the window and the curious tracks in the snow. Thank the saints, but Dunnan had dressed properly, had bobbed his hair, and was cleanly shaven. He walked straight to the sideboard and poured brandy.

Nichol had known Dunnan for several years now, and through some trying times. He had never seen him look as out of sorts as he had these past two days. One moment he was laughing, the next he seemed almost despairing. Even when Nichol had first met him, and there had been the matter of an astounding debt, he'd not seemed so ill at ease. Perhaps he really was simply extraordinarily uncomfortable in the presence of women. But no, he'd seen Dunnan with women...the sort of women that inhabited gaming hells...but nevertheless, he was not so uneasy.

A thought suddenly occurred to Nichol. Was it possible something was afoot now? Had Dunnan gone and done something stupid? He glanced at the open door, then at Dunnan. He strode across the room and closed it, then turned to face his friend.

Dunnan frowned at the closed door. "Miss Darby has no' yet arrived."

"Dunnan. You know you can trust me, aye?"

"Pardon? Aye, I do, Bain—"

"Is everything all right, then?"

Dunnan blanched. He looked again at the door. "Why would you ask such a thing at this moment, of all moments?"

"You are no' yourself. You are rather apprehensive."

"No," he said, and put down the brandy. He

glanced wildly about the room, almost as if he was looking for another exit. "I'm no' in the least, Bain. But I…well, you *know* verra well how I am when it comes to the fairer sex. I'm quite hopeless, and she," he said, gesturing to the door, "she is *verra* bonny. Too bonny for the likes of me."

"Aye, she is bonny," Nichol agreed, and felt another stab of regret and guilt and repugnance for himself. He had always considered himself a man of upstanding moral character—it was imperative to him that he was, to contrast with the man he'd thought was his father—but his actions here had been deplorable, and the knife dug in a little deeper each time he thought of it. He felt at odds with himself now. As if everything he thought he'd understood about himself was wrong. All those years he strove to be someone his father would respect, all those years he believed something must be fundamentally wrong with him, and none of it true. All those years he'd avoided intimacy for fear of exposing the vile thing in him.

Nothing was true.

He wasn't sure who he was anymore.

There was something about Dunnan's claim that rang false, too. "Are you certain there is nothing more?" he asked.

"Aye," Dunnna said, and swallowed.

Bain studied him a moment. "How is the linen trade?" He'd seen the workhouses in the distance this morning, and smoke rising from the chimneys. The work was continuing in spite of the snow.

"The linen is verra good," Dunnan said. "Better than good, if I may. I've been down to London to open a new warehouse." He abruptly drained his snifter of the brandy.

Dunnan had promised to stay away from London. He had agreed he was faced with too many temptations when he was in London. "*Have* you," Nichol drawled, trying not to sound accusatory.

"It was a little jaunt, really. Mamma accompanied me and we attended the theater—"

The door swung open and Maura stepped inside, effectively halting any more conversation on the subject. She paused just inside the door and looked at the two of them warily.

"Miss Darby," Nichol said, and cast a sidelong look at Dunnan.

He seemed to understand Nichol's look; he jerked to attention and offered his hand to Maura, intending, Nichol assumed, to help her into a seat.

But Maura ignored his hand and walked to the center of the room where they were standing. She clasped her hands tightly at her waist and cleared her throat. "Mr. Cockburn."

"Aye?"

"If we may dispense with the pleasantries?"

"Pardon?"

"If I may be so bold, then, I was brought here with the understanding that you intended to offer for my hand in marriage. Do you, or do you no', intend to do so?"

Nichol and Dunnan exchanged a look of astonishment. Nichol had never heard a woman speak so directly about such a delicate matter. Not even the Mackenzie women, whom, he had learned, were quite outspoken.

Dunnan looked almost stricken by her question. He coughed. He glanced helplessly at his empty snifter. "Well, ah…*aye*," he said with an affirmative nod of his head, and lifted his chin so that he could rub the underside of it with two fingers, as if contemplating, when, precisely, he meant to extend his offer. "I certainly *do* intend…that is, I intend if that is what *you* want. That is to say, if you will, umm…have me."

Maura cocked her head to one side and openly examined him. "I've no choice in the matter. What of your mother?"

"Pardon?"

"You are surely aware that she doesna want a union between us, aye?"

"*My* mother?" Dunnan said, sounding quite baffled.

"Aye, your mother, Mr. Cockburn. Mr. Bain's mother is no longer living."

Nichol choked down a cough of surprise.

"It would seem you are no' aware, then," she said crisply when Dunnan looked to Nichol for help. "Allow me to inform you that your mother doesna wish me to be here. She's made it quite plain to me, that she has."

"There must be some mistake," Dunnan said. "She *does* want you here, Miss Darby, on my word!"

"I think she rather likes being mistress here," Maura pointed out.

Diah, but she would have it all out, the consequences be damned, and Nichol couldn't help but admire her for it. It was precisely the sort of thing he'd do. One could not negotiate terms if one's cards were not on the table.

Poor Dunnan stared at her as if she were speaking French.

"Do you think, Mr. Cockburn, that you might have a word with your mother, then, and set the matter to rights?" she asked curiously.

Good God! She was bloody well bold and direct and Nichol couldn't have been more aroused.

"I will," Dunnan said, nodding adamantly that he would. "At once. Straightaway. Shall I ring for her?"

"No," Maura said quickly. "No' until we've come to a mutual understanding, aye?"

"Aye, of course, of course," Dunnan said, nodding even more violently, to the point Nichol worried he might damage his brain. "Would you like a wee bit of brandy, Miss Darby?" he asked, gesturing to his snifter. "I'm feeling a wee bit parched myself."

"No, thank you," Maura said pleasantly. "Now, as for your mother, I would suggest that if we are to marry, she might enjoy a long holiday. Perhaps to France."

Dunnan coughed so hard that Nichol was compelled to pound him on the back. "Miss Darby," Nichol said low, trying to warn her from taking this so far that Dunnan had no choice but to cry off. Perhaps that was her intention.

"I beg your pardon, Mr. Bain, but if you please, it would seem your role here is done, is it no'?" she asked coolly, and fixed her light blue gaze on him. She was challenging him, all right. He could almost feel the frustration radiating from her. "This concerns me and Mr. Cockburn. Is that no' so, Mr. Cockburn?"

"It certainly is. B-but I, for one, should like Mr. Bain to stay."

She shrugged. "If you wish. I've nothing to hide from him," she said, leveling another look at him. "I think you should know, Mr. Cockburn, that if you would like to make an offer of marriage, you must be prepared to make some accommodations."

Dunnan gaped at her. So did Nichol. *This woman!* She was incredible, prepared to lay out the terms of her survival here, as if she had the bargaining power. She had *no* bargaining power that he could see, but she had come in here as if she owned all of Luncarty. She had taken Dunnan's measure, had found him to be without the slightest hint of a spine, and was battling forth, and Dunnan was allowing it.

She was brilliant, and Nichol was in awe of her.

Dunnan may have admired her as well, but at present, he was quaking in his boots.

"First, I should like an allowance, aye?" she said cheerfully. "I am in need of new clothes since the ones I had were dispersed. I donna want to have to ask for every pence, sir."

Nichol thought this quite smart of her—this would be the easiest thing Dunnan could agree to. Money was not an object for him, not since his debts had been settled.

"Absolutely, Miss Darby. Consider it done," Dunnan said with great verve, and likely thought that was the end to her demands.

It was not.

"As I said, I should like some distance from your mother until such time she is at ease with our arrangement. I think it impossible that we might embark on married life with someone constantly between us, aye?"

Dunnan winced. "Now that—" he said, shaking his finger "—*that* is a wee bit more problematic, you see. I am responsible for her."

"I understand completely," she said graciously. "You are the best sort of son, sir. But is it no' possible to be responsible for her at a distance, then? It's no' as if she needs you to be her nurse."

Dunnan's face began to turn red. "We are verra close, my mother and I. Perhaps we might move her to another part of the house?" he asked hopefully.

Maura smiled. "Perhaps another house altogether. Please do think on what I've said."

Dunnan blew his cheeks out, then sucked them back in and nodded his agreement. "Is there more, then?"

"Aye. I donna know how to say this delicately, so I'll just say it, shall I? There will be no conjugal relations until we are certain we are compatible."

Now it was Nichol's turn to cough and cover his cry of surprise. Maura had just thrown down a gauntlet, daring Dunnan to pick it up. Dunnan would not pick it up. He didn't know how to pick it up.

He looked to Nichol with wide eyes, but Nichol shook his head. He could not help him with this. No man could help him. He was an island in the sea of gentlemen who would never agree to such terms.

Dunnan looked at Maura forlornly. "No conjugal felicity, madam?" he asked, his voice going higher. "Is that no' the foundation of a good marriage?"

"Perhaps it is, Mr. Cockburn, but I should think compatibility would be higher on the list than that, would you no' agree, then? I hardly know you, or you me. You have *verra* graciously agreed to marry me, in spite of my current state, which, I admit is lacking. I am grateful to you for that. But I still must insist on certain conditions, aye? I think it will benefit us both, then."

"But when—"

"If we do come together," she said, coloring a little herself, "it will be a mutual desire. I have one last demand, then."

"What could possibly be left?" Dunnan groaned. "I'm to give you my money, remove my mother and stay out of the marriage bed. What more, Miss Darby?"

"This is mine." She put her hand to her necklace around her neck. "It is all I have of a family I remember with great fondness, and I will no' part with it."

"No, of course no'," he said, flicking a wrist at her necklace. "That is the least of my concerns."

"Thank you," she said. She drew a deep breath. "Verra well, those are my terms. What are yours, then, Mr. Cockburn?"

Dunnan stared at her. Even Nichol felt a little tongue-tied. "May I think on it?" Dunnan asked carefully.

"Of course! Take all the time you need." She smiled prettily.

"I shall. But at present, I'm a bit discombobulated, I am," he said, and touched two fingers to his temple. "This has been a most unusual meeting, has it no'?"

"Well, I have given you a lot to think on, I have," she said sympathetically. "I beg your pardon for it, but I thought it important. If I may, then, I'll take my leave."

"Please," Dunnan said weakly, and gestured to the door. She twirled and walked smartly out of the room without a word, her head high.

Dunnan slowly turned and looked at Nichol. He was dumbfounded, quite at a loss.

For once, Nichol didn't have an answer for him.

He didn't have an answer for any of them. He was completely out of answers.

CHAPTER TWENTY-THREE

THE REST OF the guests began to rouse themselves at three o'clock, stumbling out of their rooms, heading downstairs to find something to eat and drink. By five o'clock, the house was alive with music and laughter.

As they were housebound, they decided on the production of a play, using the grand salon's furnishings as props. That was followed by charades, where common phrases were acted out by one team, while the other team was made to guess. They continued until a misinterpretation of a word led to a few punches between two gentlemen who had very nearly finished a bottle of whisky between them.

From charades, the group moved to games of chance. Platters of meats, bread and cheese were brought from the kitchens, and everyone helped themselves. Wine and whisky flowed, and Mrs. Cockburn, who had clearly imbibed too much, remarked loudly to all that she would host cards every Sunday once her son was married. By seven o'clock, her laugh had become loud and harsh, rising above everyone else.

By seven o'clock, everyone was loud and harsh.

Maura took herself to her room at that point. She had not found the day particularly diverting, as furious as she was with the world at large and Nichol in particular. She could scarcely bear to look at him, for each time she did, her heart twisted into a painful knot. She had decided after last night had bled into today that she would make the best of this wretched, *wretched* situation, and if she had to marry Mr. Cockburn, she would at least make certain that she had some say in what would happen to her. That's all she wanted! A voice in what was to be her fate.

Nichol sat next to her more than once, but she refused to be wooed by him. He had made himself quite clear this morning in his bed—she was not best for him. Not that Maura believed that for as much as a minute. Nor did she believe that *he* believed it. But he had made up his mind and he would not yield, would not bend his way of thinking. He was stubbornly determined to carry the mantle of *bastard*. He was a rolling stone, or so he fancied, and he would not be burdened with the likes of her, no matter what his heart might be telling him.

"Miss Darby? Are you in there?" a muffled voice called on the other side of her door. That was followed with a firm knock.

Maura stood up from her bed, where she'd been very close to tears and opened the door a bit to see who wanted her.

Miss Fabernet's smiling face peeked at her. "I've brought you something," she said.

Maura opened the door a little wider, but Miss

Fabernet pushed it all the way open and sailed into the room with an armful of garments.

"What is this, then?"

"What do you think? I've brought you some clothing."

"Oh, but that's no' necessary," Maura said. "I've a few gowns," she added, pointing to her bag.

"Are they as sad as the one you are wearing now?" Miss Fabernet asked gaily. "If they are, mine is an errand of mercy. And besides, I couldn't remain in the salon another moment. Mr. Johnson's hands take to wandering to places they ought not to go when he's pissed. He's being quite wretched this evening." She shrugged. "Otherwise, he's a perfect gentleman." She tossed the gowns onto the bed. There were four.

"Is Mr. Johnson no' married to the lass with the red hair, then?" Maura asked.

"He certainly is," Miss Fabernet said, and winked. "But you know how men are."

Maura knew very well how men were.

"Moreover, Mr. Cockburn has left the gathering to his mother, who is a dear, she is, but she does like her card games when the rest of us would prefer to sing, and she doesn't care to lose, if you take my meaning," she said, and waggled her brows at Maura.

"I'm no' surprised in the least," Maura muttered. "Where is Mr. Cockburn, then?"

"I've not the slightest idea," Miss Fabernet said.

If Maura were lucky, he'd be off thinking of a way to cry off of their supposed marriage agreement.

Miss Fabernet put her hands on her hips and

surveyed the gowns she'd brought. She picked up a green-and-white stripe and held it up, just under Maura's chin, and studied it.

"How long will you and the others stay, then?" Maura asked.

"Oh, we're off to Edinburra tomorrow if the roads are passable. We're to perform there." She tossed aside the green-and-white gown.

"You're the lucky one, are you no'?" Maura said morosely as Miss Fabernet held up a pale pink gown.

"Aren't you lucky, too? You'll have this huge house all to yourself."

"I donna want this huge house to myself."

Miss Fabernet laughed as if that were preposterous. "What of your Mr. Bain?" She glanced up and smiled mischievously. "Aren't you lucky there, as well?"

Maura swallowed down a lump of regret. "He is no' my Mr. Bain. He escorted me here, that's all. From here, he is to Wales."

"Wales!" Miss Fabernet said, and clucked her tongue. "I'll have you know there is nothing there."

"Apparently there is a man with a problem that needs solving, aye?"

"Well, that's a pity. He's quite handsome. Never mind that, are you not to marry Mr. Cockburn? He told us all about it the night before you arrived. He'd said Mr. Bain had arranged his marriage."

"Aye," Maura admitted. "But I donna want to marry him."

Miss Fabernet laughed gleefully. "Thank goodness you don't! I thought you'd lost your mind, darling, for he is quite odd, isn't he? If you don't want to marry him, you ought to come with us."

Maura laughed at the suggestion.

"I mean it with all sincerity!" Miss Fabernet insisted. "You're a fine dancer. You can sing, can't you?"

"What?" Maura laughed again. "No' well at all."

"No one said you need sing *well*," Miss Fabernet said coyly. "Sing softly if you can't carry a tune." She winked at Maura and held the pink gown up a little higher. "Yes, I think the pink. It looks lovely with your skin and hair. It is my gift to you."

"I couldna accept—"

"And I can't bear to see you in a drab gown like this one more time. You will accept, and you'll wear it now, won't you?"

"Thank you," Maura said, smiling. She began to unfasten her gown. "Where will you perform in Edinburra?" she asked curiously.

"Oh, I hardly know where. On a stage, of course, but Mr. Johnson is the one who arranges things." She twirled Maura around to undo her skirt. "It's paid work, you know. It's how we earn our living."

It sounded intriguing to Maura, to sing and dance and be paid a wage for it. "But where do you live?"

"We take rooms. Some of them are quite nice. Others, not as nice, but we make do. You should come." She reached around Maura and held up the pink gown so that Maura could see it in the mirror.

"See how rosy it makes your cheeks appear. You're very pretty, Miss Darby. You'd be quite a draw."

"A draw!" Maura laughed self-consciously. "No one would want to hear me sing."

Miss Fabernet tucked her chin onto Maura's shoulder and looked at her in the reflection of the glass. "Don't be naïve, darling. The gentlemen don't come to hear the ladies sing. That's for Mr. Johnson to do. They come to gaze at us with lust and envy, that's what. And besides, I'll teach you to sing if you really want to know."

Maura stared back at Miss Fabernet's reflection. It was absurd. But so was everything else that had happened to her in the last month. What did she have to lose? She would much rather ramble about the country dancing and singing God only knew where than end up here, married to a milksop of a man with a mother who despised the very idea of having to share her son or her house.

"What do you think?" Miss Fabernet asked.

"I think aye," Maura said.

Miss Fabernet squealed with delight and hopped back, clapping her hands. "Splendid! I'll tell Mr. Johnson straightaway. You'll not be sorry, Miss Darby. I'm Susan, by the way. Susan Fabernet."

Maura smiled. "Maura. What happens after Edinburra, then?" she asked.

"After?" Susan shrugged. "We'll return to London and craft an entirely new performance."

London! That was exciting to Maura. Granted, a theatrical life was certainly not what Maura's father would have wanted for her, or one she would ever have envisioned. But she liked to think that neither would her father have saddled her with Mr. Cockburn for the rest of her life.

Nichol had said she had no other choice. Well, now she had one.

She turned around to Susan and began to shrug out of her day gown. "I'm coming," she said firmly. "I'll see if the pink fits, aye?"

"You've made me very happy!" Susan exclaimed. "You'll not regret it, Maura, on my word," she vowed.

LATER, WHEN MAURA had dressed in the pink gown with the same white petticoat with little red hearts, she and Susan went downstairs to join what was now a very disorderly affair. There was some dancing, although it wasn't as good as the night before, seeing as how most of them could scarcely stand, given all they'd drunk. More food had appeared, and plates were passed around. There was no civility to it—they ate with their fingers, with forks scavenged from the kitchen. Mrs. Cockburn, whose ruddy face flagged her inebriation, cackled with great glee at the attempts to dance and sing.

There was no sign of Mr. Cockburn, but Nichol stood off to one side, subdued, his expression shuttered. He noticed Maura the moment she entered the room, and she felt the yearning from him, could see it in the way he looked at her. She wanted to go to him, but she wouldn't do it—the remaining tatters of her pride forbade it. He had made his decision, and she would not beg.

When the dancing was done, a game of Whist was suggested, and several of them sat at tables to play. Nichol remained where he was, his eyes fixed on Maura. Even when she wasn't looking at him, she could feel his gaze on her body. She refused the offer of wine, and after a hand or two, she bowed out of the game and let Susan take her place.

At the other table, the game had turned very competitive, and others were gathering around to wager on the hands being played. Maura had never understood gambling. She couldn't imagine why someone would want to risk the money they'd earned or inherited on chance, which, by very definition, was a mere *chance*. She found the process of betting tedious, and walked around the room, looking at things, examining them. A porcelain figure of a frog on a toadstool. A small brass sculpture of the Madonna.

She felt someone come near and glanced over her shoulder.

Nichol smiled softly. "How is it possible you are more ravishing every day, then?"

He was the ravishing one. He was wearing pantaloons, a creamy gold waistcoat and a black coat. She wanted to touch the sleeve of his coat, but said coolly, "Good evening."

"Aha, at last, the first words you have spoken to me since this morning."

She bent over to look at a small portrait of a

young woman and realized it was Mrs. Cockburn.
"I thought there was nothing left to say."

"Maura," he said, his voice low and silken.

"Am I wrong?" she asked, and straightened, turning around to face him. She wanted to see his face
when he answered. Was there more to say? Would
he say it?

"Might we walk?" he asked.

"It's freezing outside."

"There are miles of hallways, are there no'? We
can walk there. In silence," he added, glancing back
when Mrs. Cockburn suddenly shrieked with delight
at something.

"Verra well," Maura agreed, and walked with him
out the door.

In the hallway, the voices of the others began to
fade. So did the acrid smell of smoke from hearths
at full blaze all day. A full moon lighted their path
through the windows of a long hallway, helped by
an occasional candle in a wall sconce. The two of
them walked in silence, him with his hands at his
back, hers with her hands clasped before her. She
was acutely, painfully aware of him beside her, of
his physical presence, of his height, his strength.
She wanted to hate him, but it was impossible. She
longed for him.

She *loved* him.

That's what made this so very painful, so very
awkward. She wanted him to say all the things to
her that she wanted to say to him.

He paused at a window and looked up at the full

moon. "I find it curious that Dunnan had no' come down this evening."

Maura stepped up beside him to look at the same moon. "I hope he's racking his mind for a proper way to cry off, I do," she suggested.

The corners of Nichol's eyes crinkled with his smile. "If he were a wise man, he'd be looking for a way to wed you and never lose you, aye?"

The sentiment surprised her mildly, and she looked at him. "Are you no' cross with me, then?"

He turned to face her, leaning against the sill. "I was proud of you, lass." His gaze moved to her mouth. "So verra proud of you."

"Why?"

"Because you stood up for yourself. That requires courage and a leap of faith that most donna have. Dunnan didna have it, aye? He should have tossed you out on your arse," he said with a chuckle.

"*Diah,* but I wish he had," she muttered.

Nichol touched her collarbone. Maura didn't push his hand away, as much as she would like to have done. She craved his touch at the same time she cursed it. "You should no' say such things, *leannan*. He is your salvation," he murmured.

Maura snorted her opinion of that. "He is *no'*. I'll no' marry him, Nichol."

"No?" he asked calmly, almost as if he'd been waiting for her to say it.

"Are you no' surprised, then?"

He laughed softly. "Should I be surprised at something you've said at every turn, then? After the way he received you, I would no' have been surprised to hear that you'd fled."

She folded her arms. "I *intend* to flee."

"Oh? And where will you go, then?" he asked.

He was entirely too casual. He didn't believe her, she realized. He thought she was being petulant. "You think you're the only one who can fix things, do you? Well, you're no'. I'm joining the troupe."

That certainly caught his attention. He lifted his gaze from her décolletage. "I beg your pardon?"

"Aye," she said, nodding. "I intend to join the troupe. I leave with them on the morrow for Edinburra." She cocked a brow and silently challenged him to tell her she could not.

He obliged her. "Maura, you canna do that. Are you mad?"

"Why no', I ask you? *You* said I have no choice, but now I do."

"Because the living is hard. Women from the stage generally donna have easy lives. They are entirely too dependent on men in this world who donna care for them."

"Just like I am here," she pointed out.

He shook his head and put his palm against her neck. "*Leannan*, listen to me, aye? You'd no' have an easy life—"

"Is that what you think I want?" she asked, and pushed his hand away from her neck. "An easy life?"

He frowned with confusion. "Why would you *no'* want an easy life?"

"Why would I? Can you imagine anything more

lifeless than an easy life? You, of all people, know how dreadfully tedious it would be to have an easy life here. What would I do, then? Needlework unto my death?"

He put his hand on her arm to soothe her, but Maura shook it off. "Donna touch me, Mr. Bain, I beg of you," she said, surprised by how much emotion came tumbling out with her words. "Donna be tender, donna smile at me. You must know—you *must* know—what my feelings are for you. You must know how impossible it is to know you will leave me here. It is too much to be borne. It is beyond my ability to endure, seeing you walk out that door, and me to remain here with…with *them*, knowing that I *love* you, just as you guessed, knowing that I long for you and no other, and I…" She broke off, felt herself sagging. She caught herself on the windowsill. Nichol pulled her into his embrace.

"Mi Diah," he breathed. "It is just as difficult for me, Maura, you know that it is. My feelings for you are the same—"

"They're no'. If they were the same, you would never ask this of me. You would never let me go. Do you love me?"

He lifted her face in his hands. "Aye," he said solemnly. "I love you, Maura Darby. I love you above all others."

"Then donna leave me here," she said tearfully.

Nichol responded by kissing her. He put his soft mouth to hers, his breath warm, and nipped at her bottom lip.

Maura was overwhelmed with emotion, the intoxicating mix of love and adoration and desire. She felt as if she were breathing underwater, trying to kick to a surface where her thoughts weren't so muddled by the tug of her heart. She rose up on her toes, her arms finding his neck. A million little thoughts danced rapidly through her mind as her tongue tangled with his. She was sinking, dragged below the surface again, wrapped in the sensations only he could give her. She felt almost feverish, worried that she would never have this moment again, that she was grasping desperately for happiness that would, in the end, elude her.

She grabbed onto the lapels of his coat to anchor herself. Nichol moaned with his own want, and with one hand he held her tight, as he caressed her neck, her face, with the other. She could feel his arousal, could feel the beat of his heart as she pressed against him. He *did* love her. *He did.*

It was as if he heard her thoughts, for his grip of her tightened, and his fingers splayed against the side of her head as he thrust his tongue into her mouth. He twisted her about and put her back against the wall, pinning her there with his arms and legs, his hands sliding down her body, his thumb brushing across the hard peak of her breast through the fabric. Her womb fluttered, her breath left her. Tiny little waves of pleasure rolled through her, each of them bigger than the last. She wanted to remove her gown, wanted to feel his skin and the hardness of him against every bit of her. He tasted and shaped her lips as his hands explored her, and Maura thought she would come apart like a rag doll, her seams dissolving, and everything about her would flit away on some gust of cold wind.

He suddenly lifted his head. "Never doubt, Maura," he said hoarsely. "Never doubt what you mean to me, aye?" He kept his gaze locked on hers as he slid down her body, then began to kiss the skin above her décolletage, one hand spanning her entire rib cage, the heel of the other pressing against her breast. "Let's go upstairs, then," he said against the swell of her breast.

The prurient sensations unfurling within her had made her incapable of speaking. Her hands tangled in his hair, fell to his shoulders and the muscles in his back.

"Upstairs, aye? To my room," he said again with breathless anticipation. "I canna bear another moment in this hallway, no' like this."

Maura wanted it, too, she wanted it as desperately as anything she had ever wanted. But she caught his head between her hands and made him look at her. "No," she said.

He stared at her. "No?"

"If you mean to leave me here, I'll no' allow you to hurt me any more than you have, Nichol."

"You donna understand what I mean. I love you, Maura. I will never—"

He suddenly paused and lifted his head.

Maura heard it, too. A lot of shouting. Not the sort

of shouting that came with drunken reverie. This was coarse.

Nichol dropped his hands from her and stepped away from the wall, listening.

"What is it, then?" Maura asked. "Are they fighting over cards?"

But Nichol shook his head. "Something has happened," he said, and straightened his clothes, his hair. "Stay here, lass. I'll go and see." He started down the hall toward the shouting.

Maura stood there only a moment. *I will never what?* she wondered. What had he meant to say?

The shattering sound of what could only be a gunshot made her jump. She pushed away from the wall and hurried after Nichol. She was not staying put.

CHAPTER TWENTY-FOUR

NICHOL KNEW THE moment he entered the salon that Dunnan was responsible. His first, unbidden thought was that he'd been gambling again.

He took note of the three men with guns, all of them pointed at the group of actors, gathered like sheep in the corner of the room. He took note of the hole in the ceiling. And he took note of the man standing in back, casually studying a nail.

A million little thoughts raced too quickly through Nichol's mind for him to catch. The agitation, the whispers, the recognition that the man in back, in the long dark green cloak, was who he'd seen speaking with Dunnan last night. He was not a guest, not a member of the troupe as Nichol had surmised, but a different sort of visitor. The tracks of horses he'd seen in the snow belonged to this man. Whatever Dunnan had said yesterday had not appeased him, apparently, for he'd come back today.

Which could only mean that Dunnan didn't have the money he owed. *Again.*

The troupe was clinging to each other, their drunkenness pushed aside by their collective fear. Mrs. Cockburn had not left her seat at the gaming table and was looking wildly about, her aggravation clearly evident in her expression. Dunnan stood nervously between the men and the rest of them, his expression one of confusion and abject fear. Even from across the room—Nichol had entered at the far end of the salon—he could see the perspiration shining on Dunnan's face.

He surveyed the scene and weighed the options. He heard the door behind him open—Maura nearly collided with him, catching herself on his arm.

"*Diah,* I told you to stay behind," he muttered under his breath.

"What is it?" she asked, ignoring his admonishment. "What has happened?"

"Does the lass want to know what has happened?" asked the man in the green cloak. He sauntered forward. "I'll tell you what has happened, that I will, lassie. We have come to call on Mr. Cockburn, but he did not care to give us entry, in spite of having given half of England entry," he said, sweeping his arm toward the troupe. "But then again, he owes us a fair sum, he does, and he's not yet thought how to pay it."

The man had a mean way of speaking. An uneducated English accent. Nichol glanced at Dunnan.

"Mr. Cockburn!" his mother said sharply. "Is this true?"

Dunnan turned to his mother, his expression that of a child who had been caught being naughty. "Mamma, you must forgive me," he said desperately.

That settled it—Dunnan was a weak fool, and

Nichol wanted to kick himself for ever having thought to marry Maura to him.

The man in the green cloak began to walk around the room, studying the guests, his eyes on the women's jewels. "Now, I could rob you all of your jewelry," he mused as he moved by them. "Alas, all I see is cheap costume." He turned his head and looked at Maura. Nichol imagined that her necklace shone like a beacon across the room.

"Except for that one," he said, and strolled across the room.

Maura's hand instantly went to her throat.

Nichol stepped in front of her. "Who are you?" he demanded of the man.

"Me? Why I am Julian Pepper, at your service, milord," he said with a sneer, and bowed with exaggerated flourish. "Purveyor in hard to obtain goods, moneylender and governor of justice and truth." He laughed.

His clothes were expensive, yet worn. He was wearing a wig made of horsehair. His shoes were muddied, his chin rough with stubble and he smelled of smoke.

"What business have you here, before Cockburn's guests and mother, then?" Nichol asked.

Julian Pepper put his hand to his chest and reared backward. "I beg your pardon, sir, but are you the man responsible here? I thought it Mr. Cockburn."

Dunnan looked almost tearful, as if he thought he was about to meet his Maker. "I didna know how to put it all to rights, Bain, on my word, I didna know."

"Put what to rights?" Nichol asked, although he already knew the answer. He wanted to hear Dunnan say it.

Mr. Pepper looked at Dunnan, who was having trouble answering the basic question. "Shall I say?" he asked cheerfully. "He owes a bit of money, he does, due to his wagering. Uncontrollable wagering, I should amend. He borrowed a tidy sum from my benefactor."

Dunnan winced, but offered no alternative explanation.

"I told you no' to go to London," Nichol muttered.

"I didna listen!" Dunnan said tearfully. "'Tis my fault. All my fault."

"There is no dispute as to that," Nichol said coolly.

"Now then," Mr. Pepper said. "How shall we see this debt repaid, sirs?"

Someone in the troupe moved or spoke, and one of Mr. Pepper's ruffians shouted, "Stop there, lad, or I'll blast your bloody head from your shoulders, I will." The troupe sounded like a flock of morning wrens as they made little mewling cries and huddled closer together.

"See here!" Mrs. Cockburn said, and hauled herself to her feet and strode across the room to Mr. Pepper and grabbed his arm. Mr. Pepper twisted around and slapped her hard across her cheek.

Everyone gasped. Nichol was stunned, and he put his arm out, reflexively, across Maura. "Donna lay another hand, sir," he said low.

"Or what?" Mr. Pepper asked loudly. "You'll

single-handedly fight us?" He laughed. "All right then, lovie, lets have the necklace," he said, and gestured to Maura's neck.

"No," Maura said.

Pepper arched a brow. "I beg your pardon?"

"Just give it to him, Miss Darby," Dunnan pleaded.

"No," she said again, and covered it with both hands.

Mr. Pepper lifted his hand, no doubt with the intent of striking her, too, but Nichol caught his arm with strength that felt almost unnatural and squeezed tight. "You donna want to do that," he said.

"Do I not?" Mr. Pepper sneered.

"No," Nichol let go of his arm. "You'd no' get what you want for the jewelry around here. You'd need go to London to ask a proper price, and would there no' be questions about how you came upon such an astounding piece of jewelry?"

Mr. Pepper's eyes narrowed.

"What is the debt?" Nichol asked.

Pepper paused. "Two thousand pounds," he said, eyeing Nichol curiously.

That announcement was met with gasps of shock from the troupe. *God curse Dunnan.* Nichol couldn't believe he'd actually been tolerant of the bloody fool, had believed his vows that he would keep his purse in Luncarty. His estate was entailed—he couldn't draw from it. He bloody well did not have two thousand pounds to squander at a gaming hell.

"Diah save us," Mrs. Cockburn whimpered, and

stumbled backward, falling into a chair so heavily that the card table was tipped over and upended with a clatter of glasses and coins.

"Bloody hell, will you allow a man to *think*?" Mr. Pepper shouted, then turned a glare to Nichol. "I may not get what the necklace is worth, but I'll get something," he said, and tried to step around Nichol.

But Nichol blocked him, putting himself fully before Maura. "There are other ways to get what is owed."

"And what would that be?"

"Ransom," Nichol said. His thoughts were jumbled, and he grabbed at the first word in his head.

Pepper laughed.

"He's right," Dunnan said suddenly. "He is the son of the Baron MacBain of Comrie!"

Regrettably, the only other person Nichol had ever told the truth of his identity, besides Maura, was Dunnan. The man he had considered his friend, in a loose moment of inebriation, had betrayed him.

Behind Nichol, Maura gasped. She tried to move around him, but Nichol put his hand on the side of her leg, stopping her. He cast a withering gaze at Dunnan. He had been prepared to offer himself up, if only to remove this debacle from the salon and away from Maura's necklace. But the fact that Dunnan had just betrayed his trust only served to anger him more.

Pepper looked curiously at Nichol.

"Aye, it's true. First born of the Baron William MacBain of Cheverock. Now there is a man who has built his wealth and has no' squandered it on useless cards and games of chance. You may inquire of anyone in Scotland if you donna believe me."

"It's true," Dunnan said.

"Why in blazes would you offer yourself as ransom?" Pepper said.

Nichol shrugged. "There is no love between my father and me, and I donna care that he would lose two thousand pounds from his vast fortune. But I care that these people go unharmed. They had naught to do with what happened in London."

"*No*, Nichol," Maura said, her voice shaking. She gripped his arm, her fingers squeezing into his flesh. "Please donna do this."

"Quiet, woman," Pepper said, and looked at Dunnan.

Dunnan, the coward, nodded quickly. "It is true. A wealthy man, the baron. Verra wealthy."

Still, Pepper eyed Dunnan and Nichol with suspicion. He moved to stand in front of Dunnan, towering over him by a foot. "Be advised, Mr. Cockburn, that if this is some sort of trick, I'll come back to slit your throat. Don't doubt it."

"No," Dunnan said, and swallowed. "I donna doubt it."

"Well, then, lads, bring him along," Pepper said, jerking his thumb over his shoulder at Nichol. "If his father is as wealthy as that, perhaps he'll pay three thousand pounds for him, aye?" He laughed.

"No!" Maura said. She clung to Nichol's arm. "They can have it," she begged him, but one of the ruffians jerked him hard away from her.

"No!" Maura shouted again.

Nichol glanced back at her and smiled. *"Uist,* lass," he said, telling her to hush. He had a far better chance of finding his way out of this debacle without her and the others to think of. But for the first time since he'd met her, she looked frightened. Terrified, really. He realized she was terrified for him, and it speared him. No one had ever cared so much for him. All his life, he'd yearned for affection, for someone to care, but had been too fearful to allow it to happen. And now that he had it, he'd been on the verge of giving it away. If he found his way out of this mess, he would never make that mistake again. He'd wanted to tell her in the hall—he would never let her go. "Trust me, aye?" he begged her. "Donna fret, lass. *Tout est bien."*

All is well.

But Maura, her face contorted with her terror, shook her head. She knew better than that. *"Es ist nicht,"* she responded in German. *It is not.*

It didn't matter—they had him in hand, were dragging him from the salon as everyone exclaimed and threatened the men. Yet not a single one of them moved. Only Maura followed helplessly behind.

"Bain! Bain, you must believe me, I am so verra sorry for it!" Dunnan cried.

Nichol rolled his eyes, and Pepper laughed. They carried on, pausing in the foyer when Nichol insisted he be allowed to fetch his greatcoat. "And where do you mean to hold me, then?" he asked casually as he shoved into his greatcoat.

"You'll see soon enough, won't you? So, what do you say your father has a year? Twenty thousand?"

"At least," he said. Nichol had no idea what the baron was worth. He looked around him, saw the butler hiding in the hallway, watching warily. "Fillian, is it?" he asked.

Fillian cleared his throat and stepped into the foyer. "Aye, sir."

"Rouse the lad, Gavin, and tell him to prepare to ride."

"What? This isn't a bloody holiday, Bain," Pepper said.

It certainly was not. "He's my groom. He knows where to take the ransom demand, aye? Or, if you like, you can send one of your men, but my father's home is rather remote—"

"Fine, fetch him," Pepper commanded with a flick of his wrist. "Come on, then, enough talking," he said, and yanked open the front door. Frigid air rushed in as Nichol was ushered outside.

He felt strangely composed as they pushed him down the steps to waiting horses. He wasn't frightened— that would come later, when they discovered his father wouldn't pay as much as a pence to save him before he could think his way out of this. What he felt was the deadly calm of uncontrollable fury. The heartbreak of realizing when it was too late that love was possible for a man like him.

If he survived this, he would come back and kill Dunnan with his bare hands.

And then, he would settle things with Maura.

Dunnan may have left him in quite a predicament, but he'd left too many things unsaid with Maura. He'd created a problem that he needed to fix. For all of eternity. He would figure something out, because that's what he did.

If he survived this.

CHAPTER TWENTY-FIVE

THEY HEARD THE front door slam shut, and all of them leaned forward, listening, perhaps expecting them to come back. But when no one came, the room erupted into shouting.

Shouting at Mr. Cockburn for having brought them here and exposing them to this. Shouting at each other to gather their things. *Shouting, shouting, angry shouting.*

In the midst of it Maura stood, her fists clenched, her breath coming in gulps. She had never been so frightened in her life. Not when she was taken from the only home she'd ever known to go and live as the ward of the Garbetts. Not when the Garbetts sent her away to live with David Rumpkin in that nightmare of a house. Not when she'd escaped Nichol in the dead of night and fled. This fright was much deeper than any of those times. This fright was tinged with the sense of looming loss, the fear for someone else and her own inability to affect his fate.

He had sacrificed himself to save her necklace. He had done that for her. *For her.*

He really did love her, and he couldn't pretend

any longer that there was a better life for her without him.

Maura was also furious. She felt a fury so great that she could scarcely contain it. She slowly turned to look at Mr. Cockburn, who, like her, was oblivious to the flurry of activity around them. He stared at her, wide-eyed, as if he expected her to strike him and couldn't seem to brace himself for it.

"Be prepared to leave at first light!" Mr. Johnson bellowed at his troupe.

"Should we not flee tonight?" someone asked, and the group descended into a round of arguing about what they ought to do.

Maura took a step closer to Mr. Cockburn. He flinched. She took another step.

"Maura! It's decided! We leave at first light," Susan said, appearing at her side. She grabbed Maura's arm. "You'll be ready, won't you?"

Maura did not answer. She did not remove her gaze from Mr. Cockburn.

Susan disappeared with the rest of them, all of them clambering up to their rooms, arguing and shouting, some of them reliving the terror from their own unique perspective about what they'd just witnessed.

When they had gone, only Maura, Mr. Cockburn and his mother remained.

Mrs. Cockburn was sitting at the table someone had set upright, staring morosely at the floor. Somehow, half her hair had come out of its coif. She had an angry red mark on her cheek where Mr. Pepper had slapped her. She seemed suddenly much older. As Maura stood seething, Mrs. Cockburn glanced up at her son. "*Two thousand pounds*, Dunnan?"

He dropped his head forlornly.

"Do you no' have something you can sell to repay the debt, then?" Maura heard herself ask. "Acreage? Livestock? Your linen factory?"

Mr. Cockburn shook his head. "The property is entailed, aye? Bain sold what I could legally sell the last time." His voice was quivering, and he looked close to collapse. "Our linen manufacture has been hampered by competition from Glasgow." He lifted his head and looked at the both of them. "I should have told you, Mamma, that we've been struggling in the last year."

"Then why?" Maura demanded angrily. "Why risk what you donna have to risk?"

"I donna know," he said, sounding pathetically tearful now. "I canna seem to stop myself."

That only made her angrier. "Were you going to tell me the truth, Mr. Cockburn? Or did you intend to offer knowing that you had lost so much?"

He didn't answer her, but looked down at his feet.

"What are we to do?" Mrs. Cockburn asked.

"We have to help him," Maura said, uncertain if the question had been asked of her. "You must have something, sir. What of this?" she asked, and with both hands, picked up a heavy gold candelabra.

"You've several of them. Surely you've enough gold in this house—"

"Gold plate," Mrs. Cockburn said.

"Pardon?"

"It's gold plated. No' gold."

"I beg your pardon?" Mr. Cockburn sputtered. "It was to be gold!"

"I know what it was to be!" his mother said sharply, and looked away.

Maura set it down. "Then what of your china?" she asked. "Your paintings?" She looked between mother and son, wanting an answer, but both of them avoided her gaze by glaring at each other. "None of it is authentic?" she asked disbelievingly. The trappings of wealth in this house were counterfeit? They'd flitted away their fortune and had nothing to show for it? "*Diah* save you," she said, and started for the door. "An innocent man could be killed for this."

"Donna be so dramatic, Miss Darby," Mrs. Cockburn said harshly. "His father will pay his ransom."

"His father?" Maura laughed with impotent rage. "His father willna pay his ransom, madam! He does no' claim him as his son! He has all but banished him from his life." She looked at Dunnan Cockburn. "And you knew it. He told you so. You *knew* it, and still you offered him up for a ransom you knew would no' be paid." Mr. Cockburn's chin began to tremble.

Maura could hardly look at him and whirled around.

"Wait!" Mrs. Cockburn called. "Where are you going?"

"To determine how to save him, aye? I need to think. *You*," she said to Mr. Cockburn, "have destroyed me. You have taken the only thing that mattered to me, aye? You have ruined my love."

"I beg your pardon, but I donna understand," he said.

She wasn't going to waste her breath explaining to him. She walked out, striding down the hallway. Then running. Running up the stairs, down the hall where everyone was madly moving about, packing, preparing to escape.

Maura went directly to Nichol's room, throwing the door open, madly hoping that by some miracle, he had escaped, and he was there, waiting for her.

He wasn't there.

She looked wildly about, uncertain what to do. His few things neatly stacked on a stool. His plaid, which she took and wrapped around her shoulders. She went down on her knees and went through his leather bag. A few items of clothing, shaving implements. His book, *An Enquiry Concerning the Principle of Morals*. She pressed her forehead against that book and thought of him that night under the stars, casually reading as if he was seated at his hearth. There was his purse with a few pounds, a key to heaven knew what.

She gathered all his things and took them to her room. And then she paced. She paced back and forth in that small space, racking her brain for how to help him. She couldn't leave Nichol like this. He had no one. It was a horrible feeling to know one was alone in the world—the good Lord knew she understood. Nichol was just like her, he had no one.

You're a bloody fool, Nichol Bain. How could he not see that this was what made them so perfect for each other? They had only each other. He loved her—he *loved* her. And she loved him.

Maura paced until she was certain she'd worn a hole in the carpet. But when she had exhausted herself, she calmly packed her few things, and his, then lay on her bed in the pink silk gown with the white petticoat.

She didn't know how this would go, or what to expect. She was Nichol's only hope and had to fix this for him. She loved him enough to sacrifice, too.

THE TROUPE WAS up surprisingly early, given how much moving around Maura had heard through the night. But there they were, all twelve assembled in the foyer with their bags and cloaks.

Maura descended the stairs to see them off. Susan frowned at her. "You're wearing the gown from last night. Where is your baggage? Your cloak? They are bringing the coach around, Maura—you must be quick."

She took Susan's hand in hers, gripping tightly. "I'm no' going with you."

"What? Don't be ridiculous, you can't stay *here*,

not with him!" she said, gesturing at Mr. Cockburn, who was leaning against the wall as if he couldn't hold himself up any longer.

"But if I donna help Mr. Bain, who will?"

"What?" Mr. Johnson, having overheard, shook his head. "There is no need to worry, Miss Darby. His father will ransom him. Now get your things and come along now."

"His father willna ransom him, because he has no father," Maura said.

Susan gasped and looked around at the troupe. "What are you saying?"

There was too much to explain, and no time for any of them. "There are things about Mr. Bain that you donna know, aye? Believe me when I tell you that he has no one to help him but me, and I mean to do just that."

"How the devil will you do that?" Mr. Johnson demanded.

"I have an idea. And Mr. Cockburn will help me."

"He won't help you!" Mr. Johnson shouted. "He is the one who offered Mr. Bain to those villains! What makes you think he will help *you*?"

"Maura, please," Susan begged her. "Don't stay here. Come with us. We'll take care of you, you have my word."

"We will!" one of the men called from the back. "But do come along! We should be gone from here."

"Go," Maura said, and pulled her hand free of

Susan's. Susan eyed her closely, then sighed. "Very well, if that is your wish."

"It is. Susan—thank you for your kindness, aye?" Maura said.

Susan smiled a little and shrugged, then unexpectedly kissed her cheek.

"Come, Susan, it's time," Mr. Johnson called.

Susan fluttered her fingers at Maura, then hurried out the door to join the others.

When Fillian closed the door, Maura turned about.

Mr. Cockburn was leaning against the wall. He looked broken and eyed her with resignation and skepticism.

"Well, then, Mr. Cockburn, we must ransom Mr. Bain, aye? You know his father will no' pay a farthing."

"And how shall we do that?" Mr. Cockburn asked. "We've neither of us a pence to our name, aye?"

"I must sell my necklace, quite obviously," she said. "And you will help me. You owe him that much, Mr. Cockburn."

"Aye," he said wearily. "I do. I know that I do."

"First, we must learn where they have taken him," she said.

"How?" he complained.

"They will have sent a note or a messenger to Cheverock with the demand for ransom, aye? That note or messenger will lead back to them. You must first take me to Cheverock. Preferably in a coach with a team of six. We've no time to waste."

For the first time in days, Mr. Cockburn perked up a little. He straightened from the wall. "Aye, you're clever to think of it. I'll just tell Mamma."

As he hurried away, Maura said a silent prayer. If she had to endure Mrs. Cockburn for a day or two to find Nichol, she'd do it. That's how much she loved him.

CHAPTER TWENTY-SIX

GLASGOW. HE KNEW that much, at least, because they'd
passed the Glasgow cathedral, a familiar sight, and
the air had the smell of rotting fish to it, a scent he
associated with Glasgow and the trade that ran in
the River Clyde.

Julian Pepper had taken boardinghouse rooms
near the wharfs, and the constant clang of rigging
sounded as if ships were just outside the door. The
two small rooms smelled of humans—perspiration
and excrement, smoke and stale ale. Scattered on
the floor in one room were dirty, stained pallets for
sleeping.

Nichol decided he'd sleep sitting up.

In the second room, a crude table, some chairs, a
few wooden cups.

Mr. Pepper pushed him down onto a seat at the
table and poured stale ale for him, which Nichol
drank because he was thirsty and didn't know if
he'd have another opportunity.

Mr. Pepper sat down across from him and folded
his hands on the table. "Well, then, here we are. Me,
a man of the streets, and you, the son of a wealthy
baron."

Nichol said nothing.

Mr. Pepper stood up. He walked to a shelf on one wall and picked up a wooden box. He brought that back to the table and opened it, withdrawing paper, a quill and a bottle of ink. "How are you at writing, Mr. Bain?" he asked pleasantly.

"I can write," Nichol said.

"Aye, you've one leg up on me, then. I canna write but my own name. I'm not fancy like you," he said, and one of his ruffians laughed.

Nichol laughed, too. "I'm not fancy, Mr. Pepper. I'm a vagabond and have spent most of my life moving from one place to the next."

"Those are fine clothes you wear for a vagabond." He shoved the paper and writing implements across the table to him. "Pen a letter to your dear old pappa, and explain to him that for the bargain price of four thousand pounds, he might see the bright face of his firstborn son again."

Four thousand pounds. Not even the king would ransom him for that. "The debt is two thousand," Nichol reminded Pepper.

"I know what the debt is, sir. But I also know to catch the golden egg from the goose that lays it." He grinned, revealing a gap in his front teeth. "Write it, just as I said."

Nichol slowly drew the paper to him and picked up the quill. He dipped it into the ink and wrote a letter to his father.

The Honorable William L. MacBain of Cheverock, Baron of Comrie

My lord, I am writing to you as the hostage of a man who should like four thousand pounds to guarantee my safe return to the bosom of my family. I'll not burden your final days with the details of how this came to be. But as I know very well that you will not entertain the idea of paying ransom for a man you utterly revile, I will take this opportunity to say that upon reflection of your recent revelation to me, I have come to understand that the flaw in your character runs much deeper than I could have imagined. I fear it runs too deep to be repaired with a few words of prayer uttered by the vicar over your grave, and I therefore conclude that you will not find your heavenly reward. Perhaps you would find solace in knowing that you have destroyed my childhood and my happiness in retribution for having lost your own. But I regret I cannot give you that small victory, for I forgive you. I forgive you the sins you have visited on me. I utterly, without hesitation and with all due clemency, forgive you. May you rest in peace,
Nichol Iain Bain

He folded the paper and reached across the table for a candle to drip wax and seal it.

"Not so fast," Mr. Pepper said, and gestured for the folded letter.

Nichol handed it to him and watched as Pepper opened it and studied it. He waited, wondering if the man had been truthful about not being able to read. But Pepper nodded, folded the paper, then picked up the candle, tilting it a bit to drop wax on the folds to seal it.

He lifted one finger in the air and said, "Bring the lad."

Moments later, Gavin was pushed into the room. He was ashen, clearly nervous. Nichol smiled, trying to reassure him, but Pepper would not allow the lad to be soothed. He stood up and came behind Nichol, and held a knife to his throat.

"What's this?" Nichol asked, trying to keep calm. "You've been so hospitable until this moment, aye?"

"You know how to reach Cheverock, do you, lad?" Pepper asked Gavin.

Gavin swallowed and nodded slowly, his gaze on Nichol.

"Here then, pick up the letter and carry it to the old man. Wait a day for his reply, but no more. Do you understand?"

"Aye," Gavin said, his voice a near whisper.

"A full day, that is. Twenty-four hours. But not a moment more. If you've not returned by Friday, you'll find this one's headless corpse waiting for you."

"That's no' necessary," Nichol said. "It would make quite a shambles of the otherwise bonny accommodations here, aye?"

"Shut your trap," Pepper said. "Do you understand, me boy?"

"Aye, milord," Gavin said, his shaking voice giving his fear away.

"Then go on with you, deliver the letter. One more thing," he said as Gavin moved for the door. "If you think to run to the authorities, just remember that my boy Davey is not here."

"Aye, right you are," Nichol said. "We seem to be missing a ruffian."

"Davey waits in town. If you cross me, and bring the authorities down on my head, Davey will find you. But he won't kill *you*. He'll kill your mammy."

All the color drained from Gavin's face.

"All right, then, that's a bit too far," Nichol said irritably. "No need to frighten him to death before he can deliver the note."

"Just making sure he knows what I say is true," Mr. Pepper said.

Gavin looked ill. He nodded. He swallowed hard and managed to say, "Aye. I understand."

"Well, then, go on with you," Mr. Pepper said. He moved, as if he meant to knick Nichol, then laughed when Gavin began to breathe as if he might faint. "Go on, go on," he said laughingly, as if this was all just a wee lark.

Gavin picked up the letter and fled from the room.

Pepper dropped the knife, sauntered to his chair and sat. "Are you a gaming man, Mr. Bain?"

Nichol had four days to either think or talk his way out of this predicament. "At times," he said, and settled back, as if he had not a care in the world.

CHAPTER TWENTY-SEVEN

THE JOURNEY TO Cheverock might have been made much faster had only Maura and Mr. Cockburn gone, but Mrs. Cockburn was determined to come along, and she could not ride. And because the snow had made the roads difficult to travel, they were forced to wait another day.

Maura found the wait to be excruciatingly painful in the house alone with the Cockburns, who argued incessantly over Mr. Cockburn's transgressions, which apparently were many. She had nothing more to divert her than her increasingly wild imaginings of the worst possible scenarios that could befall Nichol or her.

The next day they departed at dawn and lumbered along toward Cheverock in a cramped coach with bad springs and the press of hostile bodies.

They reached Cheverock just as daylight was beginning to fade. Maura's head was pounding. She was the first to disembark, pushing open the door and leaping before the driver could come down from his bench. She strode to the door, her heart racing with all the anxiety of the journey, of not knowing, of fearing this was all for naught, that they were too late.

She knocked hard and long on the door, and after several moments, the strange thin butler Erskine showed them into a receiving room. As they waited for someone to come down, Mrs. Cockburn complained of hunger.

"Dearest, you must be patient," her son begged her.

"Donna think to speak to *me* in that tone, sir," she snapped. "Were it no' for me when your father passed, you would have found yourself living in a constant state of hunger and in much meaner conditions than you enjoy today, aye? Who do you think made the linen manufacture what it is today? *I* did. It wasna because of *you*."

"By all that is holy, please donna argue now," Maura said crossly.

"And neither should you deign to speak to me in that tone," Mrs. Cockburn said, but turned her back to both of them and walked across the room, and sat on a settee with a *whoosh* of air. "I've given all that I am to my son, and this is the thanks I am to receive? He will make a mockery of us before the world?"

These were all things she'd said in the course of their drive, in various ways, and in varying levels of vitriol. The more she railed, the smaller Mr. Cockburn seemed to get. Maura was surprised that she actually felt a wee bit sorry for him.

But she had her own worries. The Cockburns were a means to an end only, and she'd had quite enough. "Mrs. Cockburn! Kindly allow us to keep our attention on what's at stake here *now*, aye? You may lecture your son all you like when you return to Luncarty. You'll have little else to do, aye? Once word spreads, no one will want to dine at your verra long table."

Mrs. Cockburn gasped with outrage. She made a move as if she meant to launch from the settee at Maura, but that was an undertaking in the best of circumstances, and at that moment, the door opened and Ivan MacBain strode in, his face thunderous. Just behind him was Finella, whose smile constrasted brightly against her husband's demeanor. "Miss Darby! How pleased we are to see—"

"Shut *up*, Nella," MacBain said curtly.

Finella was quite taken aback. So was Maura. She swallowed down a small wave of hysteria. "Mr. MacBain, thank you for receiving us."

"What do you want, then?" he demanded, and gestured impatiently with his hand.

She didn't know what to make of his rudeness. "May I introduce Mr. Dunnan Cockburn and his mother, Mrs. Cockburn?"

Ivan MacBain didn't look at either of them, but kept his gaze fixed on Maura. "You're no' welcome here, Miss Darby."

"Ivan! What are you saying?" Finella exclaimed nervously, and tried again to smile at Maura. "We're delighted to see her again!"

"We are no', madam, and you will no' say another word," he warned his wife.

"I beg your pardon, Mr. MacBain, but I donna know what you mean," Maura said pleadingly. "I've come on a mission of great urgency, I have. I donna like to be the bearer of bad news, but something *terrible* has happened."

"Is this part of a scheme? Whilst my father lies on his deathbed? He warned me something like this might happen, that Nichol would try and wrench a few farthings from him in his final hours."

Maura gasped. "That is no' *true*!" she said with great indignation for Nichol. "He left this house with devastating news. He wants nothing—has wanted nothing—to do with the baron. Surely you must realize that is so, Mr. MacBain. He has no' come round all these years."

One of Mr. MacBain's eyes twitched. "You must think yourself quite clever, Miss Darby, aye? Nichol *came* here, knowing that the baron was close to death, hoping to gain from it. It was no coincidence that he came when he did, and once he discovered the truth, he resorted to meaner measures."

"Ivan!" Finella cried. "Donna say such wretched things!"

Maura was astonished that Ivan or the baron could believe that Nichol had come hoping for inheritance. How would he have possibly known his father lay dying? After all these years, when he'd kept a proper distance, they thought he'd swoop in at the last moments of a man's life and try to extort it? *"No,"* she said, her voice shaking with emotion. "He came because of *me*, Mr. MacBain, on my word. He would no' have come at all had it no' been for me, and the things that *I* did."

"Miss Darby, if I may?" Mr. Cockburn said.

God help her, not him, not now! Her thoughts were racing, trying to think of what to say to convince Ivan MacBain. "Mr. Cockburn, please—"

But Mr. Cockburn was suddenly in front of her, addressing the tall and imposing Mr. MacBain. "All we want, sir, is to know if you have received a demand for ransom, and if so, from where it might have come. Nothing more."

"Who the bloody hell are *you*?" Mr. MacBain said angrily.

"I am Mr. Dunnan Cockburn of Luncarty, aye? Do you know where we might find your brother?"

"How should I know? I've *never* known where he is. All my life, I have been left here to tend to our father and our legacy with no help from Nichol."

"Perhaps the news came by post?" Mr. Cockburn asked, doggedly ignoring Mr. MacBain's anger.

"No' a post, damn you, a messenger. The same lad who had come before, who do you think?"

Maura gasped. "*Gavin?* Where is he?"

Mr. MacBain looked between Maura and Mr. Cockburn. "I donna *know*," he said furiously. "Nor do I care—"

"But what did he say?" Mr. Cockburn pressed in a surprising display of fortitude. "Did the lad say where you might find him, then, were you to change your mind?"

Mr. MacBain laughed with incredulity. "Have you

all lost your minds?" he asked, looking around at them. "The lad came, presented the letter, and said he was to return within a day's time for the answer. But I told the little rat he could bloody well wait until hell froze over, aye? I've no idea where he's gone, then."

Maura's heart slipped from its moorings and began to sink away from her. She would never find Nichol now. She couldn't begin to imagine what would befall him once those blackguards knew he could not raise the ransom.

"I think you should leave," Mr. MacBain said.

"Aye, straightaway, sir," Mr. Cockburn said. "But, if I may—"

"You may no'!"

"If the lad was to return, what time might you expect him?"

"We must find him, Mr. MacBain. We donna care for the ransom. We mean only to find your brother."

Mr. MacBain looked angry and confused. *"Get out,"* he said, his voice shaking, "I want nothing to do with this, aye?" He turned and strode from the room.

Finella watched him go, then turned a tortured gaze to Maura.

"Finella," she said quickly, reaching for her hand. "He is Mr. MacBain's brother! He didna come for money, I swear to you. We only want to help him—"

"The inn," Finella said, glancing over her shoulder toward the door. "There is only one within miles, on the main road, aye? If he meant to return here on the morrow, he'd have no other place to go." She pulled her hand free of Maura's. "Now go," she whispered. "Ivan is at his wit's end, he is. He doesna mean what he says. He misses his brother, he does, but the baron." She glanced over her shoulder again. "He's confused, Miss Darby. And the baron, he… Well, he may no' last the night, aye?" She hurried after her husband.

"You are too *bold*, Miss Darby," Mrs. Cockburn snapped.

Maura was too drained to respond to the old woman now. She wanted only to find Gavin before it was all dreadfully, horribly late. She walked out of the room, making her way to the foyer and the door. She removed her cloak from the stand and threw it around her shoulders.

Mr. Cockburn was right behind her. "To the inn, then, I should think?" he asked crisply.

She glanced at him with surprise and skepticism at his newfound helpfulness. "Aye. To the inn."

THE INN WAS in Comrie, only two miles from Cheverock, and was rather busy in spite of its remote location. So busy, in fact, that Mr. Cockburn could only secure one room for the three of them. They found a table near the door—Maura insisted on that, so she could see who came and went—and were served beef stew and ale.

The Cockburns devoured their meals. Maura hardly touched hers. Her nerves had turned her belly to acid, an unsettling mix of worry and fear. She couldn't take her eyes from the door long enough to eat, certain she would miss Gavin.

It was nearly nine o'clock when Mrs. Cockburn belched and complained of a sour stomach. She insisted that Mr. Cockburn see her to the room they'd let. "Are you coming, Miss Darby?" Mr. Cockburn asked as he stood to help his mother to her feet.

"No' yet," she said. "There is no other place he can be, aye? He'll come sooner or later, I should think. I'll wait."

"Perhaps he's scurried away and willna return," Mrs. Cockburn responded.

"Come now, lass," Mr. Cockburn said as his mother began to move toward the stairs. "'Tis no' safe for a young woman to remain in the common room alone, aye?"

"I'm fine," she insisted and waved him away. There was hardly anyone left in the public room as it was—just a few men laughing and drinking from tankards. And the Cockburn driver, seated apart from them, who looked as if he was very nearly asleep in his ale.

"Donna waste your time, Dunnan," Mrs. Cockburn said as she began to weave her way through the tables.

Mr. Cockburn smiled apologetically at Maura, pushed his unfinished ale in front of her, and followed his mother up the stairs.

Maura looked into the tankard of ale, watched the wee bit of foam slowly circling around the surface. She'd never felt as despondent as she did tonight. The loss of Nichol from her life was far more injurious to her heart than anything she'd ever experienced.

And the feeling of helplessness seared the injury even deeper. After so many years of having no one who was for her, having no one she could trust, to find that person and then lose him was devastating.

If Nichol were here, he would probably tell her she was going to lose him anyway. Or would he? He'd been about to say something to her that night. That he'd never...*what?*

Whatever it was, in that moment, she had felt that the tide had turned and was no longer pulling them apart, but was pushing them together. She believed that Nichol had realized what she'd realized—for people like them, love like this wouldn't come their way very often, and they ought to hold on to it. Love that meant trust, compatibility that was strong and prurient. Neither of them had sought the rapport they'd found. Neither of them had wanted the entanglement. And yet, here she was, pining over a man she'd known for a very few days, but felt as if she knew better than most anyone else in her life.

How would she ever recover? How could she possibly carry on, as if nothing had ever happened? Unfortunately, it appeared that she was going to have to face the possibility of it, because Gavin wasn't coming to this inn.

Her wild chase would end in bitter disappointment. She was ridiculous to have believed Gavin would have been here, waiting for her as if by miracle. The lad had no money for an inn! He would be more comfortable in a stable—

Maura gasped and sat up. That was it! He'd not

pay for a room at the inn, he would bed with the horses! She abruptly rose from her chair and hurried toward the door. She pulled her cloak tightly around her and went out, running down the path to the attached stables.

It was dark inside; she needed light. She groped around on a bench beside the door, looking for any sort of light, a candle, a lantern.

She had given up a hope of finding it when the driver—*their* driver—came stumbling toward the stables with one of the inn's lanterns. His face registered his surprise when he saw her standing just inside the door. "Miss?"

"Aye, will you help me, then, sir? Hold your lantern up and walk with me, will you?"

"Walk with you? Where to?" he asked, confused as to what she could possibly want in the stables.

Maura took a breath, told herself to remain calm. "There might be a lad here, aye? That was the reason for our trip to Cheverock, to see this lad. But he'd already left."

"And you think he's here?"

"I donna know—please, there is no time to waste! Will you hold your lantern up and walk with me?"

The driver stared at her as if he thought there was something a wee bit off about her. But then he shrugged his shoulders and held his lantern aloft. Together, they moved down the center of the stalls.

The horses shifted about as the walked, looking for food or attention. But they found no other being in the stable but the horseflesh. No Gavin.

At the end of the stable, Maura sighed with frustration. "I donna believe it," she said, feeling herself close to tears. "I canna imagine where he's gone. When we were at Cheverock, he stayed in the stable there, with the horses. I thought he'd be here."

"Aye, mayhap that's where he is, then," the driver said, and yawned, clearly disinterested.

Maura blinked. Of course. *Of course.* He knew the cook there, the groom there. He would have looked for a place to sleep, some place he could trust. She whirled around to the driver. "I must go back to Cheverock, aye? At once."

"Pardon?"

"To Cheverock! He's there, I know he is."

The driver looked almost frightened of her. "Miss… I canna bring round the carriage and put the horses in their stays by myself—"

"I'll help you!" she cried, loud enough that horses began to whimper and shift about.

"You canna help me, you're but a wee thing," he said.

Maura grabbed his lapels and gave him a shake. "I must go *back*."

His expression was stricken. He looked around them, then said, "Can you ride, then?"

"Aye."

He rubbed his face. "Mrs. Cockburn will have me head, that she will," he mused.

"I'll be back before dawn, you've my word."

He looked at the horses. "Aye," he said, giving in. "Bram is restless. He'll take you."

Three-quarters of an hour later, Maura slowed the horse Bram to a walk and approached a dark house at Cheverock. A light burned in a single window on the first floor, but there were no other lights, no movement that she could detect.

She got off the horse and tied it to a post railing and walked quickly and quietly to the stables. Her heart was pounding so hard that she could hardly hear another thing. It was quite cold, and yet she was perspiring. She was entering a stable where she was not supposed to be, risking everything if she was discovered, perhaps even her neck. And if Gavin wasn't there, it would all be for naught. The past fortnight would have all been for nothing.

The stable doors were closed, bolted by a heavy iron bar. It took all of Maura's strength to lift it, and when the bar slid off to one side, it landed with a loud clang. She caught her breath and held it, listening for any sound that would indicate someone had been alerted. But all she could hear were the horses moving around inside.

She pulled one of the doors open. It squeaked horribly, and she winced, certain she would be discovered at any minute. Still, no one came. How was it possible they had not heard her? A groom? A groundsman? Could they not hear the intrusion?

She pushed the door open a little wider, hoping the moonlight would help her see. She heard some movement then, the sound of a person, not a horse, and froze with absolute fear.

"Miss Darby?"

Her relief was so strong and violent that she had to grab onto the door of the stable as Gavin stumbled forward, wrapped in his plaid. He was blinking, as if he couldn't believe what he was seeing.

"It's a bloody miracle!" she whispered, and threw her arms around Gavin. "Aye, it is a miracle, that's what it is. Is there anyone else within?"

Gavin shook his head. "They've gone to the house. The baron is dead."

CHAPTER TWENTY-EIGHT

NICHOL WAS ON the verge of sealing a deal with Mr. Pepper, he could feel it. With all the time he'd spent waiting, he'd done quite a lot of thinking—he simply had to give Julian Pepper an alternative to murder. Surely it couldn't be that difficult. Mr. Pepper did not seem the murderous sort.

And perhaps that was his overly optimistic view.

He had pondered it the first day. What was it that Mr. Pepper, with his greasy black hair and deep brown eyes, needed more than to kill Nichol when the ransom didn't come?

Nichol had come to a stunning realization as they'd passed the time playing various games of chance—for which Pepper now owed him one hundred pounds by Nichol's count—that they were really very much alike.

"What do you do for your livelihood, then?" Pepper had asked him the first night as they'd played cards and drunk the whisky he'd brought with him.

"I solve difficult problems for esteemed men," Nichol said. "Perhaps you could use my services, aye?"

Pepper had laughed. "The only difficult problem

I have is you, is it no'? No' my money Cockburn pissed away, is it? I, too, solve difficult problems for esteemed men," Pepper had said, and had clinked his tot to Nichol's, as if to salute that fact.

Nichol had seen then that they were of the same ilk, solving other people's problems. In slightly different ways, obviously, but their goal was the same.

"What will you do then, if the lad doesna return?" Nichol asked far more casually than he felt about the situation.

"Besides cut his mother's throat?" Pepper had asked.

Nichol had clucked his tongue at him, and the man had chuckled. "I donna know, to be honest. Go back to Cockburn, I suppose. Take his things and try and sell them. Furniture. Gold. Quite a lot of bother, really."

"It will be hard to reach two thousand pounds selling his things piecemeal, aye? May I suggest something else?"

Pepper sat back, amused. "Aye, and what would that be, Mr. Bain?"

Nichol shrugged and pretended to study his cards. "A stake in his linen manufacture. It's losing money to hear him tell it, but it could be quite lucrative if one were to consider markets on the Continent. A percentage is all you need, then. You can direct him. Tell him what must be done, visit him now and again, and reap the rewards."

"Visit him? I live in London, not bloody Scotland," Mr. Pepper scoffed.

Nichol played his card. "I'll no' take that personally." He took the hand.

Mr. Pepper sat back and eyed him curiously as Nichol shuffled the deck. "Why didn't you do it? Take the percentage, that is?"

"I prefer my line of work," Nichol said simply. He didn't trust Dunnan in the least, but he wouldn't offer that on the slim chance he could get Pepper to bite at this idea.

"Aye, so do I. And I'll have my two thousand pounds if it's the last thing I do. When I give my word, I honor it, and I'll have a tidy profit when your father sends his love."

"Think on what I've said," Nichol advised. "It is potentially worth more to you than two thousand pounds, it is. And besides, I'm expected any day in Wales."

Pepper laughed. "I donna believe you. You'd not go off and leave the bird behind."

"The bird?" Nichol asked.

"The lass," he said. "*Och,* you love her, seems to me." He glanced up from his cards. "Am I wrong?"

He was not wrong, but Nichol was surprised it was obvious to him. "Whether I do or no', it doesna matter. 'Tis too late for me."

"*Och,* don't be such a pessimist, Bain. Your father will send for you," Pepper said with a flick of his wrist. "No matter the acrimony between father and son, a man will not betray his blood."

Julian Pepper didn't know the baron. "I meant it is too late in my life," Nichol said. Not the least because he had made it so. He had set wheels turning that he couldn't stop now.

"Donna be a fool, Bain," Pepper scoffed.

That brought Nichol's head up. "I beg your pardon?"

"I'll tell you a story, shall I?"

"Have I any choice?"

"I had a love once. She was as lovely as a fine spring day, she was. Beautiful golden hair," he said, fluttering his fingers from his temple down his side. "I was a young man, green as grass, and I'll tell you, lad, I would have walked over hot coals for her."

Nichol smiled. He understood that burning desire.

"I loved her." Pepper paused, glanced away a moment, as if seeing her standing there. "But I was full of piss and thought I ought to have the world, too. Thought there were better women out there for me. So I left her behind. Broke her heart."

It was difficult to imagine Julian Pepper as the object of a broken heart.

He suddenly leaned across the table. "I'm forty years, lad. *Forty*. Never have I felt that way about a woman again, do you see? *Never*. That true esteem only comes round once. Don't let go what you have in hand."

"Poetic," Nichol said, and threw down a card. He didn't need Julian Pepper to tell him so—he was consumed with it. How many times had he berated himself for being so bloody stupid? He loved her, and this problem should have been the least difficult thing he'd ever solved. But he'd allowed himself to believe what his father had said of him. He had not trusted that anyone could truly want him in the same way. He had not trusted, period.

Pepper was right—he should have grabbed hold and held on to it the moment he realized what it was.

They played on as the hour for Gavin to appear neared. When Nichol couldn't bear another hand of cards, he tossed them down and said, "No more." He stood and began to pace. He'd been stuck in this hovel of rooms for nearly four full days. He was dirty and disheveled, smelled of bad ale and smoke, and frankly, it felt as if something was crawling in his stubble.

In one hour, all would be lost. He wondered how Pepper would do it. Break his neck? Weight him down and throw him into the river? Shoot him?

He was startled by a knock at the door. Pepper shoved to his feet as one of his men opened the door and walked in. Pepper moved forward, but he stopped, staring at the person who appeared in the open door behind him. It wasn't Gavin—it was Dunnan Cockburn. Dunnan swayed backward, startled by Pepper's looming presence before him.

But Pepper wasn't looking at Dunnan, Nichol realized. He was looking past him. Looking for Gavin.

Dunnan looked behind him, too, then said, "Ah, I see, you were expecting the lad, aye? He's gone home to Stirling. He was right worried about his mother, he was. I must say, Mr. Pepper, that was badly done, to instill such fear into one so young, aye?"

"What the bloody hell do you want?" Pepper growled.

"I should think it obvious!" Dunnan said cheerfully. "Why*ever* would I come to this establishment, but to pay Bain's ransom?"

Pepper looked at Nichol, but he was just as confused and shook his head. "You've been to Cheverock, have you?" he asked Dunnan.

"Aye, that I have." Dunnan hesitated. He rubbed a finger alongside his nose, then cleared his throat. "I, ah… I regret to inform you, Bain, that your father has passed."

Nichol swallowed. "He was no' my father," he muttered. "And I know he didna pay a ransom from his deathbed."

"Oh no," Dunnan agreed. "We had to be a wee bit more inventive," he said with a small, bitter laugh. "May I come in, then?" he asked, and walked in without waiting for an answer. From his coat pocket, he withdrew a leather pouch and handed it to Pepper. "You'll find it all there and more. Twenty-two hundred pounds, it is. We gave fifty pounds to Gavin— as he had quite a fright, thinking he'd find his mother with her throat cut." He paused there to give Pepper a scathing look.

Pepper paid him no heed and grabbed the pouch from his hand. He opened it, dumping the contents on the table, then counted through the banknotes and the coins. He looked up at Nichol and grinned. "It is indeed all here," he said, and looked at Cockburn. "Did you put any aside for a little wagering, Cockburn?"

"Absolutely no'," Dunnan said, and sniffed imperiously. "I am done with that, I am. Now then, you have your ransom and a wee bit more. Bain is free to go, is he no'?"

Pepper looked up at Nichol, and he looked, amazingly, a wee bit sad. "Aye, he is. I'm a man of my word." He counted out some banknotes and handed them to Nichol. "Unlike your friend, I pay my gambling debts."

Nichol had no such tender feelings. He took the money—it was seventy-five pounds, and not the hundred Pepper truly owed—and put it in his pocket. "Good luck to you, Pepper," he said.

"Aye, and to you," Pepper said, and watched him stride from that room, grabbing Dunnan by the arm and forcing him to come along as he went. The only thing he cared about was Maura. He wanted to know how quickly he could find her, gather his things, and get on a ship bound for Wales. It was too late to ride.

Once they were outside, Nichol paused to blink, blinded by the sunlight after four days in that dank room. "You've no' gone and done something irreparable, like marrying Miss Darby and bartering her necklace, have you?"

"No!" Dunnan said.

"Then how?" Nichol asked simply.

"Well, it was quite convoluted, that it was," Dunnan said. "We cobbled together enough to sell."

"We?"

"I mean Miss Darby and I."

Nichol's heart skipped. She hadn't gone with the theatrical troupe. "Where is she?"

"Can you no' see her, then?" Dunnan said, and nodded toward the water.

Nichol jerked his head up, trying to focus in the bright sun. He saw her. She was standing just feet away, wrapped in his plaid. She smiled uncertainly, as if she didn't know how Nichol would receive her. How he would receive her was with his heart bursting through his chest, as it felt it would do at any moment. He reached for her and pulled her into his tight embrace. "You're here."

"Aye, that I am. I couldna let them harm you, Nichol."

"Oh," he heard Dunnan say. "Shall I wait at the inn, then?"

"Please," came Maura's muffled reply, as her face was crushed against Nichol's chest.

"Diah," Nichol said, and let her go before he suffocated her.

"You're free, aye?" she said brightly, her eyes shining with delight. "I canna believe we managed it!"

"How?" he demanded. "Where did you get the money?"

"Oh, it's quite a story, it is. I think I shall write a book about it."

He groaned and kissed her, but Maura put her hand up between them and wrinkled her nose.

Nichol laughed. "I've quite a story, too, *leannan*. Now tell me, where did you get the money?"

"It doesna matter!" she said, laughing. "You'll be astounded when you hear how I found Gavin, the poor lad. And Dunnan! He proved to be helpful after a day or two. He was rather pleased to know he'd no' have to marry me after all. I think he was a wee bit intimidated."

Bloody coward, he was. "The money came from Dunnan, then," Nichol said.

"What? Oh aye, some of it, aye. He meant to sell his gold, but you'd no' believe it," she said, and linked her arm through his, pulling him away from the rooms of his captivity. "He and Mrs. Cockburn had quite a row, they did—Mr. Cockburn discovered that all that gold he'd spent a fortune to purchase at her behest was no' gold at all, aye? It was *gold plated*."

Nichol didn't understand the significance of this and looked at her, trying to follow.

"I think the love of gambling runs in the family," she whispered. "She tried desperately no' to be discovered, but oh, he found her out." She laughed.

Nichol didn't laugh. "Then, how, Maura?"

She smiled. "You must be exhausted, then. I'll tell you all. We've a room at the inn."

Nichol knew how. He reached for the plaid she had wrapped around her. She tried to hold it in place, but he peeled her fingers from it and pulled one end from her shoulder, so that the plaid fell open. Her throat was bare.

A wave of something so powerful went through him and landed squarely in his knees. "Maura."

"It was only a thing, aye?" she said with a flick of her wrist. "I should have given it to him in the beginning, but I am far too stubborn for my own good. What was I to do with it, really? Wear it every night to the theater?"

Nichol was overcome with a rush of gratitude at her sacrifice. For *him*. She had sacrificed something dear to her *for him* because she loved him. He'd never experienced this, had never understood how such overwhelming esteem and gratitude would fill a person's heart and eyes. *"Maura,"* he said again, but words failed him. He was too dumbfounded, too moved to express that her sacrifice was as painful for him to accept as it was elating.

She calmly returned the end of the plaid to her shoulder. "Now that you are free, Mr. Bain, you undoubtedly will want to collect your things. Mr. Cockburn was kind enough to have them brought from Luncarty, as I could no' bear to return there, given all that happened."

He wasn't listening. He couldn't take his eyes from her, couldn't believe he had almost let her escape. Julian Pepper was right—if a man were ever lucky enough to experience this sort of love, he'd be a fool to let it go.

"You need no' worry after me," she said. "I have discovered that I am quite capable of taking care of myself. I've decided I shall be off to Edinburra to meet Mr. Johnson and Susan. Unless..." She swallowed. Then nervously tucked a bit of hair behind her ear. She shrugged a little.

That small gesture was what tipped him over the edge of his astonishment. Nichol felt himself falling, both figuratively and literally, onto his knee before her.

"What are you doing?" she asked.

"Marry me."

Her eyes widened with surprise.

"Marry me, Maura."

Her eyes moving wildly over his face.

"You love me," he said. "No one could ever love me as you do, on my word. And I love you, aye? *Mi Diah,* do I love you. I canna give you a name or a home, but I swear to you, I will give you all that I am, every day that I draw a breath."

She didn't speak, and Nichol thought perhaps he'd misread the situation entirely.

"Say it again," she whispered.

"I have nothing—"

"No' that," she said, and came down to her knees before him. "Say it again."

"I love you," he said, and stroked her face. "I love you in a manner that both frightens me and exhilarates me, aye? I love you for setting this all to rights. Until I met you, Maura, I couldna see the biggest problem before me. I couldna see that *I* needed to be set to rights. It took you to do it."

She laughed. "I am astounded, Mr. Bain, that I have tolerated your pigheadedness for as long as I have."

He grabbed her arms and pulled her forward, kissing her. He stood up and helped her to her feet. "Where is this inn, then?" he muttered as he nuzzled her neck.

"Close by, thank the saints," she said as he pulled her into his side. "*Mi Diah,* but you stink, Nichol."

Nichol laughed. He laughed and laughed, loud and long, because he stank, because he'd almost made the worst mistake of his bloody life. Because he almost failed to fix himself.

Because he knew what love was.

AT THE INN, they ignored Mr. Cockburn who was tucked into a table with a pitcher of ale and ordered a bath. When they crawled under the covers of the small bed, Maura told him everything that had happened before she sank down onto his body.

He felt heartsick when she told him of the encounter with his brother. He should have gone home sooner, should have made a greater effort to stay in touch with Ivan. He felt nothing for the baron's death. If anything, with the baron gone, Nichol felt new and reborn and brimming with optimism for the future.

He understood that this depth of emotion he shared with Maura was what he should have had all along. It was the thing that had been robbed from him at a very early age, and he meant to make up for all the years he'd spent keeping to himself. And when he entered her, and slid into that state of pure, pleasurable oblivion, he could think only that this was right, this was *so* right, that he'd finally put everything to rights.

The next morning, he awoke to her warm soft body pressed against his back, and God help him, he would never do without this again.

He kissed her eyes. "We need to go," he murmured.

"Where?" she asked through a sleepy yawn.

"Wales."

"I thought it was impossible that I should accompany you to Wales."

He smiled. "I will think of something. I always do."

"What of Edinburra? I've been invited to join a theatrical troupe, aye?"

He rolled over, putting her on her back. "Is that what you mean to do, then, Miss Darby?" he asked.

She smiled up at him. "Perhaps I will. After all, I'm free now."

He kissed her. "You never answered me yesterday when I asked you to marry me, Maura. I will have your answer now," he said as his hand traveled down her body.

"I've no' decided," she said, and sighed contentedly when his hand slipped between her legs.

"No?"

"I'm still rather cross with you."

"Are you?"

"*Diah,* Nichol, you meant to see me married to Dunnan Cockburn! What am I to think?"

"I swear to you, I will spend the rest of my life

atoning for it," he said with a chuckle. "Will you marry me, then?" he asked, stroking her.

"You have me at an unfair advantage."

"Do I?"

"Aye, you do," she murmured. "But I will do it. I will marry you, Nichol Bain. You need me terribly."

Aye, he needed her terribly and forever.

EPILOGUE

Balhaire, the Highlands
Scotland
Christmas 1760

CATRIONA GRAHAM, THE Duchess of Montrose, needed something fixed at her family's estate of Balhaire. So she'd sent for the only person who could manage it: Mr. Nichol Bain.

"Donna smile at me as if I should be glad to see you, Bain," she warned him when she met him in her father's study. But she herself was smiling.

"Am I smiling? I am rather surprised, for I am no' given to smiling," he reminded her.

Catriona looked at her husband, Hamlin Graham, the Duke of Montrose. He gazed so fondly at his wife that Nichol felt as if he ought to turn away and let them have this moment. It was amazing to him that he once knew the duke to be a terribly aloof, distant man. He was wholly changed and now walked about looking besotted all the time. He wondered if he looked the same. He'd had Maura in his life for two years, and he was still just as besotted with her as he was the day she'd rescued him in Glasgow.

He was happy to be in Balhaire once more. Catriona had called him to help with Auchenard, a converted hunting lodge where she and women who needed shelter wove beautiful shawls, plaids and blankets. They had been so successful that they were beginning to send their wares to London, Dublin and Cardiff. There was a bit of a problem with Ireland, however, and Catriona needed Nichol to fix it.

Once she had explained it all, he had seen quite clearly how to set it all to rights.

"I'll pay you of course," she said.

"Aye, you certainly will," he agreed with a slight smile.

"That's quite a lot of cheek from a man who should be thanking *me*. Were it no' for me, you'd no' have found a woman who would tolerate you."

"You will claim responsibility for my wife, then?" Nichol asked, amused.

"Aye, I will. My husband is the one who recommended you to those people, is he no'?"

"That he did. Therefore, I am beholden to the duke for my utter happiness."

"And was it no' my uncle who released you from service so that you might pursue that wee issue?"

"And I am beholden to the earl for my conjugal felicity," he agreed with a smile.

"Bain! Do you no' see what those two men have in common?" Catriona asked laughingly.

"That I do, and she is bonny, she is. But she is no' responsible for my happiness. As I recall, she caused me quite a lot of despair."

Catriona laughed. "Well, then, you must at *least* allow me to claim responsibility for the musicale we are to have tonight."

"You are indeed, and for that wee bit of trickery, I am indebted to you." He bowed gallantly. It had been no small feat to summon Mr. Johnson and his merry band of actors.

Catriona laughed with delight. "You are an impossible man, Bain. But I do wish you all the happiness in this life. All is at the ready, did you hear? The troupe is in the south wing of the castle, as unruly as children, waiting to be set free to sing and dance."

Nichol had arranged this surprise at a considerable cost. He was fortunate that his work for the Welshman had been lucrative. He and Maura now had a small town house in Edinburgh, which young Gavin had been enticed to care for. They were rarely in Edinburgh, really, as his work—*their* work—had taken them all over England and Scotland. Maura had proved to be a great asset to him. She was clever—she had an amazing ability to see angles of an issue he'd failed to see.

He loved her more every day. He wanted to show her how much she meant to him, so he'd arranged this surprise for her. Catriona had been very helpful, delighting in a wee bit of subterfuge. All of the Mackenzies were happy to participate. Captain Aulay Mackenzie had brought the troupe from London on his ship and would return them to England. Aulay's beautiful wife, Lottie Mackenzie, had taken Maura to the island where she'd been raised on the day the troupe was to arrive so they could be properly hidden away before Maura returned to Balhaire.

Rabbie Mackenzie and his wife, Bernadette, had insisted that Nichol and Maura stay with them at Arrandale so that the troupe could rehearse. Vivienne and Marcas Mackenzie, and Cailean and Daisy Mackenzie had all descended on Balhaire, as well. They said they had come for Hogmanay, the celebration of the New Year. But tonight's surprise, on Christmas Eve, was the true reason they'd all come.

The laird and his wife, Margot, were also included, and pretended as if nothing was amiss at all, that they expected all their children and grandchildren at Balhaire for Christmas and the New Year.

Maura suspected nothing, which Nichol wasn't certain he trusted. Her instincts were, at times, uncanny. If she did indeed suspect, she was a fine actress. She was in a room at the castle now, having her hair dressed and donning the gown she'd had made for her in France. *Och,* but she was a vision in that gown. It was sky blue silk, the very color of her eyes, with a gold petticoat, embroidered with gold leaf, fashioned in the same vein as the dresses at the French court. He'd never seen anything as fine.

But there was one thing missing from her ensemble.

He dressed carefully that evening. All the gentlemen were wearing plaid, the ladies in their finest gowns. "You are the bonniest of them all, Maura," he said to her as she helped him with his neckcloth.

She laughed. "You would say that if I were wearing nothing at all."

"I certainly would," he said, and kissed her.

They went down to the great hall, where the Mackenzie clan had gathered for Christmas Eve dinner. Nichol poured his wife wine and handed it to her. "Are you happy, then, Maura?"

"Oh aye, it's bonny, is it no'?" she remarked, looking around at the wreaths that had been hung to mark the season.

"I mean, lass, with me."

She laughed with surprise. "*Diah,* Mr. Bain, I thank the saints for you every day. To think I might be at Luncarty just now, prepared to attend service with Mr. Cockburn and his mother." She laughed again. "You have made me happier than I deserve." She rose up on her toes to kiss him.

"Under the mistletoe!" Lottie Mackenzie said laughingly as she passed them on her way to her seat.

"Are *you* happy, then, Nichol?" Maura asked.

"*Leannan,* I will never find the words to express my utter contentment and love for you." He would have to show her instead.

Maura giggled. "You just did."

They took their seats for the meal, but before the first course was served, Arran Mackenzie, the laird, stood. "Before we begin, a bit of entertainment, aye?"

Maura leaned against Nichol. "The children, I should think. I heard them singing yesterday morning when I went out to walk."

But when the adult voices began to filter into the great hall, and the troupe proceeded to enter, all of them in green velvet and wreaths on their heads, all of them carrying candles. Maura gasped. She sat up, leaned forward, her eyes wide with disbelief. *"No,"* she whispered, then looked at Nichol. "It canna be! That's Miss Fabernet!"

He smiled.

"And there is Mr. Johnson! Nichol!" she squealed, and threw her arms around him and showered a dozen kisses on his cheek before eagerly turning to hear the performance.

The evening was everything Nichol had hoped it would be. There was much merrymaking and singing, a happy reunion between Maura and the troupe, quite a lot of dancing and laughter and more dancing. It was the embodiment of what Nichol believed he and Maura had missed in their lives before finding each other. Warmth. Family. Love.

Later, when the candles had burned down, Nichol and Maura held on to each other as they took themselves off to bed. In their chamber, she said, "It's Christmas! I have a gift for you." She went to the wardrobe and pulled out a package wrapped with a bow and handed it to him proudly.

"What is this?" Nichol asked, and untied the bow and removed the silk wrapping. He stared at the book in his hand, recognizing it instantly. It was *Treatise of Human Nature* by David Hume. His father's book. The book that he'd read as a young man and had found so enlightening.

"There's more," she said, nodding at a smaller box that had been wrapped with the book. Nichol opened it and stared at the contents. He knew it immediately—it was his grandfather's pocket watch. The same pocket watch his father had taken from him and given to Ivan before sending Nichol out of his sight.

So many emotions swirled in Nichol. Surprise and gratitude, the two constants he felt with Maura. Love. Deep affection. And hope. "I donna understand," he said.

"Look inside the book," she said.

He opened to the first page, and inside, there was a letter addressed to him. He recognized the handwriting straightaway as Ivan's.

He dropped the things and looked at Maura. "How?" he asked again.

She smiled. "We women have a way of patching things," she said with a wee smile. "I wrote to Finella, aye? Ivan had no' been told the truth about you, Nichol, but he wants to know the truth. He's the baron now, he has nothing to fear, aye? He's written to tell you."

Nichol was astounded by this gift. By this woman. He pushed aside the gifts to take her face in his hands and kiss her. "It's perfect," he said, kissing her. "A perfect gift. Thank you, Maura."

"Will you no' read the letter, then?"

"In a moment. I've a gift for you, as well."

"You already gave me a gift! I could no' have asked for more than to see them all again, aye?"

He reached under the bed and withdrew the velvet box he had hidden there.

She looked at the box, then at him. "What is this, then?" She took it and carefully opened it. Tears instantly welled in her eyes as she removed the necklace from the box.

"It's no' your great-grandmother's, alas," he said, alarmed by the tears slipping down her cheeks. "That could no' be recovered. But it is as near to hers as I could recall."

"It's beautiful," she whispered, holding it up.

"It's no' an heirloom," he said, unnecessarily. "I had it made."

She looked up at him with eyes shining with true love. "It *is* an heirloom, Nichol. This one, this is ours. We will pass it to our children, and they to theirs. This is the *best* heirloom, the only heirloom I shall ever want. This one is us."

She presented the back of her neck to him to fasten the necklace. He hoped it was near the same as the original—a ring of small diamonds with a teardrop emerald that winked at him when he removed everything but the necklace from her body and made love to her.

When they had sated themselves, they lay in a tangle of arms and legs before the fire, her head on his chest, staring at the flames.

"I had almost forgotten it, but I've one last wee gift for you."

"Nichol! You're spoiling me! What is it, then?" she asked, and lifted her head.

He stroked her hair. "Remember last month when I went to Stirling?"

She nodded.

"I had a situation that required some inventive thinking, aye?"

"Who?"

"The Garbetts," he said.

Maura gasped and sat up. "You didna tell me!"

"I didna tell you, no. I wanted to surprise you."

"What?" she demanded, pushing on his chest. "Tell me everything!"

"Here you are, lass. Miss Sorcha Garbett was scandalized when Adam Cadell cried off their engagement."

"The blackguard," Maura muttered.

"And she had no other suitors."

"Hardly a surprise."

"So I did a wee bit of matchmaking. I would say I found her the perfect match."

"Who?" she cried laughingly. "Tell me now before I perish!"

"Mr. Dunnan Cockburn. And his mother, naturally."

Maura gasped loudly and stared at him in disbelief.

Nichol couldn't help himself. He began to laugh at the thought of Sorcha and Dunnan. "And do you know the strangest part of it?" he said through fits of laughter. "They seem quite content."

Maura dissolved into laughter, too, and the two of them lay there before the fire, giggling like happy children.

* * * * *

AUTHOR NOTE

IN 1759, CARRON IRONWORKS was started in Falkirk, Scotland. It was a partnership of three men—two Englishmen, John Roebuck and Samuel Garbett; and a Scot, William Cadell. The men imported the latest technology from England to Scotland, and put Carron Ironworks at the forefront of Scotland's Industrial Revolution. I borrowed the company and two of the names (and assigned them new nationalities). I moved the company from Falkirk to Stirling to make my geography work, what with all the riding around on horseback. It would have taken too long for some of the transitions to have happened from Falkirk. And that, readers, is the beauty of fiction.

Another person mentioned only in passing here is Mr. James Ferguson of Rothiemay, Scotland. He was a real, self-taught Scottish astronomer and lecturer of note. He eventually moved to England to teach and make globes, needlepoint patterns and to paint pictures. A man of many talents.

GLOSSARY OF TERMS

Scottish Gaelic:
Bampot—a troublemaker
Boideach—beautiful
Criosd—Christ
Diah—God
Feasgar math—good afternoon
Leannan—sweetheart
Mo chridhe—my heart
Uist—hush

French:
Bonjour—good day
Bel—beautiful
Enchantée—nice to meet you
Mon trésor—my treasure
Mon Roméo—my Romeo
Pas avant que vous n'écoutiez ce que j'ai à dire—not
until you've heard what I have to say.
Sortez maintenant, imbécile—get out, imbecile
Tout est bien—all is well

German:
Es ist nicht—it is not

Mir ist es gleich was Sie zu sagen haben—I don't care what you have to say.

Schön—beautiful

Wollen Sie von hier fortgehen?—Do you want to leave here?